Stockings and Cellulite

with love
Debbie
x

Stockings and Cellulite

Debbie Viggiano

Matador
5 Weir Road
Kibworth Beauchamp
Leicester LE8 0LQ, UK
Tel: (+44) 116 279 2299
Fax: (+44) 116 279 2277
Email: books@troubador.co.uk
Web: www.troubador.co.uk/matador

ISBN 978 1848 764 361

British Library Cataloguing in Publication Data.
A catalogue record for this book is available from the British Library.

Typeset in 11.5pt Bembo by Troubador Publishing Ltd, Leicester, UK

Matador is an imprint of Troubador Publishing Ltd

Printed in Great Britain by the MPG Books Group, Bodmin and King's Lynn

Two very special people inspired me to write this book.
For Robbie and Eleanor, with much love.

Chapter One

'Happy New Year Simon.' I pecked my host's proffered cheek as a party popper whizzed over our heads. 'Absolutely fantastic party,' I lied.

'Thank you Sandra.' He squinted at me.

'Cassandra,' I corrected. Pillock.

Extricating myself from his drunken grasp, I scanned the whooping crowd for my husband. Perhaps Stevie was holed up in the kitchen with a bunch of beered-up work colleagues? Either that or flirting outrageously with anything in a skirt.

I slipped out of the room and went upstairs to collect my coat. Party music pounded in my temples. A headache threatened. Elbowing open the door to the master bedroom I froze. My brain struggled to make sense of the scenario.

I'd caught Stevie at it. On the job. Trousers down. Well, off actually. They were lying in a discarded heap on the floor along with his designer shirt – a Christmas gift from me – and a tangle of female garments. Shockwaves hit my body. I felt peculiarly detached, as if looking down on the situation before me.

Stevie was on his back, spreadeagled across the bed. A porky woman bounced around on top of him. He was naked apart from his socks. A part of me pondered whether he'd put a condom on or whether it was just socks that he bothered about these days?

The woman had large porridgy thighs, a stretchmarked tummy and banana shaped breasts. Her nipples were firmly in the grasp of both gravity and my husband's hands. The earlier glow of celebrating both my thirty-ninth birthday and embracing the New Year disappeared faster than water down a plughole. It seemed like an eternity but was probably only a matter of seconds before my presence registered.

Stevie's head snapped sideways, our eyes collided, his hands froze mid fondle before shoving the woman hard. She let out a loud squawk and slid right off the bed pulling the duvet from under Stevie's buttocks to frantically cover herself.

'Cass!' Stevie spluttered. 'This honestly isn't what it seems. Believe it or not there is a perfectly innocent explanation for what you think you've just seen.'

Did he say *think* I'd just seen?

Stevie began to dress, grabbing his shirt, hopping from foot to foot as he pulled on back to front underwear.

I didn't know what to say, or how to respond. The cat had been set amongst the pigeons and taken my tongue with it. Not one word of rebuke did I utter. Presumably it was shock.

So this was why my husband hadn't been by my side whilst Big Ben bonged the midnight hour. Clearly he'd been too busy doing his own particular brand of bonging. I extricated my coat from an untidy pile on the floor – at least they hadn't bonged all over my fake fur – before calmly walking out of our host's bedroom, down the stairs and out of the house. For a moment I stood on the pavement simply gulping in the freezing night air, then strode off toward the car. The engine turned over and I hit the accelerator, just as Stevie erupted out of the front door doing up his flies.

Twenty minutes later I killed the engine on our driveway and slumped over the steering wheel. Infidelity. That horrible deed that made the heart pump unpleasantly, turned legs to rubber, knees to jelly and was the surest way to losing a stone in weight without even trying. If infidelity could be manufactured as a diet, the financial ramifications would be endless.

Stevie didn't come home. I lay in the empty double bed dully contemplating the dark shapes of bedroom furniture in the gloom and listened to familiar background noises – the hum of the emersion heater as it warmed the hot water tank, pipes creaking, the drip-drip of a tap in the bathroom. Noises of an otherwise slumbering house.

As I lay there, utter devastation washed over me. I began to shake. Had he done this before? How many times? I couldn't think straight. We'd more or less trundled through married life happily enough. Or so I'd thought. Oh I'd always been aware my husband was a flirt. Sometimes a downright outrageous one. But whenever I'd voiced aloud objections or suspicions, Stevie had thrown his hands in the air with a look of wide-eyed innocence protesting such playful teasing was only a bit of fun for heaven's sake. How many times had I retreated, like a dog being scolded by its master, believing I was nothing more than a possessive little wife who really should muster a grip on her overactive imagination?

So was my husband a serial adulterer? No doubt I'd been manipulated and lied to on more than one occasion. Dazzled by Stevie's good looks and fobbed off by his charm, I'd clearly become blind to any extra-marital sneakiness.

What the hell was I going to do? Leave my husband? Break up the family? Consign our twin children, Livvy and Toby, to a part-time father? It was either a case of put up and shut up, or do something about it.

I stretched my legs, wincing as they encountered a chilly expanse of sheet from the unoccupied part of the bed. Turning over I huddled into the foetal position pulling the covers over my head. In a few more hours I'd collect the twins from Nell, my good friend and neighbour, and have a serious think about what – if anything – should be done.

With these thoughts tumbling over and over in my mind, sleep mercifully descended and it was almost ten o'clock before I opened my eyes again to see cold winter sunlight filtering through the open curtains.

'Happy New Year Cass!' Nell fondly clasped me to her. 'You look a sight for sore eyes. Good party eh?'

'Oh it was an absolute blinder,' I confirmed.

'Attagirl!' she laughed and nudged me heavily in the ribs. 'Must be great having a husband who isn't a party pooper, unlike my Ben. The minute anybody mentions a chance to partake in champagne celebrations, he goes straight into reverse, mad bugger.'

'Who's taking my name in vain?' The man himself wandered into the hallway, scratching his balls distractedly before readjusting his trousers. 'Don't believe one word of my wicked wife's spin, it's all lies. I'm simply a home bird and there's nothing wrong with that. If you want to go out whooping it up Nell, tag along with Cass next time.'

'I might just do that,' Nell threatened, nonetheless snuggling into Ben as he wrapped an arm companionably around her shoulder.

The pair of them seemed the epitome of wedded bliss, a couple who accepted each other's faults but happily rubbed along together – sharing, dedicated, supportive and loyal. I swallowed the sudden lump in my throat as the twins appeared at the top of the stairs, Dylan hot on their heels. An only child, Dylan always relished the company of my two.

'Aw, do we have to go now Mum?' wheedled Toby.

'Yep, come on. Let these good people have some peace and quiet.'

I gave my neighbours another hug and thanked them profusely for the extended babysitting service. With promises of doing the same for them and cries of any time, no problem, I gently extricated myself. Livvy and Toby followed me back across the grass strip that separated the two houses.

'Where's Dad?' asked Toby.

'He's, um, had to pop into work.'

'Oh. Fancy having a game on the PlayStation Livvy? Come on, race you upstairs!'

As the children thundered up to Toby's room, I wondered whether the lack of their father's presence mattered more to me than them.

Later that afternoon the twins went out to play in the cul-de-sac on their bicycles, racing around with Dylan, shrieking and screaming with laughter in the cold winter air while I sat alone in the kitchen nursing a tepid cup of coffee.

The emotional numbness had lifted enough to permit an

endless stream of tears to silently course down my cheeks. I wasn't actually crying. There was no heaving chest or breathless gulping or anguished howls. It was simply as if my eyes were leaking. Rather badly.

The sound of a key cautiously turning had my heartbeat quickening, but I remained motionless at the kitchen table.

'Cass?' Stevie called before tentatively entering the kitchen.

I kept my eyes down, staring at the skin floating on my cold coffee.

'You do realise that you're blowing things out of all proportion don't you?' he began.

I continued to look at the disgusting coffee, aware that my mouth was turned down.

'Don't you think you should at least give me the chance to tell you what really happened?'

I dragged my eyelids away from the brown liquid. 'Go on then.'

Stevie's explanation of what I witnessed was almost laughable it was so pathetically lame. Apparently Mrs Banana Breasts had been feeling faint. Stevie had taken her to the bathroom to splash her face with water, but the bathroom had been engaged. Undeterred and ever the concerned party guest, Stevie had led Mrs Fat Arse into the master bedroom whereupon she'd fainted en-route to the en-suite. Conveniently there just happened to be a double bed for her to swoon upon.

'Now she was a big girl Cass, you saw that with your own eyes. A bit of a whopper. Her arm was around my neck, weighing me down. And when she keeled over – well it couldn't be helped could it? I went down with her. Next thing I know she's made this amazing recovery, flipped me over, pinned me down, stripped me off and jumped on me.'

'How terrible,' I gasped in sympathy. 'It's tantamount to rape.'

Stevie's eyes flickered. 'I'm telling you she tricked me! I was set up good and proper and couldn't get her off. It might have looked like we were going at it, she was certainly trying, but good old Dick was having none of it. He was as limp as a lettuce. And then

5

you walked in! But I'm being absolutely honest, the intent was totally one sided – hers not mine.'

For one idiotic moment I'd nearly fallen for it. Almost believed him. Which just left one outstanding question.

'Where were you last night?'

'Ah. Now you might not believe what I'm about to tell you, but I swear it's the God's honest truth.'

Wearily I rubbed my red-rimmed eyes. 'Get out Stevie.'

As the front door banged shut, I wondered whether he'd go to *her*.

That evening, as I spooned baked beans over triangles of buttered toast, Toby regarded the empty space at the head of the table.

'When's Dad coming home?'

'Ah yes,' I quavered brightly. 'I forgot to tell you both. Something cropped up at the office and Daddy has had to go away on urgent business.'

'But he didn't say good-bye,' frowned Livvy. 'He *always* says good-bye before he goes away. Where's he gone?'

'Well, here and there,' I replied vaguely. 'It's something frightfully important and all a bit hush-hush.'

Precisely what could be so top secret that a bog standard surveyor should take off without any farewell fortunately bypassed the twins.

'When will he be back?' asked Toby cramming an entire toasted triangle in his mouth.

'Not sure,' I mumbled miserably.

The following morning, as I stared at a soggy mass of cereal willing my oesophagus to swallow a few spoonfuls, the doorbell exploded with frantic ringing. It was Nell.

'Cass, you silly cow, why the hell didn't you confide in me?'

'Probably because I was trying to come to terms with the situation before anybody else got wind of it,' I replied looking at her meaningfully.

There was almost nothing Nell didn't know about the residents of our cul-de-sac and I had certainly been deluding myself hoping the infidelity fiasco would go unnoticed.

I chucked the congealed cornflakes in the bin and made some fresh coffee for us both while Nell spilled the gossip beans. It transpired that my love rival was a neighbour. She'd moved into the ivy-clad detached at the far end about a month ago. As I scalded my mouth on boiling coffee, I tried to silently count small blessings – well just the one blessing actually. My house was the first in the road and hers the last, so at least we wouldn't bump into each other on a Monday morning when the bins were put out. Nell also confirmed that my adversary was a divorcee, had four children, and Dylan was in the same class as her eldest boy. That was only one down from the twins. Oh God. I'd have to move.

'What's her name?' I hissed.

'Cynthia.'

'*Cynthia*?' I shrieked, making Nell jump. 'Who the hell is called Cynthia in this day and age?'

'Fat old bags?' asked Nell hesitantly.

'What am I going to do?' I wailed massaging my temples.

Nell considered. 'Well, the way I see it there are three options.' She held up her fingers and began to tick them off. 'Move, stay put or–'

'Murder Cellulite Cynthia,' I growled.

Nell left about an hour later, eyes bright after such a gossip feast. This was the best scandal since Mr Witherspoon a few doors down had been rescued by the Emergency Services. Although nobody had ever fully understood quite why he'd felt the need to shove his penis up the spout of the bath tap. Especially the hot one.

Stevie sent a text proclaiming he loved me and had made a huge mistake. I let out a snarl and hurled the mobile to the floor. Fortunately we were the only house in the cul-de-sac never to have got around to laminate flooring. The mobile landed intact on the shagpile.

Settling down with a notepad and pen I made some financial calculations – essential if one was seriously considering going it alone – and happily discovered that I was not necessarily financially dependent upon Stevie. Two years ago my darling octogenarian parents had left me reeling when they died within weeks of each other. As their only daughter they had bequeathed me the entirety of their worldly goods which, although modest, was not to be sniffed at. The money had been quietly sitting in a bond earning a tidy sum of annual interest. If I was thrifty it could easily support the twins and myself.

On the pretext of wanting an early night, I was in bed soon after Livvy and Toby. In truth I wanted to privately release a torrent of weeping. Burying my face in the pillow to mute my howls of anguish, I wondered what Stevie and Cynthia were doing right now. Were they curled up together on the sofa watching telly? Cuddling? Kissing? Even worse, at it? The pain was so acute I thought it would dislodge my heart.

I eventually sank into a tortured mixed up dream. Sitting astride Stevie I repeatedly yelled, '*Liar, liar, liar*'. As I pneumatically bounced around, Stevie morphed into Cynthia. '*Bitch, tart, home wrecker,*' I shrieked lashing out with my fists. She grabbed me by the shoulders shaking me furiously. '*Cow! Pig!*' I screeched, thrashing about and wishing she'd stop rattling me so violently because my brain was starting to hurt. If only I could just bunch my fist up one more time and biff her really hard on the nose it would be – *ouch* – it would be – *argh* – what was my rival doing to me?

'Mum! Can you hear me? Wake up!' Toby was gripping my shoulders and shaking me like a terrier with a rag doll. Behind him stood Livvy managing to look both disdainful and pained.

'Do you know what time it is?' she admonished. 'It's nearly eight o'clock. We go back to school today and there's no bread to make our packed lunches.'

Oh my goodness. What sort of parent was I? Aside from a heartbroken single one of course? I leapt out of bed, experienced a bit of a head rush, then belted down to the kitchen to ransack cupboards for crackers, crisps, biscuits and anything that bore the labels monosodium glutamate and millions of E numbers. Why couldn't I be like some of the other school-gate mothers channelling my energies into raising a vegetarian family, buying organic ingredients and knocking up nutritious home baking? Perhaps if I'd been more like that I'd have had a faithful husband by my side. Meanwhile bags of crisps, sugary drinks and stale Ryvita would have to do.

Shame washed over me as I realised that wallowing in self-pity had resulted in neglecting my precious offspring. Bugger Stevie for doing this to me. For the first time since the catastrophic events of *that* party, anger reared its head.

I slapped Tupperware lids on lunchboxes and frisbeed them to my patiently waiting children. Belting back upstairs and ignoring my burgeoning bladder, I pulled my long coat from the wardrobe, grabbed handbag and car keys and legged it out to the car.

After blowing noisy kisses to the twins' rigid backs (public displays of affection were apparently uncool) on sudden impulse I headed off to Fairview Shopping Centre. There was nothing like a spot of retail therapy to lift the spirits. And right now I needed to do everything possible to keep the pecker up. Just *visualising* handing over a little rectangular piece of plastic was putting some roses back in my pasty cheeks. This was definitely going to be good. I could feel it in my water. And talking of water, I really should find a loo very soon.

Inside the shopping mall, distraction was immediate in the form of glittery denim jeans in the window of River Island. Low slung, belted and boot legged they'd look absolutely terrific on an eighteen year old. I was a battle worn thirty-nine – feeling furiously rebellious.

I strode into the disco-lit interior where blaring music instantly assaulted my eardrums. Businesslike, I began moving around the shop floor loading up. It was hot work. Ten minutes later I flung the garments over my shoulder and shrugged off my heavy winter coat. Instantly refreshed I headed off to the fitting room vaguely aware that two teenagers were regarding me with ill-concealed amusement. When I swished the fitting room curtain aside with a flourish the reason for the girls' mirth became apparent. My reflection, caught in a full length mirror and lit in a blaze of down-lighting, revealed a white faced black-eyed woman clad in nothing but a nightdress. I groaned and sank to the floor in mortification. At that moment I hated Stevie. How could I have let him reduce me to this?

I bought the jeans and several tops, one fabulously clingy making my boobs look far bigger and better than *hers*.

Once home, I dumped the carrier bags in the bedroom and sank into lethargy. Exhaustion overwhelmed me. Why was I so tired? Downstairs a pile of ironing awaited. Dropping onto the bed I closed my eyes. Just for five minutes.

Three hours later I awoke with a jolt. The school run!

Liv came through the school gates looking poker-faced and Toby was sporting a puffy purple eye. Both children flatly refused to offer any explanation until we were away from the school and on the road.

'Well?' I demanded. 'Who did this? I want names Toby, because I'm going to complain bitterly.'

Toby promptly burst into tears.

'He had a fight with the new kid in Year Four,' Livvy answered in a monotone.

'Oh indeed? And what horrible child was this? From the council estate perchance? I suppose it was one of the Sykes family. Nell said there was talk of them joining our school.' A pelican crossing loomed and I slowed down. 'Their father's in prison you know. Got caught trying to rob a bank apparently. Nell said something about him waving a concealed gun around wrapped in a carrier bag. Turned out to be a banana. You see children? This is what happens when you don't pay attention at school. If Sykes Senior had bothered to learn his times tables and worked out floor areas and angles of infra red beams, he'd have stood a far better chance of success.' I thumped the steering wheel to underline my point. 'You can't enter into something half cocked, brandishing a banana.' The last of harassed mothers with their offspring crossed the road. Shoving the gear into first I sped off. 'I'm telling you, the Sykes family make a plank look intelligent.'

'Mum,' Livvy snapped, 'the new kid in Year Four happens to

live in our road and was taunting Toby at break time. He said our dad is now his dad.'

I nearly crashed the car.

Naturally an explanation had to be given. I told the children in a matter of fact voice that Daddy and I had been experiencing difficulties and were spending a few days apart to do some quiet thinking.

'So why is Dad living with Ned Castle's mum?' asked Liv.

Good question. And one to which I didn't know the answer.

Within minutes of returning from the school run, the headmistress telephoned.

'Good afternoon Mrs Cherry.' The greeting was pleasant enough but one could detect the steel at ten paces. 'I'm sorry to have to report an incident earlier today between Toby and another pupil. I feel it would be appropriate if you could come to the school so we can discuss the matter properly.'

There then followed a bit of mutual diary checking and we agreed upon ten o'clock the following morning.

Nell, ever the good Samaritan, appeared on the doorstep at tea time weighed down with an enormous casserole.

'I'll bet you're not eating properly,' she fussed setting the dish down on the kitchen table. 'Also I've got some more info for you on *you know who*,' she rolled her eyes meaningfully.

Suddenly my legs wouldn't support me. I sat down. Despite loathing my love rival, I wanted to know everything about her. Apparently she is forty-five years old – which makes her five years older than Stevie. Hardly dolly bird material. She's also on the look out for fresh male company having just ended her *third* marriage.

'By all accounts she's looking for Husband Number Four,' confided Nell.

'And obviously set her cap at my husband, the thieving bitch!' I snarled.

The following morning I painstakingly combed my wardrobe for appropriate apparel. It was vitally important to appear well presented – impressions were everything. Miss Jenner would look up from her desk to observe a mature and sensible woman, an exceptionally capable mother of two star pupils – one of whom had regrettably strayed under the severest of provocation. Yes, absolutely.

'Mum, I'm so sorry,' said Toby miserably as he dressed for school.

'Hey! No worries little man,' I smiled and ruffled his hair affectionately. 'Playground scrapping happens all the time. Meeting the Head is just a formality,' I assured ignoring my churning stomach.

At exactly five minutes to ten I knocked on the secretary's door and was immediately led through to the headmistress's office.

'Ah, Mrs Cherry,' Miss Jenner proffered her hand and gave mine a strong shake. She was a typical headmistress – tweedy, iron grey hair and of indeterminable age.

'Miss Jenner,' I smiled graciously.

'Do sit down Mrs Cherry,' she beckoned to an empty seat in front of her desk.

As she shut the door I registered the bulky presence of another person who had initially been obscured. Seated to the side of Miss Jenner's desk was Cynthia Castle. My jaw hit the ground.

'You!' I spluttered. 'It's her!' I informed the Head.

'Please sit down Mrs Cherry.'

The cut glass voice defied argument. I sank into the indicated chair, my cotton shirt instantly drenched in sweat, heart hammering wildly. It really hadn't entered my head that Ned Castle's mother would also be at this meeting. Stupidly I'd thought this morning would be a straightforward one-to-one discussion. Faced so unexpectedly with the opposition, I completely wimped out. What a lost opportunity considering the many hours invested in daydreaming dark revenge fantasies – like liberally decorating Cynthia Castle's car with paint. And why stop at the car? I had a sudden urge to whip out a lipstick from the depths of my handbag and scrawl all over Cynthia Castle's face, but regrettably could not summon the wherewithal. In fact, it was as much as I could do to remain upright on the chair and not sprawl in an ungainly heap.

The headmistress cleared her throat, gravely acknowledged delicate issues between both parties before going on to say that nonetheless she couldn't have pupils knocking seven bells out of each other. I sat in a shocked haze watching Miss Jenner's mouth move and form words, but failed to actually *hear* anything further. When I did finally tune back in it was to catch Cynthia Castle whimpering about *her Ned* being *victimised*. Victimised? By Toby? How *dare* she! I jumped up but, sensing trouble, Miss Jenner stood up too.

I waggled a forefinger in front of Cynthia Castle's startled face and gained a smidgen of satisfaction that her eyes were round with apprehension.

'You tell *your Ned* from me to keep his fists to himself. And you can also tell him that my son's father is exactly that – *Toby's* father.'

And with that I burst into tears and stumbled out of the office.

Later that evening Stevie turned up insisting we talk. Liv and Toby were overjoyed to see their father but their reaction was tempered with caution too. They wanted explanations.

'There's nothing to explain,' Stevie confidently assured, 'everything is in hand.' He hugged them tightly before they reluctantly disappeared to watch The Simpsons.

When Stevie and I were finally alone, the urge to let rip and slap him hard was overwhelming, as if this would somehow alleviate the depth of my own emotional hurt. Instead I ranted and raged in fury and frustration releasing angst and vitriol until the dam suddenly burst and I was sobbing uncontrollably. Stevie had his arms around me in a trice.

'Stop it Cass. Please. I can't bear it.'

He couldn't bear it? Stevie was holding me so tightly my face was squashed into the soft fleece of his cream sweater. It was warm and heartachingly familiar. It was also now sodden and covered in mascara, snot trails and tears. Good. Let Cynthia Castle tenderly hand wash *that* little lot off.

'Can I come back?' Stevie whispered into my hair.

I froze. In my dreams I'd fantasised about this moment, written umpteen reunion scenes and re-played them too. Now he'd actually said the magic words. I removed my head from his chest and gazed into his soft hazel eyes with my own red rimmed road maps.

'No.'

'What? But I love you Cass! I've always loved you and I always will.'

'I love you too Stevie,' I replied. 'But not as a husband. Not any more.'

From the incredulous look on his face, one could presume things were seriously not running to plan.

'You can't possibly mean that Cass.'

'Oh but I do.'

'For heaven's sake! We go back a long way – we're a team, we belong together. Apart from anything else, what about the kids?'

Ah ha. Yes. Livvy and Toby. Stevie was playing the card that gave the ultimate knee jerk reaction.

'Stevie we might go back a long way, but we are not a team and frankly I would question we ever were. Couples who are devoted to each other are also dedicated to each other. They don't cheat on their partners or cause public embarrassment and humiliation. As for Liv and Toby, obviously you are their father and I'm more than happy for you to see them whenever you want.'

'Oh that's *aw*fully decent of you,' Stevie replied sarcastically.

'After all, you're only down the road,' I pointed out dryly.

'Listen to me Cass. Staying at Cynthia's was only ever a temporary situation whilst the dust settled with you.'

'Please. Spare me the soft soap. Where you now live and with whom is of no interest to me.'

Stevie glared at me furiously. 'Meanwhile, as it's almost the weekend, is it okay if I take the twins out tomorrow?'

'Of course,' but I was addressing his back. He stalked off to say good-bye to the twins.

The evening limped on. Pushing away the gloom that threatened to swamp me, I made some fresh coffee and settled down listing some outstanding chores, anything to keep occupied. Tomorrow I would purchase some Wellington boots for gardening, stock up on light bulbs and buy that new bolt long overdue for the garden gate.

Shopping list complete, I drove home the following morning with the tiniest sense of accomplishment stealing over me. I told myself that I'd fix that bolt without any male help whatsoever which would be yet another small inch down this new road of independence. And talking of roads, good grief, what was going on with this one?

I had encountered a junction and straight ahead was a traffic officer and stationary police car. The traffic cop gave me a hard look followed by a series of hand signals. Cautiously I proceeded towards him, trying to read his waving arms. Did he want me to pull over? What had I done? He seemed to be gesturing to the pavement. What? Pull over here? But there wasn't any space due to parked cars packed bumper to bumper. I crawled forward desperately searching for an appropriate gap to pull into. No gaps. Things were starting to get distinctly gushy under the armpits.

I risked a quick glance in the rear view mirror. The cop had his back to me and had switched his attention to other drivers who were heading up a side road. At least my now pulling over wouldn't cause a hold up.

I indicated and came to a gentle stop, but the traffic officer took no notice of me. Two minutes passed. Then three. Had he lost interest in me? I dithered. Perhaps he hadn't actually wanted me to stop at all? Yes, that was it. I'd been mistaken. Sighing with relief, I indicated, pulled out and drove off. Clearly I'd caught a lull in the traffic because there wasn't a car in sight. How strange. And quite eerie. This was usually such a busy town. I sped up enjoying the throaty hum of the engine and was happily trundling around a bend when I encountered a scene of such carnage I nearly choked on my tonsils.

A huge lorry had jack-knifed across the road. Skew-whiff to its rear was a car, squashed like a concertina, a lamp post sliced through the broken engine and embedded in the driver's seat, shattered glass everywhere. A vast fire-engine was blocking any further progress of my own vehicle, as were an ambulance and another police car, blue lights flashing as they idled at various angles across the tarmac. Firemen were reeling thick hoses off the engine, a bunch of paramedics were crouched over a stretcher, and an absolutely furious looking policeman was striding towards me yelling into a walkie-talkie. The cop was about my own age and a dead ringer for Brad Pitt. Despite the dreadful circumstances, I felt my heart do a few unexpectedly skippy beats.

The policeman raised his hand indicating I halt. I buzzed down the window.

'Hello Officer.'

I gave a winning little smile but Ploddy's face remained thunderous.

'Switch off your engine, step out of your vehicle and hand me your keys,' he barked. 'Im*med*iately.'

Cripes. Did he want to give me a breath test? Bloody hell. I'd only drunk a bit of coffee that morning. Okay, four coffees. But they had been decaff. Okay, best not to lie. Confess to the filtered stuff. These cops weren't stupid were they? Clearly they could detect dilated pupils and the shakes at ten paces. This didn't seem quite the appropriate moment to do a breath test what with a body on that stretcher and – *crikey*, it really was a body.

I suddenly felt a bit odd. With jellified legs and scared out of my wits, I craned my neck up at the policemen. He was tremendously tall, even taller than Stevie. I stared at him like a frightened rabbit.

'Have I done something wrong Officer?' I whispered.

'Wrong? *Wrong?*' he bellowed, his good looks contorted with rage. 'My colleague ahead instructed you to divert left, but you blatantly ignored him and continued forward.'

I suddenly twigged. 'Oh! Do you know Officer I wondered about that,' I gabbled with relief as understanding dawned. 'He was flapping his arms about and I thought he wanted me to pull over but I couldn't find anywhere to stop.'

'Flapping his arms about?' he hissed, chin jutting belligerently, eyes like flint. Shame he was so apoplectic. It really did spoil those devastating good looks.

'Madam, can I suggest you equip yourself with a copy of The Highway Code and study the bit about *flapping arms*.'

'Um, will do Officer,' I cranked up a nervous smile.

'Are you aware Madam that you have driven onto the scene of a major road accident?' Ploddy flung his own arms wide indicating the mayhem.

'N-no, I wasn't originally aware Officer, but I am now. I'm terribly sorry.' Heavens, he still looked absolutely livid. 'H-have I wiped out all the clues?'

Ploddy's head inclined slightly, his mouth dropped open but nothing actually came out for a moment or two.

'This is an *accident* scene Madam,' he enunciated slowly, 'not a *burglary*.'

I nodded my head. This situation was having a dire effect on my body. My bowels momentarily lurched and I clenched my buttocks tightly together.

'It's women like you that give blondes a bad name,' he growled.

I nodded away. Now what the devil was that remark supposed to mean?

The copper gave an exasperated sigh and thrust my car keys back in my hand.

'Get out!' he yelled. 'Go on! Get out of here right now before I change my mind and give you three points on your licence and a hefty fine.'

More frantic nodding. My clammy hand curled around the car keys. I didn't need telling twice.

'Yes Mr Pitt,' I bleated and hurriedly squashed myself behind the steering wheel. In my haste to get away I over-revved the engine whilst shoving the car in gear, forgot about the clutch, gave a lurching bunny hop forward and immediately stalled. By this point I was very aware that my deodorant had completely let me down.

With reeking armpits and swearing under my breath, the car engine whined before turning over. Nervously I negotiated my way around the firemen, past the ambulance and its grisly contents, zig-zagged between the fire engine and the paramedics and finally got the hell out of there.

Chapter Two

As the car jerked to a halt on the driveway, I heaved a sigh of relief and momentarily rested a cheek against the cool steering wheel.

'Coo-ee!' Nell rapped on the window making me jump out of my skin.

'God, don't do that. I've had more shocks than I can take this morning.'

'Coffee?'

'Yeah. Yours or mine?'

'Definitely yours. Ben's been in the downstairs loo and stunk out the whole of the ground floor.'

'Oh lovely,' I gave her a wan grin as I stuck the key in the lock.

'Now then Cass,' my friend plonked herself down on a kitchen stool and fixed me with a beady eye. 'You need to start getting out and it just so happens an excellent opportunity has arisen to test out your wobbly ego.'

'Who says my self-esteem is suffering?' I immediately went on the defensive.

'It's so obvious. Look at you breaking out in a muck sweat at the mere *suggestion* of going out. You'd much prefer to hide away, curled up on the sofa in your bobbly cardigan and slipper socks with the remote control all to yourself.'

My shoulders drooped. 'Am I that transparent?'

'There's nothing wrong with staying in. But not night after night.'

I hugged my coffee while Nell outlined her big plan. Basically she had a mate intent on celebrating an impending fortieth birthday with a bunch of girlfriends next Saturday in a dodgy sounding club by the name of *Passé*.

'What the hell does that mean?' I scowled. 'Past it?'

Nell shrugged. 'The club stipulates entrance is not permitted to anybody under the age of thirty.'

'Oh brilliant. So it's bound to be full of wrinklies all wearing their emotional baggage on their sleeves.'

'Nonsense. Now drink up and we'll go out and buy some new razzle to dazzle.'

'What, right now?'

'Right now.'

We drove to Fairview, hallowed stomping ground of women shoppers like ourselves. Nell fiddled with the car radio.

'Good heavens Cass, why are you listening to Radio Two?' she tweaked the volume then expertly stabbed at buttons re-programming stations. 'Nobody of our age listens to Terry Wogan.'

'I like Terry,' I retorted defensively.

'So does my Granny,' she muttered.

And so it was that I awoke, a whole week later, with a sense of nervous anticipation. One newly purchased outfit was awaiting its induction at *Passé*. On impulse I threw open the wardrobe door and lifted the regulation LBD out. One word summed up the garment. Minimalist. Minimalist in the sense that there wasn't much of it but the price tag dared to question otherwise. Bought in an incredibly giggly moment with Nell, I now regarded the dress in horrified disbelief – plunging neckline, cut-outs at the naval, slashes to the shoulders and, at the back, an open gash trailing down to the cleavage of one's backside with scissor splits around the hem's perimeter. At least they were only weeny splits. But then again they couldn't really be anything else considering the skirt only barely covered one's knickers.

I crouched down and extracted a shoebox from the wardrobe's depths and nervously lifted the cardboard lid. Nestling upon a bed of tissue paper were the sexiest stilettos I'd ever set eyes upon. Nell had taken one look and pronounced them 'fuck me' shoes. I'd purchased them on impulse whilst in the midst of an adrenalin rush, recent rejection mixing with bitterness and hurt. And now?

The only feeling coursing through me now was one of dismay. What on earth had I been thinking of? And exactly what statement would I be projecting attired in this gear? What signals would be read? *Single saddo woman – all offers considered.*

But maybe I'd feel a bit better if I *looked* better. The mirrored wardrobes reflected back a woman older than her years, careworn and pale, mousy blonde hair falling lankly to shoulders, faded green eyes distinctly lacklustre. If only fairytales didn't have the monopoly on fairy-godmothers.

I reached for the phone.

When Nell appeared later that evening, dressed to the nines and wearing enough scent to rival a perfume shop, she stared at me in amazement.

'Blimey, what have you done to yourself?' she gasped. 'You look absolutely drop dead gorgeous.'

'Oh give over,' my sun-kissed cheeks dimpled as I gave a modest twirl. It was amazing what transformation could be wrought in a spray-on tanning booth. And of course Giorgio had worked miracles with my hair, effortlessly layering and shaping so that the finished look was akin to celebrity status. It had been an absolute pleasure to watch him at work not least because of his brooding good looks, pale brown arms and curling chest hair peeping over the top of his low buttoned shirt.

'Who did this to you?' breathed Nell in wonder.

'A devastatingly handsome fairy,' I truthfully answered as the doorbell rang. 'That will be Stevie.'

'Is he babysitting?' asked Nell.

'He's having the twins overnight.'

Nell shot me a look. 'What at-?'

'Yes, *her* house.'

'Aren't you bothered?'

'Do I look bothered?' For a surreal moment I felt as though I'd dropped into a Catherine Tate *face bovvered* sketch. 'Yes of course I'm bothered. Bothered to blazes if you must know.'

I'd spent much of the day firmly pushing down mixed feelings about this impending arrangement, desperate to be coolly unfazed when in reality I was bordering the traditional estranged wife with an axe to grind. In the end I had simply pasted on a brave face and nonchalantly asked the twins how they felt about staying the weekend with their Dad in the Castle household. Toby's reply had stunned me.

'Actually Mum, I'm rather looking forward to it. Me and Ned Castle are quite good pals now.'

'O-oh! That's excellent news darling. Jolly good,' I'd warbled, swallowing the bitter bile that momentarily threatened to choke me.

I flung open the front door.

'Cass, I just want to say thanks. I know this must be extremely difficult for you.'

I nodded at my estranged husband, eyes very bright, not quite trusting myself to speak as the twins pressed their lips against my cheeks and eagerly followed their dad out into the night. Stevie started to walk away but then stopped and swung back to face me.

'By the way, you look absolutely sensational.'

Sweet. Bitter bitter sweet.

'Well done,' Nell gave me a squeeze. 'Come on, time to go and let our hair down.'

And let our hair down we did.

Nell, myself and four other girls – whose names funnily enough now evade me – began the evening in an Indian restaurant. It was all harmless fun but, as the evening progressed and the drink flowed, an onlooker might have commented we were a little *ladette* in behaviour.

Raucously we worked our way through numerous dishes, spoons dipping in pots as we tested each other's choices like Loyd Grossman in *Master Chef*. Throughout the meal we repeatedly toasted the birthday girl with an incompatible mix of Cobra, house wine, whisky, vodka and brandy coffee until our euphoria had risen to a bawdy high.

At around half past eleven the birthday girl had insisted on personally thanking all the staff for a marvellous evening and refused to leave until she'd been permitted access to the chef whom she kissed on both cheeks several times. Even the washing up boy didn't escape her praise as she gushed alcohol and curry fumes all over him.

It was almost midnight when we tumbled out of our respective cabs outside Passé. The place was heaving and within seconds of entering the crowd we were pushed apart.

'Go to the bar. THE BAR!' the birthday girl hollered.

Nell insisted on ordering three lots of doubles to save on queuing time and then bossily instructed everybody to drink up before hitting the dance floor.

'Why can't I put my drink on the shide?' I slurred.

'Coz it might get nicked or shpiked,' she slurred back.

'Good God. You mean someone might shteal our drinks?' I reeled in shock.

I possessively clutched all three glasses before downing the contents like a woman in danger of dehydration. Thus refreshed, we staggered to the large sticky circle which passed as a dance floor.

Ah yes. The dancing. It was wonderful. Feeling unbelievably free and emboldened, I stared brazenly at the other faces in the club. Hm. She was pretty. She wasn't. He was attractive. He was repulsive. And he was coming over. I toppled off my high heels and fell against Nell in such a way that I damn nearly snogged her. Oh jolly good. The guy clearly thought I was batting for the other side and had stomped off.

The women were, on the whole, very glamorous although I noticed that none were spring chickens either. Phew, what a relief. Encouraged, I plunged into the whirling throng and lost myself in the music.

Eventually I became aware that a man was dancing opposite me. He smiled. I smiled back. He smiled again and put his arms around me. How very nice. It made the tiresome task of staying upright that much easier. I gazed at his blurry face. Oh good result, he was a looker! He bent his head and gently kissed me. No tongues I hasten to add. Didn't want him thinking I was a slapper.

And suddenly it was two in the morning and the club was

closing. The looker asked for my phone number. I blinked owlishly at him without saying anything.

'Don't you want to give me your number?' he asked.

'Shorry. Can't seem to remember it.'

He dug about in his pockets and instead scribbled his telephone number several times on a bit of paper which he tore into smaller pieces.

'Just in case you lose one of them.'

At the time this had seemed to make perfect sense.

Nell materialised by my side urging we must hurry as the others had secured waiting cabs. I lurched after her into the bitterly cold night air just in time to wave good-bye to three of the girls. The remaining party comprised of Nell, myself and the birthday girl who had begun to turn a rather nasty shade of green.

''uck it,' she gulped.

'Yeah fuck it,' Nell giggled moronically.

'No *buck*et!' I translated as the birthday girl leant into the open door of the taxi's passenger side and regurgitated into the floor well.

The cabbie was understandably furious. He rushed to the slumped birthday girl and hauled her upright. Straightening up she promptly puked down the front of his jacket.

The sound and smell of a person being sick is not conducive to one's own feel-good factor. Within moments Nell had upchucked all over the taxi driver's shoes. The taxi driver was now incandescent with rage, arms going like windmills as he broke into a stream of invective. At that precise moment a police car cruised past. Hearing commotion it braked, reversed back and swung a left through the entrance gates, bouncing gently over the nightclub's forecourt before drawing up alongside the cursing cab driver.

'It's the filth,' screeched Nell. 'Run!'

'Nell!' I bawled back, which was quite unnecessary given the fact that she was clinging to me and her ear was centimetres from my bellowing mouth. 'They ain't called filth no more.'

What had happened to my voice? I sounded like an EastEnders actress.

'Wot they called then?' Nell seemed to have morphed into Pauline Fowler.

'Um,' I tried to focus on her as I considered. What was that programme called? Ah yes. 'The Bill.'

I suddenly registered the presence of two ferocious looking policemen. Or was it one? I refrained from blinking and waited for the double image to blend into one stern and horribly familiar face. Dear God. It was only Brad Pitt.

'Ploddy!' I squeaked.

'Wot happened to Bill?' asked Nell screwing up her eyes myopically.

'Madam, don't I know you from somewhere?'

I gaped. 'Er, well, um, ah,' I waved my hands about waiting for the brain to make contact with the mouth and give a plausible explanation. Ploddy gave one look at my flapping arms and grimaced.

'It's you. The female motorist who can't read hand signals.'

Nell gave the copper a cross-eyed gaze. 'Oi Billy Wossaface,' she poked Ploddy hard in the chest. 'That's me friend yer insultin'.'

Ploddy caught Nell's hand. 'I'm warning you not to do that again Madam.' He glanced back at me. 'So we meet again. And this time you are drunk and disorderly in public.'

I opened my mouth to protest. Drunk? Who *me*? How outrageous.

Ploddy's radio crackled into life and he responded. Something about calling an ambulance and a situation under control. Nell and I were made to sit down with our heads between our legs. An ambulance arrived and took away the birthday girl who had suspected alcohol poisoning. Ploddy frogmarched us towards the squad car.

'I wanna solicitor!' bellowed Nell. 'This is false arrest.'

Ploddy shut the door on us before settling himself into the front next to a female cop. They exchanged glances. She was a slim brunette with finely chiselled bone structure and porcelain skin. She looked like one of Charlie's Angels and I took an instant dislike to her.

'I assume both you ladies are local?' asked Ploddy. 'Please tell me where you live so I can get you home and off the street.'

I felt a sudden surge of excitement. Secretly I'd always wanted to ride inside a police car. I leant forward and tapped Ploddy on the shoulder.

'Mishter Pitt, could we poss'bly drive home with the blue light flashing and the bee-baw on?'

Forty-eight hours later, Nell and I were *still* awaiting full recovery.

'But you must agree Cass, it was a hell of a night wasn't it?' She was anxious for confirmation that I had enjoyed my debut night with the girls.

'It was certainly an experience,' I answered carefully.

'So who was the gorgeous guy you were smooching with?'

'Haven't a clue.'

'Did you give him your telephone number?'

'I can't remember,' I truthfully replied.

That evening, over the regulation beans on toast (I had yet to get to grips with the current menu in this house) Toby questioned whether I had plans to find a job.

'No. Why do you ask?'

'I just sort of wondered. Now that Dad's left,' he trailed off.

I flinched. 'We haven't yet discussed the finer points of our separation.'

Toby tried again. 'Aren't you ever bored at home all day Mum?'

'Good heavens no! A woman's work is never done. There are windows to clean, groceries to buy, the car to wash, housework, gardening, laundry, ironing, bedding to change-'

'Okay Mum, I get the picture. Even so, you must sometimes feel lonely not having anybody to talk to while we're at school.'

'Don't be ridiculous Tobes,' Livvy scoffed. 'Mum doesn't do proper conversation.'

'How *dare* you be so condescending young lady,' I snapped.

Liv immediately dropped the haughty expression and apologised.

'I didn't mean to be rude Mum but, well, it's just that you don't really talk about anything other than Coronation Street, what's for tea, or the escalating price of a loaf of bread.'

'I see. And at the grand old age of nine and a half you're able to parlez politics, eulogise about the economy, discuss the pros and cons of a single currency and give an informed opinion on whether fox hunting should be outlawed?'

'Actually Mum yes, within reason. We do current affairs at school and Mrs Carpenter encourages us to debate. Whereas you don't even buy a newspaper and haven't the faintest idea what's going on in the world! And incidentally fox hunting has already been outlawed.'

And with that my daughter scraped back her chair and excused herself from the dinner table on the pretext that she would be reading in her room, leaving me mouthing like a goldfish. What the heck was she off to read? I thought it was Harry Potter. Evidently it was The Times or Observer.

Yes, well, we'd soon see about that!

And so it was that I found myself detouring, after the school run the following morning, to the local newsagent. Inside the shop I stood before rows and rows of national newspapers and deliberated. Two had instant appeal. *Pop Star Arrested* screamed one headline. In my opinion the newsworthiness of this item was pure gold. I gave myself a mental smack and studied the explosively angry newspapers. *Our Third World Hospitals* blasted one paper with a distressing picture of an old lady prostrate on a gurney. Oh dear. I didn't want to read about that with my morning coffee. *Clegg ConDems Cameron*. No thanks, I loathed politics. What was that one? *Earthquake Death Toll Still Rising*. Oh God. It wasn't that I lacked compassion – heavens I had buckets of the stuff – it was just that it was all so terribly dire and dismal. My personal life was depressing enough without reading heartache on a global scale. I'd much rather read *Is Nicole Preggers Again* and *Are You a Chav*.

After several dithery moments I opted for two bulky papers which promised in-depth accounts of the money markets and discussion of foreign policies. That would make good starter reading. And was it psychological or was I already feeling more boffin-like as I approached the counter, intellectual fodder tucked under one arm?

'Just these?' asked the bored gum chewing teenager with a plethora of zits across his forehead. Ripe too, particularly that one to the side of his nostril.

'Yes thanks,' I gave a geeky smile. 'Can't wait to get home actually, put the kettle on and get stuck in. See if share prices are rising and how the tootsies are doing.'

'Footsies.'

'Those too,' I smiled brightly.

'The teenager switched the gum from one side of his rotating jaw to the other. 'Those sort of papers bore me to shit.'

I blinked. 'Um, right. That reminds me. My friend asked me to pick up her daily paper too.' I reached out and grabbed a definite trash job blaring the headline *What Becks Did Next*. 'She's really into Beckham,' I added by way of explanation.

'Aren't all the women?' the teenager leered. 'Bit of a bad boy on the quiet, our David. This time it's a hairdresser blowing her kiss-and-tell trumpet, alleging it wasn't just his hair that had a blow job. Even gives the length,' he nodded sagely.

'Well that can't amount to much,' I commented. 'He was virtually bald the last time I saw a picture of him.'

'Ha ha, very amusing,' winked the teenager. 'Victoria's apparently gone ballistic. Walloped him with a frying pan by all accounts.'

'Really?' I enquired licking my second finger and frantically flicking to *continued on page 5 column 2*.

Back home, I was in the process of devouring the trashy news rag from cover to cover when the doorbell rang.

'Only me,' Nell trilled through the letterbox.

As we sat companionably in the kitchen sharing a lunchtime sandwich, Nell knocked me sideways with the news that she'd recently applied for a part-time job as a classroom assistant and, moreover, been offered the job.

'But I thought you loved being a stay-at-home mum,' I gasped in astonishment.

'Sure, but sometimes I feel like Shirley Valentine. I caught myself grumbling to the toaster not so long ago. The grey matter is definitely not what it used to be and I thought this opportunity would be a perfect compromise.'

'Working with kids? Your grey matter will keel over completely!'

'Nonsense,' she pooh-poohed. 'I'll be polishing up on multiplication tables which will enhance mental arithmetic skills, my general knowledge will increase on a daily basis and there will be proper grown up conversation in the staff room at break times. Brilliant!'

'Won't Dylan miss you?' I bleated, which was actually Cassandra-speak for *I will miss you.*

'Silly! Dylan's timetable is the same.'

For some ridiculous reason I felt insanely jealous. But before I could question why, the telephone rang.

'Cass it's me,' said Stevie. 'I think it's time to do some frank talking.'

'What do you want to talk about?' I asked, knowing fully well the answer.

'Us of course.'

'Right. This evening okay?'

'All right. See you about sevenish.'

After Nell had gone I spent the remainder of the day seriously thinking about the pros and cons of reconciliation.

When Stevie eventually pitched up, his usual confidence and charm were missing. Instead he looked anxious. Worried even. He hovered uncertainly in the hall.

'Well come in,' I said leading him into the kitchen, the only room where a crisis was always aired.

'Thanks.'

This was weird. He was behaving like he was a stranger in the place.

'Sit down,' I indicated a stool.

He pulled out the stool and perched uncomfortably. I did a

double take as he gave his palms a quick wipe against denim clad legs. He really *was* nervous!

'Look Cass, I'm not going to beat about the bush. I've thought long and hard about this and I think honesty is the best policy.'

'Absolutely,' I agreed.

And then my husband spread his palms across the kitchen table in an apparent gesture of truthfulness and launched into the Mother of All Confessions. Now whilst I am sure it was wonderfully therapeutic for him to release a long overburdened conscience, funnily enough it had quite the opposite effect on me. In fact as Stevie sat, visibly swaying with giddy relief, it was as much as I could do not to take a leaf out of Victoria's book and resort to ransacking the saucepan cupboard.

His flirtations hadn't been confined to merely the females I'd suspected, but included proper dalliances with girls who'd never even occurred to me. Women who'd been friendly with me. Smiled like Judas to my face.

'Alice?' I interrupted sharply.

'Yes, Alice in Accounts.'

And not just Alice but also Rachel, Sophie, Kylie-

'*Kylie*? But she can't be more than twenty years old!'

'I can't help it if I'm attractive to younger women.'

'Well you could have bloody well said no!' I thundered, standing up and knocking my chair over backwards.

'You're right, I should have said no. But I didn't and I'm sorry.'

Finally Stevie took a deep breath and spilt the Cynthia beans.

'Honestly Cass, she meant nothing. None of them meant anything.'

'Is that meant to make me feel better?'

'For what it's worth, yes. Forgive me Cass. Please. Let's start again.'

'I'll think about it and let you know,' I hissed.

'Can't you tell me now?' he implored.

'No. I need to think about it quietly. On my own.'

Preferably when I'd worked through the seething fury that was engulfing me.

After Stevie had gone and the twins were in bed, I sank into the sofa and bathed in the television's soothing cathode rays. I found my mind wandering and, after Nell's revelations regarding her new impending job, idly considered the possibility of part-time work for myself. If this separation became permanent, serious thought would have to be given to generating my own income. There was also a secondary factor which had everything to do with Livvy's stinging remarks regarding my inability to hold an intellectually interesting conversation. Before the twins came along I had worked as a legal secretary. Perhaps I could make a minor comeback?

I sighed and switched off the television. Hauling myself from the depths of the sofa, on a whim I decided to turn out and tidy up my chaotic wardrobe. I could start with that muddled handbag mountain. Best to check inside them too and empty out any disgusting old tissues.

I sat back on my heels and opened the clasp of the sequinned clutch bag I'd taken to *Passé*. Inside a tiny scrap of paper nestled in the folds of the lining. Ah yes. The looker's telephone number. I stared at it and considered. Why should Stevie have the monopoly on affairs. Hang on a minute Cass. Who said anything about having an affair? You're just talking about making a telephone call. Having a conversation. Nothing more.

I dialled the number.

Chapter Three

It took several attempts to ring the looker's number without hanging up half way through. Finally, when I did manage to nervously punch out all the numbers, I spent an hour talking to a total stranger!

The looker's name was Jed, he was two years younger than myself, divorced and had a little boy. The conversation concluded with arrangements to go out. As I hung up the phone I exhaled shakily. Oh my God, I had a date!

When Livvy and Toby returned from tea with Stevie in *that* house, I immediately set about using my subtle powers of persuasion to extract information. Nosy-parkering in other words.

'Mum!' Livvy eventually howled. 'Please stop quizzing us.'

'I'm only asking if you had a nice time,' I shot my daughter a wounded look, whipped up a bit of lip tremble for added effect.

'Yes, we did.'

'Was the pizza nice?'

'It was okay.'

'And, er, was Cynthia nice?'

'She was okay.'

Cow.

'And was Daddy nice to Cynthia?'

'He was okay.'

'Right. So-'

'So everybody was nice and everything was okay. Okay?' Livvy growled before thumping off to her room, Toby hot on her heels so desperate was he to avoid a grilling.

Well honestly! And I hadn't even got close to asking the really pertinent questions – like whether Stevie was sharing Cynthia's bed or sleeping on the sofa.

'I'm just popping over to Nell's,' I called up the stairs. 'She's started her new job and I want to know–'

Two bedroom doors banged simultaneously. Oh well.

'So how's it going?' I asked my neighbour as I tucked my legs under her kitchen table and took a sip of coffee. 'On second thoughts let me guess. The teachers are overworked, there's a complete lack of class control and your days are spent watching thirty snotty nosed children beat each other up.'

Nell laughed. 'It's going brilliantly actually.'

She then launched into a summary of amusing anecdotes the little darlings had uttered, the titillating conversation of the hallowed staff room and pointed to an invitation propped against the toaster for a 'Brainstorming Evening'.

'To raise funds for the school – promises to be a good laugh.'

'I'm so pleased for you,' I said, feeling anything but.

What was the matter with me? Was I jealous of Nell's job?

Back home, the sour mood persisted. Irritably I concluded the wardrobe tidy-and-chuck-out session.

The following morning I hauled two bulging black sacks down to the car. I dropped the twins at school and detoured via the charity shop to dump the discarded clothing. My wardrobe was now so tidy it was virtually empty. Sighing, I pointed the car in the direction of Fairview.

The next few hours were a blur of frantic purchasing as, like a woman possessed, I trotted the perimeters of both the lower and upper mall not once, not twice, but three times. Eventually, defeated by the awkwardness of carrying so many bulging bags, it was time to call it a day. I'd nip home, unload the goodies and with a bit of luck have time for a quick coffee before collecting the twins from school.

I tottered across the car park, arms like stretched spaghetti, to Aisle J. That was strange. Where was my car? I could have sworn it had been parked here. Perhaps it was in the next aisle? No. The one next to that? No. Oh for heaven's sake Cass. Right. Start at the beginning.

With a sense of rising panic I searched up and down each of the car park's individual aisles wearily trailing umpteen shopping bags. At this rate I would be late picking up the twins. In desperation I telephoned the school from my mobile and put the secretary in the picture.

'I'm sure the car can't be far away,' I tinkled apologetically.

The secretary didn't tinkle back and instead droned on about no late class provisions for pupils and that alternative arrangements should be made for Olivia and Tobias.

'I'll ask my neighbour to collect the children, she's Dylan Lambert's mother.'

'Dylan has already left for the day with his grandmother for a dental appointment. Mrs Lambert was unable to collect her son herself because she's assisting with computer club at the school she works for.'

'I see.'

My thoughts darted about, desperate to find a solution. Stevie worked in London and was miles away. Maybe the twins could start walking? But what if they took that lonely shortcut across the park and through the woods?

The secretary cleared her throat indicating she was about to broach a sensitive subject.

'Mrs Cherry, there is one possibility. I could contact Ned Castle's mother on your behalf – Mrs Cynthia Castle?'

'Yes, yes. I know who Mrs Castle is,' I whispered into the handset, shoulders drooping. Tears momentarily threatened. 'Right-oh,' I warbled. 'That's an excellent idea. Please would you be so kind as to call Mrs Castle and, er, convey my grateful thanks.'

I hung up, beset with rage. She was the last person on this planet whose help I wanted. Fuckity fuckity fuck. And where the hell was the bloody car? Clearly some robbing bastard had nicked it. I hoped it ran out of petrol and the bugger got stranded. Preferably on a busy roundabout. Seething, I rang the local nick.

'Police and make it snappy,' I rudely instructed the operator. 'My car has been stolen.'

I was curtly informed a squad car was within the vicinity and would arrive shortly. Indeed, just minutes later, a police car purred to a standstill.

I launched into a ranting diatribe before the policeman was out of the driver's seat.

'We should take a leaf from the books of other cultures,' I stormed, well and truly in my stride. 'If a man steals, chop his hand off. That goes for everything – whatever they do, chop it off. Hands, arms, legs, the lot.'

As the policeman turned to face me properly, the breath whooshed out of me.

'Oh!' I gasped with horror. Brad Pitt. This was all I needed. What a sodding day this was turning into. 'Er, hello. Again. My car seems to have been stolen.'

'So I gather Madam,' Ploddy replied gravely. He produced a slim notebook. 'Let's start off with some details. Your name?'

'Mrs Cassandra Cherry,' I mumbled. Of all the policemen in the force, why did I keep running into this one?

'Make and model of the car?'

'Nissan Almera.'

'Colour?'

'Blade Metallic.'

Ploddy's pencil momentarily hovered before writing the word silver.

'Registration number?'

Damn. I'd hoped this piece of information wouldn't be necessary.

'Mrs Cherry?'

'The registration number. Y-e-s. The registration number is, let's see, the reg-ist-ra-tion number is…it's ah…it's ah…it's ah–'

'Madam, you do *know* your car's registration number?'

Two pink spots scorched my cheeks. 'Of course I know my registration number,' I snapped. 'It's LV – no! It's LX, yes definitely LX and…um…then a couple of numbers…followed by something something something.'

'Is that it then? Just an L and X?'

'One moment Officer,' I clenched my teeth. 'I will telephone my husband for the exact information.'

But Stevie was out of the office and nobody knew when he'd be returning. Upon trying his mobile, it was switched off.

'Has the husband been stolen too?' Ploddy quipped.

Bastard! My eyes instantly flooded with unshed tears. I blinked desperately, willing the waterworks to subside.

'As a matter of fact,' my voice wobbled dangerously, 'my husband has indeed been stolen.'

Ah. That had his attention.

'Stolen by another woman,' I enlightened him. 'And do you know what Officer, hm? Well I'll tell you! I wouldn't have minded so much if it had been some eighteen year old little strumpet with a pert behind, big baby blues and even bigger mammaries,' I paused, struggling not to hyperventilate, 'but she wasn't remotely like that. My husband was stolen by a middle aged Plain Jane with stretchmarks that could challenge National Railways and a backside the size of an armchair. So do you appreciate that you've touched a bit of a raw nerve and do not come anywhere close to comprehending exactly what my FEELINGS ARE ON THIS MATTER?' I bellowed into his face.

Oh God. I'd probably get arrested now for being abusive or disturbing the peace or something. I put my head in my hands and viciously rubbed the heels of my palms over my eyes, thoroughly upset by the series of unfortunate events that seemed to be invading my life at the moment.

An expression flickered across Ploddy's face. Sympathy? Compassion? He snapped his notebook shut.

'I trust you have documentation for your vehicle at home Mrs Cherry, so perhaps it would be better to access that data and let us know accordingly. Meanwhile I would be more than happy to run you home. I seem to remember you don't live far away,' he added pointedly.

And so for a second time I found myself sitting in a squad car. Ploddy shifted the vehicle into gear and headed towards the exit which took us through a second car park. It was awfully similar to the car park we'd just left. In fact, it looked identical. A horrible churning began to play in my stomach.

'W–would you mind terribly if we could divert to Aisle J only I need to, well, just check something out.'

Ploddy looked at me but didn't question the request. Obligingly he turned the wheel and crawled along Aisle J. And there was my car. Just where I'd left it earlier that morning.

'Could you stop for a moment?'

'Is everything all right Mrs Cherry?'

'Ah ha ha ha, you're never going to believe this!'

'Try me.'

Half an hour later, still smarting with embarrassment, I detoured to the newsagent's to buy the local paper.

'You won't find any Footsie stuff in this one love,' the same spotty teenager advised.

I handed him some loose change. 'Actually I've bought this particular paper for a completely different reason.'

'Oh yeah? Don't tell me. You read all about Beckham's botty, got a bit hot and bothered and now you want to look up local private masseurs.'

'Idiot,' I grinned. 'I shall be reading the Employment columns. I want a job.'

Driving into the cul–de–sac, I psyched myself up to tackle the final hurdle of this interminable day.

Cynthia Castle opened her front door wide, pencil thin eyebrows arched, mouth pursed like a dog's bum. The twins mumbled good-bye as they came out.

'Thank you,' I said stiffly.

Once home I settled down with a strong coffee and read the Jobs Offered pages. There was very little available on a part-time basis with a secretarial background. However, my eyes alighted on an agency advertising for temporary secretaries. Hm. A temporary job would give my rusty skills a chance to test the secretarial waters so to speak.

I glanced at my watch. Five minutes to five. The phone answered on the first ring.

'Starting Point Recruitment Agency,' purred a female voice.

'Oh! Hello. Er, I'm thinking about returning to work.'

Seconds later I had a registration appointment scribbled in my diary which just happened to fall on a Friday, the same day as my impending date with Jed.

When Friday dawned, I set off to the agency feeling rather buoyant. Pushing open the swing door I was immediately engulfed in soft carpeting, computer screens and telephones. Butterflies took off deep in my stomach as a coiffed consultant by the name of Carmel invited me to sit opposite her.

'Let's start by compiling your Curriculum Vitae,' Carmel smiled. 'When did you last work Mrs Cherry?'

'Almost ten years ago, just before my twins were born,' I replied apologetically. 'I've kept my secretarial skills up typing occasional survey reports at home for my husband when his secretary was up to her eyeballs-'

I broke off as it dawned on me that the secretary had probably been up to her eyeballs with my husband's dick rather than dictation. I was almost ambushed by a fresh outbreak of tears. God, when would this angst cease?

'That's fine Mrs Cherry,' Carmel assured. 'All that remains is a small typing test and then it's just a case of waiting for temping appointments to roll in. This will be the perfect introduction to ease you back into full time employment.'

That afternoon whilst cruising the aisles of Tesco, my mobile chirruped into life. It was Carmel rather tensely informing me that one of the agency's regular temps had broken her wrist and, with a sense of urgency, asked if I would be prepared to take over the booking on Monday.

'Yes of course,' I beamed into the handset, 'but don't forget to remind the company that I can only provide cover until three o'clock because of the school run.'

'That shouldn't be a problem,' Carmel assured.

I hung up feeling tremendously excited.

Later that afternoon Stevie knocked on the door ready to

collect the twins for the longest period in *that* house so far. I wouldn't see the twins until Sunday teatime.

'Cass?' he asked in a wheedling tone which instantly irritated me. 'Have you thought any more about us getting back together?'

'I'm still thinking about it,' I snapped. 'Although frankly, after listening to your litany of legovers, I wouldn't get your hopes up.'

'You know you don't mean that Cass. You're still angry – understandably so – but you'll calm down eventually.'

I swung round furiously. 'Oh will I?'

'Yes, of course. It's just that I'd like to get back to normal, preferably as soon as possible. I want to get on with my life.'

My eyes rocketed open in disbelief. '*Your* life? And what about *my* life, or is this just about you?'

'I meant *our* lives getting back to normal. Apart from anything else, Cynthia's sofa is doing my back in.'

I froze. So he wasn't sleeping in her bed after all? Or was he? Was he telling the truth? Or was he lying? Would I ever recognise when he was being honest or whether I was being spun a pack of lies? The very thought of never knowing for sure sent my stomach churning. Could I resume living by his side knowing I would be in a constant state of turmoil? I had a mental vision of riffling through the pockets of his suit at the end of every working day. Feverishly scrolling through the text messages on his mobile. Possibly even ringing a few numbers I didn't recognise just to see if the voice that answered might be female. And then what? Hang up? Or blindly wade in asking impudent questions with somebody who might innocently turn out to be a female tax consultant? If our relationship stood any chance of reviving and surviving, then trust was paramount. But I no longer trusted Stevie. In fact, I didn't think I'd ever trust him again. My head felt dizzy and I clutched hold of the doorframe to steady myself.

'Are you okay?' Stevie had a protective arm around my shoulder in a flash.

'Fine thanks,' I tetchily shook him off just as the twins appeared.

'Cass I'd better go, Cynthia's got a big roast in the oven for all of us.'

'Oh yummy yummy. Well run along then,' I spat.

'Don't be like that Cass. Please. Could you let me have some sort of answer fairly soon?'

After he'd gone I moodily plucked an apple from the fruit bowl and bit into its lacklustre skin. Huh, just like mine. Yuck, it was badly bruised. Like my heart too. Suddenly I whipped round and flung the apple at the kitchen wall. It splattered against the paintwork leaving a trail of pulp and sticky juice in its wake.

'Bastard!' I shrieked at the disgusting mess and promptly burst into tears.

Oh God, this was no good. Jed would be here in a couple of hours. I needed to calm down. Have a bath. Get ready.

I blew my nose on a sheet of kitchen towel, cleared up the mess and went upstairs. While the bath was running I routed around in the medicine cupboard looking for something to sooth frazzled nerves. What was this? Suppositries. A periodic requirement but only good at soothing frazzled piles – the result of bearing two babies in one go. I sorted through the packets and selected some hayfever tablets. *May cause drowsiness.* Excellent. Three of them should calm me down. Along with a good stiff drink.

Jed was greeted by a lethargic woman with dilated pupils.

'Hi!' he greeted.

'Hi!' I gushed back.

'You look fabulous,' he smiled appreciatively.

'So do you,' I blurted.

It was true. Jed was even better looking than I remembered. Olive green eyes, dark hair and extremely white teeth. I wondered if they were bleached. Best not to ask at this stage. Maybe later, when he'd unbuttoned a bit. Perhaps he could even tell me who his dentist was.

'Ready?' he asked offering his elbow in a charming old-fashioned gesture.

He led me to his Porsche Boxster and opened the passenger door. I sunk into the leather depths. Oh very nice. Yes, very nice indeed. I tucked my legs in and let him shut the door.

We drove to a quaint pub and started the evening off sitting before a warm log fire, heads together chatting. I sipped a gin and tonic while Jed stuck to mineral water. A sense of relaxation stole over me which I suspected was nothing to do with the mix of pills and alcohol but everything to do with Jed.

Eventually we went through to the pub's dining area which was all knotty wood and low beams. Lots of atmosphere. Inevitably the conversation touched on our respective failed marriages and we exchanged sob stories. Surprisingly, when I told Jed how I'd found Stevie *in flagrante*, instead of becoming angry or upset I found myself seeing the funny side. I won't pretend I creased up slapping my thighs with mirth, because I didn't. But somehow a shrug of the shoulders and a rueful smile helped soften a distressing memory.

Driving home, was it my imagination or had the atmosphere changed? All previous banter seemed to have been left behind in the pub. I sat tensely in the passenger seat. Jed drew up outside the house, the engine turning over throatily. There was a pause. A sense of waiting. What now? What was the form? Issue an invitation for coffee? Sit at the far end of the sofa? Work our way towards each other? Make mad passionate love whilst the dodgy springs protested? I was completely out of touch regarding rules of the dating game.

'Can I ring you sometime next week?' he asked.

'Y-yes, of course,' I stuttered. 'Thank you for a wonderful evening.'

'It was a pleasure.'

And then Jed simply leant across the small divide between his seat and mine, cupped my face in his hands and planted a soft kiss on my lips.

I spent the remainder of the weekend feeling strangely uplifted. Now why was that? It was almost as if an invisible pair of rose tinted glasses had been perched on the bridge of my nose transforming the world into a much nicer place to dwell. Was this experience merely a histamine hangover or had optimism genuinely entered my life? As I stood over the ironing board gazing out of the kitchen window, a beam of sunlight pierced the grey clouds and haloed them with silver linings. It made me feel as if I were suddenly seeing light after being in a very dark tunnel.

I wasn't naïve or foolish enough to believe I'd fallen in love after one date with a stranger. Of course not. But I did believe that one date with another man had altered my perception about Stevie.

As the weekend rolled into the start of a new week, I rose half an hour earlier than usual to prepare for *Operation Return to Work*. I gulped nervously. This was top secret stuff. Nobody knew about it, not even Nell with whom I usually confided everything. The secrecy was partially due to cowardice – what if the whole thing was a disaster? That was why discretion was tantamount. Once the booking was complete and depending upon its level of success, then and only then would I convey to everybody my successful return to work. Or not as the case might be.

'Hey Mum!' Livvy stared at me in surprise. 'You look-'

'Yes?' I asked eagerly standing before her in my new black-as-midnight suit.

'Has somebody died?' Toby cut across his sister.

'Of course not!'

'Why are you all dressed up?' asked my son who, by sheer dint of being born with a willy, possessed the enviable male knack of getting straight to the point.

'Are you seeing a solicitor?' asked Livvy, her eyes narrowing dangerously.

'N-no. Whatever makes you ask that?' I stuttered.

'Daddy wondered if you might be taking legal advice before you make a decision about a reconciliation,' she explained.

'Oh did he now?' I flushed angrily. 'And why is Daddy discussing grown up matters with you?'

'Because I asked him.'

'Well in future don't!'

'So where *are* you going?' asked Toby.

'To the doctor,' I replied crisply.

'With full make up and dressed to impress. Are you having a smeary test?'

'Thank you Toby,' I spluttered, 'that's quite enough of that sort of talk.'

Finally, after a last minute game of hide and seek looking for the car keys, we headed out the front door.

'Ooh what's the occasion?' Nell appeared on her driveway within seconds of my locking the front door. Damn.

'Dentist,' I explained hurriedly.

'You told me it was a doctor's appointment,' Toby accused.

'Correct on both accounts,' I smiled tightly. 'Doctor first and then the dentist. Must dash,' I fluttered a hasty wave at Nell's astonished face before legging it to the sanctuary of the car.

Forty minutes later I parked in the staff area at the rear of a Victorian terrace. I gazed up at the elegantly old fashioned building and read the words *Morton Peck & Livingston* etched in gold across the windows. With mounting excitement, I grabbed my handbag from the passenger seat and marched up to the front door, heels clicking confidently over the paving stones.

Inside, a generous hallway doubled as a reception area. A peroxide blonde receptionist with heavy make up and an orange tan was clearly in the middle of juicy gossip with a fellow colleague.

'I told her fair and square,' the blonde sniffily informed her pal. 'I said that if she didn't tell her mother then I most certainly would. After all, I've known Mirium for years. *Years!*' the blonde shrieked. 'What on earth would Mirium think if she discovered I'd known all along what her own *daughter* was up to?'

My ears wiggled appreciatively as I stood and patiently waited. My goodness, what on earth was Mirium's daughter doing? Evidently it was more than raiding the biscuit tin after hours.

'Yes?' the blonde snapped, unprepared to divulge further details of Mirium's daughter in front of a stranger.

'Hello, I'm the temp.'

'Sit down,' the blonde waved a bejewelled hand at a row of hard chairs. 'I'll let Mr Morton know you're here.'

I sat on one of the uncomfortable chairs until the Senior Partner's arrival. He was a short man somewhere around mid-forties with a pale non-descript face. On the bridge of his nose perched a pair of rectangular glasses through which he coldly observed me. It would be fair to say that a bag of frozen peas emanated more warmth than Mr Morton.

'Mrs Cherry?' he enquired giving my outstretched palm a brief shake. 'Please come with me.'

We went up a flight of stairs, across a landing covered in threadbare carpet and through a side door which led into Mr Morton's office. There was a distinct air of dreariness, no doubt generated by years of regulation brown gloss and scuffed beige walls. A vast table smothered in rows of stacked files edged one wall. Opposite was a battered desk layered with bundles of ribboned documents, scribble pads and an ink blotter. A Dictaphone machine lay abandoned in the middle of this organised chaos.

Mr Morton motioned me through an internal door to another room which was, by comparison, about the size of a cupboard. I tried to work out the mathematical formula for squeezing my frame into the space between typist's stool and keyboard area and momentarily felt like Alice in Wonderland before she drank her shrinking potion.

Mr Morton rattled off a logging on procedure and password before giving a guided tour of the secretarial desk and its burgeoning In Tray. My duties were pretty simple really – field calls, organise the diary and type at one hundred miles per hour.

'I'll leave you to it then,' he said before reversing out of the cupboard.

I slotted a cassette into the dictation machine and started typing. The desk was pushed up against an outside wall set with a small barred window. I beavered away, my back to Mr Morton's office, face pointing toward the meagre light attempting to filter through the iron bars. Thank goodness this was only a temporary booking, the whole environment was too depressing for words.

The lunch hour was pretty much non-existent. I managed to find the Ladies and a concealed tea and coffee machine along a dark corridor, but upon returning to my desk with a limp sandwich, Mr Morton instantly materialised by my side requesting an urgent document for a two o'clock Probate appointment.

Time slipped by at a frightening rate. I was sure the hands of the clock didn't gallop as quickly when pottering about at home. Suddenly it was time to dash off on the school run. I hurriedly logged off and delivered the remainder of typing to Mr Morton's desk.

'Well Good-bye,' I trilled. 'See you tomorrow morning.'

'Where the devil do you think you're going?' Mr Morton barked.

'Er, did the Agency not explain about my children?'

'Haven't you got a childminder?' Mr Morton asked incredulously.

There then followed a lot of huffing and puffing before he finally dismissed me, muttering about beggars not being choosers.

Ruffled, I turned on my heel and stalked out. I thanked my lucky stars for opting to temp before jumping straight back into the unchartered waters of permanent employ.

That evening just as I'd flopped down in front of the television, the telephone rang. It was Stevie.

'Cass, enough is enough. I really do think it's time to stop dangling me on a piece of string. Can I please have a straight answer from you? Preferably now and not after Who Wants To Be A Millionaire?'

I hastily killed the television's volume. 'Yes Stevie. Of course. No more prevaricating.'

'Well?'

'I care about you Stevie. Really I do.' I heard his sigh of relief. 'But–'

'Oh Cass, no buts please. Let's just get back together and get on with our lives.'

'Stevie I do indeed want us to get on with our lives. But not together.'

'What the hell do you mean *not together*? How else but not together?'

'I mean living apart. Separate lives.'

'Listen to me Cass, you've had a devastating experience and you're still reeling. You're hurt–'

'Hurt?' I gave a mirthless laugh. 'Do you have any idea of the depth of my hurt?'

'Yes, yes, of course.'

Stevie gave a sigh of exasperation and I could almost visualise him making a gesture with his hands, pushing my answer away – an answer he didn't want to accept.

'Stevie, hurt doesn't just go away. You can't stick a plaster on it.'

'Of course not. But in time the pain would recede. Eventually it would go away.'

'I don't think so. I think it would always be there, festering.'

'Nonsense,' he scoffed. 'Time is a great healer. Everybody says that. It's a phrase that's as old as the hills.'

'Look, I'm sorry, but after that incredible confession cataloguing precisely how many affairs you embarked upon, I simply can't trust you any more.'

'They weren't affairs!'

'Oh?'

'They were mere *distractions* and meant absolutely nothing.'

'Well unfortunately they meant something to me,' I countered. 'And your *distraction* with Cynthia Castle sent me to hell and back again. Maybe I could forgive you in time – but I'm absolutely positive that I would never forget. It would always be there Stevie, rearing its ugly head, causing arguments and endless regurgitated hurt.'

'Cass please, I'm begging you now,' Stevie's voice cracked slightly. 'I know what I did was wrong. I've behaved abominably over the years.'

'Damn right. And made out that I was some sort of irrational, overly-possessive basket case.' My voice rose and my heart started to palpitate unpleasantly. 'When I think back on all the times you didn't come home, all the times I'd ring one of your mates or a colleague – even your secretary *dammit* – apologising profusely for interrupting their evening and asking if they'd seen you or knew of your whereabouts, making excuses that you'd probably told me but I'd been too preoccupied with the twins to take on board what you'd said – wining and dining a client, attending a boring function

'– how humiliating was that for me? And how embarrassing for those people having to think up lies to cover your backside?'

'Cass, listen to me. Hands up! I led you a merry dance. I admit that I made out you were imagining things. Yes, I am mostly the guilty party.'

'What do you mean – *mostly* the guilty party?'

'Well it takes two to break a marriage you know. You can't put all the blame on me.'

'Are you saying that I'm responsible for your affairs?'

'Only in the sense that you *were* always preoccupied with the twins. There was never any time for me.'

For a moment I felt wrong-footed. Had I neglected my husband then? Was it actually *my* fault he'd sought solace elsewhere? I cast my mind back to the early days of motherhood – the endless sleepless nights with two babies being fed on demand. I'd come to know exactly how a dairy cow felt as two little mouths clamped down on me. Eventually I'd resorted to bottle feeding. But barely had that got off the ground when the colic set in. And no sooner had the colic resolved then the teething had started. Perhaps, instead of shuffling exhausted from the nursery back to my bed, I should have cellotaped my eye-lids open and slipped into a French Maid's outfit. Injected a bit of oo-la-la into my sex-starved marriage? And then I came back to the present.

'Okay, maybe I was permanently exhausted in the early days and unable to give you my full attention. But that doesn't excuse you for the more recent flings. It certainly doesn't justify your affair with Cynthia. In fact Stevie, how *dare* you try and point the finger of blame at me.' Tears stung my eyes. But they weren't tears of sorrow or self-pity, they were tears of anger. And justifiably so. 'How bloody *dare* you!' I shrieked.

Stevie instantly realised he'd overplayed that particular hand and tried to retract the statement.

'Calm down Cass, I'm not saying it was *all* your fault because it wasn't. You were a wonderful wife and an excellent mother-'

'Oh good. I'm glad to hear you say that Stevie because for one moment I thought you were trying to lay all the blame at my door.'

'No, no, not at all,' he soothed.

'Excellent. So let's get this conversation back on track. Where was I? Oh yes, separate lives-'

'Cass you're making a mistake-'

'No! Hear me out please. I need to be true to myself from now on. I don't want any reconciliation. In fact,' I took a deep breath, 'I want a divorce.'

Chapter Four

Following my request for a divorce, Stevie's immediate reaction was one of dismissal.

'You're not thinking properly Cass,' he'd stormed. 'When you've removed your brain from your backside we will resume discussing our future. A future *together*.'

Work provided a welcome distraction even if Morton Peck & Livingston's staff were as much fun as a leaking roof. On the home front I had since owned up about my whereabouts between nine in the morning and three in the afternoon. Both children seemed relieved that I was out of the house every day and otherwise occupied. Another happy diversion came in the form of Jed who telephoned me on my mobile in Friday's lunch hour.

'Am I speaking to the gorgeous Cassandra?'

Swooning slightly, I squeaked confirmation into the handset.

'I know it's rather short notice, but I wondered if you'd like to go to the cinema this evening?'

I squeaked a bit more as mutual times were agreed. It was only after Jed had rung off that I realised a small matter of babysitting arrangements were outstanding.

Hastily I punched out Stevie's mobile number.

'Have you come to your senses yet regarding our reconciliation?' he barked.

'Er, no. Would you like to see the twins tonight while I go out?'

'Are you asking me to babysit my own children?' he asked incredulously.

I considered. 'Yes.'

He sighed irritably. 'Of course I'll have them, but Cynthia is having a Girls' Night In tonight. It might be better if I see them at home.'

Home. He still thought of our house as his home. It was inevitable that at some point we would need to get around to sorting out the house, its ownership, our belongings.

'We still have talking to do,' I ventured.

'Damn right we do,' Stevie huffed. 'You need to stop and think carefully before making nonsensical demands like divorce.'

'If you live in a glass house you shouldn't throw stones.'

'What the hell's that supposed to mean?'

'Did you ever stop and think carefully before permitting Cynthia Castle to strip you down to your socks and impale upon your person her PERMANENT DEPOSITS OF SUBCUTANEOUS FAT?' my voice rose to a shriek.

There was a moment's silence.

'I'll see you at seven,' Stevie snapped before hanging up.

A hand lightly touched my shoulder. I looked up, cheeks pink with anger, to regard Mr Morton boggling at me.

'Er, could you type this up Mrs Cherry?'

Blast and damnation. He must have heard everything. But did it really matter? Especially when Carmel telephoned with the good news of another booking next week for a law firm in nearby Boxleigh.

'And you have made them aware about the part-time hours and the fact that half term is looming?' I whispered into the handset.

'The Personnel Officer is desperate to secure any sort of available assistance so I can promise it isn't a problem,' Carmel assured.

Before leaving Morton Peck & Livingston for the last time as a temporary employee, I made discreet enquiries via Reception as to who was the matrimonial solicitor. An appointment with Mr Livingston was pencilled into my diary.

Stevie turned up at six, an hour earlier than arranged and consequently caught me wearing just a bath towel and applying full party make-up.

'Going out with Nell?' he enquired.

'No.'

When I failed to elaborate Stevie followed me into the bedroom, observing my indecisive wardrobe riffling.

'Sorry, do you mind?' I jerked my head toward the open door indicating he leave.

Ten minutes later I tiptoed downstairs in a cloud of perfume intent on blowing hasty kisses to the twins before scampering round the corner to wait for Jed. Stevie was watching television, a child tucked under each armpit. The bottom stair creaked and Livvy turned.

'Wow, you look nice Mum.'

Stevie instantly disentangled himself from the children and followed me to the shoe cupboard.

'Who did you say you were going out with?'

'I didn't,' I said just as the doorbell rang.

Stevie got there first.

'Er, hi. Is Cass there?' I heard Jed ask.

I rammed my feet into a pair of stilettos.

'Are you taking my wife out?' Stevie spluttered.

'Jed!' I trilled, barging past Stevie. 'How lovely to see you.' My eyes were wide with unspoken meaning which I desperately hoped he would cotton on to. I turned back to my slack-jawed husband. 'Back about midnight. Toodle-oo!'

As we drove off, Jeff gave me a side-long look.

'Cass, I'm not getting into a tangled web am I?'

'Not at all!' I laughed shrilly. 'That's my ex. He's simply seeing the children while I'm out. No big deal. We're cool,' I was appalled to find myself slipping into Toby-speak. Jed looked unconvinced.

The evening was blighted from the start. At the cinema we watched a romantic comedy, but all hopes of flirty hand holding were off the agenda. Afterwards we went to a little eatery which lacked any sort of atmosphere and reflected the widening chasm as Jed mentally distanced himself. I found myself jabbering nonsense to fill the silences. Flustered, I began to feel more and more upset.

When Jed dropped me home I was horrified to see Stevie silhouetted in the lounge window like a sentinel. After a few agonising seconds, Jed cleared his throat.

'Cass, exactly how *ex* is your ex?' he asked.

'Well, you know, *ex* as in over and done with.'

'But not divorced?'

'Oh yes definitely. Well, you know, almost definitely. It's just a matter of finalising things.'

'So you've got your Decree Nisi?'

I bit my lip and didn't answer.

Jed took a deep breath and contemplated his hands folded firmly in his lap.

'Cass, I'm terribly sorry, but I'd rather steer clear until your husband is most definitely a fully fledged ex-husband.'

So that was that.

'And you've got the nerve to bang on about *my* adultery!' Stevie hissed as I drooped through the door.

'I have not committed adultery with anybody,' I snapped. 'I've simply been out to dinner with a friend. Now please leave my house because I'm not in the mood for an argument.'

'This is my house too Cass and don't you bloody forget it.'

With that he snatched his jacket from where it lay over the banister and stomped off into the night, the door slamming behind him.

The following day I caught up with Nell who kindly agreed to look after the twins when I have my appointment with Mr Livingston, the matrimonial lawyer.

'Are you sure about going through with a divorce?' she asked placing a large mug of steaming coffee in front of me.

'Absolutely. Stevie confessed to a list of conquests *this* long,' I held up my hands indicating a gap of several feet. 'The man could have given me an ST.'

Nell looked momentarily stumped. 'Sanitary towel?'

'No, you know, sexually transmitted lurgy stuff.'

'Oh, right. That reminds me of a joke,' she broke into a few guffaws.

I flashed a wounded look over the rim of my coffee cup.

'I'm not taking the Mickey, honest. One of the teachers told me this one.'

I sighed. 'Go on.'

'Two guys are chatting over their pints together. One said to the other, "Did you get your test results from the doctor?" and the other guy morosely answered, "Yeah. Looks like all those years of phone sex has caught up with me. I've got Hearing Aids".' Nell paused expectantly. 'Cue laughter,' she prompted.

'Sorry, I'm miserable at the moment.'

'Then don't divorce Stevie!'

'I'm dejected because of something else.'

'What?'

'Do you remember that chap I met at Passé?'

'The looker?'

'Mm. Well, he took me out the other day and again last night.'

Nell instantly straightened on her stool. 'Go on.'

'And then he dumped me.'

'Dumped you? But I thought you'd only just got acquainted?'

'Yes, we had. But then he met Stevie.'

'Why the devil did you introduce him to Stevie?' she squawked.

I gave her the low down concluding with Jed disappearing over the horizon in his natty little sports car, never to be seen again.

'I see,' she considered. 'Well, if the boot had been on the other foot Cass and you had driven to Jed's only to find wifey waving him off, what would you have thought?'

Point taken I suppose.

'Listen, I'm having a little dinner party in a couple of weeks. Why don't you join us?'

'No way. I'm not up for any of that being-paired-off-with-the-spare-berk-nonsense.'

'He's not a berk,' she giggled.

'Ah ha, so there is a spare man!'

'He's a vicar, very nice and you're coming.'

Time was passing quickly now that I was working. Suddenly I was once again donning my black suit, this time for Hempel Braithwaite along Boxleigh's bustling high street.

The receptionist, in complete contrast to the last one, was a merry faced girl in her early thirties with a mass of brown bubbly curls haloing her head.

'Can I help you?' she smiled.

'Hi, I'm the temp, Cassandra Cherry for Mrs Grace Herbert in Personal Injury.'

'I'm Julia. Take a seat and I'll let Grace know you're here.'

As I sat down, I had an awful moment of déjà vu and fervently prayed Mrs Herbert wouldn't be in the same mould as Mr Morton. Thankfully she wasn't. Grace Herbert was a dear little apple dumpling of a lady with several chins, ample hips and ankles that folded over the sides of her sensible shoes. Mrs Herbert peered at me over pince-nez spectacles attached to silver chains as she extended a hand in greeting.

'Hello my dear. I hate formality so do call me Grace. I just know we're going to get on like a house on fire. Capricorn?'

'Er, no, it's Cassandra.'

Out of the corner of my eye I saw Julia stuff a fist in her mouth. She looked like a definite mate.

'No dear, your birth sign.'

'Oh! Yes, I believe so.'

'Excellent!' Grace beamed as she led me out of reception and along a corridor. 'I get on extremely well with Capricorns.'

'Jolly good,' I smiled uncertainly.

Was that the only qualification required then? Never mind being able to type at one hundred and twenty words a minute or demonstrate a good telephone manner. Just make sure your birth sign was the goat and rest assured you were unlikely to lock horns with this particular solicitor. How eccentric.

The day went quickly and the work was – dare I say it – a piece of cake. Dictation was clear with impeccably given instructions so it was virtually impossible to make mistakes. My fingers whirled over the keys producing reams of printed documents and, as the hands of the clock nudged towards midday, I asked Grace if she would like a cup of coffee.

'Ooh lovely dear. Three sugars please and put some of the

sweet stuff in yours too. It's very good for shock and I can tell you've had a few lately.'

Definitely eccentric.

I went off in search of the kitchen faintly amused. What did she know about my life?

All too soon it was time to get Livvy and Toby from school.

'Cheerio dear. See you tomorrow. You go and see to those lovely twins of yours.'

'Will do,' I smiled.

I couldn't wait to see my children's happy faces as they spilled through the school gates with their friends. Swinging my handbag jauntily over my shoulder, I was half way across the car park before being brought up short. How did Grace Herbert know my children were twins? I stood stock still until a car tooted me out of its way. Oh how silly Cass! The agency must have told her. Of course.

But the following day Grace Herbert stunned me by making reference to the legal appointment with Morton Peck & Livingston. I was one hundred per cent positive I hadn't mentioned anything about it in conservation. Her blue eyes twinkled over her little spectacles as she smiled mysteriously at me.

'Sometimes I'm privy to certain information dear.'

I wasn't at all sure I understood that comment.

Once home I telephoned Stevie to advise him of the impending appointment with the solicitor. I didn't want him being unprepared for the letter that would duly plop through Cynthia's letterbox.

He gave a sigh of resignation. 'I can't believe you're doing this Cass.'

'Stevie please. I don't want to start arguing. I just want to get on with my life.'

'We don't need to be divorced for you to get on with your life.'

I thought back to the fiasco with Jed.

'I think it's better this way.'

'Are you absolutely sure this is what you want?' he asked grimly.

I took a moment to desperately try and recapture just the smallest of sparks. Sadly there wasn't even a splutter.

'Quite sure.'

'You won't turn into one of those bitter and twisted women who withhold access or use children as an emotional weapon?'

'Of course not!' I retorted, deeply offended.

We then had a surprisingly amicable chat about finances. Stevie said he was prepared to sign over the entirety of the house to me on condition I accept only a small monthly payment for the twins. The mortgage was paid off two years ago so the house represented a solid amount of equity. If I drew upon my bond's annual interest and continued temping, then financially things would be stable.

'Tell this legal bod to keep it straightforward. I'm not messing around with solicitors myself, so just give me the paperwork, show me where to sign and we'll split the bill. Agreed?'

I couldn't say fairer than that.

As I approached Morton Peck & Livingston's building the following afternoon, I repressed a shudder. Shouldering open the door, nothing had changed. What a dreary place.

'Cuthbert Livingston, pleased to meet you Mrs Cherry.'

My solicitor shook my hand before indicating a chair opposite his desk. Dapper and with a warm manner, he was nothing like Mr Morton.

Nervously I sat down. While Mr Livingston selected a clean page on his scribble pad and searched for a functional biro, I glanced around his office. Fake wood panelling encased all four walls. Grey light filtered through dusty Venetian blinds. Battered filing cabinets lined the far end of the room. It was with a pang of sorrow that I realised the first steps to formally ending my marriage should end in such a gloomy room, in utter contradiction to the way it had all begun. A warm day, bathed in lemon sunshine, a young bride floating amidst a sea of white lace, tumbling hair sprinkled with a rainbow of confetti.

The receptionist suddenly barged in bearing a tea tray. With a jangle of cheap bracelets, she set down the regulation china and stale shortbread, simpered to Mr Livingston and even managed to bare her bleached teeth in my direction. Clearly paying clients were entitled to a free smile. I gave a chilly one in response.

After the best part of an hour outlining general divorce procedure and taking copious notes, Mr Livingston told me not to worry about anything and to leave matters in his capable hands.

'Is that it then? Don't you need any proof of adultery?'

'Not at all Mrs Cherry. The days of private investigators jumping out of bedroom wardrobes and catching couples playing *coitus* are long over.'

'I saw my husband and Cynthia Castle with my own eyes. Believe me Mr Livingston, neither of them were playing quoits.'

I continued to work at Hempel Braithwaite and found myself enjoying it. Julia, the receptionist, was definitely a new pal.

'So how are you getting along with our Gracie then?' she asked one lunchtime over a whiffy egg mayo bap.

'Fine. She's great to work with. Just a bit, oh I don't know–'

'Weird?'

'A little,' I admitted. 'She seems to know an awful lot about me and my personal circumstances, but I'm at a loss to understand how.'

'She's known as Godly Grace in the firm.'

'Why?'

'Because she's psychic.'

'Don't be daft,' I guffawed and promptly choked on a crumb. Julia thumped my back until I could breathe again. 'You mean,' I croaked, larynx struggling for complete recovery, 'that she wraps a shawl around her head, pops a pair of gold hoops in her earlobes and then consults a crystal ball?'

'Sort of, but without the props.'

'Oh don't be ridiculous. You don't believe all that mumbo-jumbo do you?'

'I'm telling you Cass, Grace Herbert could probably tell you what colour knickers you're wearing *and* when you last bonked your husband.'

Even I didn't know what colour underwear I'd hurriedly pulled from my knicker drawer earlier this morning. Grotty Grey probably. And as for when I'd last – well it was unthinkable.

'Gracious,' I eventually replied.

'Gracious Grace,' Julia giggled. 'Ask her to give you a reading some time. She's really rather good.'

As another working week drew to a close the Personnel Officer, Susannah Harrington, summoned me to her room. Tall and thin with a beaky nose, iron grey hair and coal black eyes, she wouldn't have looked out of place as the Governess of a female prison. Susannah was, in fact, absolutely charming but her officious presence automatically reduced me to check stockings for ladders and fingernails for dirt.

Timidly I tapped upon her door.

'Come,' a voice boomed from within. 'Don't look so scared Cassandra,' she chided as I scuttled over to her desk. 'This isn't a disciplinary hearing. In fact,' she rearranged some paperwork and then switched her telephone to voicemail, 'I want to praise you.' She smiled and the austere features instantly softened.

And it was indeed high praise, so much so that Hempel Braithwaite wished me to join them permanently as a floating secretary.

'How wonderful!' I enthused before realising the ramifications of full time work. 'But, I'm so sorry Susannah. I have to stick to temping because of my children you see.'

'I fully understand my dear and that is exactly what Hempel Braithwaite would like you to do. But within our stable of employment rather than the recruitment agency's. We suggest you carry on working from nine to three and spend school holidays with your delightful children, but on the proviso you work exclusively for this firm.'

'I don't know what to say,' I gasped as the full realisation of what Susannah was suggesting hit me. My God! How absolutely brilliant – I wouldn't need a childminder and I'd be earning a guaranteed regular wage.

'Just say yes dear. We will give you a fixed rate of hourly pay which will be higher than the agency's rate, but no doubt lower than we are currently being billed by them. So, what do you think?'

'I think, well I think yes! Thank you! Thank you so very much!'

Meanwhile Julia's gossip regarding Godly Grace had left me both intrigued and curious, so much so that I succumbed to a 'reading'! However, unlike Julia, I was not remotely sold on Grace's so-called predictions. Okay, a few trivial incidents were accurately touched upon, like the time I fell off my bike as a child. But what child hadn't ever fallen from their bike? Liv and Toby were mentioned, but I wasn't convinced Grace hadn't somehow found out about them previously. She mentioned my pending divorce – a lucky guess? – and the fact that Stevie was 'a loveable rogue dear, but definitely a rogue'. Yes, well, I would imagine a good percentage of divorced men were dumped on the grounds of them being *lovable rogues*. Personally I preferred to call them unfaithful bastards.

Regrettably it wasn't a thrillingly atmospheric reading. Grace didn't slip into a trance across a tasselled tablecloth. Instead she matter-of-factly stated that I'd already met my future husband – naturally a soul mate – and would be married by the end of the year.

Right. So exactly who was this hunky soul mate? I'd been out with precisely one man – Jed. That friendship had barely wobbled off the ground before it came to a big fat full stop. That left the competition being divided between the postman with teeth so stained by nicotine they resembled a burnt picket fence, or the newspaper boy with hair raising halitosis. The fact that one was old enough to be my father and the other young enough to be my son was mere detail.

I politely thanked Grace for her amusing predictions privately thinking she was as nutty as a fruitcake.

That evening the telephone rang.

'Are you still on for tomorrow night?' Nell asked anxiously.

Hell. I'd forgotten about her dinner party and the blind date.

'Can't wait,' I fibbed wondering if this would be a convenient moment to develop a throbbing migraine and bail out, but Nell was two steps ahead of me.

'I was just phoning to make sure you weren't getting cold feet.'

'Ha ha – as if! Although I'd feel a lot happier knowing you and Ben won't be nudging each other smugly over the petites pois if, by some dint of good fortune, this chap and I do happen to hit it off.'

'Don't be daft, we wouldn't dream of doing that. Anyway, it's only a bit of fun.'

'So where exactly did you and Ben meet this vicar?'

'Oh Ben's played golf with him a few times,' she airily dismissed my interrogation. 'Clive occasionally makes up a four with Bill and Fiona, but it would be fair to say that he's more their pal than Ben's, and I gather Fiona is really into the church scene. She just *adores* Clive.'

'Well clearly he must have something going for him other than a heavenly handicap.'

After Stevie had collected the twins the following evening, I stood nervously in Nell's kitchen sipping chilled Chablis. My neighbour was extremely pink in the face, flapping arms at me as I got under her feet. Every now and again Nell would peer fretfully through the oven's glass door at a duck sizzling away before darting off to the hob to stir a scrumptious smelling plum sauce. A mountain of chocolate profiteroles balanced precariously on a crystal platter nearby. All evidence of Marks & Spencer's packaging had been disposed of. Fiona's culinary reputation was apparently legend-like and Nell was determined to pass off the evening's efforts as entirely her own.

'Please do not mention anything about the packaged or processed food that is normally consumed in this house.'

'What's wrong with that?' I demanded, chippy from alcohol on an empty stomach.

'I'd just prefer you not to breathe a word.'

'Dear God,' I rolled my eyes.

'And don't say the God word either. Clive thinks it's blasphemous. Shit!' squeaked Nell. 'They're here.'

Ben answered the door while Nell hastily despatched Dylan to his bedroom, a brand new DVD tucked under one armpit and under dire threat not to reappear for precisely one hundred and twenty minutes.

I scuttled into the lounge clutching a refreshed glass of wine just as Fiona and Bill wandered in trailing a camp looking man. From that moment I just *knew* the evening was doomed.

Ben led the introductions.

'This is Cassandra, and Cass this is Bill-'

I shook hands and fixed a smile on my face.

'And Fiona-'

'How do you do!'

Bill and Fiona, dressed in matching Pringle sweaters, made an obvious public statement that they were Mr and Mrs and belonged exclusively to each other. Both sported the permanently ruddy complexions of those who loved the great outdoors. It was very apparent that Fiona did not possess any pot or tube bearing the words *face* and *cream*.

'And finally this is Clive.'

Tall and thin with a receding hairline and bobbing Adam's apple, Clive limply shook my hands.

'I gather you play golf?' I smiled.

'Only when there is time, which is regrettably short. Are you partial?'

'No, not really. Ambling across a huge field sporting a pair of outrageous checked trousers and dropping my sticks in the sandpit isn't my idea of fun, ah ha ha ha,' I trilled merrily.

Clive looked pained. 'The correct phraseology is *green, clubs* and *bunker*.'

Jerk. I tried again. 'I gather you're a vicar?'

'Yes.'

I blinked. Was that it then? No wish to elaborate? I nervously cast about for a conversation filler.

'I've just remembered a religious joke I heard somewhere,' I brightly informed my uninterested audience, 'Oh yes, you'll love this,' I slapped my thigh and winked at Fiona. 'Did you hear about the agnostic dyslexic who questioned whether there was a Dog?'

I promptly convulsed, clutched my sides and wheezed at the carpet.

Fiona looked blank. 'Not sure I understand that one actually.'

I hastily excused myself on the pretext of giving Nell assistance, leaving them to talk about birdies and bogies. Such ridiculous terminology. Why on earth had I agreed to this?

'What do you think then?' Nell nodded her head in the direction of the lounge as she inserted hands into huge oven mitts.

'You've got to be joking.'

Dinner was served. The drink flowed and things began to liven up. Clive was a pompous bible basher who repeatedly waved his fork around to emphasise a point whilst taking us all on a verbally guided tour of the New Testament and predictions within Revelations.

'Oh yes, it's all there,' he informed. 'Pestilence, plague, disease, flooding, earthquakes. Just take a look around the four corners of the world and see for yourself.'

Hell this man was depressing. I flung some more wine down my neck. I was bored silly and not more than a little tipsy. When Clive finally paused for breath I jumped into the gap and excitedly told everybody about Grace Herbert and her psychic predictions.

'Ah. A charlatan in league with Satan,' Clive nodded knowingly.

'What *are* you talking about?' I squinted across the table, stabbing my own fork around in mid-air. He wasn't the only one in the room with a monopoly on the cutlery.

'Evil souls conjuring demons and devils.'

I banged my fork down on the table so hard everybody visibly jumped. 'That's just typical of people like you Clyde.'

'Clive.'

'Whatever. The trouble with you is that you're narrow minded, bigoted, fusty, crusty, blinkered and biased. You vicars smugly sell your Alpha courses, sit in church with your happy-clappy congregations, sing a few pop songs passed off as modern day hymns all the while with your heads stuck firmly up your bums.'

Fiona gasped, Bill blanched, Nell began making frantic head

twitching gestures and Ben snorted with unsuppressed laughter, but there was no stopping me now.

'Wasn't Jesus a psychic, hm? Answer me that one! He knew all about when he was going to die, who would betray him and how he would rise again. And what about his miracles eh?'

'Oh does this Grace Herbert do miracles too?'

'Every day!' I howled indignantly, although admittedly I had yet to see her multiply her packed lunch into a board room banquet or place her hands on the photocopier and heal it from jamming. 'And what about David Blaine?' I demanded, 'I've seen him levitate right off the pavement. Nobody accuses him of being in league with the devil do they?'

'I think you'll find Jesus is incomparable to David Blaine,' the Adam's apple in Clive's neck was yo-yoing furiously up and down his windpipe.

'How so?'

'Because Jesus was the Son of God, whereas David Blaine is an illusionist.'

'Don't you try and pull the wool over my eyes Clint. I'll have you know that I am *more* than familiar with the Da Vinci Code.' I nodded my head sagely and tapped the side of my nose with a forefinger for good measure. Except my nose seemed to have relocated and I ended up poking myself in the eye instead. With a streaming eyeball I turned to address Ben and Nell.

'A wonderful evening dear neighbours but sadly all good things must come to an end. Fabulous grub Nellie-Wellie. Good old Markies eh?'

Chapter Five

I awoke the following morning with a headache and a misty memory nagging my conscience. Had I made inappropriate conversation? Something to do with a religiously psychic evil charlatan posing as Jesus and floating off a sidewalk? I had a nasty feeling I owed Nell an apology.

Half an hour later, hair still wet from the shower, I sat in Nell's kitchen clutching a mug of coffee.

'I'm so sorry,' I wailed, 'I don't know what got into me.'

'An awful lot of wine?' she ventured with a wry smile. 'Don't worry. I forgive you. It was quite funny actually, particularly when you interrupted Clive's lecture on Genesis.'

'What lecture?'

'You told Clive that after God created man He'd taken one look at Adam and declared 'I can do better' before collapsing into hysterics over the After Eights.'

'Geez.'

'Oh forget it Cass, it couldn't matter less. Now then, tomorrow it's Valentine's Day. Are you going to buy anybody a card?'

'Like who?'

'What about Jed? Perhaps you could re-establish links now that you've started proper divorce proceedings.'

'I don't think so,' I sighed.

I briefly pondered whether Stevie had bought a card for Cynthia Castle. Bastard. With a bit of luck Cynthia might squash his penis flat.

So I purposefully ignored Valentine's Day and instead flung myself into half term activities with Livvy and Toby. But even though spending quality time with the children was great fun, there was a frozen space deep inside me which felt out of sorts. Like having an ice cube lodged in one's heart.

I sometimes caught myself aching for a pair of warm arms to embrace me. But not Stevie's. Perish the thought. No, I wanted the comforting and nurturing arms of somebody who loved me both deeply and unconditionally.

One evening, long after the twins had gone to bed, I dolefully rummaged in the larder for a bag of toffee popcorn before switching on the movie channel. I selected a Bridget Jones film. She was a singleton wasn't she? Maybe she had a leaf I could borrow from her book of life.

I poured myself a stiff gin and tonic and settled down to watch. Within moments I was hooked. Entranced, I flung my head back and poured toffee popcorn straight from the packet into my open mouth. It cascaded over my face and showered off sideways into my hair. No matter because Bridget was skiing in her own inimitable style down a vertical ski slope straight into a pharmacist's, winning a slalom championship en-route.

By the time I'd worked my way through a second sizeable gin, it came to me with resounding clarity that all my problems would be resolved if I went skiing. I sipped some popcorn and flung gin all over my face before staggering upstairs to bed.

Thus I returned to my job upbeat and full of optimism. As I shot into the Pay and Display car park, I spotted one remaining space and bee-lined towards it just as a gold Rover appeared in my rear view mirror. The driver revved impatiently and attempted to squash past in a bid of out-manoeuvring. Narrowly avoiding a nasty prang, I zoomed into the remaining slot.

The man's horn blared. Unfazed I gathered up my handbag, umbrella and car keys only to discover the driver getting out of his car. Oh joy.

'Oi you!'

Ignoring him, I tossed my head back and briskly strode off.

'Hey I'm talkin' to you Missus Fancy Raincoat!'

I stopped and gave him a cool look.

'Yes?'

'That's my parking spot you've just nicked.'

'I think you'll find this is a public car park.'

'That as may be, but the unspoken rule in this *particular* car park is those that get 'ere at this time of mornin' pick their spot and stick to it. An' that's *my* spot.'

'Well we'll have to agree to disagree on that. Good-bye.'

'You haven't heard the last from me,' the man yelled furiously.

Oh Lord. Anxious to put distance between us, I quickened my pace. Deciding not to take any chances, I broke into a run.

Julia looked up from her switchboard as I crashed into Reception. 'Goodness, you're keen to get here!'

'That's me,' I scraped a shaky hand through my hair. 'Ready, willing and able.'

'I'm very pleased to hear it,' purred an oily male voice. 'How wonderful it would be if all women were as enthusiastic as you.'

I spun round to find myself staring into the depths of charcoal pinstripe so sharply tailored it could possibly inflict wounds. My gaze travelled up to a wickedly grinning raffish face.

'Mr Collins,' he stuck out his hand. 'And I do believe you are Cassandra?'

'Yes,' I gasped as my hand was captured in a handshake like no other. For one crazy moment I thought Mr Collins was about to lift my hand to his cupid-bowed lips. Instead he grinned like Bruce the Shark encountering Nemo.

Brilliant. In the space of five minutes I'd encountered both the car park lunatic and the office wolf.

I caught Julia's broad wink as Mr Collins led me out of Reception and off to his office where the touchie-feeliness continued for a few minutes longer disguised under the cloak of gallantry. Warm fingers brushed the nape of my neck as he thoughtfully took my coat. My backside was given the tiniest caress as he oh-so-thoughtfully whipped out the typing stool. An arm glided around my shoulder as he cosied down, cheek to cheek, on the pretext of showing the location of keyboard and mouse. When an arm suddenly brushed across my breasts as he tapped in a password I shoved back the typing stool. The castor wheels squeaked in protest as they viciously ran over Mr Collins' soft leather slip-ons. He let out an undignified squawk.

'I'm *sooo* sorry Mr Collins,' I apologised, cupping my hands to my face in a gesture of horror but managing to execute a perfect clip on his chin in the process. 'Oh *God*! I'm just *sooo* sorry.'

'Quite all right. No worries,' he squeaked, nervously backing away.

The rest of the morning mercifully passed without incident.

At lunch time I grabbed my bag, keen to be off to the travel agents to pick up a couple of ski brochures. But on approaching my car I was brought up short by its appearance. The windscreen was decorated in lemon Post-it stickers, all covered in abuse and clearly the poetic work of Mr Angry. I looked around. There was his car. Right by the entrance. Despite finding an alternative parking space, clearly he had felt it necessary to vent his spleen.

Irked, I peeled off the stickers along with a plastic envelope. Oh terrific. A parking penalty. In my haste to scarper to safety I had completely overlooked a little matter of feeding the ticket machine. Stuffing everything in my handbag, I started up the car and headed off to the travel agents.

Emerging back into the sunny high street a little while later, I felt a glow of achievement. Folded under my arm were two holiday brochures sporting leaping snowboarders hurtling through space, salopetted legs tucked under jacketed torsos.

At five minutes to three, Mr Collins thanked me profusely for my wonderful typing, spot-on spelling and immaculate presentation before clearing his throat.

'Cassandra my dear, would you like to meet up later for a drink – purely to discuss clients of course. It would give you the chance to get familiar with some of the cases, legal policies and so forth.'

'Well how very kind of you Mr Collins,' I demurred. 'But I have my children keeping me extremely busy this evening.'

Mr Collins raised his palms in a gesture of backing off. 'Of course, of course. Have a lovely evening Cassandra dear.'

In the car park Mr Angry's gold Rover was still in situ. Slipping behind the wheel of my car, I foraged around in my handbag for a pen and paper. No paper. Rooting around in the glove box, I discovered an old letter. The envelope would suffice. Smoothing out the creases, I began to write.

Starting up the car's engine, I furtively glanced about before reversing backwards. Straightening up, I let the car trundle toward Mr Angry's vehicle with a growing feeling of daring-do and not a little giggly. But the smile was wiped off my face when noting a second gold Rover had materialised from nowhere and parked alongside Mr Angry. Hell. Which car was his?

I pulled up the handbrake and cogitated. Surely it was the one nearest the entrance? Scanning the area to make sure nobody was about, I eased open the driver's door. Which one? This one! Oh God, no, no, it was that one! Wasn't it? Dithering, my eyes flickered back and forth from one identical car to the other. This one!

Head down, I scuttled the short distance throwing in a couple of guilty zig-zag turns for good measure. Carefully I placed the envelope under the Rover's windscreen wiper before scampering back to my car and gunning out of there.

The following morning I parked right at the other end of the high street in a different Pay and Display.

At lunchtime Mr Collins suggested we partake in a spot of lunch together, purely to discuss clients, their cases, legal policies and so forth. I thanked him and said I already had an appointment. I pulled on my coat, aware that Mr Collins was staring lasciviously at my black stockinged legs, and set off to the Travel Agent to book a week's Easter skiing in Risoul.

That evening I tossed a brochure apiece at the twins. 'Tell me what you think of this!'

'Wow!' Toby sucked in his breath.

'Oh Mum, this is so cool!' Livvy exclaimed.

'Isn't it just!' I grinned happily as the doorbell rang.

Feeling decidedly chipper and half expecting it to be Nell, I skipped down the hallway trilling, 'I'm coming, I'm ca-ha-ha-humming!'

I flung the door wide but my smile died. For there on the doorstep, wearing a particularly pained expression, was Brad Pitt aka Ploddy.

'Oh. It's you.' I stared at him in the glow of the outside courtesy light.

'It is indeed me,' Ploddy confirmed gravely. He raised his hand, holding aloft an envelope. 'Does this belong to you?'

I gulped. '*Poss*-ibly.'

'The envelope bears your name and address.'

'Ah yes, in that case it is definitely mine,' I whispered.

My eyes snagged on Ploddy's vehicle parked on the driveway. A gold Rover.

'Mrs Cherry I came to the conclusion some time ago that you were something of a character, but nonetheless felt compelled to visit you for an explanation. Why do you feel I should,' he paused to read my writing, 'partake in a spot of anger management?'

I cleared my throat. 'I'm terribly sorry Mr Pitt. There's obviously been a dreadful misunderstanding.' Miserably I gave the explanation.

'I see,' said Ploddy eventually. 'Not road rage but Pay and Display rage.'

Was I mistaken or did his lips twitch with the ghost of a smile?

As I sat, the following morning, with Mr Collins perched in close proximity on the edge of my desk, I irritably wished the man would stop invading my personal space.

'And here's another sentence that requires slight tweaking.'

His body leant in closer as he regarded my monitor, a wrist brushing against mine as he suggested changing a full stop to a comma. I gnashed my teeth and tried not to asphyxiate over the keyboard as wafts of aftershave assaulted my respiratory system.

'Absolutely first class Cassandra. You really must let me thank you properly for all this marvellous work you're producing. What about lunch?'

'Would this be to discuss your clients, their cases, legal policies and so forth?'

'Absolutely!'

'Then I'll have to decline because I really like my lunch hour to be a total respite from work.'

'Ah.'

As I was powdering my nose in the Ladies, Julia swung through the door and cheerfully greeted my reflection.

'Hi! How are you getting on with the office letch?'

'Tell you in Starbucks?'

'Sure. I'll give you some tips on how to fend him off.'

'Do you speak from experience?'

'One hundred per cent.'

At a quarter to three Mr Collins materialised by my desk, noisily clearing his throat. I removed my headset and glanced up.

'Now Cassandra my dear, you look absolutely exhausted working those poor little fingers to the bone. I really do insist you join me for a spot of sups this evening. I know a wonderfully cosy little bistro.'

But my ready excuse died on my lips as, without any announcement, a glamorous middle aged brunette swept into the office. Mr Collins jumped like a scalded cat and shrivelled before my eyes as he bowed and scraped all over the place. I gave the haughty stranger a curious look which she immediately caught and volleyed back with a supercilious stare.

'Mrs Cherry, would you be so kind as to make coffee for *Mrs Collins*?'

Mrs Cherry eh? That was a first.

Five minutes later I returned with the coffee only to find Mr Collins pulling on his coat while Mrs Collins impatiently tapped a well shod foot.

'Ah, change of plan Mrs Cherry,' he blustered whilst attempting to squeeze past me, stomach touching his backbone lest some part of his body touch mine in wifey's presence. 'Sorry about the coffee, we're going out for a late lunch.'

'Super,' I smiled brightly. 'You must take Mrs Collins to that marvellous bistro. You know, the one you constantly want to take me to – purely to discuss your clients, their cases and legal policies of course.'

'Ah ha ha ha,' Mr Collins laughed looking slightly sick.

I went off to the kitchen to tip the unwanted coffee down the sink with a smile on my face.

The weekend's arrival had me hitting the shops with the twins to get kitted out with our ski gear. Stevie turned up to collect the children just as I was trailing bulging shopping bags through the front door. He had some rather unexpected news.

'Cynthia's moving.'

'Moving? As in moving *away*?' I boggled. 'Where does that leave you?'

'Exactly where I am at the moment.'

I gazed at him uncomprehendingly.

'I'm buying Cynthia's house,' Stevie explained. 'It was only ever a temporary situation Cass. I knew it. She knew it. And now she wants a fresh start somewhere else.'

'Oh she does, does she?' I rounded on him, suddenly furious. I was aware of the twins sloping past, silent and anxious, but I couldn't zip my mouth. 'After wrecking our marriage, *Cynthia* wants a fresh start.'

'Cass it was my fault, not Cynthia's.'

'Your fault...her fault...whatever!' I spat. Upstairs I heard bedroom doors tactfully closing. 'I think it's pretty damn rich that she's moving lock, stock and barrel to start all over again after a relationship breakdown – a relationship that barely lasted two months – while I'm still here facing the neighbours and embarrassment after years and years of marriage.'

'Cass, would you just calm down and–'

'Calm down? And now,' my voice rose shrilly, 'and *now*–'

'And now we're going to be permanent neighbours.'

I stood there, chest heaving, fists clenched angrily. Stevie stared at the floor, scuffing the heel of his shoe backward and forward before breaking the silence.

'Sounds to me like you still care Cass,' he said softly. 'We could call the divorce off. It's not too late.'

'You're right,' I exhaled slowly. 'I mean you're right it's not

Cynthia's fault. If it hadn't been her, it would undoubtedly have been somebody else. So no, Stevie, the divorce goes ahead.'

When Stevie finally left, taking Livvy and Toby with him, I felt edgy and unsettled. It didn't help having the entire house to myself without the twins' noise. God it was quiet. And lonely.

Grabbing a bottle of mineral water from the fridge I wandered into the lounge and flopped down on the sofa. Flicking through the satellite channels, I tried to lose myself in a house makeover programme. Distraction came in the form of a rather hunky male presenter urging a middle-aged couple to rip out their pre-war Formica kitchen and replace it with a contemporary work of art.

I took a sip of mineral water, fidgeting restlessly. Maybe it would help if I had my own home project to concentrate on – something to throw myself into, keep busy and stave off loneliness. A kitchen refurb perhaps? The more I thought about it, the more I liked the idea. And why stop at the kitchen? Why not redecorate the entire house? Maybe get shot of some scruffy furniture along the way. Ousting the old marital bed would be quite symbolic. I wouldn't mind a sexy leather sleigh bed. It would certainly have Nell arching an eyebrow in disbelief.

I fiddled with my wedding and engagement rings while I cogitated. They twirled around my finger, their familiar chinkety-chink playing over and over. Suddenly the rings jammed painfully against my knuckle. I stared at them in bemusement. What was the point of getting a new bed to mark a fresh start when I was subconsciously clinging to married woman status? I should have taken the rings off ages ago. Indeed, many a woman would have hurled them at her unfaithful husband long before now, never mind one that had fornicated before her very eyes.

I grimaced at the memory. It still hurt. I wondered if the emotional fall-out would ever completely go. The light caught and played on the dainty cluster of diamond chips, sparks shooting off like miniature fireworks. Pretty rings. Inexpensive. It was all we could afford at the time. Stevie had kissed me and promised that one day I'd have an eternity ring too. Needless to say that had never happened. And now it never would. I looked at the rings on my finger for the last time before slipping them off.

As I drove to Hempel Braithwaite on Monday morning, I did some financial calculations. My money bond's annual interest was ready to be drawn. There was enough to take care of a kitchen and maybe a bit more too. I liked the idea of having a project to throw myself into. Even my dreams last night had been hectic with designers and luvvies re-decorating the house. I'd stood in the midst of chaos shrieking, 'I can't *possibly* have yellow paint Laurence – it will clash with my hair.'

In Reception Susannah Harrington was waiting for me.

'Good morning Cassandra dear. Let me introduce you to Morag McDermott, one of our dynamic solicitors in Company and Commercial.'

I shook hands with a dour looking thirty-something female who looked as dynamic as a pair of old socks.

'Morag will be your boss for the next three weeks while her secretary holidays in America.'

'Pleased to me you,' I smiled at Morag while my tummy contracted. I wasn't getting good vibes from Ms McDermott at all.

I settled down to work and tried to tune out the poisonous atmosphere emanating from my new boss.

As the week progressed, my misgivings about Morag proved unhappily correct. At around eleven every morning she would storm into our shared office apparently nursing a monumental hangover. She would then slam things around her desk, growl into a mobile and achieve absolutely nothing. Come noon, in a fit of bad temper, she would wordlessly stalk out without a backward glance. Invariably, just as I was reaching for my coat to go home, Morag would stagger through the door wafting whisky fumes and declare *we* had a lot of work to do.

So far I'd managed to avoid a drunken screaming match as invariably she would sit down, nose dive on to the ink blotter and snore robustly.

But on this particular morning Ms McDermott happened to

be waiting for me, an expensive shoe tapping impatiently.

'What time do you call this?' she snapped.

Do not rise Cass, do not rise. I looked at my watch. 'Five minutes to nine,' I carefully replied.

She flung a tiny plastic cassette at me. I dodged and it landed on my desk's surface with a light clatter.

'I want this typed and ready for half past nine on the dot.'

And a very good morning to you too Morag McCow. Just what was this female's problem? Either she had rampant pre-menstrual tension or one hell of a personality disorder. God help me if it was both.

At noon Morag once again disappeared with no explanation whatsoever and didn't return until I had logged off and was buttoning up my coat. But instead of sinking soporifically down on to the ink blotter, she instead collapsed upon her chair, placed her head in her hands and surrendered to uncontrollable sobbing.

My instinct was to rush over and offer comfort, but she wasn't the most approachable of people. I didn't want her blotchy face rearing up and snarling at me to bog off. In the end I made do with awkwardly patting her shoulder.

'Er, Morag? Can I make you a cup of coffee?' I asked gently. She peered at me vacantly through brimming eyes. 'Morag? Have you had bad news?'

She gave the smallest of nods. 'Yes,' she whispered. 'Terrible news. My husband doesn't love me any more.' Her face crumpled. 'I've only been married six months.'

Ah.

Over the next few days I got to know the real Morag. She was actually an extremely nice lady with a heart as soft as a strawberry centre. Her entire family lived in Scotland and she had nobody in the South of England other than her estranged in-laws.

'I was initially so wrapped up in my marriage and work that I didn't really make any friends down here,' she confessed one day.

'Well you can certainly count me as a mate. It's the weekend tomorrow. What about we have a get-together on Saturday night. The twins will be at my ex's so I won't have to hurry home.'

'I'm available all day,' Morag hinted, looking at me hopefully.

I smiled. 'Unfortunately I'm not. I'm checking out new kitchens but you're welcome to keep me company.'

'Oh no thanks,' she wrinkled her nose. 'The excitement of whether to choose ash or cherry wood cabinets would be too much for me.'

'Don't mock,' I waggled a finger playfully. 'This is my new project designed to keep me busy and buoyed up.'

'Are you still feeling terribly raw?' she asked looking sympathetic.

I shrugged. 'It's getting better. See you tomorrow evening.'

The following morning I beetled off to the local DIY store's kitchen department. An earnest salesman tapped the vital statistics of my kitchen into a computer. Hey presto! In no time at all I was being shown a computer generated virtual tour of a kitchen Delia would die for.

'I want it,' I squeaked excitedly.

'I'll get the fitter to give you a call. Are you around this afternoon?'

I didn't have long to wait.

'Hello, is that Mrs Cherry?'

'Speaking.'

'My name's Euan. I'm the fitter who will be installing your new kitchen. Would you mind if I paid a brief visit just to verify the drawing measurements and check out power point locations?'

'Not at all,' I replied. 'When do you want to come?'

'Well I've actually got a slot right now.'

I hung up feeling tremendously excited. Things were already starting to move on this new project.

When I opened the door to the fitter, I literally caught my breath. It was as though I'd been slugged in the stomach by a bag of cement. He simply oozed sexiness. I invited him in, all the while blushing furiously and feeling ridiculously tongue tied.

'I suggest that if you're removing the breakfast bar and relocating this row of cabinets, it might be prudent to put in a bank of electrical sockets in this area.' Euan's eyes were a mesmerising sapphire blue fringed with long sooty black eyelashes. My own mousy-browns positively shrieked with jealousy.

He smoothed the drawings out against the worktop with strong looking hands. I was shocked to find myself wondering what those hands would feel like travelling over my body.

'Mrs Cherry?'

'Oh please, call me Cass.'

'Cass?'

'Mm.' I liked the way he said my name.

'Cass?'

'Mm, mm.'

'Er – do you agree Cass?'

'Oh sorry! Yes, that sounds absolutely fine. Fantastic. Ha ha!'

I hadn't a clue what he'd been talking about.

'Is it just the kitchen you're doing up?' Euan asked conversationally.

'Well I started off thinking it would just be the kitchen but,' I shrugged and gave what I hoped was a mysterious little smile, 'I imagine it might extend to other things – some new furniture maybe. Top of the list is a sexy leather bed,' I grinned.

'A sexy leather bed eh?' Euan murmured.

Was it my imagination or had the room suddenly gone terribly still. And if I wasn't mistaken, was that not a twinkle in his eye? Too late I realised this wasn't Nell I was gossiping with.

'Y-yes. Amongst other things of course. Well thank you so much for your time Euan,' I smiled brightly, determined to put the conversation back on a businesslike track. 'See you again soon.'

That evening Morag picked me up in her natty little sports car and together we drove into Boxleigh Village. She'd somehow managed to secure a booking at an exclusive Italian trattoria which usually required a fortnight's advanced booking. I pondered how she'd achieved this. Perhaps she'd ventured down earlier in person and bandied her not inconsiderable chest around in front of the mesmerised maitre-d'.

I sipped my wine and listened as, bit by bit, Morag once again took me through the meltdown of her fledgling marriage.

'I hope you don't mind me repeating myself Cass, it's just that it helps to talk about it.'

'Of course,' I nodded my head, understanding exactly what she meant.

'It was destined to fail from the start,' she grimaced. 'When I met Gordon he was a debonair fifty-two year old with a senior partnership in a top London law firm.' She took a sip of wine. 'And very definitely married.'

'Oh dear.'

'Yes. Oh dear. He captured my heart within moments of our meeting and within days we'd embarked on an illicit love affair. It was giddy stuff. A month later Gordon declared he couldn't live without me unless I was permanently by his side – as his wife.'

There was a pause while a waiter took our orders.

'And then he got divorced,' I prompted her.

'Yes. A quickie divorce followed. Meanwhile I transferred to Hempel Braithwaite to escape the gossip. We then had a discreet civil wedding with me congratulating myself on bagging such a dynamic, successful and distinguished husband.'

'But you haven't really told me *why* it all went wrong,' I regarded her over the rim of my wine glass.

'It went wrong when I pointed out that I was in my mid-thirties and horribly aware of the ticking biological clock. I wanted to start making babies, but Gordon already had three children to fund in private education with expensive lifestyles. He told me to direct any maternal energy towards my new step-children.'

'Easier said than done.'

'Too right. His girls positively reviled me. I was the *other woman* who had broken up their parents' marriage. So then the arguments started with me constantly bitching and sniping.'

She broke off as the waiter re-appeared bearing plates of spaghetti carbonara.

'It got so bad we were barely civil to each other. And then one day Gordon simply moved out. Just like that,' she clicked her fingers. 'Initially I didn't know where he'd gone. Eventually a colleague gave me a tip-off and I tracked him down.'

'Where was he?'

'Back with his first wife.' There was a pause while Morag wrestled with her emotions. 'What am I going to do Cass?' she looked at me with watering eyes over her untouched meal.

'I'll tell you exactly what you're going to do – you're going to bounce right back and get on with life!' I sucked a long tendril of spaghetti into my mouth. 'Who needs men anyway?'

'My vibrator is very good at a lot of things but it can't make babies.'

The couple at the next table choked on their garlic bread.

On the way home Morag drove like a man – fast and aggressive. As she flew down the outside lane of the carriageway it was with a sinking feeling I spotted a blue flashing light in the passenger wing mirror. A split second later a wail rent the cool night air.

'Bugger,' Morag declared. 'Is he after us?'

I twisted my neck to look over my shoulder. Head lamps flashed in confirmation. Morag slowed and pulled onto the hard shoulder before unfolding her shapely legs from the car to greet the police officer.

'Good evening Madam, do you know what speed you were travelling at?'

As soon as I heard his voice I froze.

'Before we go any further,' Morag imperiously informed, 'I'd like you to know I'm a solicitor.'

'That's nice. And I'm a police officer,' Ploddy confirmed the obvious.

I pulled up my collar and slid slowly down in my seat while Ploddy asked if the vehicle belonged to Morag and requested sight of her driver's licence.

Irritably Morag flung open the driver's door. 'Pass me my bag Cassandra,' she snapped.

I leant across the driver's seat and silently placed the little clutch bag in her outstretched palm. Upon hearing my name, Ploddy peered enquiringly through the open door. As he stared at me in disbelief I could feel myself beginning to squirm. Was he the only police officer in Kent?

'A very good evening to you Mrs Cherry.'

'Thank you – and to you too Mr Pitt.'

Ploddy stared wordlessly at me before giving the smallest shake of his head.

Eventually the roadside meeting concluded with Morag being instructed to attend the local police station with all sorts of documents.

As we set off home at a sedate forty, she gave me a sidelong glance.

'He was almost worth getting nicked for. Did you see his eyes Cass? God they were absolute heaven. And what about those wonderful broad shoulders?

'Mm.'

'I hope he's on duty when I pay the local nick a visit. He can certainly put me in handcuffs any time. I wonder what his name is. How does he know you?'

'Don't ask,' I groaned.

Chapter Six

Once the twins were back from their weekend with Stevie, we sat down together we went through a collection of home style magazines.

'Can we have our bedrooms made over?' asked Livvy.

'But I thought you loved Barbie,' I said.

Livvy stuck two fingers in her mouth and made gagging noises. 'I did – when I was *five*.'

'Mum, we're going to secondary school next year,' Toby pointed out. 'What do you think my mates are going to say when they come over? Hey, like the Action Man wallpaper bud.'

'Point taken,' I grumbled.

I left them to it and wandered off to my own bedroom. Standing in the open doorway, hands on hips, I assessed the room and tried to visualise ideas. I would definitely buy that leather bed. A jumbo one allowing plenty of room to stretch arms and legs like a starfish. A mental picture of my kitchen fitter rolling around with me on the mattress suddenly popped into my head. I rubbed my forehead in bemusement. Now where had that idea sprung from?

At work the following day, as the hands of the clock edged toward lunchtime, Morag tossed her handbag across her shoulder and confidently sashayed out the office to visit the police station with her documentation. She returned an hour later po-faced and disappointed.

'He wasn't there.'

'Who?' I asked as I pressed buttons and sent a document off to print.

'Your policeman friend.'

'Believe me, that man is no friend of mine,' I insisted, picking papers up from the print tray.

'God he was a stunner.'

I was too busy thinking about another stunner to comment.

The stunner in question rang my mobile an hour later.

'Hello Cass? I need to talk to you about local tiling and plastering where the breakfast bar is to be removed. I also have some suggestions about the downlighting.'

'Right, fire away.'

'I think it would be better to meet up and discuss it – then we can both be sure about what we want out of this.'

'Er, right.' For a moment I wasn't sure if he was talking about the kitchen or us.

'Excellent. I'll pick you up this evening then, about seven.'

'That would be heavenly,' I gushed into the handset. 'I-I mean, fine. Whatever.'

My face was flaming as I ended the call. You idiot Cass. For God's sake get a grip. Your workman was simply suggesting an informal business meeting to discuss an impending job. A contract. Not a date. Got it? Right. In which case, why weren't we having the meeting on site so to speak?

I immediately whirled into action and telephoned Stevie to ask if he would have the twins for a little while this evening.

'Sorry Cass, can't do. I've got a date with a racy little blonde number.'

Well it hadn't taken him long to move on from Cynthia had it? Or me for that matter? What about all those tear jerking pleas for reconciliation?

In the end I telephoned Nell, managing to catch her on a staff room tea break.

'Any chance of you having Liv and Toby for a couple of hours this evening?' I asked breathlessly.

'Tell you what Cass, why don't I give them their tea and then they stay for a sleepover. You can return the favour for me when Ben and I go out to celebrate our wedding anniversary tomorrow. It would be nice to know we can continue the party once back home – if you catch my drift.'

'Deal!'

The day wore on with my mood getting more and more excitable. In total contrast Morag was sinking into a grey depression.

'Fancy going for a drink after work Cass and drowning a sorrow or two?'

'I'd love to,' I lied, 'but truly can't. Got to sort out this new kitchen business.'

'Oh well. Guess I'll have to have an early night then. Just me, a brandy and my vibrator.'

I made a tutting noise. 'You could always watch a movie you know.'

Morag perked up. 'Good idea — me, the brandy, vibrator and a blue movie.'

I shook my head and smiled. 'See you tomorrow.'

Once home, I quickly gathered uniform for the following day and walked the twins over to Nell's. Scampering back across the grass strip between the two houses, I tossed my jacket over the banister and trotted up the stairs. What was I going to wear this evening? Half an hour later the bed was piled high with rejected clothing. I charged back down the stairs and dashed over to Nell's.

'I need to borrow something,' I panted desperately.

'Sure. What do you want — milk? Bread?'

'No. Cropped jeans, stiletto heeled boots and a plunging top to show off my cleavage.' Nell gazed at my drooping chest with an expression of disbelief. 'I know my bosoms are currently in the grip of gravity but a Wonderbra will sort that out — can I borrow one of those too please?'

'You'd better come in. I thought you were having a business meeting with your kitchen fitter?'

'I am. Just want to make an impression that's all.'

'With your boobs jacked up to the moon?'

'Oh for goodness sake!' I sighed in exasperation.

Several hours later I lay in my bed — alone — mentally hugging myself. I wasn't remotely tired and recognised the tell-tale signs of having a thumping great crush on Euan.

We had started off nursing drinks in a cosy pub, chatting about the suggested plastering and downlighting ideas. That had taken —

ooh – about five minutes. Having dispensed with the formalities, we then went on to the informalities. Like the fact that Euan was separated from his wife. Although somewhat confusingly he was still living with her. However, this bit was speedily glossed over – something about waiting for a stale property market to recover in order to achieve peak price on the marital home. A distant alarm bell did faintly ring but was firmly ignored, especially when Euan went on to reassure that he and the wife were married in name only and it was strictly separate beds.

We sat drinking and talking until finally, with a deep sigh of regret, Euan looked at his watch and said he had to be going. No sooner was I firmly ensconced in his passenger seat, he leant across the handbrake and pulled me toward him for a very thorough kissing.

'When I drop you home, will you be asking me in for coffee?' Euan grinned wickedly at me, his face suffused in the orange lights of the car park.

'No!'

'Never?'

'Not yet.'

'Ah,' he grinned, 'so it's just a case of biding my time and being patient.'

As his car pulled up outside my house, Euan caught my hand in his. 'I'll see you soon beautiful lady,' he promised, drawing my hand to his warm lips.

Moi? A beautiful lady? I wriggled delightedly as I hugged the memory of his words to myself. Pulling the duvet tightly up under my chin, I drifted into an untroubled sleep with a smile on my face.

Morag was in a much more upbeat mood the following day.

'Feast your peepers on that!' she grinned. 'Doesn't it make you positively salivate with longing?'

It was a fulsome article on the joys of holidaying in the Caribbean. A photographic layout showed turquoise water lapping white sand, remote islands smothered in green palms along with an arty-farty shot of stacked conch shells. I nodded my head in agreement.

'I really can picture myself stretched out on that sand,' Morag said wistfully, 'some handsome ebony guy with a big todger massaging me with coconut oil and plying me with rum before whisking me off for a thoroughly good seeing to.'

'Sorry to bring you back to reality, but this post needs signing off before I collect the twins.'

Morag sighed and picked up her fountain pen.

'I miss sex,' she stated as her flashy signature scribbled across the A4.

'Right.'

'I need sex like food and water.'

'Right.'

'I'll have to do something about it. Soon.'

'Right.'

On the drive to school I idly reviewed my own sex life. Non-existent unless I included last night's erotic dream involving Euan.

Nell walked Dylan over that evening before going out to celebrate her wedding anniversary. As Dylan disappeared to join the twins on their PlayStations, my neighbour lunged forward grabbing my wrist in a Machiavellian grip.

'Not so fast! What's with the sparkly eyes, dewy skin and backward smile?'

'Eh?'

'You keep grinning like the village idiot.'

'Don't be daft!'

'Are you in love?'

'Oh bog off Nell. Go and have a brilliant evening with Ben and bonk him senseless when you get back home.'

'Yes I will,' she assured. 'But you and I have some serious catching up to do.'

The working week zipped by and all too soon it was another Saturday. Within minutes of the twins leaving for Stevie's, the telephone rang.

'Is that the gorgeous Cassandra?'

'Euan!' I coiled a strand of hair around one finger like any girl in the first flush of crush.

'I want to whisk you away from the washing up.'

'Excellent news.'

'I'll pick you up at eight.'

When I opened one eye the following morning I wasn't sure if I'd had another erotic dream or not. I sneaked a sideways look. No, it had definitely been the real thing. Lying next to me was my kitchen fitter.

I truly had not intended to leap into bed with a virtual stranger – and on the second date no less. The fact that I had previously put fresh linen on the bed, exfoliated my entire body, carefully dressed in sheer black stockings and squirted every nook and cranny of my skin with scent was nothing more than appalling coincidence.

After being wined and dined it had seemed only polite to offer a nightcap of some sort. Trembling with nerves, I had barely set down the coffee cups rattling away in their saucers when Euan had wordlessly picked me up in his strong arms, strode up the staircase and tumbled me onto the bed.

Like a scene from a romantic film my hair had billowed out, fanning itself attractively across the pillows. As Euan stared down at me in the rosy glow of lamplight, I could almost hear the accompaniment of film music rising to a dramatic crescendo as he grasped his leather belt and tore at the buckle fastening.

'God you're beautiful Cass,' he'd declared as his trousers were carelessly tossed to one side. 'You are the most gorgeous, sensual, sexy, desirable woman I have ever met.'

I'd occasionally been called attractive or pretty in my time, but never had so many flattering adjectives been used to describe me of all people. It was heady stuff and I urgently felt the need to qualify those words.

And suddenly I was in the grip of a living fantasy. Never before had I felt so desired and desirable. The writhing female throwing herself with great gusto into a sexual marathon was no longer a middle aged woman with an overstretched tummy from a double pregnancy. Nor was her waistline marred by one too many chocolate biscuits or her thighs dimpled with a smattering of cellulite. In her place was a blonde bombshell that sizzled and spat with newly discovered sexual energy.

At around midday, just as he was leaving, Euan planted a lingering kiss on my upturned face.

'Cass, we are at the beginning of a very special chapter in our lives.'

I grinned by way of response. I hadn't the energy to formulate actual words.

And so began a discreet romance. I hugged the secret to myself, not daring to tell a soul, terrified in case Livvy and Toby found out and wanting to protect them above all else.

The days blended into one another and suddenly the Easter holiday loomed along with the impending ski trip. Typically, having now met a gorgeous chap, I found myself not wishing to leave him for a whole week.

Late one afternoon Nell tapped on the back door just as I was making a coffee.

'We have some serious catching up to do,' she sternly informed me.

'Oh? What about?'

'Don't play the innocent with me Cass. Come on. Make me a coffee and tell me about this man you've met.'

'What man?'

'The chap who's going to fit your new kitchen one of these fine days.'

'It's all in hand,' I assured. 'Just as soon as the twins break up from school.'

'The only fitting schedule I want to know about is how this guy is fitting into your personal life.'

'There's nothing to tell. We've just been out for a drink a few times.'

'And?'

'And, well, that's it really.' I placed a steaming mug before her. 'He's a mate.'

'As in *play*mate presumably.' She folded her arms across her chest and adopted a bossy tone. 'Cass this is like pulling teeth. Utterly painful. Now come on. Spill the beans.'

'What beans?'

'The sexy ones. Is he good in bed?'

'Nell, what sort of a question is that!'

'A nosy one. And don't pretend you haven't bonked him because you've got a red flush spreading up your neck. Which is probably where the expression *scarlet woman* comes from,' she nodded knowingly and dipped a Hob Nob in her mug.

'Oh all *right!*' I threw my hands up in a gesture of surrender. 'What precisely do you want to know?'

'Good girl,' she grinned rubbing her hands together. 'Let's start off with the most important question first. Has he got a big willie?'

That evening the telephone rang but all I could hear was heavy breathing.

'Hello?' I asked cautiously.

'Do you see how I'm panting for you Cass?' laughed Euan.

'Very funny.'

'Can I come over this evening?'

'Sorry but I have to say no.' Much as I was longing to see Euan, the twins would be at home and I wanted my private life kept well away from them.

'But Cass, you're off to Italy this weekend. When am I going to see you?'

'I could see you for a couple of hours tomorrow, but it would have to be late afternoon when the twins are with their dad.'

'Okay. See you then.'

It had dawned on me some time previously that, with Euan in my life, it was essential my underwear was up to scratch for any impromptu bedroom liaisons. It was no good giving come hither looks togged out in grey undies. Thus I had recently invested in a stash of sexy lingerie. Running my fingertips over a purple bra boasting maximum plunge, I pulled a matching thong from the drawer and topped it all off with a floaty robe.

When Euan eventually turned up for our rendez-vous, it was

not Cassandra Cherry, part-time secretary and harassed mother, who greeted him. Oh no. In her place was a sensual being. As Euan shut the door and properly registered my attire, his eyes gleamed with appreciation.

'Bloody hell Cass, that's one heck of a dressing gown.'

The entirety of our time together was spent in bed, mattress springs wildly protesting as Euan embarked on what an onlooker could be forgiven to think was a wrestling session.

The twins and I were awoken by the clock radio blaring into life at five the following morning. Our flight was hellishly turbulent.

'This plane is better than the Corkscrew at Alton Towers,' declared Toby.

The initial relief of exchanging an airbus for a coach on terra firma was short lived. As our burly driver navigated narrow mountain passes and repeatedly swept around hairpin bends, it seemed as if the massive vehicle would tumble at any second down the sheer drop. On more than one occasion my stomach wanted to cosy up with my tonsils.

Eventually we rumbled into the picturesque village of Risoul which sported scenery straight out of a winter wonderland movie. To our right, in the distance, skiers in brightly coloured snowsuits flashed like colourful ants against a backdrop of glistening white.

The hotel was rustic in a cuckoo clock sort of way. The proprietor, Pierre, greeted his weary arrivals with smiles and largesse, before showing us to our family room.

Liv and Toby peered into cupboards and poked around before throwing open the wooden French doors which issued onto a balconied veranda. Icy air blasted around the room.

'We can chuck our ski socks out here at the end of the day Mum,' Toby suggested. 'Dylan told me they get really whiffy.'

'Your socks are whiffy all the time,' Livvy flashed back.

'Don't start!' I bellowed. 'Shut those doors please Toby. I want the pair of you to come with me. There is ski equipment to collect.'

Much later, while the twins were cleaning their teeth before bed, I discreetly sent Euan a text message.

Wish you were here.

He didn't reply.

Standing nervously with the rest of the adult beginners on the nursery slope the following morning, I could see Liv and Toby making pals in the Children's Club ski group. I cast about for somebody to strike up my own friendship with.

'So what do you think of Risoul?' I smiled at a big bottomed woman to my right.

'Not bad,' she shrugged her well padded shoulders.

'And what do you think of,' I glanced about, 'the scenery?'

'Not bad.'

At that moment our ski instructor arrived. Jean-Paul had the sort of smouldering looks and sexy accent guaranteed to make most females weak-kneed.

'Wow,' I murmured to the big bottomed woman, 'I bet I know what you think of him!' I gave her a wink and cheeky grin. '*Not bad!*'

She stared at me. 'I wouldn't know. I'm gay.'

'Zees morning,' Jean-Paul addressed his motley group of beginners, 'we learn 'ow to snow plough.' He adopted a wide pigeon-toed stance. 'Eez eemportant for stupping.'

Jean-Paul slid slowly down the slope's incline by way of demonstration before executing a perfect halt.

'What you theenk?' he asked me.

Personally I thought he had an excellent butt and a damn good pair of thighs.

That evening I locked myself in the bathroom with my mobile and tapped out a second text message to Euan.

Still wishing you were here.

And then I reluctantly switched off the handset. As anybody knows, a watched phone never rings. Or, in this case, never bleeps.

The following morning I eagerly fell on the mobile phone convinced it would yield a text message from Euan. Disappointingly the handset remained silent.

Bit by bit our holiday rhythm got underway. All three of us

would rise fairly early to do a six hour stint on the ski slopes. The twins would impersonate a pair of supple elastic bands while their mother creaked stiffly up and down the mountain slopes. Periodically I tried contacting Euan but with no success.

On the last day, Jean-Paul pronounced everybody good enough to ski a red run. The slope was littered with soft mounds of snow, as if an army of mad moles had been tunnelling upward. From our great height I could see Risoul spread below like a white tablecloth embroidered with fir trees. I gulped and tried to concentrate on the ski instructor.

'We do leetle turns around zee moguls,' Jean-Paul instructed. 'Après moi s'il vous plait.'

Setting off, I was aware of a tight knot of snowboarders coming up from behind. As they swooped closer, their boards hissing in the snow, my concentration began to unravel. Suddenly one of them shot right across my path and upset my balance. Within seconds I was hurtling off, out of control. My stomach shot into my oesophagus as I gained upon the boarder, my skis bouncing right off the mountain. I must have looked a bit like a leaping thoroughbred at the Grand National, but with none of the grace. And suddenly I was on top of him, smashing into his body, sending the pair of us crashing down on an icy patch.

There was a horrible crunching noise as skis and board briefly entangled before both my skis came right off my feet, deflecting to the side. But my ordeal wasn't over. I might be down, but I was still travelling.

'Argh!' I screeched in terror as I slid head first down the mountain. Mercifully I hit a mogul and veered sideways into a soft bank of snow.

Shocked, I watched the world from an upside down view, as waves of pain ricocheted throughout my upper body. My right cheek was burning as if torched by flame. The snowboarder tore off his board and bounded over to my side.

'Hey, are you okay?'

'Funnily enough,' I hissed, 'I am *not* okay. I think my neck's broken.'

I sat up and flexed my neck from side to side.

'Your neck isn't broken.'

'What do you know,' I snapped. 'At the very *least* I've broken my jaw.'

'Your jaw is fine but I think you might have left half your cheek on the ice back there.'

The man pulled off his visor and I gasped. It was *him*. Brad Ploddy Pitt! Out here in Risoul!

I ripped my goggles from my disbelieving face as he, in turn, stared incredulously at me. At that exact moment, a woman scrunched to a halt by his side spraying us both with snow.

'Is she all right? What happened?' The woman removed her super trendy sunglasses and I immediately recognised Ploddy's female sidekick. She stood looking poised and elegant, as if modelling skiwear. She had the most fabulous slanting cheekbones. Lucky cow. I wasn't sure I even had cheeks any more.

'You catch up with the others Selina while I make sure Mrs Cherry is okay.'

Selina looked incredibly put out.

'Oh. I'll see you at the bottom then.'

She set off with a flair that had me gnashing my teeth. Why didn't I look like that? Or have a figure like hers? She even had a sexy name. I stared after her sourly.

Ploddy retrieved my scattered skis and poles. Whenever I had the misfortune to be making a prize prat of myself, this infuriating man always seemed to pop up out of nowhere. Mind you, he had been the one at fault, snowboarding so close to me. Perhaps I could take the moral high ground this time? That would be good. I mentally rehearsed an appropriate rebuke.

Tell me Mr Pitt, what on earth were you thinking of? Were you not aware that mountains – like motorways – have speed restrictions? Might I be so bold as to suggest you partake in a spot of signalling before overtaking next time?

Tetchily I snapped my boots back on the skis and glared at Ploddy.

'I do hope Mr Pitt that in future you will demonstrate more

consideration instead of haring along like a lunatic, flattening innocent skiers in your wake.'

Ploddy's eyebrows shot up into his woolly hat. 'I beg your pardon Mrs Cherry but it was *you* haring along like a lunatic. Your skiing was erratic, uncontrolled and downright dangerous. Quite frankly you were a disaster waiting to happen.'

My aching jaw gaped in astonishment. Was this moron blaming me?

Ploddy's face was suffused with anger as he hunkered down over his snowboard and strapped his feet into position. Straightening up, his expression softened. But only by a smidgen you understand.

'Clearly you are shaken up. Can I escort you safely down the mountain and buy you a hot sweet tea?'

I closed my mouth and blinked a few times. Oh God Cass, don't start crying.

'Er, thank you but that won't be necessary,' my jaw wobbled violently. 'I'm actually with a group and they're waiting for me.' I nodded my throbbing head in the direction of Jean-Paul who, standing with the others, was looking up expectantly.

'Well let me at least take you back to your instructor.'

He pushed off, his snowboard expertly negotiating the mounds while I nervously trailed after him. As we drew up by the group, Ploddy stretched out a gloved hand and lightly touched my arm.

'By the way, my name is Jamie. Not Mr Pitt,' he grinned. He had very strong white teeth and the smile transformed him.

'Right,' I said weakly.

On the flight home I leant back in my seat and sighed deeply. Like one's first amour, the snowy love affair with Risoul would never be forgotten. Meanwhile I wondered if Euan had forgotten about me.

As soon as we were home, the twins went off to Stevie's, eager to show off their bronze medals and certificates.

Stevie was taking the following week off work as part of his annual leave and both children were staying with him. Which was just as well as the kitchen refurbishment was ready to start. If Euan turned up. I suddenly had doubts.

But Euan did turn up, his van stuffed to bursting with kitchen flat packs. He boisterously greeted me, slapping my backside with gusto before gluing his lips to mine. His unshaven stubble brushed painfully against my scabby cheek.

'Cass baby,' he whooped. 'Open up that garage door so I can unload this little lot and then you can unload me.'

'Why didn't you respond to my texts?'

'Because I lost my mobile. Left it lying around somewhere.'

'Well why didn't you ring me when I got home?'

'Because your number was programmed into my mobile silly.'

'Oh. Right.'

In no time at all saucepans, pots and pans spilt into the hall in a merry riot of stainless steel and non-stick Teflon while Euan dismantled the kitchen.

As the week progressed I thought I would end up screaming if I didn't escape the relentless boom of Euan's portable radio, the incessant thumps and bangs or the chaotic mess. Respite was required. Gazing across a sea of tools and discarded packaging, I signalled to Euan that I was going out before disappearing to Nell's for peace and girl talk.

'How's the kitchen coming along?' she asked.

'Euan's doing the finishing touches as we speak.'

'Goodness, that's fast work.'

'He likes to knock contracts out quickly, time being money and all that. All week he's started work early and finished extremely late. He's certainly packed in the hours.'

'Presumably that's not all he's packed in?'

'Don't be smutty.'

'Then don't be coy,' Nell countered. 'Come on, talk to me. What's he like in bed? You look a bit peaky actually. Is he wearing you out? Have another Hobnob.'

'If you must know I feel exhausted,' I confessed. 'The man's insatiable.'

'Well I hope he's also wining and dining you and not just bonking you senseless,' she said tartly.

'As it happens,' I beamed, 'Euan's taking me out tonight to celebrate the completion of the kitchen.'

When I returned home a couple of hours later, I caught my breath. Everything had been cleared away and Euan was down on his hands and knees washing the floor. I stared in open admiration at the beech cupboards and display cabinets, the new-fangled oven and the shiny black worktops running the length of three walls.

'It looks fabulous,' I yelled over the blaring radio, just as the doorbell rang. 'Won't be a mo.'

I shut the kitchen door against the background noise just as the doorbell rang a second time. No doubt it was Nell wanting to eyeball the new kitchen. Or Euan. Or both. Instead I came face to face with Ploddy. Or, given that I now knew his name, Jamie.

The ski suit had been exchanged for the familiar policeman's uniform. I glimpsed the gorgeous Selina in the passenger side of the waiting squad car. She caught me looking and gave a marrow freezing glare in return.

'Hello Cassie,' Jamie said and peculiarly my tummy flipped. Nobody had elected to use that particular short form of my name before. I liked it. Somehow it sounded...endearing. I gazed up at him, as if seeing him for the first time.

'I was passing and thought I'd make a quick detour to see if you were now fully recovered from your fall.'

My hand automatically touched the side of my face which was still slightly tender.

'That's very kind of you. I'm not so bad thanks. And, er, how are you?'

I suddenly felt horribly shy.

'I'm fine. Top of the world actually after all that mountain air. A great stress buster.'

'Oh yes, absolutely,' I nodded. 'Your job must be terribly stressful – intercepting burglars, chasing thieves, wrestling with gangsters, busting international drug rings-'

Jamie threw back his head and hooted with laughter which had a detrimental effect on Selina. Her mouth had all but disappeared and she was looking frostier by the moment.

'My particular line of police work is not so exhilarating Cassie. It's more often than not attending traffic accidents, curbing late night drunken revelry, hunting vehicles stolen from car parks that mysteriously turn up in other car parks.' His lips twitched. 'I'm just teasing Cassie.'

I snatched another peek at the scrumptious Selina who was now impatiently drumming her fingers on the dash.

'Well, at least your everyday police routine is uplifted by the perk of working with a beautiful partner,' I nodded in the direction of the squad car.

Jamie followed my gaze. 'My girlfriend.'

I felt momentarily winded and heard a sharp intake of breath. Apparently mine.

'Gosh!' I exhaled frantically. 'Lucky you!' Oh God, why had I said that? It made me sound like a dyke or something. 'I mean, lucky her.' Hell. Now it sounded as though I fancied him instead. 'What I mean is, how lucky for both of you.'

'Is it?'

'Oh absolutely because you can work together and, er, go out together and at the end of every day you can both go home together, so that's very lucky indeed.'

'I see,' replied Jamie looking confused. 'We don't actually live together, just occasionally date. But we certainly work together and I guess I'd better get back to the job. I'm very glad you're okay Cassie.'

Jamie gave me another smile. It lit up his face. I felt strangely weak and leant against the door frame. At that precise moment Euan stuck his head around the kitchen door.

'Cass!' he bawled loud and clear. 'How about you wiggle into your posh purple underwear for me?'

Chapter Seven

By the time Monday morning arrived I was emotionally the worse for wear. I couldn't wait to get to work and lose myself in legal documents. Anything to blot out the disastrous events of the weekend.

At lunchtime, Morag caught me in the corridor just as I was drooping out to get a sandwich.

'Ah ha!' she pounced. 'Hold it right there Cass, I'm joining you. A little bird tells me you were in Cavendish's on Saturday night and caused quite a rumpus.'

'Please don't ask.'

'Of course I'm going to ask! Hey buck up Cass,' Morag nudged me in the ribs.

'I don't know why you're so chipper.'

'Because it's good to know I'm not the only one having a shitty time.'

So, in due course, we settled down in Starbucks and I told her how both my professional and private relationship with Euan had abruptly ended.

As I'd stood in my new kitchen delighting in the transformation, Euan had swept me into his arms.

'I desire a beautiful evening with my beautiful lady,' he had huskily whispered before kissing me tenderly on the lips. Naturally I'd melted to goo.

Euan had booked Cavendish's, a local award winning bistro which sported sky high prices which would ordinarily have left me gasping for an oxygen mask. The atmosphere was dreamy. Candles floated in bowls of pink liquid and white roses in silver vases adorned the crisp linen. A gurgling fountain lit with fairy lights was the restaurant's centrepiece. A discreet waiter materialised by our sides. The wine list was offered in murmured tones.

We were half way through our exquisite meal in a packed restaurant when a red haired woman catapulted through the door. It crashed back on its hinges causing several heads to look up. A waiter rushed to greet her but was shoved to one side.

'Where is he?' she screeched. 'Where the fuck is he?'

I craned my neck to see what was going on.

'Someone's in hot water,' I whispered to Euan.

He glanced up and froze, fork suspended between plate and mouth. The woman's furious eyes were darting from table to table, scanning the seating arrangements. Her flint grey eyes honed in on our table and, in that moment, I just knew.

'You *bastard*!' she shrieked, swiftly weaving through the dining room's obstacle course of customers, tables and chairs.

'Euan?' I bleated.

'*Euan*?' she mimicked.

The previous background babble had become a highly charged silence with all eyes firmly on table eleven.

'Who are you and what do you want?' I quavered.

'I'll tell you exactly who I am,' the woman waggled a polished talon at me which she then prodded me hard in the shoulder with.

'I'm his wife. Got it? His *wife*. And what I want-'

prod prod

'Is for you-'

prod prod

'To get your claws-'

prod prod

'Out of my husband-'

prod prod

'You WHORE!'

And with that she lunged at the ice bucket and slung a load of freezing slush over my head. Before I'd even managed to react, my dinner plate had been flipped into my lap.

There was a collective gasp around the restaurant followed by an electrified buzz as diners began nudging each other. The waiters gathered into a five strong group and frogmarched the raving redhead off the premises. Chuntering broke out with disgusted looks being tossed my way. For make no mistake, the crowd's sympathy was firmly with the wronged wife.

'You lied to me!'

Nothing like stating the obvious.

Euan didn't look up or even answer. I dabbed ineffectually at my hair with a sodden tissue. Fortunately the congealed mess in my lap had collected in the linen napkin spread over my thighs. With shaking hands I dumped it on the table. Mustering the vestiges of my dignity, I strode out of both the restaurant and Euan's life.

Throughout the ensuing week I deliberately kept myself busy in the evenings, painting the newly plastered kitchen. As I viciously rolled emulsion across the ceiling I kept hearing Euan's wife's angry diatribe playing in my head. She'd called me a whore. I wasn't a whore, but by God she'd made me feel like one. My mind flew back to the night I had discovered Cynthia Castle with Stevie. I felt tarred with the same brush. Cheap.

'What's for dinner Mum?' Toby wandered into the kitchen.

I chucked the roller in its tray and scratched my head vigorously. 'Something quick and easy. How about egg and chips?'

'All right.'

'How was school today?' I dropped a kiss on his forehead before turning to wash the roller out in the sink.

'Okay. We had a puberty talk.'

'Ah yes.' I had mentally mopped my brow upon signing the school's consent form, relieved that they were taking charge of this potentially tricky subject.

'Remind me Mum, what does ejaculate mean?'

'Gosh…well now…um-'

'Don't worry Mum, I'll look it up in the dictionary.'

'Excellent idea!'

I squeezed the roller out just as Livvy came in.

'When's tea?'

'Soon,' I replied wiping my hands dry.

'Hey, you'll never guess what.'

'What?' I shook oven chips into a pan.

'Sadie's dad's going into hospital,' Livvy informed with round eyes. 'For an operation on his bum hole.'

'Why's that?' asked Toby banging a large Oxford dictionary onto the kitchen table.

'He's got piles.'

'Piles of what?'

'Piles of dangly bits. Like grapes.'

'Well I'm sure Sadie's Dad would like to keep his bottom private,' I shut the oven door and gave a tight little smile indicating the end of this indecorous conversation.

'How do you get piles then?' Toby persisted.

Livvy inclined her head to consider. 'Sadie thinks it's something to do with reading a newspaper on the toilet.'

I hid a smile in the palm of my hand and thanked God for my children. Despite a failed marriage and an abortive relationship which had ended so horribly, I was still lucky. Unlike Morag, who went home to an empty house night after night, I had Livvy and Toby. They filled my life with their own special brand of love, warmth and happiness.

Meanwhile Morag, utterly fed up with her own company in the long evenings, button-holed Julia and I in the corridor one afternoon.

'We need something to perk us up,' Morag declared. 'I for one am hacked off about the current lack of male company in my life. And I'm missing sex,' she added as an afterthought.

'I'm totally disillusioned with my boyfriend,' grumbled Julia. 'His head is on a permanent swivel ogling other women. I honestly wonder why he bothers going out with me.'

'Well I'm never going out with another man again,' I declared. 'They're all cheating bastards.'

'No they're not,' Morag put an arm around my shoulders and gave me a hug. 'We've just been a bit unlucky that's all. Let's go on the prowl. Check out a few bulging trousers and see what's up for grabs.'

'That sounds like one-night stand talk,' Julia looked fearful.

'Nothing wrong with a high quality one-night stand Jools,' she countered. 'You need to loosen up and let your drawers down once in a while. So that's settled then. We're having a girls' night out.'

'Oh God,' Julia and I murmured in unison.

Morag wasted no time in getting her entertainment project together. One hour later she pinged Julia and I an e-mail.

Re: Girls night

Date: This weekend

Itinerary: Cocktails at Pinks, nouvelle cuisine at Scooby's, clubbing at Razz.

As Saturday morning dawned, I felt flattened by depression. The temptation to simply stay in bed and miss Morag's scrupulously planned event was overwhelming. However, I knew my working life wouldn't be worth living if I dared to cop out. Moodily I flung back the duvet cover and headed off to the shower.

Pinks was packed. Nell, always up for a giggle, had joined us and appeared to be getting on like the proverbial house on fire with Morag and Julia.

We perched on tall stainless stools around a tiny monopod table slurping concoctions with dodgy names like 'Raucous Ride' and 'Blow Job'. Handsome bare-chested barmen wearing black trousers and dickie-bows mixed and shook martini shakers behind a chrome bar. Pretty waitresses scantily clad in fuchsia leotards, fishnets and stilettos weaved through the table islands holding aloft loaded drinks trays.

After a couple of fruity cocktails to loosen the mood, we took ourselves off to Scooby's. The cuisine was so nouvelle it was practically raw and the portions so miniscule it did nothing to mop up the alcoholic haze Morag and Nell were now firmly enveloped in. Morag insisted we try out a selection of house wines. She was in fine fettle by this point and went on to loudly regale us and most of the restaurant with risqué humour.

'So this kid went up to his dad and said, "Dad, I don't understand the difference between *potential* and *reality*." And his father said, "Son I will demonstrate the difference. Firstly, ask your mother if she would sleep with Robert Redford for One Million Pounds".'

'If he was still thirty years old then you could count me in,' Nell bawdily thumped the table making Julia jump.

'Definitely,' Morag nodded approval. 'Anyway, this father then told his son to go and ask his sister if she would sleep with Justin Timberlake for One Million Pounds. The kid was somewhat confused but agreed and went off to see his mother.'

'I could never ask my mother if she wanted to sleep with Robert Redford,' Julia fingered her pearls primly.

'Don't suppose your old mum would be interested anyway,' Nell giggled. 'I know mine wouldn't. Too busy sticking her dentures in a night glass and slapping face cream all over her wrinkly bits.'

'My mother doesn't wear dentures,' Julia looked shocked. 'She's only sixty and she still thinks Tom Jones is sensational.'

'Well that's sorted then. She can give old Tom a good knobbing instead,' Nell sniggered before tossing back her wine.

'So the kid says, "Mum, would you sleep with Robert Redford for One Million Pounds?" and his mother replied, "Don't tell your father, but yes I would." The boy then found his sister and asked her, "Would you sleep with Justin Timberlake for One Million Pounds?" and the sister replied, "Most definitely I would."

'Don't blame her,' Nell nodded in agreement.

'So the kid went back to his father and said, "Dad I now understand the difference between *potential* and *reality*. Potentially we are sitting on two million quid but in reality we live with two slappers".'

Cue lewd laughter from Nell and laddish shoulder clapping from Morag. Julia and I glanced at each other. Her expression said it all. I gave the smallest nod of sympathetic understanding. Only a few more hours of this *fun* evening to get through.

Fortunately the night club was within walking distance so Nell and Morag linked arms and took a tottering lead in the direction of Razz.

'Why does Morag always have to get sloshed?' moaned Julia.

'Because she's lonely and nursing a broken a heart.'

'What's Nell's excuse then?'

'She's got a lovely husband but he's rather staid and doesn't take her out very often. She's just making the most of a girls' night out.'

'Well if I were her I'd be at home enjoying every minute of my husband's company.'

'Depending on which side of the fence you're viewing from, the grass can always look greener,' I pointed out.

At the club's entrance black bouncers immaculately turned out in top hats and tails ushered us into the semi-gloom. Space was a luxury as we jostled towards the bar, elbows tucked in, blinking against strobe lights. The soles of our stilettos adhered to a floor already covered in spilt drink.

I peered through the gloom. Clientele ranged from lads and lasses in their early twenties to men and women in their forties. There was a tacky glamour about the place, from the loud décor to the funky music.

Clutching newly purchased beverages we huddled together around the dance floor watching the scene. Suddenly there was a tap on my shoulder. Swinging round, I was stunned to find myself looking at Ploddy. I mean Jamie.

'Hello Cassie!'

He sounded delighted to see me.

'H-hi!' I stammered back, heart flipping all over the place. What on earth was he doing here? No doubt the stunning Selina wasn't far away.

'I don't usually come to places like this,' said Jamie.

'Me neither,' I hastily agreed.

'Really? You gave me the impression you were quite partial to a bit of a boogie.'

Ah. *Passé*.

'Once in a very blue moon,' I assured. 'So why are you here?'

'Stag night.'

'We meet again,' cooed Morag barging into the conversation. 'Aren't you going to introduce us Cass?' She was staring at Jamie with a predatory gaze. And who could blame her? He looked absolutely divine dressed from head to toe in designer black, hair gelled into contrived carelessness.

'Jamie, this is Morag.'

'Well hello,' she gushed in her best I-want-to-have-sex-with-you voice. 'You are the naughty policeman who booked me for speeding!' She ran the tip of her tongue across her pink lips and jostled her bosoms for effect.

'I am indeed. It's very nice to meet you again,' Jamie replied. 'Would you excuse us a moment – Cassie?'

Suddenly I was being propelled toward the dance floor. In my peripheral vision I saw Morag's jaw being overcome by gravity. Nell and Julia were also wearing gobsmacked expressions.

The music was fluid and pulsed with a sexy repetitive beat. Jamie smiled as we started to dance. Every now and again he drew me close so we moved together, bodies touching. I'm not sure how long we danced for – certainly a while. Eventually he returned me to the girls. Morag's mouth was still hanging open.

'I'd better get back to the others,' he said, 'and make sure the bridegroom-to-be isn't totally smashed. It was good to see you again Cassie.'

'You too,' I croaked. The words died on my lips as Jamie bent down and pecked my cheek. The kiss scorched my skin.

'Well,' spluttered Morag as Jamie disappeared into the crowd.

'Fancy that,' I clutched hold of her to steady myself.

'I do actually,' she quipped.

That night I slept restlessly, plagued by weird dreams with lustful undertones. I had been invited to a private ceremony where Charles and Camilla were renewing their marriage vows after a spot of bother with a kiss-and-tell tart. Jamie and I were among the invited elite.

In this vision I was amazingly thin and staggeringly beautiful.

Jamie was initially delayed due to crucially important police work arresting Britain's Most Wanted Man. When he arrived he momentarily held up Charles' and Camilla's vows because he insisted kissing me passionately to which I responded with alacrity.

'Terribly sorry Charlie,' said Jamie eventually. 'Do please continue.'

'Will do old chap.'

As the ceremony drew to a close I realised both Charles and Jamie were dressed in pristine jodhpurs and riding boots. They leapt astride a pair of waiting polo ponies while Camilla whinnied at me to follow her. She then proceeded to give me tips for second marriages. I was just debating the finer points of wearing oyster pink instead of cream when the clock radio blared into life ruining everything.

For a fuzzy moment I half expected the telephone to ring with Jamie inviting me out on a date. And then I remembered that he already had a girlfriend – the gorgeous Selina.

The following week I was working for Morag which made it far easier to chat about men (or rather the lack of), our respective divorces (very messy in her case) and beauty treatments.

'So what do you think?' I jabbed a finger at my corrugated brow. 'Should I give botox a whirl?'

'Oh for goodness sake Cass, there are far more important things to consider than the state of your forehead.'

'So it *is* a state!'

'It's our sex lives that are a state,' Morag waggled her finger at me.

'Oh God,' I groaned.

'It's no good praying. We need to do something about it ourselves. Now look at this,' Morag shook open a newspaper and spread it across her desk. 'The local rag. Read, study, learn. Particularly the Lonely Hearts column.'

'What – right now?'

'No, we'd better knuckle down to some work for the time being. Swot up at lunchtime. Circle the suitables and we'll have a post-lunch meeting. Grab Julia and ask her for some input too.'

A couple of hours later Julia and I sat on our favourite park bench in the warm Spring sunshine. With something akin to morbid fascination, we boggled over all those Desperately Seeking.

'I'd say that ninety nine per cent of these are complete non-starters,' she snorted derisively. 'I mean just look at this one – *fabulously firm fifty five year old seeks suitable playmate that is still moist.*'

'Ooh, I think I've found a possible. Listen! *Forty-something male, tall, attractive and well educated seeks similar lady for friendship and possible romance.*' My red biro flagged the advert.

'Hm,' Morag considered as she later read my choice of advert. 'Sounds a bit too good to be true. However, nothing ventured, nothing gained. Ring up the voicemail number.'

'But I thought Mr Bradbury was due in for a meeting?'

'He is, but not for another hour. Meanwhile,' she poured over the newsprint tapping her pencil against her teeth in consideration, 'I shall have the sexy thirty-two year old male who would like to meet a glamour girl for fun nights.'

Trust Morag to wade straight in at the deep end.

Her potential amour was keen enough to respond within ten minutes, but it was a disastrous conversation. The stranger kept demanding to know her bust measurement which infuriated her.

'All *right*!' she raged. 'You know Jordan? Well my tits make hers look like two fried eggs on an ironing board. So now that bit of detail is out the way, tell me the length of your dick because unless it can match my fifteen inch vibrator you are on to a complete non-starter.'

He hung up.

I had to wait until the evening before my chosen guy from the lonely hearts column telephoned. Amazingly he was very pleasant to talk to and with growing interest I listened to him chat a little about himself. His name was Ken, he was an architect, divorced and forty-five years old with two grown up children and four grandchildren. My eyebrows shot up into my hairline. He and his offspring had clearly got off to a very early start in the baby-making department. We accordingly arranged to meet at a local Harvester on Saturday. I pondered how romance might flourish surrounded by families with children baying for flame grilled burgers.

'How will we recognise each other?' I asked stifling a giggle.

'Why don't we be traditional and wear a flower in our lapel,' Ken suggested.

'Okay. Carnation?'

'Why not!'

Excited, I immediately telephoned Morag to share my news.

'Bugger the lonely hearts column,' she growled. 'I've revised my opinion and now think it's a waste of effort.'

'I thought you might at least be pleased for me.'

'I am Cass. I'm just a bit frustrated at the moment. Sexually frustrated no doubt. Let's try speed dating instead.'

'Well by all means find out more about it,' I ventured cautiously, 'but don't commit me to anything until Saturday night is out the way first.'

I hung up the telephone just as Livvy appeared in the doorway.

'Oh there you are.' She flapped a brightly coloured piece of paper in my direction. 'It's Sophia's tenth birthday next week after school and she's having a pony party. Can I go?'

'A pony party? Gosh, that's a first.'

Parents were getting ever more competitive about who could provide the most original party for their little darling. Whatever happened to good old musical chairs or a visiting magician pulling a bunny out of a hat?

Saturday dawned and, with it, a sense of anticipation. Taking advantage of the twins being at Stevie's, I took a long time getting ready.

Flipping a classical CD into the hi-fi, I sighed happily as the light staccato notes of Vivaldi's Four Seasons reverberated around the house. Humming along, I tipped bubble bath and aromatherapy oils into the tub and lit scented candles for good measure, revelling in a mixture of hot water and musical quavers.

I swept into the local Harvester dressed in jeans and a floaty top complete with carnation corsage looking a great deal more confident than I felt. Almost instantly I spotted Ken, even though he wasn't wearing a buttonhole. Instead he was clutching a very large bouquet of carnations, rosebuds and frothy gyp. As our eyes collided the breath caught in my throat. It would be fair to say that the flowers were the best part of the evening.

Ken jumped up from his stool in the bar area and waved in my direction. I pasted a smile on my face and waved gamely back.

'How simply wonderful to meet you Cassandra,' Ken took my hand and raised it to his lips. 'Now my dear, what's your tipple?' he patted the empty stool beside him.

A bucket of gin sprang to mind. Ken was gracious and charming, but he had clearly lied about his age. And not just a little fib but a serious whopper. Forty-five eh? That would have been about twenty years ago. His teeth were perfect, but then dentures were never anything else were they? And his thatch of dark hair bore more than a passing likeness to an acrylic toupee. I had nothing against pensioners. I just didn't want one as a boyfriend.

I sat and made polite conversation while my dashed hopes sank to my strappy sandals, through the scuffed wooden floorboards, down to the cellars under the bar and merged with the very foundations of the building. Shifting my coccyx on the hard stool I feigned interest in Ken's garden, car, tool shed, grandchildren and goldfish until Ken arrived at the raison d'être for his marriage collapsing.

By this time I was yawning into my glass and briefly pondering if wifey's departure had anything to do with the fact that Ken could have bored for England. Or perhaps she'd simply tired of competing with the goldfish?

I gazed into the depths of my spritzer, gloomily watching tiny bubbles fizz and pop. Was this my lot then? A series of disastrous liaisons? This one wasted on a man grappling wretchedly with lost youth, another with the married Euan and – last but not least – Jed who had driven off never to be seen again.

I buried my face in the heels of my hands, rubbed my tired eyes and groaned with dismay. Instantly Ken was all concern.

'My dear Cassandra, are you all right? Have my painful marital tales distressed you?'

I flushed guiltily, aware that I'd switched off and hadn't a clue what he'd been talking about.

'Um, yes, a little Ken,' I spotted an excuse and swam hastily toward it. 'I do sympathise.' If I chucked in a few more compassionate murmurs then Bob would surely be my uncle.

'I knew you'd understand,' he grabbed my hands enveloping them within his dry papery grasp. 'I told my Violet before she took off, impotency is suffered by millions and nothing to be ashamed of.'

'Absolutely,' I nodded, privately calculating the odds on a swift extrication and fleeing home.

What with the bouquet and the finger fondling, any onlooker would have been forgiven for thinking we were having a starry-eyed moment. Apprehensively I glanced from my captured hands to his smiling crinkled face awake to the fearful possibility that he was moments from zooming in for a romantic clinch. He clearly regarded this particular moment as recognition of just that.

'You're wonderful Cassandra,' he gushed. 'At last a woman who understands.' He leant in closer, flimsy translucent lips heading towards mine. Like a deflecting magnet my body abruptly arched backwards and I nearly fell off my stool.

'Ha ha!' I attempted a tinkling laugh which instead came out as a strangled neigh. 'Yes I do understand Ken. Really I do. I'm a fellow sufferer you see.'

'Really? But I didn't think women-'

'Oh but yes – they do! Not as much as men of course, but it's still a real bugger.'

'Good Lord.'

'Take Evening Primrose Oil and you'll be as right as rain in no time.'

'Evening Prim-?'

'That's the one. Meanwhile it's been an absolute pleasure, but I must go. Relieve the babysitter of my, um, triplets. Two sets of them. Rather exhausting and all under five. Thank you so much for the beautiful flowers. Toodle-oo.'

And with that I turned on my heel and fled.

The following evening, when Stevie walked the twins home, I was greeted by one sullen daughter and a tight lipped ex-husband. Toby appeared to be the only one in high spirits, managing to aggravate Livvy even further.

'Miss Stroppy Socks is having a moody!' he gleefully informed.

'That's enough Toby,' I ordered as Livvy barged straight past me and boycotted her father's attempt to kiss her good-bye.

'What's that all about?' I jerked my head towards our daughter's retreating back.

'I think it's my new girlfriend. Liv didn't take to her too well. Probably the age gap.'

Ah. Well Cynthia Castle hadn't exactly been a spring chicken had she? Stevie obviously had a thing about older women. Perhaps this one was a grandma. Or even a great-grandma.

'Charlotte is eighteen,' Stevie added.

'Eighteen?' I repeated gormlessly.

The number, like a shiny coin, rolled slowly through my frozen thought processes before dropping somewhere in the region of my oesophagus, momentarily strangling me. *Eighteen?* Jealousy curdled in my stomach. Whilst I had been out fending off an amorous pensioner, he'd been canoodling with a mere stripling only nine years older than Livvy. No wonder our daughter had the hump.

Livvy was very subdued over the Cocoa Pops the following morning.

'You okay Miss?'

She shrugged, eyes cast down. 'I hope none of my school friends ever meet Charlotte. It would be dead embarrassing.'

'I don't think that's likely to happen,' I assured. 'Why does she bother you so?'

'She tried acting like she was my big sister and she's not!' Livvy spat.

'I expect Charlotte was just trying to get some rapport going between the two of you,' I suggested. Why was I defending a child–woman I'd never met?

'She kept prattling on about nail polish and make-up, what clothes I liked and whether I fancied Usher.'

'I see.' Who was Usher?

'If she wants to be my new best friend she'd better wise up. Like understanding my heart belongs irrevocably to Mika.'

'Well quite.' And who the heck was Mika?

At work Morag insisted on listening to a blow by blow account of Saturday night and predictably split her sides.

'What a hoot,' she chortled as I glared at her sourly. 'Oh Cass, buck up for heaven's sake. Just write it off as experience. Meanwhile we'll push on with Plan B.'

'Which is?'

'Speed dating of course.'

Oh yes. Wasn't that a sort of musical chairs situation with a flirty little interview thrown into the mix? I had a horrible vision of talking to a room full of Ken look–a–likes all miserably clutching their lost libido and pick-me-up prescriptions.

'You know Morag, I think I'd like to grow old gracefully on my own. Life is a lot simpler without a man in the equation.'

'Nonsense. You're just a bit disillusioned at the moment. Mark my words Cass, we're going to find ourselves a pair of stunners in the not too distant future.'

Morag was, if nothing else, doggedly persistent.

As I sat outside the school gates that afternoon, I was pleased to see Livvy had perked up. She bounced out of school with Toby bringing up the rear, laughing with a gaggle of friends.

'Hey Mum,' she plonked herself on the back seat, 'did you hear about the man who asked a piece of string, "Are you a piece of string?" and the string replied, "No I'm afraid not".' She roared with laughter. 'Do you get it Mum? A frayed knot. Mum?'

But my concentration had lapsed elsewhere. Where exactly had Stevie met this Charlotte? In a pub? A club? McDonalds? The make-up counter in Boots? The fact that she was only eighteen irritated me. I tried to analyse why. After all, plenty of men went out with girls young enough to be their daughters. And then I realised that I, too, was old enough to be this girl's parent – a harsh reminder that I was half way through my life whereas she was youthfully poised on the first rung of adulthood. No matter what trendy clothes I wore or how I contrived to knock a few years off the hands of time, it was superficial. Nothing could alter the fact that my next birthday was the Big Four O. And for an added kick in the teeth, here I was back on that first rung, just like Charlotte. But whereas her future was a blank page ready to be put into print, mine was a case of having scribbled through everything previously written in order to redraft the chapters.

Stevie telephoned that evening.

'Hi Cass, can I have a word with Livvy please?'

'She's in the bath. Shall I get her to call you back?'

'Yeah. I want to see if she's calmed down and let her know she's my number one girl.'

Ah yes, the Charlotte Factor.

'I think she needs to have some questions answered,' I ventured.

'Really?'

'Absolutely. Like, er, where you both met. And how serious the relationship is. Oh, and what her parents think of you – that's if you've met them. Have you?'

'So many grown-up questions from a mere child.'

'Well quite.' I flushed. 'And don't forget the little matter of their respective taste in pop stars.'

There was a pause.

'I see. Well as Livvy has such a comprehensive list of points to discuss, I'll wait and chat to her in person.'

Later that evening, after a hot bath, I scrutinised my face in the steamed up mirror.

'Why are you staring at yourself mum?' Toby appeared by my side and reached for his toothbrush.

'I'm thinking about trying botox.'

He rinsed and spat. 'What's botox?'

'Special injections that fade wrinkles. I was wondering if it might help me look eighteen again.'

He wiped his mouth on a hand towel leaving a trail of toothpaste.

'You don't need it Mum.'

'Really?' I perked up.

'Course not. You look great. For a wrinkly.'

'Thanks.'

'Any time Mum.'

I chucked the towel in the laundry basket and switched the bathroom light off.

Chapter Eight

The following afternoon I drove to the local riding stables to deposit Livvy with birthday girl Sophia for the eagerly awaited pony party. Toby was not impressed at being dragged along to watch.

'Aw Mum, I don't want to watch a bunch of girls riding a group of mangy horses.'

'Stop whinging, it's not for long.'

At the riding school there was a sense of organised chaos. Twenty rheumy-eyed ponies lethargically plodded into the indoor school. Bit by bit children were paired up with ponies, stirrups adjusted and girths checked.

Livvy climbed onto a nearby mounting block and hopped onto the back of an ancient Exmoor named Molly. It looked suspiciously like a dishevelled donkey. Was this perhaps Molly the Mule, descendent of Muffin?

As Livvy settled into the saddle, I felt beset with anxiety. What if Molly was only pretending to be an old nag and underneath all that long hair lurked a thoroughbred bronco intent on bucking my daughter off? Visions of my own pony mad youth were instantly recalled. Riding bareback. No hard hat. Effortlessly popping my precious pony over five foot fences. Blissfully unaware that horse riding was a sport that had cost some riders their mobility, indeed their lives.

A slip of a girl – all of eleven years old – materialised by Molly's neck, apparently the lead rein assistant.

'Er, I think not,' I called to the riding instructor. I scrambled over the wooden barrier separating the arena from the spectator stand and jogged over to my endangered daughter. 'I'll be the lead rein assistant.' Livvy looked mortified. 'I love horses you see,' I explained to the astonished instructor. 'It's their smell – can't get enough of it,' I inclined my head next to Molly's muddy cheeks and breathed deeply. 'Mm, wonderful,' I heaved as a mixture of ammonia and ungroomed hair shot up my nostrils.

And so for the next thirty minutes, much to Livvy's chagrin, we shambled around the arena with me tugging at Molly's bridle in order to make the wretched creature move even a leg, let alone gallop off with her hooves cheekily flicking upwards.

'Okay everybody,' the instructor said, 'when I shout *stop* I want all of you to gently pull the reins. Okay? Stop!'

'HEEL!' I yelled at Molly. The instructor glared at me. 'Sorry. Thought it was a dog. Just for a moment.'

'Mum,' Livvy hissed. 'Would you *please* go away?' An awful lot of eyes stared in my direction. Livvy leaned forward in her saddle. 'Go and have a coffee with the other parents.'

I gave the instructor a tight smile. 'Well I think she's doing splendidly and clearly doesn't need me any more.'

The eleven year old silently materialised by Molly's side and I smartly headed off towards the café.

Inside Toby was mindlessly stuffing pocket money into a fruit machine. The birthday girl's mother was setting out sandwiches and sausage rolls on a long trestle table with a couple of other school mums assisting. Perhaps they'd like a hand? As I made my way over, a tall man seemed to step out of nowhere and touched me lightly on the arm.

'Hello,' he smiled pleasantly. 'Can I get you a coffee?'

Ah. The birthday girl's father.

'How very nice,' I beamed up at him.

Sophia's father indicated an unoccupied table in the corner and went off to get the coffee. Moments later he was back bearing a tray with two steaming mugs and a plate of chocolate biscuits. What a charmer. He set the tray down, swung his legs over a seat opposite and extended a rough hand across the table.

'I'm Matt by the way.'

I shook his hand. 'Cassandra,' I replied. 'Mm,' I took a sip.

'Delicious. Thanks very much for this.' I took another sip and discreetly checked Matt out over the cup's rim. He was certainly nothing like his prim and proper wife who always dressed in a very uniformed way – navy skirt, white shirt, flat loafers. Matt, by comparison, was scruffily attired in jeans so distressed they were mere threads away from nervous breakdown. Rusty coloured hair curled in unruly fashion over a frayed collar and – goodness – was that a gold hoop in his left ear?

'The party's going well,' I nodded toward the ponies plodding around, heads drooping lower and lower. Jolly good. With a bit of luck Molly would keel over any second from exhaustion and I could legitimately pluck Livvy into the safety of this café. Matt picked up on my fretfulness.

'Don't worry, the ponies are all bomb proof. I take it one of those kiddies belongs to you?'

I gave him a strange look. 'Well, yes. And you too surely?'

'No, it's only the ponies that are mine.'

'Aren't you Sophia's father?'

'Nope. I've got a few daughters but, to the best of my recollection, none of them are called Sophia.' He grinned disarmingly. 'Allow me to introduce myself properly. Matthew Harding. I'm the owner of this place.'

I felt myself flushing. 'I'm so sorry. I thought you were someone else. What must you think of me accepting an invitation for coffee with a total stranger?'

Matt glanced towards the arena. The children were all dismounting now and the ponies were being led away. He looked back at me.

'Cassandra, I can see you will need to return to your daughter very shortly. But to answer your question frankly, I was taking a chance upon you being single. I'm just an old rogue attempting a chat up number on you,' he gave a rather endearing shrug and his hazel eyes twinkled mischievously. Gosh, he was quite attractive actually.

'That's okay, I'm not married,' I blurted foolishly. 'Well, I am, but not for much longer if you see what I mean. That is, I'm not with anyone at the moment.' Oh cringe. Talk about sounding desperate. I'd be throwing myself at him over the coffee cups in a minute. At that precise moment the fruit machine began to judder like an overloaded washing machine. It gave three deafening clangs and spewed out a cascading shower of silver.

'YES!' Toby punched the air in delight. 'Mum! There's enough money here for your buttocks injection.'

That night I lay in bed going over the afternoon's events with a secret smile on my lips. On the bedside table was Matt's equestrian business card. He'd pressed it into the palm of my hand before disappearing. His last words had been for me to call him.

At Hempel Braithwaite I began a lengthy float assignment for one of the Senior Partners. Martin Henniker was to be my boss right up to when the children broke up for the long summer holidays. As the working day unfolded, I realised that he and I were never going to bond. Words like unpleasant, nasty, disagreeable, sarcastic and downright rude would not have been inappropriate to describe him.

Morag pinged me an e-mail that we meet for lunch vis-à-vis speed dating. I groaned into my keyboard. I really didn't want to do this just yet. Especially now I had Mr Harding's telephone number. But Morag wouldn't take no for an answer.

'We'll go this Friday,' she insisted.

Julia, disillusioned with her current inattentive boyfriend, was joining us.

Once the twins were tucked up in bed and well and truly out of earshot, I barricaded myself into the kitchen and settled down by the phone to ring Matt. Apprehensively I punched out the numbers. There was something about a woman ringing a man which made my toes curl. However, I'd been reluctant to give out my number in case one of the twins had answered the phone. It had been Matt's suggestion that I call him instead.

'Cass!' he sounded genuinely delighted to hear from me and the usual small talk ensued for a minute or two. Eventually Matt steered the conversation to Saturday night.

'I'd love to take you to a little restaurant I know. Traditional cuisine. Cosy atmosphere. Can't go wrong,' he assured. 'It will give us a chance to talk quietly and find out a bit more about each other.' There was a small pause while he let me digest this. 'And Cass, I do want to find out more about you.' Another pause. 'A lot more,' he whispered. I instantly broke out in a muck sweat.

As Speed Dating Day finally dawned, I took one horrified look at myself in the mirror and, in the lunch hour, dashed out to a local beauty salon for a spray on tan and nail extension appointment.

The combination of freshly applied glowing tan and beautiful nails left me feeling strangely empowered. I waggled my nails at Morag who endorsed them with a nod of approval.

'I think we're going to have a great evening Cass.'

'We'll see.'

'It will be like mulling over a scrumptious box of chocolates and handpicking our favourites.'

A little before seven, having waved the children off with Stevie, I met up with Morag and Julia in Browns, a snazzy jazzy bar already elbow deep in hustle and bustle. A set of plans had been laid down which kicked off with consuming one glass of something lightly alcoholic in order to muster a bit of the old Dutch courage. Naturally, five minutes later we were on our second with Morag lining up a third for herself. She tipped it down the hatch before inhaling and exhaling several times like a panic attack victim.

'That's better,' she smacked her lips appreciatively. 'My veins are waking up now. Meanwhile ladies,' Morag looked solemnly at Julia and me, 'love is in the air. Let us go forth and find our soul mates.'

We arrived at the local banqueting hall, usually booked for wedding parties, where an efficient woman of about my own age greeted us. She consulted her clipboard before handing out name badges and a printed sheet of potential suitors.

I discreetly glanced about and suddenly wanted to vomit. Dear God. There was Cynthia Castle. Don't let her see me please. Oh too late. Our eyes clashed together and rolled in mutual dismay. Appalled, Cynthia made a desperate effort to put distance between us and cannoned blindly into another woman. Could things get any worse? Apparently not.

A horribly familiar pensioner was working the far corner looking for potential date victims and – deep joy – Ken was edging his way towards the reversing Cynthia. Wallop! Good manners forced her to smile an apology. Ken was beaming away, ultra white dentures flashing. Excellent. There really was such a thing called karma.

Mrs Clipboard clapped her hands for attention.

'Everybody follow me please.'

She led us into a vast meeting room and gave a speech of welcome. The men were invited to sit down on one side of a long length of tables that ran around the room. The men were to remain seated at all times. The women were to sit opposite. Each 'couple' would have just a few minutes to talk to each other. If you liked what you saw, you ticked the relevant box on your dating sheet. When the signal was given, the women were to move up one place for the next allotted interview until finally everybody had met each other. At the end of the evening, if respective ticks matched up, potential couples were permitted to exchange telephone numbers.

And suddenly, like impatient horses jostling together at the starting line of the Grand National, the women were elbowing and shoving their way towards the seats and we were off!

I found myself sitting opposite a nerdy looking male with a little boy's side parting.

'Do you do this often?' he leant in over the table.

'Er, no. Do you?'

'Yes. All the time. It fills a void in my life.'

'I see.'

'You have a nice tan.'

'Thank you.'

'And very nice nails.'

'Thank you. And you have–' it was surely only polite to return the compliments, 'um, a very nice side parting.'

The signal sounded and I moved to the next chair. The faces blurred into non-descriptiveness. Eventually I found myself sitting opposite Ken. He was quite unabashed and I was beyond caring.

'Cassandra! My dear lady, how simply wonderful to see you again. How are all your children?'

Oh yes. Exactly how many sets of twins, triplets and quads was I meant to have?

'They are very well thank you Ken,' I carefully replied. 'Ned, Ted and, er, Fred are with their Daddy for an access visit. Mandy, Andy and, um, Pandy are with the au pair.'

'I had no idea you were such an Earth Mother,' said an amused male voice. Not Ken's. As I turned to look at the guy sitting next to him, I gasped in horror. It was Ploddy. Brad Pitt. I mean Jamie. The signal went and suddenly I was sitting opposite him.

'Cassie,' he smiled warmly.

My heart did a few skippy beats and my armpits instantly broke out in a gushing mess. I hastily picked up my list of names and began to fan myself with it.

'Whatever was that all about?' Jamie inclined his head in Ken's direction.

'Nothing. Crossed wires. Sorry.'

'So how are you? In this light I can see your face has completely healed.'

'Yes. All better,' I touched my cheek. 'It's just the heart that's taking it's time to mend.' I flinched. Damn. Why had I said that? It wasn't even as if Stevie had sole responsibility for the current state of my emotions. Euan had contributed to the upheaval too.

'Ah yes, a heart's scars can run very deep,' Jamie nodded sympathetically. There was something about the tone of his voice that had me looking at him sharply.

'Are you speaking from personal experience?' I held my breath.

'Oh definitely.'

For a moment Jamie looked so haunted I felt as though I were encroaching on some sort of terrible personal grief. I mentally slapped my forehead. Of course! That's why he was here! He must have split up with the luscious Selina. Clearly the experience had knocked him sideways. Left the poor man devastated.

Suddenly I felt my hopes surge. Might I be the one to help him get over her? For one wild moment I had a vision of us both ticking our respective boxes and walking off into a romantic sunset together. And then I squashed the thought flat. If Jamie and the stunning Selina were no longer an item, what chance had I got of wowing him? How must he regard me? A scatty female who periodically lost her car, *still* didn't know its registration number, deposited cryptic messages on drivers' windscreens, slipped into seductive lingerie for her workmen and spouted ridiculous lists of fictitious offspring to the general public. And by comparison he'd had the gorgeous Selina, every inch the sexy cop in her hip hugging uniform, brandishing a lethal weapon as she adopted a movie star pose, pouty lips ordering baddies to freeze because they were under arrest. How could I compete with that? There was no way I could tick his box. He was way out of my league. I felt bemused that such thoughts had run through my head and, more incredibly, that I had even entertained them. I peered up at Jamie under my eyelashes. He looked a million miles away.

'So that's why you're here?' I asked.

'Hm?' Jamie's eyes jerked back from some faraway place.

'You know – because of what happened with Selina.'

Jamie frowned. 'Selina? Oh she and I split up.'

'Well yes, obviously,' I nodded my head and looked down at my list of names. I hadn't ticked one single box. The signal went. Forcing a bright smile I stood up. 'I hope you find someone else soon.'

Jamie's expression changed in a flash. He smiled back at me and I noticed how his eyes crinkled attractively at the sides. 'Oh but I already have,' he murmured.

Disappointment washed over me. I wondered who the woman was. Another female cop? So why was he here? And then I rallied.

Why was I putting myself through this dating nonsense? When would I learn that love hurt? I mentally shook myself. Love? What on earth was I thinking about love for?

Eventually the interviews finished and I still hadn't ticked anybody's box. What was the point? I realised with a jolt that the only box I'd wanted to tick was Jamie's.

Morag was thoroughly over-excited. 'Did you see him?' she asked rolling her eyes theatrically and nodding her head in Jamie's direction. He was surrounded by a flock of hopeful looking women. 'I ticked his box and I am almost one hundred per cent certain he's ticked mine.'

Suddenly I wanted to be out of this place and in my own home. As I hadn't ticked any boxes there would be no mutual exchanging of telephone numbers and therefore no reason to prolong the agony by staying. I began making my excuses and was on the verge of ringing for a taxi when somebody lightly tapped me on the arm. I spun round and was suddenly face to face with Cynthia Castle.

'F-For what its worth,' she stammered, 'I want to apologise.'

I stared helplessly into her round beseeching face. For a moment I couldn't speak. What was there to say? Never mind Cynthia, Stevie was a cad? If it hadn't been you Cynthia then it would have been someone else? Instead I found myself asking something completely different.

'What went wrong between the two of you?'

She gave a mirthless laugh. 'He found someone else of course. Traded me in for the babysitter.' I looked at her blankly. The babysitter? My hand flew to my mouth. Of course – Charlotte!

Morag awoke me from a deep sleep the following morning.

'Do you know that mean sod didn't tick my box,' she ranted.

'Which mean sod?' My tired eyes sought out the digital numbers on the alarm clock. Quarter past eight!

'That policeman friend of yours.'

'I keep telling you, he's not a friend of mine. I don't even know him properly.'

'Why didn't he tick my box?' she demanded. 'I mean, didn't I look great last night? And what about my personality? Am I not full on and fizzy? Not to mention my bust size. I thought men liked large bosoms and mine are big enough. Aren't they? Cass? Cass?'

I yawned and stretched. 'I'm here Morag and you are utterly fab. The man is evidently blind to your considerable charms and therefore not worth bothering about. Did you get any other guys' numbers?'

'Several actually,' I could hear the smugness in her voice. 'I'm meeting up with a rather nice chap tonight. His name is Ivan. What about you?'

'W-e-ll, I didn't do as well as you but I am out tonight with a guy called Matt Harding.'

'Ooh wonderful Cass. Do you know, I think things are looking up for us both.'

After we'd rung off with promises to have a dating post-mortem on Monday, I flopped back on the pillows and let my thoughts stray to Matt.

He wanted me to meet him later at the stables. It was to be a casual sort of date – go and see the horses, have a look around the yard, then out for a bit of lunch. After the monumental effort invested in last night's debacle, I was determined to do exactly the opposite for tonight.

At around six I had a quick shower and slipped into a pair of faded jeans. As my face was still golden with fake tan, I kept make up minimal with just a slick of lipstick.

Matt was out in the yard when I drew up alongside a battered old horsebox. He was talking to an owner who was expressing concerns about her lame mare. As my shoes crunched over loose gravel he glanced around and his face lit up. The owner thanked him for his advice and Matt turned to welcome me properly.

'Hey, you look amazing,' he kissed me lightly on the cheek. 'Sorry I'm not all set for you and smell a bit ripe, but it's been one of those days.'

I grinned back. He did whiff mildly of horses but it wasn't unpleasant. I found myself relaxing.

'Let me show you around the yard. Afterwards I'll fix you a big drink and ensconce you in front of the telly while I have a very swift bath.'

There were effectively two yards split between private owners and school hacks. The liveries' horses were polished and well bred compared to the riding school nags. Noble heads with pricked ears popped over stable doors as we approached. Some of the ponies nudged our hands, looking for sugar lumps or wanting their noses rubbed. Others munched hay, dropping it untidily over their doors while Matt patted necks and tweaked ears.

Yard inspection over, we walked up to the house. It was impressively large and smothered in ivy. Matt showed me into a comfortable but well worn lounge. He splashed a hefty measure of gin and not much tonic into a cut glass tumbler. A pretty girl of about seventeen wandered in.

'Hi,' she smiled and lifted a hand in greeting.

'This is Joanie, one of my daughters,' Matt said.

'One of many,' the girl said wryly. I wondered exactly how many.

Joanie made polite small talk with me while her father disappeared upstairs. I had the impression she'd done this several times before with various female friends of Matt's.

When Matt returned his hair was curling damply over a clean T-shirt and he was wearing sawn off jeans.

'Ready?'

I threw the gin down my neck, grabbed my bag and hurried after him.

'Nice to meet you,' I called over my shoulder to Joanie.

A little while later we pulled up outside a quaint olde worlde pub near the river.

'How lovely!' I exclaimed in delight. 'All these years of living in this area and I had no idea this place existed.'

'A well kept secret,' Matt smiled as he helped me out the car and slung an arm companionably around my shoulder.

We sat in an alcove by a tiny picture window overlooking the river. The rough wooden table boasted a candle centrepiece stuffed into an empty wine bottle, its waxy sides melting in artistic rivers down the glass. Dinner was enjoyable and, by the time we'd reached the coffee and mints stage, I had a potted history of Matt Harding.

Without a doubt I liked him. I could sense the feeling was mutual and that he'd like to see me again. However, Matt made my own emotional baggage look like a mere weekend carry case. Two ex-wives for starters. The third and current Mrs Harding was soon to join her predecessors. In addition to Joanie, there were four more daughters resulting from the second and third marriages plus two step-sons he'd inherited from the third marriage. Clearly, from the way he spoke about the boys, there was a genuine fondness. Matt waved away my one failed marriage and a pair of twins as a mere blip. He freely confessed that the first Mrs Harding had been traded in for the second Mrs Harding who had, in turn, gone on to duly trade Matt in. Undeterred he'd picked himself up, dusted himself off and simply resumed life eventually dating one of the grooms. In time she became the third Mrs Harding.

'So what on earth went wrong this time around?' I asked.

Matt sighed. 'Do you know Cass, it's difficult to define any one specific thing. Rather it was a combination of many effects. Overall though it amounted to the laxative effect.'

'Sorry?'

'We irritated the shit out of each other.'

Back at the stables I clambered out of Matt's car and walked over towards mine. Matt ambled alongside me. After I'd lowered myself into the driver's seat, he leant in and kissed me very gently on the mouth.

'You know Cass,' he murmured, 'you don't have to go.'

The invitation in his voice was unmistakable. I looked at him. There was a warmth between us which was both easy and casual. But that last word neatly summed it all up. Casual. If I followed him back into his home and up to his bed, it would all be so very casual. And casual sex just wasn't my scene. After the earlier heady madness with Euan that had abruptly ended in such a humiliating shambles, I knew that whilst rebounding from a failed marriage might have fun moments, regularly falling into other men's beds really wasn't me.

I touched his cheek.

'You are one very nice guy Matthew Harding. But I'm going home.'

'Hey no problem. Can I call you?'

'Of course.'

And then he kissed me one more time.

I was awoken the following morning by the phone shrilly ringing at half past seven. Anathema on a Sunday. Snarling with bad-temper I snatched up the receiver.

'Morag,' I barked into the handset. 'I'm going to bloody kill you.'

'Sorry Cass, did I wake you up?' asked Matt. 'I'm always forgetting normal people don't rise until after ten on a Sunday morning.'

'Oh God Matt, I do apologise.'

'Just because I've been up since six feeding horses I automatically presume the rest of the world is as wide awake as me. So how about I let you drift back to your dreams but later on you come over for brunch?'

'That sounds good,' I smiled into the handset.

When I resurfaced it was to greet a beautifully warm day. As I drew up outside Matt's front door I neatly side-stepped bees buzzing fatly around a flowerbed of lavender.

'Come in, come in!' Matt threw open the door. He steered me down the hall, through the kitchen and out onto the patio. A little table was laid up complete with a jug of Pimms. Cubes of ice, fresh fruit and mint bobbed about in the ruby liquid.

'You be Mum and pour the drinks and I'll be back in two ticks.'

When Matt reappeared he was bearing a tray of granary bread and butter, a plate of Parma ham, mixed cheeses and a dish of pickles and chutney.

'Mr Harding I'm impressed.'

'Oh my culinary skills are legendary. Don't tell everybody,' Matt glanced about furtively, 'but I also do a very mean beans on toast.'

'A man after my own heart!'

It was nice sitting in the warm May sunshine sipping fruity Pimms and getting mildly tight.

'Do you fancy a walk?' Matt asked after we'd cleared the table together and loaded the dishwasher. 'I'd love to show you Poppy and her new foal.'

Poppy was Matt's thoroughbred mare currently in her own exclusive paddock and quite a trek away. Matt's land ran into considerable acreage. We strolled along a dirt track that ran parallel to the yard before meandering through various fenced off fields. Matt pointed out cordoned off areas that were being rested. These meadows were thick with lush grass sprinkled with buttercups and daisies. The track rose on an ever inclining gradient. Puffing alongside Matt, I looked back at the stables tucked away at the bottom of the hill looking like a picturesque sight from Toy Land.

We climbed over a five bar gate and dropped down into an emerald meadow. An enormous bay mare with a coat like polished mahogany stood protectively over a gangly filly. The foal gave a tinkling whinny to its mother who softly whickered back. Head up, ears pressed forward, acutely alert she monitored our steady approach. Matt was talking in a low voice, soft, almost hypnotic. Good heavens, I'd heard about people like this performing horse whispering or whatever it was called. All the same, Poppy was a big girl and I didn't fancy my chances if she suddenly decided to bolt in our direction. I nervously stepped behind Matt and peeked around his shoulder.

'Darling Pops, good girl,' he cooed.

Darling Pops broke into a prance, majestic neck tucked in, tail swishing. I shot anxiously behind Matt again and resisted the urge to cling to his broad back. Poppy came to a shuddering standstill in front of Matt, eyes rolling dramatically before snorting a greeting down her equine nose. A fine spray of snot showered Matt's shirt. He laughed uproariously before patting the mare's neck.

'You naughty girl Pops, look what you've done to Daddy's shirt.'

He rubbed behind her ears. The filly was curious but kept her distance, hugging her mother's rump. Poppy nudged Matt's pockets and he rewarded her with a carrot. She snatched it up greedily before turning and trotting off, her pretty baby skipping skittishly in her wake.

I exhaled with relief at the mare's departure and stepped out from behind Matt.

'Sorry Cass, do horses make you nervous?'

'A bit I suppose. Silly really, I used to ride all the time when I was a kid. I guess it's been too long since I handled them.'

'Poppy wouldn't hurt a fly otherwise I wouldn't have brought you up here. Come on, let's get back to the house and I'll make us another jug of Pimms.'

I stole a surreptitious glance at my watch. 'Much as that sounds tempting, I'm going to have to be on my way. Liv and Toby are due home in another hour or so.'

'What about a very quick coffee instead?'

'Go on then you smooth talker.'

We cut across the rested meadows which were horse free and, bit by bit, the view of the stables grew larger. There were several riding school hacks in the yard. Children were hopping about on the ground, trying to scramble onto fidgeting ponies. Suddenly something prickly pierced my foot.

'Ouch!' I yelped slapping my ankle and hopping about on one leg like one of the kids in the yard.

'Are you all right?'

'I must have brushed against a thistle.'

'Okay now?'

'Yes, I think so.'

We resumed walking but I'd only taken a few steps when another hot sting needled into my lower leg.

'Bloody hell!' I screeched swiping the palm of my hand against my jeans. 'What the heck was that?' I cast about wildly scanning the ground for thorny thistles, but the grass was short and tufted. There wasn't a weed in sight. And then I heard a low humming. The blood drained from my face.

'Cass?'

'There's a wasp up my trousers. Argh!' I shrieked as a third sting scorched my thigh, this time accompanied by the unmistakable sound of furious buzzing. Worse still, the trapped insect was heading towards my privates. 'Help!' I bleated.

'Get your trousers off,' Matt ordered.

'No way, somebody might...ARGH!' I bellowed as several stings machine-gunned into my thigh. My hands slapped blindly in an effort to kill it before havoc was wreaked in my pants.

'For heaven's sake Cass TAKE YOUR BLASTED JEANS OFF,' roared Matt tugging at my zipper.

'I can't! People might see me.'

Of that there was no doubt. Down in the yard all the kiddies had stopped dead in their tracks to gape in our direction. Even the ponies had ceased fidgeting and were staring agog. My brain briefly wrestled with the fight or flight syndrome. After two dithery seconds it plumped for flight – regardless of the fact that the wasp would be travelling with me. Frantically I began running about in circles.

'COME HERE!'

'No – ARGH!' I screamed hysterically as the wasp's next sting set my groin on fire. Whimpering pathetically I charged blindly towards Matt. He launched himself at me with a spectacular rugby tackle and suddenly I was free falling. Holding me still with one hand, he yanked with the other at my zipper. My legs flailed about wildly – death by wasp sting being more preferable than stripping in front of an entire riding school. But Matt clung on. In a matter of seconds he'd hauled my jeans down to my knees, regrettably taking my pants with them.

'IT'S OUT!' he yelled, as a battered looking wasp took off to freedom.

But I was deaf, dumb and blind to the loathsome insect's departure and remained locked in terror, kicking my legs out, staggering unsteadily to my feet and breaking into a clumsy waddle with my jeans and spotted knickers at half-mast.

A quick glance at the riding school was enough to confirm that everybody was thrilled to bits by the spectacle of a bare bummed female attempting an Olympic sprint with dropped trousers. Still shrieking my head off, I lurched forward in a frenzy of shuffling until a combination of trailing denim and gravity sent me crashing back to the ground.

Winded, I lay face down and had a close encounter with a startled ladybird scurrying up a blade of grass. Matt rushed over and gallantly yanked everything upwards. He then pulled me to my feet where I stood unsteadily, shaking like an aspen.

'Okay folks, show's over,' Matt called to the gawping riding school. Still they stared. 'CLEAR OFF!'

Wide eyed children slowly clattered off, occasionally sneaking backward glances. Some were openly giggling. Trembling violently I hung my flaming face in mortification.

Matt put a strong arm around my waist and helped me hobble back to the house.

'You're not going anywhere Cass until you've had a whacking dose of antihistamine and some hot sweet tea.'

'I hate tea,' I bleated ungratefully but, once inside Matt's house, did as I was told. He was all concern and blamed himself. Once again the jeans were tugged down as Matt dabbed a noxious smelling solution over the red welts. I sat on the sofa like an obedient child, stripped to my knickers swallowing antihistamine and syrupy tea. Matt squatted down in front of me, placed his palms lightly on my shoulders.

'How are you feeling?'

'Better.'

'Good.' He leant forward and gently kissed the tip of my nose.

'You're a nice man,' I mumbled. 'Very nice actually.'

He smiled and kissed my nose again. Then my mouth.

'You don't have to go home you know,' he murmured, long fingers tangling in my hair.

I drew back. 'That's what you said yesterday. And even though

I'm sitting in your house half dressed having indecently exposed myself, I really can't – well you know.'

'Sure. But can we do this again? Preferably without the waspy bit?'

I grinned and nodded.

On Monday Morag, Julia and I met up for lunch. Julia had secured five potential 'dates' as a result of Saturday night and was cautiously excited. Morag had ticked off numerous names in a determined effort to get her money's worth and had half a dozen names on her own list. Ivan's name, however, had been scrawled out.

'I thought you fancied him?' I queried. 'In fact, didn't you have a date with Ivan on Saturday night?'

Morag gnashed her teeth. 'Yes. In fact I ended up spending the entire weekend with him which was a catastrophic mistake.'

Julia and I exchanged looks.

'What happened?' we chorused.

'He was like a bloody snowstorm.'

'Terrible dandruff?'

'No, it was more a case of wondering when he was coming, how many inches it would be and how long it would last.'

Julia and I looked appalled but Morag suddenly brightened up and fixed us with a determined smile.

'Never mind. I've another eleven names to work through. Surely one of them will have a bit of mileage.'

Chapter Nine

Matt telephoned that evening asking if we could meet up at the weekend.

'Ah, that's a bit awkward. The twins will be with me.

'Hey no problem. Bring them over too.'

'Okay. Brilliant!'

And thus I discovered that there were advantages dating a man with truck loads of emotional baggage – he didn't mind the kids coming on dates too. Although – hang on a minute – I hadn't actually told the children I was dating. Nor was I sure I wanted to.

That evening I thumbed absent-mindedly through a furniture catalogue while cogitating how to approach the subject of Matt with Livvy and Toby. Flattened by worry and a ridiculous sense of guilt, I ended up ordering a four poster princess bed with frills and froth for Livvy and a metal bunk bed and desk combo for Toby. Would the promise of new bedroom furniture appease the children if I introduced Matt? Their birthdays were only a few weeks away. It could be part of their present.

'Is there anything else you'd like to order Madam?' asked the disembodied voice belonging to Customer Services.

'Most definitely,' I replied.

Seconds later I had ordered my longed for leather bed. I hung up and stared at my credit card. It had taken such a battering it was a wonder there weren't any dent marks across its plastic surface.

As the weekend loomed, I still hadn't broached the subject of Matt to the twins. Taking the bull firmly by the horns, I innocently asked the children over dinner how they would feel if I occasionally went out with a man.

'What? You mean as in having a boyfriend?' asked Livvy.

'Yes, I guess so.'

'Aren't you a bit old to have a boyfriend?' Toby frowned.

'Of course I'm not too old! Boyfriends and girlfriends aren't just for teenagers you know.'

Livvy glanced sideways at her brother. 'Dad's got a girlfriend.'

'Yes but he's a man.'

Oh joy. My son was already a male chauvinist.

'Toby, older women are allowed to date too,' I pointed out huffily. 'It's not just middle aged men who have the monopoly.'

Livvy dipped a sausage in her gravy. 'Mm. And Dad's a bit of a goer too. First it was Cynthia. Now it's Charlotte. I think it's only fair Mum should have a boyfriend too. If she can get one of course.'

Toby gave me an assessing look. 'Yeah. You might not manage to find one very easily Mum.' He patted my hand consolingly. 'But I guess I don't mind you trying.'

'And me,' Livvy bestowed a kindly smile in my direction. Almost as if I was being humoured.

'Well thank you dear children for giving me your permission to date. And for your information Toby, there *is* somebody who wants to take me out, despite my being a dinosaur.'

'Is he a dinosaur too then?'

'Oh for heaven's sake!'

'Who is he?' asked Livvy.

So I told them a little about Matt Harding. Toby listened grimly.

'What does he do?' he asked.

Good grief. He sounded more like a father than a son. He'd be asking me what Matt's intentions were next.

'He owns and runs an equestrian centre.'

Livvy's eyes lit up. 'Cool.'

'In fact he owns Molly, the pony you rode at Sophia's birthday party.'

'Wow!' she clapped her hands gleefully. 'Oh *wow!*' Does that mean I can go riding regularly? Can I Mum?'

'Maybe.'

Later, when the twins were out of earshot, I telephoned Matt to firm up arrangements.

'Are you sure you're up for this get-together with my two in tow?'

'Definitely. You mentioned that you used to ride horses and I gather Livvy enjoyed the pony party, so why don't we do something altogether with a few gee-gees chucked into the equation?'

I was amazed. And incredibly pleased. And quite pathetically grateful actually. Ringing off I hastened to the bottom of the stairs and immediately bellowed up to the twins. Their reaction was to whoop uproariously like delinquent yobbos.

'But listen kids,' I warned, 'please behave. Don't embarrass me by squabbling and being – well you know,' I trailed off beseechingly.

'Don't worry Mum. We won't be the children from hell,' Livvy smiled.

'Unless of course we think Matt Harding is hell,' muttered Toby ominously.

Saturday dawned bright and clear. When we arrived at Matt's house he wasn't there. Instead Joanie answered the door.

'Dad's at the yard. Go down, he's expecting you,' she smiled at the kids and Liv grinned shyly back. Toby, however, gazed dispassionately at Joanie's good natured face before curling his lip.

'Is she my future step-sister?' he jerked his head at Joanie's retreating figure behind the door.

'Don't be so ridiculous Toby!' I spluttered. 'Matt is simply a friend, okay?' I caught his wrist and yanked him round to face me. 'I said *okay*?'

Livvy gave her brother a push. 'Stop being stupid Tobes. What's the matter with you?'

Toby gave his sister a retaliatory shove just as Matt suddenly swung into my line of vision. Terrific. His first impression of us all as a family was a harassed mother refereeing two children on the verge of punching each other's lights out. I gave them both a discreet prod in the back.

'Pack it in *now*,' I hissed.

Toby continued to bristle with hostility.

'Hello all!' Matt lifted a hand in greeting.

'Hi!' Livvy beamed. She didn't give a hoot whether Matt Harding had two horns and a devil's tail. Her expression was *lead me to your ponies*.

Toby remained chilly, his face aloof. Ooh would I have something to say to this son of mine later.

'Ah ha ha ha,' I laughed nervously. 'Matt, this is Livvy and Toby.'

Toby rolled his eyes condescendingly. Oh God, I really wasn't sure if this was such a good idea after all. But Matt was unfazed by Toby's arctic response. He led us off towards the stables, all the while chatting about Poppy and her little filly. Within minutes Livvy was eating out of the palm of Matt's hand. Toby remained resolutely silent, although I could see he was reluctantly interested.

We crossed to the riding school side of the yard where ponies were tethered to posts, dusty coats being vigorously groomed, while others rested between rides. The place was a hive of activity with busy stable girls mucking out, changing water buckets and stuffing hay into vast string nets.

'There's Molly!' squeaked Livvy pointing to a shagpile rug with meter high ears.

Ah yes. The mule.

'Would you like to ride her?' asked Matt.

'Yes please,' Livvy dimpled. She rushed over to stroke Molly's velvety nose and kiss the tiny star on her forehead.

Toby feigned disinterest. With an apparent air of boredom he wandered over to a pony whose stable door proclaimed the name Chester.

'He's a good'un,' Matt joined Toby and patted the pony's flecked neck. 'Would you like me to tack him up for you?'

'Whatever.'

I burned with embarrassment.

Unperturbed, Matt called a stable girl over to show both children how to groom and saddle up the ponies. Their attention thus diverted, Matt caught me by the hand and led me in the opposite direction.

'I'm so sorry about Toby,' I apologised, my voice catching. 'I don't know what's got into him. He's not usually like this. He's a good boy really.'

We'd stopped outside a stable with a tubby grey mare inside.

'This is Blue,' was all Matt said. He opened the stable door and fussed over the animal like an over-protective parent, talking to her all the while as he put tack on and adjusted stirrup leathers. Eventually he turned back to me. 'Blue's an old timer and safe as houses to ride. She'll look after you. That's what Toby's doing Cass. Looking out for his Mum. Letting me know that if there's any nonsense then I've got him to deal with. One or two of my kids behaved in exactly the same way to old girlfriends. Goes with the territory eh?'

I realised with a jolt that I was not fully au fait with how the children perceived their parents pairing off with other partners. Toby didn't seem to mind about his father having a girlfriend although Livvy had been furiously indignant about Charlotte. I wondered what thoughts ran through their minds as they juggled two parents and two separate homes with potential new partners falling into the mix? I realised some sort of talk was long overdue.

Matt led Blue out of the stable and gave me a leg up before mounting an enormous piebald the size of an elephant.

'This is Tiny,' he laughed as we plodded out of the yard and up the dirt track lane.

It had been a good couple of decades since I'd last sat astride a horse. As we gently hacked through woods and out the other side to winding rural lanes, the years slipped away. Leg muscles groaned but I ignored them. Blue maintained a shambling trot in order to keep up with Tiny's long swinging gait.

Two hours later, my thigh muscles screaming with protest, we jogged back to the yard. My ability to rise to the trot had long been abandoned for ungainly bouncing.

Matt effortlessly slid off Tiny. However, Blue had a girth like a water barrel and my legs appeared to have set like concrete around her middle.

'Don't tell me,' Matt teased. 'You've enjoyed yourself so much you don't want to get off.'

'Actually, I don't think I *can* get off. I'm not joking, I'm stuck.'

'Let me help you.' Matt efficiently removed my booted feet from the stirrups. 'Lean forward – no *right* forward – over her neck.'

He pushed my stiff legs back until I was spread across Blue's back like a rolled up carpet. Perhaps I could just fall sideways into his arms? I dropped stiffly to the ground.

'Are you all right?'

'Yes,' I gasped. I was still in my riding position but minus the pony. I smiled gratefully at two stable girls who materialised from nowhere to lead Blue and Tiny away. 'I'll soon limber up.'

'Okay then, what about some refreshment?' Matt rubbed his hands together.

'Ooh,' I smiled through the pain. 'That sounds wonderful.'

I waddled after Matt, discreetly tugging at the seat of my trousers which had welded to my bum. *Ouch!* It wasn't just my lower limbs that were sore.

Just at that moment Toby came clattering into the yard with Livvy, pink cheeked and sparkly eyed and evidently in high spirits. Thank goodness his sour mood had lifted. Or had I reckoned on that too soon? As Toby locked eyes with Matt his face set in a grim mask.

'We're going up to the house for a sandwich,' Matt called. 'Want to come?'

'No,' Toby snapped.

Livvy shot her brother a venomous look before turning apologetically to Matt. 'We'd love to – just as soon as we've helped feed the ponies.'

'Sure. You know where to come when you're ready.'

On the brief stroll to the house neither of us spoke. I was mortified by Toby's insolence.

Matt inserted a key into the front door. 'Are you sure you're okay?'

'Fine,' I chirruped. Actually I was in agony.

'Sit down,' Matt pulled a chair out by the kitchen table.

I clomped towards it, moving from the hip like a cowboy in a Western. Positioning myself in front of the chair, I briefly hovered before collapsing backwards, legs splayed open.

Matt washed his hands and then swung into action. An enormous platter of cling-wrapped sandwiches were extracted from the fridge. Then it was off to the larder where, like a conjurer, he produced boxes of fairy cakes and Eccles buns, then back to the fridge again to haul out ice cold cans of lager.

'Here's to an afternoon pleasantly spent,' he toasted and tapped his tinny against mine. I gamely clanked back.

Just at that moment the twins burst in trailing two other children, a boy of about eleven and an older girl around thirteen.

'Hi,' the strangers chorused as they plonked themselves down at the table, outstretched hands claiming sandwiches. I boggled at them. Were these more offspring?

'This is Petra and Jonas,' said Matt. 'They have a pony of their own stabled here and argue constantly about who has first ride, so they both help out at the yard to earn extra rides on my ponies. Consequently they treat my house like a second home. But I don't mind because their Dad happens to be my best mate.'

Petra and Jonas smiled and it became apparent that Livvy and Toby had made a couple of friends. Petra's eyes kept darting curiously in my direction.

'You look familiar,' she furrowed her brow. 'Do I know you from somewhere?'

'I don't think so.'

The children demolished almost all the sandwiches and fairy cakes before excitedly heading back to the yard.

'Don't be too long,' I called after the twins, 'we'll be heading home soon.' If I ever managed to raise my backside from this chair.

Matt began clearing the table and loading the dishwasher.

'Don't you mind Petra and Jonas pitching up as if they own the place?'

Matt bent down to stack a plate. 'Not at all. I went to school with their Dad and I've known Petra and Jonas all their lives. They're like family to me, especially after their mother died.'

'God how awful. When did that happen?'

'Four years ago.'

'She was obviously young. Whatever did she die of?'

Matt straightened up from the dishwasher. He blew out his cheeks in a flummoxed gesture. 'Philly had an undetected congenital heart condition. She died from degeneration of a heart valve. When I stop and think about it, there's still a feeling of stunned disbelief. I guess it will never completely go away. Even now it seems impossible that Philly has gone. She was always roaring around – everything she did was at one hundred miles per hour. And she was such a happy person. Always laughing about something. And then suddenly she was lying in a morgue – dead from acute heart failure. Mac was devastated and went to pieces. For a while he kind of lost his marbles and gave us all quite a scare.'

'What about Petra and Jonas? Are they at risk of this happening to them?'

Matt chucked a dishwasher tablet in amongst the crockery. 'Thankfully not. Mac had them off to the doctor for a full heart scan and both kids were given a clean bill of health.' He slammed the dishwasher shut and turned a dial.

'Is your friend okay now?'

'When you have kids you can't sink forever. Thankfully he got through it and is swimming again. In fact, he even hinted that he'd met somebody meaningful quite recently.'

'Well good for him. Life goes on and all those other clichés.'

'Yep.' Matt tossed an empty cake box in a recycling sack before crouching down in front of me. I swallowed nervously as a pair of hazel eyes zoomed in on mine. Was he about to make some sort of romantic advance? With my frozen muscles I was incapable of jumping up and running around the kitchen table, Benny Hill style.

'You haven't budged from that position for the last hour. Are you quite sure you're all right?'

'Actually, I seem to have set like jelly in a mould. I think a hot bath might help. *My* bath,' I added hastily as the hazel eyes lit up like headlamps.

With supreme effort I hauled myself out of the chair and

toddled to the door, anxious to put a safe distance between Matt and myself. The children were duly rounded up and shepherded to the car. They clambered into the back while Matt folded me up like a deckchair and slotted me in behind the steering wheel.

'Are you okay to drive?'

'Sure, it's nothing a soak won't put right.'

He leaned into the open window and lowered his voice. 'Do you want me to pop round later and soap your back?'

'Thanks but I have a loofah.'

'I could give you a massage,' he smiled hopefully.

'Maybe another time,' I kissed him chastely on the cheek before turning my attention to the back seat. 'Children, do you have something to say to Matt?'

'Thank you very much,' they chorused.

'You're welcome,' Matt raised a hand to them before turning back to me. 'I'll call you soon,' he promised stepping back as the engine turned over.

On the journey home I detoured via the local chemist.

'Why are we stopping?' asked Toby.

'Here,' I thrust a fiver into my son's hand. 'Go and ask Nisha for a pot of Sudocrem.'

'Isn't that for babies' bottoms?'

'Just do it Tobes.'

After a steaming bubble bath and a copious application of healing cream, I spent the evening pottering. Shoving a pile of ironing in the airing cupboard, quite by chance I overheard the twins in conversation. They were chatting about their trip to the stables and meeting Matt. Talk was somewhat fractured by the periodic yelling of "Die you moron!" at the computer screen.

The bedroom door was ajar. I tiptoed across the landing, like an improbable ballerina up to no good.

'Well I liked him,' I heard Livvy say.

My ears pricked up and began flapping in earnest.

'He was a total prat,' growled Toby.

Pause for much erratic button stabbing.

'Jonas and Petra were good fun.'

'Yeah.'

Stab, stab, stab.

'Do you think Mum's in love?'

Tap, tap, tap.

'Yesss!' my son roared. What? I wasn't in love at all. 'I've *killed* it! Next level coming up Liv. Nah, of *course* Mum's not in love.'

'How can you be so sure?'

'Because Matt was a jerk and Mum wouldn't fall for a jerk.'

Oh wouldn't she? Somewhere along the line I'd once married one.

I did a few seconds of noisy throat-clearing before barging in Toby's bedroom.

'Hi guys!'

No response.

I leant over and pressed the off button. 'I *said* hi guys.'

'Aw whadya do that for Mum?' they complained in unison.

'Time for a talk.'

They caught my tone, shot each other a look before giving me their full attention.

'About today,' I ventured.

Two faces peered at me silently.

'Did you enjoy it?'

Two nods of the head.

'Did you like Matt?'

Only one nod of the head. Livvy. I looked at Toby, an eyebrow arched enquiringly. 'Well?'

'He's okay I guess. I deliberately let you down Mum and I'm really sorry.' And with that he burst into tears.

An emotionally exhausting family session then followed. All three of us aired and discussed our respective feelings on the dramatic change of events in the last five months that had led up to the point we were now at. The *divorce* word was brought out into the open for the first time.

'Your dad and I have desperately tried to smooth the edges on everything that a permanent split entails,' I said gently. 'Above all else, we love you both dearly.'

'But not each other,' sniffed Toby.

'We do love each other but not in the way that married couples *should* love each other. All that matters now is that you get to see both of your parents as often as possible. Dad's even bought a house in the same road so he can be near you.'

'So how does Matt Harding fit into the shape of things?' asked Toby.

'He's a friend,' I replied firmly.

'But is he your *boy*friend?' Toby persisted.

'I don't think of him that way. He too has children who are in exactly the same situation as the two of you, so he understands how you feel. Matt just wants to be friends too.'

'So you don't think you'll marry him one day Mum?' Livvy asked.

'Of course not! I like Matt a lot. But like is *like*, like isn't *love*. And much as I like Matt, I don't see myself ever falling in love with him. But-'

'What?'

I hesitated. 'Nothing really. Just that maybe it would be nice to fall in love again one day. In a hidden corner deep within every human being there is a part of us that yearns to be loved and *in* love. But for now there is nobody. And there may never be. All that matters right now is you two. Understand?'

They nodded and then we all hugged and sniffed a bit.

'How about we raid the freezer and have some cheer up nosh?' I gave them a watery smile.

The twins didn't need to be asked twice and catapulted down to the kitchen. Out came the raspberry sorbet, the dregs of an old tub of Cornish Vanilla and a rather congealed tub of Strawberry Sundae. Ice-cream was greedily scooped out and scattered with colourful hundreds and thousands and topped with ripples of fudge sauce.

'God this is disgusting,' I groaned.

'But utterly delicious,' Livvy grinned.

In the midst of this ice-cream mayhem Matt telephoned.

'Hi Cass. I just wondered if you and the kids fancied a get-together tomorrow?'

I nervously patted my posterior. 'More horse-riding?'

'For the kids yes, but not for you and me.'

Matt then went on to explain that his widowed mother was visiting for family lunch and we were very welcome to join in.

'Cass, it's a totally informal lunch where my noisy children will display disgusting table manners, talk with their mouths full, drop food everywhere and maybe lip my poor old mum. It's most certainly not a "Meet the Mother" situation, I promise.'

'Ha ha,' I laughed, almost choking. Had I been that transparent?

'Liv and Toby can mess about down the stables with my bunch while you help me cook lunch.'

'Did you say *help* you? As in *assisting* with cooking?'

'Yup. Good heavens Ms Cherry,' he teased, 'you didn't presume there were romantic connotations behind the invitation did you?'

'Not at all Mr Harding,' I quipped back. Well actually yes. How disappointing. Suddenly I felt confused. Whilst I wasn't wishing to take a flying leap into Matt's bed, nonetheless there was something very pleasant about the playfully flirtatious undercurrents. But then again I didn't seem to know what I wanted from this relationship. Correction. *Friendship*. It was no good giving the twins weighty assurances that Matt Harding wasn't falling-in-love material or telling myself – much as I liked the guy – that I didn't want to take things further when I seemed more than happy to participate in teasing banter. I sighed heavily. God this dating lark was perplexing.

'So is that a yes?'

'Absolutely, we'd love to come to lunch.'

'Good. See you at nine.'

'Nine in the morning?' I squeaked. 'I thought you said *lunch*?'

'I did, but I also said you were helping me, remember?'

When I cautiously poked my head around Matt's kitchen door the following morning it was with an element of surprise that I saw Petra and Jonas at the kitchen table hoovering up piles of buttery toast. Despite having had their own breakfast, Liv and Toby swiped a couple of wholemeal triangles from their proffered plates.

'Good grief, doesn't their father feed them?' I hissed at Matt.

'I told you before Cass, this is their second home. They'll probably join us for lunch too. And talking of lunch, we need to make a start.'

'Bit early isn't it?'

'Not for what I have in mind,' he waggled his eyebrows and smiled suggestively.

Oo-er. Thank goodness the children were still here. But not for much longer judging from the amount of chair scraping going on as they stood to leave, heads bowed together in a giggling huddle. Moments later they'd peeled off to the stables leaving me alone with Matt. I felt a small frisson of panic. However, the only vibrating gadgets that he produced were those stowed away in kitchen cupboards. A rather phallic looking blender was deposited on the work surface along with a battery powered cheese grater.

'Neat,' I commented picking up the latter for inspection. 'I haven't seen one of these before. What are we making?'

'Lasagne,' replied Matt setting down a chopping board and vicious looking knife. 'Here. You chop the basil and beef tomatoes and,' he stretched sideways digging around in an overloaded vegetable rack, 'these red onions too.'

I turned and stared at him aghast. 'But we can buy lasagnes by the trolley load in Tesco.'

'That as may be, but they wouldn't taste like the ones we're going to make.'

'I thought you were a beans on toast man!' I accused.

'And so I am. But occasionally I enjoy cooking properly and anyway, where my mother is concerned she wouldn't expect anything else.' He placed some parmesan in the grater and set to work. 'She's Italian and would revile any convenience foods cooked in a supermarket foil tray.'

Just as well she didn't regularly park her bottom around my kitchen table then.

An hour or so later Matt was ready to line several baking trays with thin rectangles of pasta and a mixture of meat sauce. As he deftly set about layering and stacking, I admired his culinary skills.

The final layer was topped with mozzarella, ricotta and flakes of parmesan. One by one the trays disappeared inside a vast kitchen range.

'However many people are we catering for?'

'A small army.'

Within minutes a delicious aroma pervaded the kitchen. Matt directed me to the cellar for red wine while he scrubbed pots and pans. I left him to it and explored the ground floor of the house en route to the cellar.

Large lofty rooms led off from the hallway. There was a faded elegance about the place but it was a bit too tatty for my liking. I would definitely have drawn the line at those mud encrusted Wellington boots abandoned in the lounge.

When I eventually returned with a couple of bottles of Chianti, Matt was putting the last saucepan away.

'Half eleven,' he said checking his wristwatch. 'Not bad timing. In fact,' he looked at me speculatively, 'we've got time to be naughty.'

I instantly positioned myself on the other side of the kitchen table ensuring an enormous obstacle was firmly wedged between his body and mine.

'Shall we indulge?'

'In what?' I squeaked.

'A glass of robust red or a good slug of gin?'

Relief washed over me like a tidal wave. He was merely bandying words about suggestively, that was all. It was a simple case of partaking in some mildly flirtatious chit-chat.

'In that case I'd love to be naughty,' I chortled provocatively. Steady Cass. Keep it light. Don't send out the wrong signals. 'Wine please.'

'You are a wicked wayward woman Cassandra Cherry,' Matt declared. He rummaged in a messy drawer for a corkscrew and then selected a couple of glasses from a cupboard.

'Cheers!' I toasted. 'I didn't realise you were half Italian. Can you actually talk the language?'

Matt regarded me for a moment, dropped his voice an octave

and launched into a fluent husky Italian. I gasped wantonly with surprise. Thank God the guy didn't talk like this all the time. There was no telling what havoc it could wreak with my hormones.

'Buon giorno, come va?' he murmured seductively as strong brown hands suggestively wandered over his body, slowly fingering each individual button on his open necked shirt, travelling down and down and down a bit more, lightly grazing the zipper on his faded jeans. My eyes bulged. Did he want to take his clothes off for me?

'Dove si trova la lavanderia automatica?'

'That was beautiful,' I whispered hoarsely.

'Don't get too worked up,' he laughed mischievously, 'I was only dropping hints about you doing a spot of laundry. Come on, let's throw some salad together to go with lunch.'

Good natured Joanie was despatched to collect her grandmother from the station and over the next twenty minutes or so a steady troop of youngsters filed into the kitchen two by two, a bit like the animals from Noah's Ark. Matt introduced them as each slouched past, shoulders hunched in the posture all teenagers seemed to adopt. Four girls were daughters from his second and third marriages and were staying for the weekend. Two lads were boyfriends of two of the daughters. Another two boys were step-sons from the current marriage who wanted to stay put until their mother was properly sorted out in her new home. One was a step-son's girlfriend and another pair I recognised from earlier that morning as being Petra and Jonas.

'And I do believe these two are yours,' concluded Matt as the twins traipsed after the others down the hallway, for all the world as if they lived in this house too.

Matt poured my third glass of wine. It had been a long time since breakfast and I was a little tipsy.

'I can hear Joanie's car. Mama has arrived.' He slung a dishcloth over his shoulder and went off to greet her.

'What's her name,' I called after his departing back.

'Mia.'

Mia. Mama Mia. I giggled. Here I go again. I snorted into my wine glass. My My. Mama Mia waddled into the kitchen, a formidable sight swathed from head to toe in black widow weeds and clutching a handbag the size of a small suitcase. Introductions were made and then everybody got down to the business of eating. Lunch was an informal affair with almost everybody dressed in stable gear and smelling absolutely outrageous. Mismatched cutlery was noisily extracted from a drawer, plates were grabbed at lightning speed from cupboards and mountainous servings were heaped into various landscape arrangements across individual platters. What seemed like hundreds of teenagers then scattered and regrouped to various corners of the house to eat – be it prostrated on a floor in front of a handily available television, ensconced on a sofa, reclining in an armchair, or squashed around the kitchen table. I could see the twins found it refreshingly decadent compared to my own ideas of where and how meals should be taken. I was very alive to the fact that not one single person had washed their hands before eating. Indeed, even the twins were sporting filthy hands and black fingernails.

However, no amount of germs or grime could detract from the deliciously aromatic food being forked up by one and all. More wine was brought up from the cellar and I reasoned that a fourth glass was surely permissible now my stomach was full of blotting paper. I gazed blearily around at my fellow luncheon companions and gave a contented sigh. Best not to drink any more though. The brain was ticking over nicely but I suspected it might not fully connect to the mouth.

Despite Mia's many years in England, she spoke with a heavy accent and I struggled to understand her, although it would be fair to say she battled to comprehend me too.

'I hava terrib arthrite,' she was telling me. 'Needa walk stick anda beega willchair summatime.'

'Oh dear, I'm sorry to hear that.'

'Ver pain.'

'Do you take tablets?'

'Huh?'

'Doo yoo take painkillers?'

Mia stared at me in bewilderment. I looked fuzzily at her. Had a nasty feeling I'd actually asked her whether she pained takekillers. No matter.

'Drugs,' I tried again.

'Droogs?'

Might be best to mime. 'Drugs,' I repeated carefully. Lest there be any further doubts I leant over the kitchen table and, with an index finger pressed firmly against one nostril, gave a glaringly obvious impression on how to snort a line of cocaine. Mia instantly looked liked she'd swallowed a gobstopper.

'Droogs!' she exclaimed, eyebrows disappearing into her hairline as the dawn came up. 'Nonna my familia tayka droogs, nevair, my chillren are all gooda chillren, my son ees gooda boy.'

I boggled at her. What had her son got to do with prescription drugs for arthritis? Perhaps it was time to change the subject.

'Are you going on holiday this year?' I asked politely before taking another sip of wine. Somehow the glass missed my lips and banged painfully against my front teeth.

'Mebbe,' Mia glared at me. 'Mebbe Eeetally.'

'Oh right. Will Mebbe be very hot?'

Matt appeared to be weeping into his lasagne.

When Joanie drove Mama back to the station I was left with a sneaking suspicion I'd failed to make a good impression. Oh well. It wasn't like she was going to be my future mother-in-law.

However, I deeply regretted drinking too much and consequently not being able to drive. Matt came to the rescue driving us home in my car with Joanie following behind in her little Renault.

As he drove, Matt gave me a sidelong look. 'Half term starts tomorrow. Have you got any plans?'

'As a matter of fact yes. I've been toying with the idea of doing some decorating and having some new flooring put down. That should keep me busy while the kids are off school.'

'That's nice. Bit boring for the kids though. Why don't you let Liv and Toby spend the week up the stables giving me a hand and in exchange they can have riding lessons?'

'Ooh can we Mum?' Livvy begged.

'Well I–'

'Please Mum,' Toby implored. 'It will be dead boring at home with you up to your armpits in dustsheets.'

'They're more than welcome,' Matt assured.

'Well, if you're sure, that's very kind of you.'

'Yay!' the twins cheered as the car came to a standstill on our drive. The back doors opened and they tumbled out in high spirits.

I turned to face Matt. 'You are such a nice man. A very, very nice man.'

'So you keep telling me,' Matt smiled wryly. He leant across the handbrake and brushed a fleeting kiss against my cheek. 'Come un raggio di sole hai illuminato la mia vita.'

Heavens. I palpitated a bit before clambering unsteadily from the car.

Chapter Ten

As the week progressed the temperature soared setting a record for early June. Matt kept his promise providing holiday jobs at the stables for Livvy and Toby. I kept myself busy appointing a carpenter who replaced the worn shagpile with golden floorboards.

To say I felt huge gratitude to Matt was an understatement. I really liked the guy but, confusingly, couldn't seem to work out my feelings toward him. He was great fun, kind and attractive. So did I fancy him or not?

One late afternoon, after the carpenter had departed, I drove to the stables to collect Liv and Toby. I found them stuffing hay nets and in deep conversation with Petra and Jonas.

'Aw Mum, give us ten more minutes,' Toby wheedled.

'Make it five,' I smiled and went off in search of Matt. I was aware of Petra staring after me.

'Why does your mum look so familiar?' I heard her say.

Matt was in the indoor riding school giving a private dressage lesson. I watched from the seated area until he'd finished, then put up my hand to catch his eye. He immediately waved and strolled over.

'Sorry if I hum a bit,' he leant across the wooden divide and planted a kiss on my cheek. Ah good, no lips. But ridiculously I felt disappointed. Why?

'Now then Mr Harding. You've been an absolute brick this week allowing Liv and Toby up here to hang out and get under your feet. I insist on showing you my appreciation and gratitude.'

'Ooh promises promises. Keep going Cass. This is music to my ears.'

I gave him a light cuff. 'I want to cook you a really special dinner to say thank you. Something Italian eh?'

'Right.' Matt paused and stared down at his riding boots.

'Oh. Is there a "but" coming up?'

'No, not as such. It's a very nice gesture Cass and I'm touched but-'

'I knew it!'

'But you really don't need to do that. And apart from anything else, I know you can't cook.'

'Don't be rid-ic-ulous,' I spluttered, 'of *course* I can cook – when I want to – and I'm not taking no for an answer.'

Matt raised his hands in surrender. 'Okay, no problem. In that case I would be delighted to accept your invitation. And when is this veritable feast taking place?'

'Tomorrow evening. My place.'

'I shall look forward to it.'

'Good,' I grinned, 'that's settled then.' I turned to walk back to the children but Matt caught my arm.

'Oh and Cass?'

'Yes?'

'You can be pudding.'

'Ha ha!'

In actual fact, the very thought of a sexy close encounter with Matt had me breaking out in a complete muck sweat. But perhaps I was just nervous, after the previous disaster with Euan. Yes, that was probably it.

It was only as I lay languishing in the bath later that evening that I realised what an idiotic suggestion it had been to insist I cook for Matt. I should have suggested a table for two at The Rose and Crown. Nothing wrong with a bit of gastro pub grub. But no. Stupidly I'd led him to believe that, when I had the whim, my culinary skills eclipsed Jamie Oliver. What the hell had I been thinking of? Dolloping Dolmio over a bowl of soggy penne was a no-no. This was a man who'd been raised at his mama's knee with the finest in home cooking.

The following morning, the moment Stevie had collected the twins for the weekend, I hastened to the kitchen to pour over my cookery books. It turned out to be just the one book – *The Best of Baking*. As I flipped through three hundred pages of buns, breads, pastries, gateaux and cookies, realisation dawned that a starter of fairy cakes followed by Victoria Sponge for mains and pancakes for pud was simply not on. Where was the recipe for Fettuccine Alfredo or Pasta e Fagioli when I needed it? And even if I had those recipes would I know what to do with them?

I reached for the phone and tapped out the number of Carlo and Luigi in Boxleigh High Street.

'Hello…Carlo? My name is Cassandra Cherry and I wondered if you could possibly help me out of a tight spot?'

At half past six I drew up outside Carlo and Luigi's restaurant and loaded my boot with several foil trays containing professionally cooked delights. Fifteen minutes later it was carefully transferred to my own oven on a very low heat, as instructed by Carlo, in hardly-ever-used casserole pots. Five minutes later every foil tray had been disposed of in a black sack and dumped in the wheelie bin outside. However, the dustmen had yet to come a-calling and the wheelie bin was bulging with household detritus. But my plans hadn't come this far to be thwarted at the eleventh hour by an overflowing dustbin. After a thorough pummelling, the topmost bag of garbage had been squashed into the receptacle. Unfortunately the lid remained obstinately raised, but no matter.

Matt arrived with two bottles of red Chianti tucked under each arm.

'You rather enjoyed this the last time we indulged,' he smiled and carefully set the bottles on the kitchen table. 'All we need now is a line of cocaine and the evening will be perfection.'

I winced at the memory. 'Not funny Mr Harding.'

Matt busied himself looking for a corkscrew and glasses. 'Mm. Something smells good,' he sniffed appreciatively.

Feeling terribly smug, I bustled over to the oven and dished up.

'The evening shall commence,' I announced, 'with minestrone verdure con crostini.'

'Hey not bad pronunciation Cass,' said Matt sitting down at the table. He dipped his spoon into the hot liquid. 'Very nice. In fact delicious.'

'Medaglione di manzo,' I placed the mains on the table with a little flourish. Matt eyeballed the delicate medallions of beef, wilted spring spinach and just-so creamed mash plus a boat of peppercorn sauce with an expression of incredulity.

'Cass I take absolutely everything back about you not being a cook. This is seriously impressive.' He popped a tender medallion in his mouth and rolled his eyes appreciatively. 'Heaven. You must have been chained to the kitchen all afternoon.'

'Oh it was nothing,' I said quite truthfully.

Finally, dessert.

'A small confession,' I declared placing a dish of tiramisu upon the table. 'Pudding is courtesy of Sainsbury's.' Well there was no point in lying all the way was there?

Much later, feeling incredibly mellow from so much wine, we sank into the sofa side by side to watch a late night movie. It seemed only natural for Matt to put an arm around me as he flicked through the channels. What was it with men and remote controls?

'Ooh, naughty channel,' he commented.

I stiffened.

On screen a bronzed blonde with massive fake breasts woodenly invited viewers to press the red button on their remote control *now*.

'What happens if you press the red button,' I croaked.

'The blonde and her female chum will romp in the buff wearing only whipped cream on their bits and pieces,' Matt laughed.

I shifted uneasily on the sofa.

'Fancy it?' whispered Matt pulling me closer. I was enveloped in a bear hug and suddenly on intimate terms with an Aramis scented armpit.

'Ah well now, don't let me spoil your fun. I'll just go and wash up and leave you to it eh? And then I'll pop back in time for the movie.'

Matt turned his body into mine at exactly the same moment I made to get up. Instead of finding myself released and unfettered I was instead nose to nose with his face, his lips a mere two millimetres from mine. The hazel eyes bore into mine, searching for just the smallest of signals that would indicate the green light and *go, go, go*. I stared back wide-eyed and terrified, hands clasped tightly in my lap, torso stiff and unyielding.

Suddenly Matt released me. There was a pause and then he switched the television off.

'You know I really would like to get to know you better Cass. Much better. But I truly don't know how to go about it. One minute we're larking about, swapping banter, having a laugh and flirty chit-chat. And then suddenly you're backing off with red flags waving and whistles blowing. To say I'm confused is an understatement.'

'I'm so sorry,' I whispered. 'I do like you Matt. Truly I do. It's just, well, I don't seem to know what I want myself half the time.'

'Cass, I guess we're all looking for someone, be it consciously or otherwise. It's human nature to seek out a partner, spouse, soul mate – call it what you will. I know I'm looking. Three marriages under my belt and here I am, a forty-three year old saddo *still* looking. *Still* hung up on the fact that somehow, somewhere, there might be *some*body waiting for me. I may never find her but I know in my heart I will never stop searching. I like you Cass. *Really* like you. And I'm happy to be your friend and see you casually with or without your kids. But I'd rather you tell me now if I'm wasting my time romantically. I don't want to embarrass you making clumsy passes if you're just looking for a platonic friendship.'

I seemed to be rapidly blinking. Couldn't stop actually. With an effort I tore my eyes away from his face, unclenched my rigid hands and took one of his in mine.

'I adore seeing you Matt,' I hesitated, choosing my words carefully. 'You're a fantastic guy – great fun, kind and sincere. And you're quite right. I'm looking for someone too. Eventually. But I foolishly threw myself into a very brief relationship not long after my marriage ended and it was a disaster. However, the experience taught me that I'm not cut out for having an intimate relationship with another man without, well, being in love I suppose. And right now,' I glanced up at his serious face, 'you're special, very special, but–'

'You're not in love,' Matt finished my sentence for me and I nodded slowly.

We sat there for a moment just looking at each other. Eventually he stood up.

'Cass, I'm going home now but I'd still like to see you in the future – if you want to that is.'

I gulped a bit and gave a weak smile. 'Of course I do. You're my friend Matthew Harding. And good friends are awfully precious.'

Together we walked to the hallway, our arms loosely around each other's waists. But upon opening the front door I froze.

'Oh my God!'

Matt followed my horrified gaze.

The incriminating sack of rubbish placed so carefully in the wheelie bin only a few hours earlier had been raided and ripped apart by a pillaging fox. Tin foil dishes and cardboard lids emblazoned with the homily 'Carlo and Luigi' were scattered across the drive. As realisation dawned, Matt turned back to regard my red-faced embarrassment. He started to chuckle. Then his shoulders shook. Suddenly he keeled over hugging his belly as hilarity convulsed his body. Seconds later a fit of giggles bubbled up within me. And suddenly we were clutching each other, doubled up with mirth.

'You are incorrigible Cassandra Cherry,' Matt wiped his eyes. 'And actually,' he gently took hold of me, 'what you did tonight demonstrates that I truly am a very special friend. Thank you.'

And with that he dropped a warm kiss on my forehead and wished me goodnight.

Reversing his car down the driveway he suddenly stopped and buzzed the window down.

'Can I call you tomorrow?'

'That would be great,' I replied truthfully.

He gave a cheery little toot and I waved until the car's red tail lights disappeared. Sighing, I turned on my heel and went in search of a fresh black sack.

As good as his word, Matt telephoned the following morning suggesting lunch. I readily agreed, eager to dispel any awkwardness following last night's cards-on-the-table confession.

When I arrived at Matt's he was in the yard messing about with a small wirehaired terrier, attempting to throw a deflated football for the little dog who was determined not to relinquish his toy without a good deal of growling and head shaking. Matt saw me approaching, rubbed the dog's head and walked on over.

'How's the best cook in the world?' he teased by way of greeting.

We fell into an easy stride together, his arm around my shoulder but in a chummy way rather than a flirty manner. It was honestly as if nothing had ever happened.

We lunched at a quaint inn tucked away on the borders of woodland. Over a Ploughman's we chatted and joked. At some point Mac, the widowed father of Petra and Jonas, cropped up in the conversation.

'He's a bit down at the moment,' Matt confided.

'Well it can't be a bed of roses raising two young children single-handedly.

'Tell you what,' suggested Matt, 'how about a bit of a get-together next weekend. I'll invite Mac over. Liv and Toby can hang out with Petra and Jonas. Perhaps you'd like to bring a girlfriend along and we'll make it a bit of a social thing. If the weather carries on being as beautiful as today I could even do us a nice barbie.'

'Okay,' I enthused.

My first thought was Morag, but then I hesitated. What if she got plastered and became lewd and loud? Perhaps Julia would be the safer option. But if Morag later found out she'd been passed over in favour of Julia, my working life probably wouldn't be worth living.

'Anyone in mind?'

'W-e-ll, I'm good pals with a girl at work. She's actually one of the solicitors. But despite having a tremendously responsible and sobering job, she can in fact be a bit-'

'Irresponsible and not so sober?'

'Er, well, only out of hours.'

'I'm intrigued Cass. Do elaborate.'

'Her name's Morag. She's attractive and vivacious but she can be rather, well, all sort of heaving bosoms and full on.'

'All heaving bosoms eh? Well that's sorted then. She's definitely invited.'

'Okay, I'll square it up with her tomorrow when I'm back at work.'

I didn't manage to touch base with the lady in question until lunchtime.

'Why are we rushing?' complained Morag as we headed to the park at a trot. 'What's wrong with walking?'

'I need air,' I gasped, 'fresh air. I'm working again for that awful Martin Henniker this week. He's so noxious I feel like I've been poisoned.'

'Oh yeah,' Julia nodded her head as she puffed along on the other side of me, 'his new secretary walked out last week. She only stayed two days.'

'Yes well never mind Hideous Henniker,' Morag collapsed onto the hard slats of our park bench. 'I've road tested this little lot,' she produced her speed dating list complete with scribbled out names, 'and they were all crap.'

'You slept with all those men?' I gasped.

'Oh Cass for goodness sake stop being such a prude,' she scrunched the list up and lobbed it at a nearby litter bin.

I turned to Julia. 'How did your date turn out with Wosser-name?'

'Miles,' Julia beamed.

'What sort of a name is Miles?' snorted Morag.

'A nice name. He's a sweetie and I like him.'

'Men,' Morag grumbled, 'are a pain in the backside. They're like a blender – you need one but you're not quite sure why.'

Julia and I laughed and joined in good-naturedly.

'They're like commercials – you can't believe a word they say.'

'Or like mascara – they run at the first sign of emotion.'

We creased up.

'Attagirls,' whooped Morag happily. 'Men are like popcorn – they satisfy you but only for a little while.'

'So you won't be interested in a bit of a blind date this weekend?' I asked slyly.

'I never said that,' Morag sat up straight giving me her undivided attention.

So I told her about meeting up with Matt and his widower pal.

'Oh why not,' she sighed. 'I've damn all else to do.'

As the week progressed the sun shone ever warmer and my thoughts turned to summer holidays. I found myself slipping into the travel agents and grabbing an armful of holiday brochures.

'Are we going abroad Mum?' Livvy asked that evening, fingering the brochures longingly.

'Looks like it,' I grinned.

'Oh yeah,' enthused Toby. 'Disneyland here we come.'

'I was thinking more Europe actually.'

'As long as it has theme parks Mum I'll be more than happy.'

'There will be a beach with an in-built wave machine and you will be deliriously happy,' I informed my son.

But when I telephoned to book the holiday of my choice, it appeared that everything suitable had been snapped up months ago.

'If you give me a definite time frame Mrs Cherry I can investigate global cancellations and last minute availability,' said the travel agent.

'Well okay, just so long as you understand I don't want to be sent off to some godforsaken third world country. I don't want food poisoning, diarrhoea, cockroaches, toilets that are only holes in the ground, stinking drains, rats, dead cats-'

'Yes I get the picture Mrs Cherry,' the travel agent interrupted. At the other end of the line I could hear the continual tapping of keys. 'Ah! This looks promising but availability is for one week only. There are just two small apartments left at The Gardens, self-catering, in picturesque Benalmadena.'

'Where's that?' I asked none the wiser.

'Spain.'

'I'll take it.'

Just as the day was drawing to a close, my long awaited new bed was delivered. I was not disappointed. The elegant chocolate leather contrasted richly against the cream bedroom carpet completely transforming the room.

However, there was a bit of a setback with Liv and Toby's respective beds. Stupidly I hadn't realised they were flat packed and required home assembly. Two pairs of blue eyes gazed expectantly at me.

'Sorry kids but I'm not even going to attempt it.'

'Call Dad,' Livvy suggested sensibly.

After just two rings a girl breathlessly answered. I say *girl* because she sounded about twelve. Presumably this was Charlotte the Teenage Mutant Tartlette.

'Hello, is Stevie there please?'

A small pause. 'Who's calling?'

Was it my imagination or did she sound suspicious and proprietary?

'His wife,' I replied as the bitch within me inexplicably roared to the surface. Almost immediately I felt contrite. Charlotte was not the cause of my failed marriage. 'One moment. BABE!' she foghorned. *Babe?* 'It's your EX-WIFE.'

I caught my breath. Well that had put me in my place hadn't it? My shoulders sagged. Oh so what? Did I really care? She was quite right. I was Stevie's ex-wife and it was only a matter of time before

157

a piece of paper formalised that fact. Why should I mind if Charlotte was being territorial?

Seconds later Stevie came on the line. I quickly explained about the twins' beds.

'Hey no problem Cass. I'll grab my toolbox and pop over right away. Can't have the kids disappointed.'

'Thanks, I really appreciate that.'

Ha! That would show Charlotte a thing or two. I might be the ex-wife but Liv and Toby were still his children.

When Stevie later sauntered past my open bedroom door and spotted the new leather bed dominating the floor space, he couldn't help doing a double take.

'That's...exotic.'

I felt acutely embarrassed. The bed seemed to silently pulsate with sexual energy.

'It's posturepaedic. Good on your back.'

'I'll bet,' Stevie winked.

'It's good for *bad* backs,' I explained irritably.

'Whatever dongs your gong Cass! What have you done with the old bed?'

'It's in the garage awaiting a trip to the rubbish dump.'

'Don't chuck it. I'll collect it at the weekend and stick it in one of my spare bedrooms.'

An hour later Stevie slung a screwdriver in his toolbox and straightened up.

'Thanks very much for your help,' I said stiffly.

Livvy's room looked indescribably pretty, the princess four-poster hung with the palest of pink voile curtains. And Toby's room was now more pre-teen than playschool with its bunk bed and desk combo.

It was gone midnight when, with a small thrill, I clambered under the duvet and spread-eagled my body across the king-sized mattress. I briefly wondered whether I would ever share a bed with another man again.

On Saturday morning Morag arrived in her gleaming little sports car. Low slung and sexy, it was great for two people but totally impractical for squeezing in Livvy and Toby. Grumbling hugely, Morag climbed into my filthy but sensible family hatchback.

'I won't make much of an impression turning up in this hillbilly wagon.'

'With looks like yours you don't need to rely upon a sports car for props,' I soothed.

'Do you think?' Morag perked up.

It was true that she looked lovely, dressed in a plunging white top and pristine designer jeans.

At the yard, Toby and Liv spotted Petra and Jonas and immediately ran off to join them. Morag and I went straight up to the house. The side gate was open so we strolled round to the back garden. Matt was fanning a smoking barbecue and chatting to another guy who had his back to us. At the sound of our footsteps Matt looked up, his face splitting into a welcoming grin which grew even bigger when he copped Morag's billowing cleavage.

'Well hello girls,' he beamed giving me a firm kiss on both cheeks so that he then had an excuse to kiss Morag twice. His eyes kept zooming in on her cleavage. Judging from the way she had switched to jiggle mode, Morag was not offended. She was impressed enough with Matt to step her forceful personality up another notch and was now doing a superb impression of Miss Piggy, all fluttering eyelashes and lots of hair flicking.

'I have to say Morag, Cass described you perfectly.'

'Hmm?' Morag simpered. She even sounded like Miss Piggy. Any minute now she'd be calling him Kermit.

'Cass said you were very — what was it? All heaving bos-'

'Buzzes,' I interrupted, flashing Matt a stern look. His eyes were dancing with mischief. Morag looked perplexed.

'As in buzzy,' I explained.

'Oh yes I am a very buzzy person,' Morag said eagerly.

But I was no longer looking at her. Instead I was staring in disbelief at the other man who had turned to face us and was looking pretty stunned himself. Morag followed my gaze and her mouth dropped.

'You!' all three of us chimed together.

Matt looked pole-axed. 'Er, do you all know each other?'

'We've bumped into each other here and there,' Morag replied coolly.

'What a small world,' mused Matt.

I stared at Ploddy – Jamie. 'You are *Mac*?'

'Mac is a shortening of my surname. A nickname if you will. I don't mind what you call me,' he shrugged, 'so long as it's not Mr Pitt.'

I flushed.

'Who's Mr Pitt?' Matt asked.

'I haven't the faintest idea.'

'How about a nice drink?' I changed the subject with forced gaiety and lunged at a jug of ruby liquid on the garden table. 'Mm Pimms, delicious. Cheers everyone!'

I took an enormous swig of the fruit and mint concoction just as the twins erupted into the garden closely followed by Petra and Jonas. I sent up a silent prayer of thanks for the distraction of children.

'Dad we're starving. Is the barbecue ready yet?'

I reeled. Petra and Jonas belonged to Jamie? He in turn was staring at the twins.

'But I've seen Liv and Toby on numerous occasions at the stables. I've even let them ride my kids' pony.' Jamie scratched his head in bemusement. 'I had no idea you were their mother.'

At that moment Petra gave me an odd look, as though seeing me for the first time. 'I've just remembered why you look so familiar.'

'Oh?' I suddenly felt horribly nervous.

'Yeah, it's coming back to me now. You were in the field the other week with Matt. That's right. You were running around in the noddy and Matt was chasing you,' she started to laugh. 'God it was seriously funny. We were all killing ourselves in the yard,' she broke off to clutch her sides. 'And Matt was slapping your bottom... ah ha ha ha!' she doubled up with mirth. 'And your backside was wobbling all over the place,' she grabbed her buttocks and jiggled them about while snorting and gasping for breath. 'And then you fell flat on your face and your bum was *still* wobbling even when the rest of you had stopped moving.'

The only sound now was of Petra's raucous laughter as she staggered about hugging her torso, clearly at the painfully funny stage of hysterics.

'How *dare* you tell such filthy lies about my mother,' Toby spat and launched himself at Petra.

The two children crashed to the floor and instantly began pummelling each other. A moment later Jamie was on to them, yanking both children to their feet.

'ENOUGH!' he bawled.

Toby was white faced and thin lipped with rage, his fists clenched impotently by his sides.

'My mother doesn't run around in the noddy,' he hissed furiously.

'And she hasn't got a wobbly bottom either,' Livvy piped up indignantly.

'A wasp went up my trousers,' I explained hoarsely. 'Stripping was the only option.'

'Oh God I'm so sorry,' Petra was mortified. 'I didn't mean to make fun. I had no idea it was something so frightening.'

'Right you two,' Jamie said. 'Shake hands. I'm not having any bad feeling.'

Within seconds the children had dismissed the matter in the way only children ever do and disappeared inside the house for Cola.

'Okay,' Matt grinned, 'enough drama. Let's have those fillet steaks!'

Any lingering awkwardness was instantly dispelled. The food was delicious and the drink flowed. In due course the children peeled off to the stables. Jamie, possibly because of his daughter's earlier faux-pas, seemed to go out of his way to be attentive company and I felt myself warming to him more and more. He made me laugh and I began to feel so at ease with him I started to suspect something was going on between us – and it was something I liked.

It also became apparent that Morag was extremely taken with Matt. She flirted outrageously and eventually bullied him into a guided tour of the stables, leaving Jamie and I alone together. We sat companionably in the low afternoon sun, watching the broadening shadows. Eventually Jamie got up and refreshed our glasses.

'So. You and Matt?'

'Friends,' I replied firmly.

Jamie took a sip of his drink. 'He's a great guy. We've been pals for more years than I care to recall.'

I remembered with a jolt that Matt had talked about knowing Jamie since school days. How he'd gone through the grief process with Jamie when his wife had died so suddenly. I cleared my throat.

'Matt told me that you were a widower.'

Jamie contemplated his glass for a moment. 'Yeah,' he pulled a face. 'Did he tell you about Philly?'

'No,' I lied, not wishing for Jamie to think Matt indiscreet. 'Do you want to tell me about it?'

'Sure, why not.' Jamie paused for a moment, seeming to pick his words with care. 'I lost Philly four years ago. Nearly lost my mind too. Matt was brilliant. Along with my family, he was instrumental in shouldering a lot of grief.'

I didn't know what to say for a moment. I'd lost my husband but the circumstances were very different in that Stevie was still alive. My loss wasn't remotely comparable to this man's.

'Philly had an undetected heart condition.'

'How awful,' I murmured.

'I can still remember that morning so clearly, like a film running through my head. We'd just made love,' he shrugged apologetically. 'Philly's hair was all tousled. She'd smiled at me and said she was going to have a shower. Moments later the shower sprayed into life, the water drumming against the glass door. It was a Sunday morning and I hadn't felt any need to get up and start rushing about. So I'd flopped back down on the mattress and drifted into a light sleep. Thirty minutes later I'd opened my eyes to hear the shower still running. In that moment, instinctively, I knew something wasn't right.'

I stared at Jamie, transfixed. 'What did you do?'

'I called her name. There was no reply. The shower was still tapping a beat against the glass door. I hauled myself off the bed and called her name again feeling a terrible sense of foreboding. When Philly still didn't respond I levered the door handle down. Clouds of steam enveloped my vision and for a moment I just stood blindly in all this fog. And then the draft from the open door tugged at the steam, pulling pockets of it apart. Philly was slumped in the shower base, her legs curled awkwardly to one side. Her head was resting uncomfortably against the shower door and a curtain of wet hair hid her face. For a moment I was paralysed with shock and couldn't move. Then I lunged forward, tearing at the door. Philly sprawled across the bathroom floor. God I'll never forget that moment for as long as I live. Her hair fell back from her face like wet seaweed and suddenly I was staring into dead eyes.'

Jamie's voice momentarily caught and I automatically stretched my hand across and touched his. He caught hold of it. Curled it into his palm.

'Coming to terms with it was … difficult. I saw her face all the time. I'd walk into a room and see her profile in the print of a wallpaper pattern, or the silhouette of her body in rumpled bedclothes. It drove me mad. Couples who had been friends felt awkward. After a while they avoided me. Apart from Matt.'

'He's a nice guy,' I murmured.

'Oh he's that all right,' Jamie nodded. 'My children were bereft and I'm not proud to admit that I was no help to them in the beginning. Matt saw Petra and Jonas every day. Bullied them into coming to the stables and got them riding which acted like a kind of therapy for them. It took a good couple of years for Petra and Jonas to become the carefree children they are now.'

A silence fell between us for a minute or two.

'And what was your therapy?' I eventually asked.

'Mine?' Jamie gave a mirthless laugh. 'Oh for a while I was an embittered ranting lunatic. But life with all its harshness goes on doesn't it? It's a case of get over it and get on with it. Either that or give up. Throw in the towel. But you can't wallow forever when you have two children to care for. So my kids ultimately got me back on track. I'm good now.'

I was very aware that my hand was still within his. He made no attempt to release it. Suddenly I wanted the moment to never end. Right then I could have sat in Matt's garden and held Jamie's hand until the end of time.

'Enough of my heavy talk. What about you? Still going for divorce?'

'Oh yes. I'll keep the married name though – *Cherry* is prettier than my maiden name.'

'Well don't leave me guessing,' Jamie teased and squeezed my hand. 'What was your maiden name?'

'Haddock,' I grinned ruefully. 'At school I was called Fish Face.'

'Ah,' Jamie nodded sympathetically. There was a small pause. 'So how did you get on at the speed dating gig? Did you find anybody?'

'Oh that. No,' I gazed at my drink miserably. 'I'm giving up the dating game. Can't seem to work out the rules. And you?'

'The person I was interested in didn't tick my box.'

'I'm sorry.'

'I haven't given up hoping that she might change her mind though.'

I carefully removed my hand from Jamie's. It didn't seem appropriate to continue letting him hold it now that he was expressing interest in somebody else.

'Are you hoping for a reunion with your female colleague?'

Jamie looked startled. "Selina? Good Lord no! Actually, the lady I was referring to is somebody I've liked for quite some time. I've been bumping into her on and off for several months now. I wanted to ask her out ages ago but I wasn't sure whether she was single in the true sense of the word. She gave me the impression at one point that there was another guy on the scene.'

'She sounds a bit flighty,' I sniffed.

Jamie laughed out loud. 'Really? I don't suspect she's that at all. More,' he considered, 'completely unaware how captivating she is and sorely lacking in self-esteem. As a result she needs handling carefully. A kid glove approach.'

I nodded miserably thinking that I wouldn't mind a bit of the kid glove approach myself.

'Cassie?' Jamie shifted in his chair. Was it my imagination or was he giving me a smouldering look? If I wasn't feeling so deflated I'd have attempted a few smoulders back. 'I'm surprised you haven't worked it out. I'm talking about–'

At that precise moment Morag and Matt returned in high spirits. Morag seemed to be fizzing and bubbling all over the place.

'Ooh Cass this naughty man is utterly de*light*ful,' she cooed. 'I think I'll have to marry him.'

Matt roared with laughter. 'Lovely lady, I would be delighted to have you as the fourth Mrs Harding.'

Morag seemed to find this terribly funny and screeched with laughter. Jamie set about attending refills and finding a soft drink for me while Matt broached the subject of holidays. Now this was a subject I could definitely get enthusiastic about! Excitedly I joined in and told everybody about the impending Benalmadena trip.

'Pretty place,' commented Jamie. 'I've been there. Where are you staying?'

'The Garden Apartments.'

'But I know them! They're up a bit of a steep hill but still close enough to the sea. It's a quiet residential road – no yobs.'

I sighed with relief. 'The travel agent said I was very lucky to get the booking – there were only two apartments left.'

'Were there now,' Jamie murmured. 'When did you say you were going?'

'Third week of July. Not long to go now,' I smiled happily.

Evening came. It was still light but rapidly cooling down so we moved inside.

'I'm feeling hungry again,' Morag complained.

'Who fancies a takeaway and a movie?' Matt asked.

The children melted off to another room with an assortment of Matt's children and step-children to watch their own choice of movie while the adults grouped around Matt's prized fifty inch big screen, eventually with vindaloos balanced on knees.

A couple of hours later Jamie called out to Petra and Jonas.

'Come on kids, it's late.'

I got up too. It was way past the twins' usual bed time.

Matt gave Jamie and I big bear hugs as he said good-bye. I suddenly realised that, despite Morag standing in the hallway, she wasn't actually saying farewell.

'I'm not coming with you,' she mouthed to me.

'What do you mean?' I mouthed back.

Morag took me to one side while the twins provided a noisy diversion looking for trainers. 'I'm staying the night with Matt.'

'Bit soon isn't it?'

'At our age Cass, life is too short not to dive into things head first. I'll be round for my car tomorrow and will give you a post-mortem of what Matt was like in bed.'

Oh God.

Chapter Eleven

Finally all the children had their belongings. They ran ahead of us as Jamie and I walked to our respective cars. He touched my arm causing such a jolt of electricity I almost rocketed out of my skin.

'Sorry, didn't mean to make you jump. I just wanted to say that it was really good to see you this evening,' he smiled.

We came to a halt by my car. 'Oh and it was absolutely marvellous to see you too,' I gushed and then instantly cringed. Steady Cass. Jamie took a step closer and brushed his lips lightly against my cheek. For an awful moment I thought my knees were going to give way. Jonas let out a low wolf whistle.

Jamie grinned. 'Kids eh?'

My cheek sizzled and scorched all the way home.

'Mum?' Toby asked as we drove along. 'Isn't Matt your boyfriend any more?'

'Matt was and still is my friend Toby. But I think he could be Morag's new boyfriend.'

'Are you upset?'

'No. Why should I be?'

'Well, I thought you wanted a boyfriend and to fall in love and everything,' he shrugged.

'If you are referring to that little chat we had a while ago, I said I'd *like* to fall in love again *one day*, but that doesn't mean to say it will ever happen and I certainly wasn't anticipating Matt to be The One.'

Toby looked thoughtful. 'What about Jamie? He's really nice. Why don't you go out with him?'

Yes why didn't I? The day had been nothing short of wonderful culminating in a delightful evening spent in the company of a man who I had felt increasingly drawn to. I genuinely clicked with him on a deep level. Jamie had bared his soul to me in the garden talking about his dead wife, discussing immensely personal and private feelings. I suspected he didn't talk like that to any old Tom, Dick or Harry. And there had been something else, something unspoken, those nuances of body language that I'd initially interpreted as flirting. There was no doubt about it, Jamie made my heart race. Even now my cheek was still burning from that kiss. But, confusingly, he'd mentioned the speed dating gig and gone on to talk about another woman he was interested in. Apparently not Selina, but nonetheless somebody else. I sighed.

'Well?' Toby persisted.

'Look Tobes, much as I appreciate your concern, it's not as simple as that. For a kick off, Jamie hasn't even asked me to go out with him.'

'But what if he did?' Liv piped up. 'Would you Mum? Would you go out with him?'

'Kids, can we just drop the subject please.'

The following morning Stevie turned up to collect the old double bed languishing in the garage.

'Morning,' he gave me a curt nod.

'Hi. I'll just get the garage key and – oh!'

I gasped with pain as Stevie grabbed my arm in a vice-like grip. He spun me round to face him.

'Have you got a man in the house?'

'I beg your pardon?'

He stalked over to Morag's sports car and kicked an alloy wheel.

'I presume this piece of turbo testosterone *shit* that's been parked on your drive *all night* belongs to a *man*.'

I didn't know whether to slap his face or burst out laughing. Just who the hell did he think he was? I'd suffered his constant infidelity, embarrassment amongst the neighbours, humiliation at our children's school, and currently he was knocking about with a girl young enough to be his daughter. And here he was audaciously questioning my personal life! We stood glaring at each other. Suddenly Stevie raked a hand through his hair and apologised.

'Sorry. I'm bang out of order.'

'Too right.'

'I can't help being jealous.'

'Oh grow up Stevie. The sports car is *oestrogen*-laced and belongs to a girlfriend who is such a man eater she should have Government Health Warnings stamped all over her. In fact I seriously advise you to collect the bed and scarper before she returns and pins you down upon it.'

Stevie instantly perked up, doubtless nothing to do with any potential man in the house but everything to do with being ravaged by a nymphomaniac.

Morag made an appearance late afternoon grinning like the proverbial Cheshire cat who'd found double cream instead of skimmed milk. Matt dropped her off and gave a brief toot and a cheery wave. Morag stood, girly and giggly, twiddling hair around one finger and issuing dinky little waves at the retreating car.

'God he's divine,' she gushed. 'Absolute knock out. Go and put the coffee on Cass and I'll tell you all about it.'

I wasn't entirely sure I wanted to hear about Matt's performance under the duvet but Morag was determined to take me through the whole event kiss by hungry kiss, quiver by feverish quiver.

'I looked fabulous Cass.' Modesty had never been a strong point of Morag's. 'Naked but for a pair of leather riding boots.'

I boggled into my coffee mug. 'And, er, Matt? Was he in riding boots too?'

Surely it was only polite to ask.

'In the buff and tied to the headboard.'

'Right,' I croaked.

'I strutted about brandishing an enormous lunging whip and demanded to be called Miss Spanky.'

'Goodness. And did he oblige?'

'Oh yes,' she purred, eyes glazing at the memory. 'I'm going to wear rubber next time.'

'Excellent,' I muttered. 'More coffee?'

'I won't actually Cass. I want to get home and have a nice hot soak and an early night. We didn't do much sleeping last night,' she winked.

I'd barely waved Morag off when Nell turned up on the doorstep.

'Hello!' I beamed. 'You'll never guess what – oh! What's the matter?'

My neighbour looked dreadful. Dark circles shadowed her red rimmed eyes. She stumbled over the threshold and collapsed, sobbing, on my shoulder. Gently, I led her into the kitchen. Digging around in the fridge, I produced a bottle of wine.

'Drink,' I ordered.

Nell obediently glugged and, in halting gasps punctuated with stutters and shrieks, imparted the cause of her terrible distress.

'I'm pregnant.'

'But Nell, that's marvellous – isn't it? You always wanted a brother or sister for Dylan. What does Ben think?'

'Ben has no idea.'

'But why ever not? Why haven't you told him?'

'He'll go ballistic Cass.'

'Don't be so silly. He'll be over the moon.'

'Take it from me. He won't.'

'This is ridiculous, I can't believe I'm even hearing this.'

'It's an unplanned pregnancy Cass.'

'So? Surely it's no big deal. After all, it takes two to tango. This is as much Ben's doing as yours. Why is having another baby such a problem?'

Nell fell silent and momentarily contemplated her fingernails.

'What I'm about to tell you is highly confidential.'

I regarded my neighbour in horror. 'You're not about to tell me this baby is another man's?'

She shook her head and gave me a watery grin. 'No, of course not.'

I exhaled noisily. 'Well thank heavens for that.'

'Nonetheless, it's still private stuff. Ben's a proud man – he'd die of embarrassment if he got wind that you knew – so Mum's the word right?'

'Of course.'

'A few months ago Ben re-mortgaged to finance setting up business on his own. He truly thought it would be a get-rich-quick thing. Business started off promisingly – until the customer went bust. Meanwhile Ben has incurred costs that run into thousands of pounds,' she pulled at her hair. 'So I took the job at the school to help out financially. But how can I work with a new baby? And babies cost money Cass! Even second hand stuff is pricey. And what about all those sleepless nights again? For months on end? Maybe years? Dylan was *five* before he went all the way through the night.' She looked exhausted just thinking about it. 'I don't think I can go through all that again.'

'Oh Lord,' I sucked in my breath, momentarily overwhelmed by both Nell's revelation and her honest reaction about the impact of a newborn. Even taking the financial ramifications out of the equation, I could totally identify with the endless sleepless nights and never ending exhaustion. 'Look Nell, this has come as an enormous shock to you and, for the moment, you just need to take a step back and calm down. Get used to the idea. In a few more weeks you'll be thinking completely differently and the pair of you will be over the moon.'

'Ben won't be.'

'Of course he will!' I soothed.

'I'm not going to tell him.'

'Oh Nell, don't be daft. The problem isn't going to go away by you not telling Ben. You're going to get big at some point. How are you going to pass it off?'

'I won't let myself get big.' Her lip wobbled dangerously, 'I'll get rid of it.'

I stared at her, shocked. 'Terminate? Nell I don't think you could go through with such a thing. I know you too well. You'd never forgive yourself.'

'Well that only leaves adoption and I definitely couldn't do that. I'm fresh out of other solutions.'

'Nell you simply *must* talk to Ben. Everything will be all right. You'll see.'

'Maybe. I'd better get back. Thanks for the shoulder.'

I closed the door after her pensively. Thank God I didn't have her dilemma. My own life was difficult enough, but at least I was in the driving seat with no complications. One never knew what problems were hurtling around the next corner of life.

I bent down to tidy a pile of jumbled shoes and resolved to buy a shoe rack for the cupboard in the hallway. As I stooped and stacked, I couldn't help thinking how good it would be if problems could be sorted like the pile of unruly shoes. Sighing I straightened up. I needed to throw myself into a new project. Something to take my mind off depressing problems. I stood back and surveyed the hall's paintwork. Tatty. Like the entire house actually. I nodded decisively. Redecorating would be my next assignment.

'But why white Mum?' Livvy asked later.

'Because I like it.'

'But it's not actually a colour,' Toby protested.

'White is clean,' I nodded knowingly at Livvy, 'and terribly contemporary.'

Bingo! *Contemporary* was a word Livvy adored. In her eyes the word could do no wrong conjuring up a picture of hip coolness. And anything *cool* was definitely *in*.

However, I had a suspicion that my overwhelming desire to paint everything white was psychological rather than fashionable. It represented wiping the slate clean. Starting again. And the urge to spill white silk into a virgin paint tray and roller it over every vertical surface ran so deep it was almost a physical craving.

The children chose their own colour schemes for their bedrooms. Livvy opted for the palest of pinks. Toby selected a combination of retro green and electric blue to be painted on alternating walls which promised to be eyeball stingingly hideous.

That night I lay awake fretting about Nell and her unwanted pregnancy, feeling more and more repulsed by the suggestion of a termination. It was unthinkable for Nell to end something that was only just beginning. Before I drifted off, I determined to try reasoning with my friend.

The following evening, while the twins were lost in The Simpsons, I stuck my head around the living room door.

'Just popping over to Nell's.'

No response.

'I'll be ten minutes.'

Silence.

'Don't answer the door to anybody. Livvy? Toby? Are you listening to me?'

Two grunted acknowledgements.

I stuffed my feet into a pair of trainers and crossed the grass strip between the two houses just as Ben's car swung into the cul-de-sac. Damn. Nell opened her front door and stood silhouetted in the hall light as Ben's car purred to a standstill.

'Hi!' I grinned at them both.

'Well hello stranger,' smiled Ben slamming the car door and slinging his jacket over one shoulder. 'It's not often *two* good looking women greet me at the end of a hard day's work.'

Nell threw me a questioning glance. I gave a meaningful look back. She frowned.

'I was going to ask Nell if I could pinch a couple of tea bags,' I smiled brightly.

'Since when have you ever drunk tea?' Ben looked amused.

'Oh it's not for me. It's for the twins. They wanted to try it. But not to worry, I'll go to Tesco. I need loads of other stuff anyway.'

'Well there's no need to rush off,' said Ben. 'Come in and have a coffee with us.'

'That's very kind but I won't. I only wanted to say hello anyway. Haven't seen you for ages Ben. So hello! And, er, good-bye.'

'Cass?' Ben called after me. 'Are you okay? Not lonely or anything? You're very welcome to come in. Have a drink and a pow-wow.'

'Oh!' I brightened perceptibly. 'That would be-'

I caught sight of Nell standing behind Ben, an index finger making slicing motions across her throat. My eyes bulged a bit as I caught her drift.

'-highly inconvenient I'm afraid.'

'Really?' Ben looked perplexed. 'I was hoping you girls might indulge in some gossip and leave me free for a swift half at the local.' He was already sliding back into his jacket and taking a tentative step down the driveway.

'Excellent idea,' I strode determinedly over to Nell. 'See you later.'

'What time do you want me back darling?' Ben called to his wife.

'As soon as possible,' Nell replied through gritted teeth as she pulled me into the hallway and shut the door on her bemused husband. 'What in God's name are you playing at Cass?'

'Have you talked to him yet?'

'No.'

'Why not?'

'Because I don't want to. I can handle this on my own.' She strode angrily into the kitchen and started banging things about, shaking oven chips into a tray and sloshing baked beans into a saucepan.

'Nell please. Don't do it,' I begged.

'Cass, I'm going through hell enough without you standing there pleading with me. I need to psyche myself into this operation, not have you talk me out of it.'

'Nell, don't do it. You will bitterly regret it.'

'I don't have a choice,' she cried in exasperation.

'How do you know you don't have a choice until you've talked to Ben?' I shouted. 'This has everything to do with him too you know.'

'IT'S MY BODY!'

'Sure it is,' I yelled back, 'and you're his wife and THAT'S HIS BABY!'

'It's not a baby,' Nell growled.

'No? What is it then?'

Nell gave me a stubborn look. 'Nothing more than a rudimentary collection of cells.'

'With a heart beat,' I added.

She glared at me and then heaved a sigh. 'Look, I know you mean well Cass and I'm grateful that you care.'

'Of *course* I care,' I cried.

'But my mind is made up. I have no choice in the matter and I'm going to terminate.'

'And how are you going to pay for it?' I asked.

'I'm going to get a bank loan.'

'And keep that secret from Ben too.'

'Yes. I will keep everything secret from Ben. *Every*thing.'

'I don't think so,' said a voice.

Nell's face went the colour of putty. I spun round to see Ben standing in the kitchen doorway.

'I only came back to dump my briefcase and heard raised voices. I think I've got the gist of what you've both been yelling about. Now if you don't mind Cass, I think Nell and I have some talking to do.'

Appalled, I quickly glanced back at Nell. She was staring past me, looking at Ben in wide-eyed horror. Suddenly her legs gave way. Slowly she slithered down the kitchen units until her bottom came to rest against the floor. Her hands fluttered up to her eyes and softly she began to weep.

'Ben I-'

'Thanks Cass, I'll see to her. She'll be fine.' Ben's tone was curt and dismissive. I nodded helplessly and stumbled out.

Over the next few days I didn't see or hear anything from either Nell or Ben. There didn't seem to be anybody at home when I knocked on the door. Telephone calls went straight to the answering machine and text messages were not responded to. I wondered where Dylan was. Staying with his grandparents? I felt dreadful that my attempt to privately reason with Nell had backfired so abysmally, that I'd been pivotal in Ben finding out in such a clumsy way. It filled me with both anguish and guilt. I wondered how my dear friend was, where she was and whether she'd already had the termination.

The weekend arrived. Moments after the twins' departure to Stevie's, I flung myself energetically into decorating. Hunkering down with my precious white paint, I tipped it extravagantly into a brand new paint tray. It rippled out like a flowing white ribbon. The smell shot up my nostrils and saturated the air.

Outside it was gloriously hot. The sun's rays filtered through the open windows as I beavered away in a pair of denim shorts and a tatty old T-shirt. With every stroke of the roller a sensation of peace stole over my soul. Life could be manic, but right now I was calm and in control.

At almost midnight I washed out the roller and paint tray. I was just folding up dustsheets when the doorbell shrilled into life. Given the late hour, I cautiously peered through the front door's spy hole. Seeing Ben on the other side of the portal did nothing to calm my nerves.

'Have you come to read the Riot Act?' I asked warily, inching the door open.

'Not at all,' he gave a wan smile. 'Sorry to visit so late but I saw the lights were still on.'

'Where's Nell?' I peered over his shoulder.

'In bed. She's whacked. Not just from the pregnancy but from carrying the burden by herself. Can I come in?'

'Yes of course, sorry.' I ushered Ben into the kitchen. 'Apologies for the paint pong.' I sat down heavily on a chair opposite him. 'Where have you both been these last few days?'

'Away, just the two of us. We left Dylan with my mother-in-law and went off to do some frank talking. Mull things over without interruptions.'

'I see.'

'I want you to know Cass that I'm very grateful you tried persuading Nell to talk to me. She was wrong to keep everything a secret. Inadvertently discovering the truth was the best thing that could have happened.' Ben steepled his fingers thoughtfully for a moment. 'There's no way I would have wanted my wife taking herself off to some backstreet abortionist, frightened and alone, bearing the burden single-handedly.'

I exhaled shakily. 'Oh, thank God. I knew everything would be all right if Nell talked to you.' I gave him a wobbly grin. 'So how are you feeling about being a father again?'

There was a pause.

'I'm not going to be a father again.' Ben's eyes bored into mine. 'Nell will indeed be having a termination. But we'll face it together. I'll support her all the way through and at no point will she be on her own.'

'No Ben, please don't–'

'Cass, stop right there. No, listen to me,' he cut across my protests. 'It's important Nell goes into this operation in the right frame of mind. Currently she's calm and focused and I don't want anything knocking her off balance. Do you understand?'

'What are you saying?' I whispered.

'I'm saying,' he rubbed his eyes wearily, 'that I want you to leave Nell alone for the time being. Don't be offended by this request Cass – please. She can't be distracted. Nell will come to you when she's ready.'

I awoke the following morning at dawn, my sleep interrupted after nightmares of aborted foetuses swimming about in goldfish bowls. How could Ben be so detached? This was his *child* he was terminating. For all Ben's assurances about being there for Nell and undertaking the procedure together, at the end of the day it was just his wife who would suffer the invasion of a surgical instrument removing life in one scrape. Just his wife left to pick up the pieces of hormonal havoc and wrestle with a ton of guilt.

I flung back the covers and slipped into my discarded old shorts and T-shirt. Padding barefoot down to the kitchen I found the coffee jar. Waiting for the kettle to boil, I levered open a tin of shiny gloss paint.

By lunchtime my eyes were sore and gritty but the reward was shining skirting boards and gleaming doors. The open windows permitted another fragrant summer's day to creep into the house, diluting the stench of gloss.

Stomach rumbling violently, I headed back to the kitchen leaving decorating paraphernalia strewn over a dust sheet. As I ripped open a packet of ham I was aware of a car engine. Slapping some butter on a rather stale slice of bread I heard the car purr to a halt outside. I paused, mid-spread, as a door slammed. Did I have a visitor? The doorbell burst into life.

Abandoning the buttery knife, I hastened through the hallway and found Jamie standing on the doorstep.

'Hi!' he greeted me with a dazzling smile. He looked utterly divine. 'I popped by to see if the twins wanted a lift to the stables. Petra and Jonas have been asking after them.'

Oh. So he hadn't actually come to see me. I mentally slapped myself. Stop it Cass, the guy is way out of your league.

'That's really kind of you Jamie, but Liv and Toby are with their Dad at the moment. They'll be very disappointed to know they've missed out on a pony ride. The pair of them are potty about horses at the moment.'

'Never mind. Tell you what, why don't I take you to the stables instead? We could say hi to Matt. And I know for a fact your chum is there.'

'Morag?'

'The very one and same.'

'That would be wonderful,' I gabbled. 'I mean it would be wonderful to see Morag. And Matt of course.' Steady Cass, don't get all skittish.

When Matt opened the front door he looked distinctly bleary eyed, his clothes and hair thoroughly rumpled.

'Thank God,' he gasped. 'The Emergency Services finally responded to my frantic call. May Day! May Day! Bring in a stretcher,' he moaned in mock despair, staggering about and clutching his groin. 'Morag's a lovely girl Cass but she's exhausting me. Come in quick before she wrestles me to the floor demanding to have her wicked way all over the Wilton.'

I giggled and followed Jamie in.

Morag was in the kitchen and clearly dying to show off her ability to entertain, even if it was in somebody else's house. She set about producing hunks of fresh granary and an awesome tomato soup that definitely wasn't Mr Heinz. Her attempt at cosy domesticity was a little spoilt by a T-shirt with *I swallow* emblazoned across her bosom.

For the next couple of hours I bathed in euphoria, revelling in the proximity of Jamie sitting next to me at the kitchen table, the closeness of his toned frame blotting out frets about Nell and last night's fractured sleep.

Half an hour before the twins were due back, Jamie drove me home but this time Petra and Jonas were in the back.

'See you Cassie,' he said softly as the car pulled up outside my house. Tingles wiggled up and down my spine. I *loved* the way he said my name. He didn't make a move to kiss me. I hesitated a moment, lest he should change his mind. He didn't. Ah well. He had his children with him of course! Maybe he'd kiss me next time. Next time? Sighing ruefully I hopped out of the car.

'See you.'

Inside the house I caught sight of myself in the hall mirror and let out a strangled yelp. Lank hair, dark circles under bloodshot eyes, a shiny face and a flourishing spot on a paint-speckled chin.

On the school run the following morning, Toby calmly announced he had discovered the meaning of the word *lesbian*. Swerving violently, I only just managed to avoid flattening a lollipop lady. I glanced at my son in the rear view mirror.

'Is this playground tittle tattle?'

'No Mum. George Newman's mother has left his dad for another woman.'

'No!'

'It's true.'

'Good heavens. Poor George.' Frankly I wasn't altogether surprised. Mrs Newman bore a striking resemblance to Gordon Brown in drag.

'And George is fretting about classmates finding out. I mean, imagine if his mum turns up at Parents' Evening or Sports Day with her dyke in tow!'

'I'm sure his mother will be sensitive to the situation. And don't use words like *dyke* Toby. It sounds disrespectful.'

'So? George's mother wasn't respectful about her son's feelings on the matter. And now he has two mothers to contend with.'

'Yes, I suppose he does. I wonder what he calls the other woman?'

'I've already asked him. It's *Bitch*.'

'Right,' I said faintly. This topic of conversation needed changing.

'What are you studying at school at the moment?'

'We did antonyms last week,' said Livvy. 'Opposites,' she explained catching my puzzled expression. 'For example, the antonym of *high* is *low* and the antonym of *bottom* is–'

'Willie,' interrupted Toby grinning.

'Why do you have to ridicule everything?' Livvy howled.

'I am not!' shouted Toby. 'My willie *is* opposite my bottom so there.'

'Enough!' I bellowed pulling up outside the school gates on yellow zig-zags.

Throughout the week I kept a look out for Nell, but our paths didn't cross. I didn't even see Dylan so presumed he was still at his grandmother's. And then one evening, just as I'd dished up the twins' dinner, there was a knock on the door. Standing on my doorstep was Nell. We fell into each other's arms.

'I've been so worried about you,' I sniffed into her hair. 'I'm so sorry about the crass way Ben found out. Do you forgive me? Are we still friends?'

'Yes and yes,' Nell hugged me tight. 'I know you had my best interests at heart Cass.'

I led her through to the kitchen. 'Have you had the op yet?'

'Not yet,' she pulled a stool out and sat down.

'You're going through with it?'

'Oh I'm definitely having a termination.'

I bit my tongue, determined not to say anything. Ben's words were still ringing in my ears.

'I look at Dylan,' continued Nell, 'and realise the child we already have must come first – not a child that isn't yet in this world. We don't want Dylan's life turned upside down by the impact of a new baby, having to move from this house into something smaller. A flat maybe.'

'Why would you have to move?'

'To reduce the mortgage. Reduce bills. And that would entail being cramped with less living space and no garden. So you see Cass, I've got to go ahead with it.' Her eyes suddenly brimmed but she kept the tears in check. 'I'm going in this Friday while Dylan is at school and then I'll have the weekend to recuperate.'

I nodded sadly. 'If I can do anything to help. Anything. You know where I am.'

After Nell had left I felt both upset and disturbed. I needed to distract myself.

'Tobes?'

'Yeah?'

'I'm going to start painting your room, you'll have to sleep on the sofa tonight'

'Cool Mum!'

It was therapeutic rollering paint over walls. And right now I needed to let my mind drift.

Spreading out large squares of plastic sheeting, I taped them carefully into place and bent down over a large tin of retro green paint. As I levered off the lid and peered inside, the colour momentarily took my breath away. It looked like something out of Steven Spielberg's Special Effects Department. Hadn't Mr Spielberg once employed it as the blood of that hideous creature in *Alien*?

I tipped the paint into a plastic tray, half expecting it to smoke as it rippled forth.

A little while later I washed out the roller and paint tray before repeating the whole process again, this time with electric blue.

When Toby peeked around the door to say good-night his face split into a huge grin.

'This is brilliant Mum.'

'Glad you like it,' I smiled lobbing a paintbrush at the tray before standing back, hands on hips, to survey the finished result. Not bad. Not bad at all actually.

The week passed without incident until Friday late afternoon. I'd barely returned home from work and the school run when the doorbell rang. And rang and rang and rang. What on earth-?

'I'm COMING,' I yelled irritably. 'Livvy? Toby? Why can't one of you answer the door sometimes?' No response. In the next room a television burst into life. I hastened down the hallway as the doorbell gave another spate of urgent rings.

As I opened the door Nell catapulted into the hall, tears streaming down her face.

'Help me Cass,' she implored. 'Oh dear God please help me.'

She collapsed against me, wracked with sobs. I wrapped an arm around her shoulders and gently steered her into the kitchen.

'There there, hush,' I patted her back as if comforting a small child.

'I've run away Cass,' she gasped.

'Run away?'

'From the hospital.'

'Why?'

'I realised I couldn't go through with it. Ben went off to a vending machine for a cup of coffee. As soon as he disappeared I snatched up the car keys and raced out to the car park. Drove like a madwoman home. I saw your car on the drive. Needed to see a friendly face.'

'Okay,' I stared at her. Tried to collect my thoughts. 'But running away isn't the answer. You have to tell Ben you've changed your mind.'

'I can't do that Cass. And anyway, Ben will probably leave me now. It'll be divorce. Oh Christ, what am I going to do?' she collapsed over the table, head banging the fruit bowl, tears splashing all over the Granny Smiths.

'Everything will work out,' I said patting her hand, 'one way or another.' I sounded more confident than I felt. 'Let's have a coffee.'

I made to put the kettle on just as Nell's mobile erupted into life. She ignored it. Moments later a merry jingle penetrated the heavy atmosphere announcing a voicemail message. Sniffing and wiping the backs of her hands across her face, Nell checked the display.

'Ben again. That's the seventh time he's called now.' She switched the mobile off.

'Aren't you going to listen to his message?'

'No.'

'Nell,' I said gently. 'This isn't right. You will have to talk to Ben at some point. Without communication, nothing can be resolved.'

She looked at me miserably before nodding her head slowly. 'I know,' she mumbled. 'You're right. Can't hide. Got to sort it out.'

'Attagirl,' I squeezed her hand.

Scraping her chair back she stood up.

'I'll just use your loo and then I'll be on my way.'

Two minutes later Nell reappeared, white faced and stricken.

'I'm bleeding,' she croaked. 'I think I might be miscarrying.'

Grabbing her mobile, I switched it back on and found Ben's number. He answered immediately, distraught. Rapidly explaining the situation, I told him to be waiting for me. I then hauled the twins away from the television and bundled them into the back of the car, wide-eyed and incredulous, and drove an hysterical Nell back to the hospital.

It was very late when Ben knocked, hours later.

'How's Nell?' I asked.

'Recovering. A scan revealed the foetus had no heart beat. The surgeon presented Nell with two options – either let Mother Nature take its course or have the pregnancy surgically removed. She opted for the latter. Despite causing havoc with the surgeon's operating list, the procedure was carried out earlier this evening.'

'Right.' I didn't really know what to say.

Ben raked his hair. He looked all in. 'On a positive note, if Nell hadn't run away she'd never have discovered the foetus had died.

She'd have gone in for the operation believing herself to be some sort of murderer. I hadn't realised the extent to which she'd been torturing herself.'

I nodded. 'Give her my love.'

I spent the entirety of the weekend once again keeping busy, decorating Livvy's room. Anything to stop myself from thinking. There was so much I didn't want to think about. Nell's loss. And Jamie's. A widower with two children to raise. His face seemed to permanently encroach on my thoughts these days. I couldn't quite work him out. Every time I saw him he acted like he was really keen on me. And yet it never seemed to come to anything. Was I so out of touch that I couldn't work out whether a guy was genuinely interested or simply pursuing a platonic friendship? I tried to bat the thoughts away. The trouble was, they kept boomeranging right back.

I washed out the brushes and paint tray. A sense of satisfaction stole over my soul. The house had been stamped from top to bottom with my own personal signature. Not one trace of Stevie's presence remained. It looked great – and felt even better.

At the office, Morag caught up with me in the corridor.

'Hello stranger!' I smiled.

'Sorry, work's been manic with lunch hours thin on the ground. But not today! Park. Usual time. Tell Julia too.'

A few hours later we sat on our favourite bench enjoying the sunshine.

'Matt's away this weekend,' Morag informed, 'taking two of the children to some County show.' She took a bite out of her apple. 'So, what are we going to do?'

'Do?' Julia frowned.

'Yes, do. You know I hate my own company, so let's have a get-together.'

'Okay,' I agreed. 'Girls night in. Your place?'

'Don't be ridiculous Cass,' Morag snorted. 'Girls night out.'

Uh-oh.

Chapter Twelve

I hadn't been home long when Nell surprised me by popping over for coffee and a catch up. Despite appearing fairly upbeat, she confessed to sudden moments of black gloom. Pondering what might have been.

'I don't like crying in front of Ben,' she stared unseeingly through the kitchen window, her eyes suddenly welling.

I patted her hand. 'It's okay to feel sad you know.'

She blinked furiously and gave a watery smile. 'What I need is a damn good night out.'

'Really? Well your luck is in! Liv and Toby are with their dad this weekend and if Ben's up for babysitting Dylan, look no further than *moi*.'

'Oh I'm up for it all right,' Nell said with uncharacteristic fierceness.

'Morag has a propensity to party quite hard,' I warned. 'Promise me you won't overdo it – if at any point you want to go home then you must say so.'

'Yes, yes, yes,' Nell snapped irritably. 'Sorry. Mood swing.'

On Saturday evening, a little after seven, Nell and I met up with Morag. She was aided and abetted by two legal cronies called Heather and Siobhan from rival firms. Julia and her pal, Kirsten, completed the group.

Tumbling into two minicabs between us, we drove to Maidstone where Morag assured the group that a good time would be had by all. Like a ship in full sail she glided into a heaving wine bar, the rest of us bobbing about in her wake. Our leader somehow managed to appropriate the only tiny unoccupied table left. Moments later

Morag was armed and dangerous with a large gin and a second lined up. I was alarmed to see Nell following Morag's example.

'Do you think that's wise?' I jerked my head at her glass.

'Oh shut up Cass. I know you mean well but frankly, right now, I couldn't give a–'

'All right, all right,' I stuck my hands up in a backing off gesture. 'Just concerned that's all.'

'Well don't be,' she took a swig from her glass. 'I'm fine. I just want to have some fun and put the last few weeks of unbearable crap behind me.'

I nodded, smarting slightly from having been firmly put in my place.

The drink flowed and with it a gabble of conversation and indiscreet shrieking. Nell had become belligerently punchy and was furiously offloading buried resentment over Ben and his abortion pressure. Her usually respectable accent had completely disintegrated.

'Fuckin' dictator,' she slurred to Heather. 'S'my body innit? Wot right 'as any man to tell a woman wot she can do wiv 'er body, eh?'

Heather promptly nosedived into her gin sobbing profusely.

'I've had an abortion,' she howled. 'I've never told a soul before now. I don't know why I'm telling you.'

Nell flung an arm cosily around Heather's shoulders. 'It's coz we're *mates*. Probably *soul*mates.'

'Really?' Heather bleated pathetically. 'How terribly nice. I've never had a soulmate before.' She gazed at Nell as if she were the Holy Grail.

The pair of them had attracted the attention of two sniggering guys who were nudging each other and rolling their eyes. They were clearly under the impression the two girls were a raving pair of dykes. Nell glared at them in outrage.

'We're not lezzies you know!' she yelled indignantly. 'S'all right when you blokes get tarty wiv each other though innit?' She stood up and pointed a manicured finger at them. 'Bloody pansies you lot are on the footy pitch – runnin' around in yer itsy-bitsy shorts, cuddlin' an' snoggin' at the goal posts, leapin' on top of each other an' shovin' yer lunchboxes in each other's faces.'

'Oh God,' I muttered to Morag as the Manager zoomed towards our table. 'Here we go.'

And go we did. Straight out the door.

As Nell and Heather staggered about on the pavement, Morag rubbed her hands together gleefully.

'Excellent,' she purred. 'This is turning into a cracking evening girls. Now follow me.'

We trooped off into – no surprises here – a nightclub. By Morag's reckoning no night out was complete without a serious bop.

'When are we going to eat?' I complained, desperately trying to ignore my rumbling stomach.

'Don't worry, I'll find us something later,' promised Morag.

Oh joy. That meant a late night food poisoning session at the decrepit kebab van already parked and poised opposite the club.

The evening passed in a noisy blur of movement. It was only when a bouncer spotted Nell energetically tap dancing to Leona Lewis' *Bleeding Love* that we once again found ourselves being rounded up and propelled toward the street.

'I can't stand piss-takers on the piss and disrupting the dance floor,' the bouncer curtly informed my neighbour.

'How dare you!' Nell squawked. 'If you weren't seven feet tall I'd punch yer lights out.'

'Good-bye,' the bouncer coolly replied.

'Sorry,' I muttered. 'She's had a bit of a tough time lately.'

Julia and I were the only ones sober, the others being catastrophically paralytic. By this point my hunger was so profound the kebab van's health and hygiene standards were not even a consideration. All I wanted was food. And if it meant eating dodgy meat stuffed inside a blackened pitta with a smattering of salmonella nestling amongst the ketchup and onions, then so be it.

I'd just handed over my fiver (*fiver?*) and was possessively clutching my meal parcel to my bosom when all hell broke out behind me. Morag was having a fast and furious row with a female homeless person. Julia and I stared at each other in shock. A homeless person on the street here?

'How *dare* you ask me for money!' Morag shrieked. 'I suppose you want dosh to pour alcohol down your throat?' she spat, almost asphyxiating the vagrant with her gin sodden breath. 'Or perhaps you want to inject another vein in your arm eh? You no-hopers cost working people like me a bloody fortune with your rehab clinics and your psycho-babble counselling.'

'I want something to *eat!*' growled the tramp furiously. 'You think I live like this out of *choice?* How *dare* you patronise me? Don't you think I'm humiliated enough without rich bitches like you having a pop at me? I'm fucking HUNGRY!' her snarls rose to a crowd attracting crescendo.

'Here,' I shoved my kebab into the woman's filthy hands realising with a shock that she wasn't an ancient bag lady but younger than me.

Julia had managed to hail a minicab and I hastily bundled Morag toward the open rear door.

'Shut up and get in,' I hissed, shoving her into the car's interior. 'Where's Nell? Oh for God's sake!'

For reasons known only to Nell, she had shimmied up a temporary makeshift barrier surrounding a roadwork excavation. She'd also managed to prostrate herself in a most undignified position and split her trousers in the process. Heather, Siobhan and Kirsten were staggering around the base of the metal fence debating how to rescue Nell. Seconds later the fence toppled over. As Nell crashed into the four foot excavation laughing like a deranged hyena, the taxi driver decided he'd witnessed enough mayhem and wanted nothing more to do with us.

'Hop it love,' he ordered Morag.

'Don't be ridiculous.'

'Out!'

A police siren wailed faintly in the distance.

I stood on the kerb feeling like a despairing sheepdog trying and failing to round up its dysfunctional flock. What the hell was everybody doing? Professional women, some of us *parents* for God's sake, behaving like a bunch of teenage delinquents.

'Never again,' I waggled my finger in Morag's face. 'Never, ever again.'

'What are you on about Cass? This evening has been an absolute blinder.'

The following morning I swam to the surface of wakefulness and realised that I had absolutely nothing to do. It was no good telephoning Nell for a post-mortem as she'd probably have a monumental hangover. Ditto Morag. And because the twins were at Stevie's, I didn't even have the excuse of going to the stables and accidentally-on-purpose bumping into Jamie.

Jamie. Popping into my head *again*. I recognised that I had a thumping great crush on the man. There. I'd said it. I tried to analyse why I was so drawn to him, apart from the fact that he was seriously good looking. Well, for starters I enjoyed his company. I sensed he was a very deep person which gave him strength of character, something Stevie had lacked. I instinctively knew Jamie to be a guy who was loyal and true. Matt had more or less confirmed this too. I would have bet my last pound that Philly, Jamie's dead wife, had never waited up into the small hours wringing her hands and despairing where her husband was. Or had a romantic occasion in a restaurant ruined while her husband made eyes at the waitress. And no doubt later exchanged telephone numbers. I had been secretly delighted that Jamie had been impervious to Morag's bosomy charms on each occasion their paths had crossed, whereas Matt hadn't been able to resist, allowing her to bed him instantly. I believed Jamie was an honourable man, one that could be trusted – unlike the Stevies and Euans of the world.

I sighed. It was no good hankering after the man. He'd had several opportunities to ask me out but nothing had come of it.

I stretched my arms and legs languidly. Perhaps I could just stay in bed all day? Yes, why not. I'd relax under the duvet and relish my new bed. I spent the next five minutes extending and elongating my body into various positions until I realised I was utterly bored.

Throwing back the covers, I bounced out of bed and drew the curtains. Outside it was pouring with rain. There was nothing else for it. I'd have to wile Sunday away at Fairview instead.

An hour later I'd spotted a drop-dead-gorgeous fuchsia pink dress. I scuddered to a halt and pressed my nose up against the shop's backlit glazing. A mannequin modelled the garment to anorexic perfection.

Inside the privacy of my changing room I stripped off. Probably best to remove my pants too so no knicker line marred the soft clinging material. It was only when I was down to my birthday suit and lit by the cubicle's harsh fluorescent lighting that I froze. My hand, outstretched toward the dress's hanger, paused and hovered mid-air. Staring back at me from the unforgiving multi-angled mirrors was a slim but thoroughly untoned woman with a baggy baby belly, stretch marks and cellulite. By dint of design, the mirror showed off this disgusting reflection from both the front, side and – if I jiggled round a bit – the back too. Oh God. Just look at that rear! I was mesmerised by its ugliness. I assumed a lap dancer's pose, spread my legs and slowly bent over. Instantly my bum inflated to the size of a baby elephant's. Transfixed, I swayed from side to side. Yep. It definitely looked like the back end of a bus. Suddenly my cubicle curtain swished open to reveal a teenager with a mass of open pores. We stared at each other through my parted legs.

'Oops. Fort me mate was in this one. Sorry.'

The curtain fell smartly back into place. Seconds later I heard a fit of stifled giggles and hoarse whispering.

'I just walked in on this bollock naked old girl swingin' 'er arse about like she woz in some porno movie or sumfink, ha ha. She should be so lucky, sad cow. You should've seen it! An' it was sproutin' hairs all over the place too.'

Was it? I jiggled back round to view my botty, roughly pulling the cheeks apart. Good heavens, she was right. I'd have to have a Birmingham or whatever it was called. Smarting with humiliation I erupted out of the cubicle. But the girl had gone. A changing room assistant gave me an astonished once over. Wrapping the curtain around me I shot back inside muttering furiously to myself.

'Well at least I only have a hairy back passage and not prolific lip hair that extends up my nasal passage. Ever heard of a nose clipper? Or a hedge trimmer in your case?'

My shoulders drooped. The teenage girl was right. My body was in dire need of toning. And what better time to firm up now that Spain was only a few weeks away?

I returned the pink dress to the wary changing room assistant and instead ventured off in search of a sports shop. Ten minutes later my carrier bags contained a sensible pair of running shorts, a couple of cotton T-shirts, sturdy trainers and a baseball cap. Might as well look like a total Chav at the same time.

Once home, I immediately changed into the new sports gear. Virginal white trainers firmly laced and double knotted, I opened the patio doors and stepped out into the damp garden. It had finally stopped raining.

I bounced about on the spot for a bit before breaking into a gentle jog.

'What *are* you doing?' Nell's pale face peered over the fence, laundry basket perched askance.

'Getting fit,' I puffed as I pounded my way to the bottom of the garden. All thirty feet of it. 'You look rough.'

'And you look a right proper Charlie.'

'Second lap coming up.'

Actually this felt rather good. Muscles were doing their stuff and the old heart was steadily banging away under the ribcage. I trotted past the apple tree and on towards the rose bush – a distance of about five feet. As my trainers thumpity-thumped past Nell again, she rolled her eyes.

'You're wearing the grass out Cass,' she chided. 'Look!'

Sure enough, a visible path of flattened green blades could be seen.

'Why don't you jog on the pavements or around the park like other sensible adults?'

'Oh I give up,' I declared irritably, coming to a standstill. 'Fancy a natter?'

'Let me peg out this washing and I'll be right over.'

Over a cup of extra strong coffee, it transpired Nell was not a happy lady. Desperate to regain her normal bounce after the accidental pregnancy, she confessed her emotions were akin to a rollercoaster.

'I'm all over the place Cass. One minute I'm fine, the next I'm incandescent with rage and wanting to punish Ben,' she inhaled deeply and closed her eyes for a moment. 'I know he was talking sense at the time and – for a while – I went with his logic. But then I got all emotional although Ben didn't. Why didn't he get emotional Cass?'

'Men are different,' I shrugged. 'Nature programmes them differently.'

'You can say that again,' she flared. 'Now it's all over I'm finally starting to come to terms with it all. Meanwhile he's the one sobbing into his pillow every night.'

'Perhaps his tears are a delayed reaction.'

'Huh. I've had to listen to him regurgitating matters, asking stupid questions like what colour eyes and hair the child would have had. It makes me want to slap him really hard. Of *course* I've quietly voiced the same questions. Before everything went wrong I constantly day-dreamed about whether it was a boy or a girl. Who it would look like. Take after. But it's irrelevant now.'

'Things will return to normal eventually. It doesn't help that your hormones are still all over the place. Maybe you should both have some counselling together.'

'I don't go for all that self analytical nonsense,' Nell frowned. 'I just wish the whole sorry saga had never happened and things could be the way they were.'

'They will be. Eventually.'

Nell contemplated her fingernails for a moment. 'The thing is Cass, this whole blasted pregnancy thing has actually left me feeling incredibly broody.'

'That's not surprising really. It's just hormonal. A phase that will pass.'

She grimaced. 'Before all this happened, a baby was the last thing on my mind. And now I can't stop obsessing about it.'

'You could always get a dog,' I joked.

'Hey, that's not a bad idea,' her eyes suddenly sparkled with a light that hadn't shone in weeks. 'A little puppy. All cute and wiggly with a fat tum-tum.'

'Nell I was just larking about.'

'Many a true word said in jest. Yes, I'll have a little puppy instead.'

I looked at my neighbour's set jaw. 'Oh terrific. Just don't tell Ben it was my idea okay?'

As the start of the working week once again got under way, Morag, Julia and I met up at lunchtime and congregated on our favourite park bench. I told them about the recent changing room debacle and my resolution to tone up.

'Don't talk to me about exercise or diets,' groaned Morag sinking her teeth into an acre of wholemeal stuffed with greasy bacon. 'In the last four weeks I've lost three pounds only to put it all back on again. I nearly bought a book that boasts thinness can be achieved through self-hypnosis.'

'What stopped you?' Julia asked.

'Because when I flicked through the pages the message was simply *think* yourself smaller. Well I don't need to buy a book to tell myself that!' Morag snorted derisively. She rooted inside a paper bag emblazoned with a local baker's name and produced a vast flapjack.

'Mm. Dee-*lic*-ious. And positively oozing with calories.'

Julia and I glanced at each other.

'So when are you starting this Think Yourself Smaller diet?'

'Oh I already have,' Morag replied airily. 'Which reminds me.' She paused and glared menacingly at the flapjack before launching into a sing-song mantra. 'I-am-thin. I-am-skinny. I-am-sooo-thin-thin-thin. Skinny-skinny-skin-neee.' She stopped and smiled. 'There, all done.' With that she began to greedily shove the flapjack into her mouth.

I stared at her in disbelief. 'Is that it?'

Morag gave me a sideways look. 'Not quite.' Her hand burrowed into her vast organiser handbag and reappeared clutching a pot of Omega 3 tablets.

'These little babas are excellent for cleaning one's clogged up arteries.' She rattled them in my face. 'So it's a case of chant your mantra, eat your sin, swallow a pill and get wonderfully thin.'

'Was that rhyme in the book?' asked Julia.

'Nope. I made it up.' Morag rammed the last of the flapjack into her mouth. 'Mm yummy. I can almost feel the weight dropping off.'

'I've got to go,' I stood up brushing crumbs off my lap.

'But it's only half past. No need to rush off surely?' Morag asked.

'It's the twins' birthday tomorrow. I've bought their cards but I must nip into Game and Next. Splash out on a wad of gift vouchers for them. They're at that age where I haven't a clue what to buy.'

'How old will they be?' asked Julia.

'Ten.'

It was only natural that Stevie should join in on the birthday celebration too. The following afternoon he left work early and arrived not long after I'd returned from the school run. It was very much a family affair with the annual iced cake and ritual lighting of candles. The children made wishes as they blew out their candles, filling the air spiralling smoke. Stevie and I immediately launched into an off-key rendition of *Happy Birthday* while Liv and Toby looked both proud and faintly embarrassed. The digital camera immortalised their smiles, this year for two separate photograph albums.

'Now hold it right there,' grinned Stevie, 'and I'll go and get your presents.'

He disappeared out to the car, reappearing moments later with enormous boxes.

'Goodness, whatever is all this?' I asked.

Toby caught sight of a brand name on the side of one carton.

'It's a media centre!' he screeched excitedly.

Livvy gasped. '*Two* media centres!'

'Well,' Stevie shrugged modestly, 'it's not your birthday every day is it?'

He swiftly set about installing everything.

'Where's the hard drive?' I peered all around the monitor, getting in the way.

'There.' Stevie tapped the back of the flat screen.

The doorbell rang.

'Won't be a mo',' I said jogging across the landing and bouncing down the stairs like a kangaroo – exercise was still very much to the fore of my mind. I opened the door to a willowy blonde.

'Hi!' she squeaked in a little girl voice. 'I'm Charlotte. Can I have a word with Stevie please?'

I gaped at the vision on my doorstep – a sort of early Britney Spears with breasts almost big enough to rival Morag's décolletage.

'Um, yes, just a minute,' I stammered before bounding back upstairs. Stevie was now in Livvy's room.

'Er, Charlotte's here.'

Stevie reversed out from under Livvy's desk. 'I'll pop back tomorrow,' he promised, 'and help pack up the old equipment. If you like I'll flog it on e-Bay for you.'

'Okay. Great,' I stared blankly after him as the front door banged shut.

I felt strangely out of sorts. For a couple of hours there we'd slipped back to being a united family doing things together with our children. But within seconds the past had crashed away hurling me back to the present so that once again I was just another single parent.

The feeling didn't abate until lunchtime the following day when I once again sat with the girls on our park bench.

'You're in shock,' advised Morag.

'But that's ridiculous,' I spluttered. 'I don't even want to stay married to Stevie. Why do I feel so rattled?'

'Because,' Julia proffered, 'in your heart of hearts you are wondering if the divorce is now a wise thing.'

'Rubbish,' snorted Morag. 'Of course Cass is doing the right thing. Stevie is a serial womaniser. Can't keep his todger under wraps for more than five minutes without brandishing it about at parties, office do's, high days and holidays.'

'Steady,' I gulped. 'That's my husband you're talking about.'

'*Ex* husband. This is nothing more than shock. You're jolted. You've been delivered a nasty kick in the teeth. By your own admission you have stated a girl stood on your doorstep, a mere stripling of a teenager no less, moreover looking like a certain pop star–'

'Oh Morag drop the court room drama speak,' I interrupted irritably. She'd be saying wherein, heretofore and aforementioned next.

'I'm just stating the obvious Cass. This girl is eighteen. You are nearly forty. It was a blow to meet your husband's girlfriend and realise he's pressing such youthful flesh. And that you aren't.'

That last remark hung heavily in the air. Let's face it, I wasn't even pressing old flesh. I set about savaging a lettuce leaf from my Tupperware crammed with rabbit food.

'How's Matt and Giles?' I growled, keen to change the subject.

'Miles,' corrected Julia instantly looking gooey.

I glanced at Morag who also appeared to have gone dewy eyed, sausage sandwich suspended halfway to her mouth.

'Matt is quite simply divine,' she purred.

Jolly good. So it was just me not having any fun then.

Stevie returned early evening to complete the installation of Livvy's media centre.

'How long will you be?' I asked.

'About an hour or so.'

'Would you mind terribly if I popped out for a bit? I won't be long.'

'Not at all, go ahead.'

I scampered off to my bedroom and quickly changed into the new running gear. Cracking the door open, I peeked furtively up and down the landing. The coast was clear. I ran down the stairs and out the front door.

Sprinting along, I felt faintly smug. I might not be eighteen or have a taut body, but by golly I could still run. Okay I was running downhill, but so what? Look at me go! I was like a greyhound!

I streaked on, round the corner, down to the village Post Office where the ground levelled out, around another corner and belted on towards the Common. This bit wasn't quite as effortless as the Common tended to go up hill and down dale. Struggling now to maintain the impetus, I laboured past a bench where a gaggle of jeering teenagers mocked me. I shambled breathlessly out of their line of vision and collapsed behind an ancient oak. Stupidly I'd left home without a bottle of water.

I bent forward, hands to knees. Panting hard, I contemplated a smooth brown pebble lying next to one trainer. Why was I rushing? Life was too short to charge about. Walking was just as good as jogging.

I set off again, this time adopting a strolling rhythm. Bowling along, I decided to enjoy the leafy scenery around me. Under a clump of tall rustling elms frolicked a family of squirrels, tails rising and falling in squiggly arches as they made sudden darting movements. Branches hung low, worshipping the sun's rays, freckling green leaves with lemon light. The grass was strewn with tiny daisies, their saffron centres fringed by petals edged in pink stain, as if a child had lightly daubed them with a felt pen. I was instantly transported back to my school days, sitting on the playing field making fairy crowns with daisy chains.

When I eventually got home, I found Stevie in Toby's room enthralled with the new machinery. As the TV burst into life on the flat screen Livvy posted a CD into an invisible slot, instantly cancelling the newsreader's monotony with an explosion of rap.

'These machines are something else Cass,' Stevie shouted over the din.

I nodded my head in agreement and kicked off my ripe trainers. Leaving everybody to it, I padded back downstairs to the kitchen for a glass of cold cranberry juice. Tipping my head back I glugged straight from the carton just as the doorbell rang. And there on my doorstep, for the second consecutive evening, stood the beautiful Charlotte.

She was dressed in a tiny cropped T-shirt and bleached jeans embroidered with a rainbow of thread. The denims were artfully ripped, frayed and distressed to within an inch of fashionable life. The non-existent waistband was slung so low it was almost indecent. I was hideously aware of my own dishevelled appearance and damp T-shirt which – I discreetly sniffed the air – even now was emitting the whiff of sweaty armpits. I squirmed with embarrassment as Charlotte daintily wrinkled her nose.

'Is Stevie still here?' she squeaked.

'Um, yes. I don't suppose he'll be much longer,' I mumbled wondering why this young girl felt the need to collect Stevie for the second night running.

'Shall I wait?' she asked pointedly.

'I'll call him for you,' I quickly replied. 'STEVIE!'

My estranged husband instantly appeared on the landing.

'Been drinking blackcurrent Cass?' he grinned coming down the stairs.

'Cranberry actually. Why?'

'You're sporting a colourful moustache. And you've spilt some down that awful T-shirt.'

At work Martin Henniker seemed to have become a permanent thorn in my side, Susannah Harrington having had no success in finding a permanent secretary.

'The man's a psycho,' declared Morag. 'I've got a horrible feeling you could be stuck with him for some time Cass.'

We had shifted our lunch time rendez-vous to a pavement café, basking in warm summer sunshine as the traffic rumbled by.

'Meanwhile,' said Morag changing the subject, 'last night was the best ever with Matt.'

'Why, what did you do?' asked Julia.

'I rode Matt around the bedroom.'

'Rode? I quizzed, chasing a cherry tomato around my paper plate with a plastic fork.

'As in horse riding. Matt was a wild stallion and I had to tame him.'

'Good grief,' Julia muttered.

'How did you do that?' I asked with a perfectly straight face.

'Well, after I'd successfully lassooed him, I hurled myself on his back and grimly hung on while he plunged about attempting to throw me off.'

'Is this Matt we're talking about?' Julia frowned.

'That's right.'

'Not a horse?'

'No, Matt was the horse.'

'But not really?'

'No of course not,' Morag cried in exasperation. 'We were *pretending*.'

'Okay. Carry on.'

'Where was I?'

'He was trying to chuck you off,' I pointed out.

'Oh yes. So I wrestled and fought with him, smacked and whacked his rump with a riding crop and finally he quietened down enough for me to pat him gently and murmur that he was a good boy, a very good boy, and good boys are always rewarded.'

'What was his reward?' Julia croaked.

'I became a mare of course.'

I concentrated tremendously hard on a squiggly piece of pasta. 'What happened next?'

'He covered me.'

'Covered?' Julia's eyebrows shot off her forehead.

'In other words Matt gave her one,' I explained.

'He most certainly did,' breathed Morag. 'And then we both plunged about doing masses of whinnying and snorting and it was incredibly raucous and mind blowingly *awesome*.'

I boggled into my skinny latte, feeling utterly worn out just *listening* to her sexual epic, never mind taking part in it. Was this where I'd gone wrong with Stevie? Would I have held onto my erring husband if I'd been blessed with Morag's sexually rampant imagination? All those years of lying in the missionary position when clearly I should have pranced around the bedroom on all fours and neighed upon climax.

That evening there was a tentative knock on the door. It was Nell.

'Would you like to see my puppy?' she beamed proudly, the way only new mothers do.

'Oh Lord. You've gone and done it then?' I stuffed my feet back into previously discarded work shoes. The twins fell in behind me as we followed Nell across the narrow grass strip that separated the two houses.

'Don't crowd around it,' I warned the children as Nell reached into her pocket for the door key. 'The puppy may be scared if it's only just left its mother. And don't grab or fight over who is having first cuddle. And don't shout, we don't want to frighten – oh!'

I broke off as an enormous and thoroughly overexcited Red Setter bounded over to Nell before swerving off in my direction. The dog goosed me hard in the groin before careering over to Nell's fluffy slippers which it proceeded to rip to shreds.

'Naughty!' Nell chided in a baby voice. The dog broke into a round of deep baritone barking.

'Nell that is *not* a puppy,' I yelled over the din.

My neighbour smiled indulgently. She reminded me of one of those awful parents who make out their wayward child is 'just playing' while little Freddie bashes thump out of everybody.

'She's only five months old Cass and an absolute poppet. Come here Rocket,' she cooed.

'Rocket?'

'Mm. But I might change it.' Nell considered. 'I like Lucy.'

'Won't a name change confuse her?'

'Let's see. Lucy, Lucy, L–*ooo*-cy.' There was no response. 'Oh well. Rocket, Rocket, R*oh-oh-oh*-ket.'

'She doesn't seem to recognise her official name either.'

'All in good time Cass. I particularly want you and Rocket to get acquainted because I know you're well and truly into your keep fit lark – and toning up very nicely too,' Nell nodded at my flabby arms and legs, 'and what better exercise than a brisk walk or refreshing run with a doggy? So you can borrow Rocket anytime you like Cass.'

Oh fabulous. Clearly going for a run without Rocket was not an option.

'So let's make an arrangement right now, hm? How about tomorrow after work?'

'Can't wait,' I smiled through gritted teeth.

Chapter Thirteen

The next several days saw me lacing up my trainers and pounding the local pavements, sometimes with the twins in tow on their bicycles, other times leaving them with Nell while I went out and jogged steadily on my own. Rocket had a tendency to pull like a steam train on the lead which was surely doing wonders for toning my upper arms. I'd also come to the conclusion that my neighbour's dog was definitely a few Bonios short of a full box.

One Saturday morning I decided to jog to the local park. Taking a short cut through the cemetery, I puffed along beside Rocket as we passed rows of lichen stained headstones. I gave an involuntary shiver, anxious to leave an area where grief and tears seemed to permanently hang in the air.

We shot through a gap in the hedge and out on to adjacent parkland where the mood instantly lifted. Swings and climbing frames in bright primary colours nestled next to an emerald green cricket pitch. An overlooking pavilion was spray-canned in a riotous rainbow of graffiti.

Bending down I released the catch on the leash. Rocket, just like her name, shot off like a pre-programmed missile. Breaking into a gentle jog I paced after her. Clearly she thought it was a game of chase. She happily frolicked ahead before sharply turning round to face me, barking rowdily a few times and then careering off. This pattern continued until my mobile phone trilled the arrival of a text message. It was from Morag.

Don't panic but I'm in hospital. Mistook a daffodil bulb for an onion. The doc has told me I'll be okay but not to expect to come out until Spring.

I hit the call button.

'Very droll,' I deadpanned into the handset.

'Thought you'd appreciate it,' she chortled. 'Fancy coming to a party tonight?'

'I'd love to, but aren't you out with Matt?'

'Oh definitely, but it's a fancy dress party and the host says the more the merrier. You don't have to go to any elaborate measures or anything.'

'I knew all those years of watching Blue Peter were worthwhile. I shall concoct something amazing out of sticky back plastic and cardboard,' I laughed. 'Are you sure I won't cramp your style? I don't want to play gooseberry to you and Matt.'

'Not at all,' Morag replied. 'Anyway Mac will be there. You know – Jamie.'

At the mention of his name, I froze. Even though I was on my own, merely thinking about him had me blushing bright red. I swallowed.

'Are you still there Cass? I think you're breaking up on me.'

'Still here,' I croaked.

'Good. Come to ours around sevenish.'

Lost in thought, I nearly walked into a tree.

Right Cass. Let's have a little think about this. You've privately admitted to having a massive crush on Jamie. So here's your chance to pull out all the glamour stops.

Spirits lifting, I whistled Rocket to heel and snapped the leash back on. She trotted along beside me looking hot and bothered, tongue hanging out and panting heavily. A bit like me when I thought of Jamie.

Back home, as soon as the twins had gone to Stevie's, I whirred into action cutting up black sacks and tin foil, stapling here, nipping and tucking there. Somewhere in the back of my wardrobe were some silver stilettos and a sparkly belt. There they were! Perfect. Next came the truly challenging part. Attempting to transform the face. If only one could nip and tuck the slackening jaw line.

At quarter to seven, full of nervous anticipation at seeing Jamie again, I drove to Matt's. Interesting that Morag had said to meet at *our's*. She was obviously spending the bulk of her time there.

'Wow!' gushed Morag as she admired my synthetic ensemble. 'Plastic fantastic! Who are you meant to be?'

'A visitor from another world,' I intoned in an alien voice. I followed Morag's undulating bottom, tightly encased in straining jodhpurs, into the hallway. I wasn't entirely sure her 'think thin' diet was working. However, she looked amazing and I told her so.

'Thank you,' she said giving a little twirl. 'I'm a show jumper.' I took in the beige breeches, white shirt and smart show jacket, no doubt filched from one of Matt's daughter's wardrobes. I'd never seen any horsy gels looking quite like Morag with her top three buttons undone, an over-abundance of cleavage spilling forth, or swapping traditional riding footwear for thigh high patent leather boots. Only someone like Morag could pull the whole thing off and look ravishing with it.

'Hi Cass,' greeted Matt pecking me on the cheek. He was decked out in a red hunting jacket and cream jodhpurs. 'You look stunning. Gin and tonic?' he thrust a crystal tumbler clinking with ice and lemon in my direction. I glugged gratefully just as the doorbell rang again. In strode Jamie, naturally dressed in his dark police uniform which sent my pulse rate soaring. Predictably my face reddened. He greeted us all warmly and gave me a very thorough once over.

'Sexy,' he winked.

I nearly choked on my lemon. Was he flirting? Or was I misreading a simple compliment?

The party was in full flow when we arrived. Music blasted from an enormous plasma screen set high on the wall. An assortment of pirates, pink ladies, noblemen and queens were already bevvied up and boogying to the beat. Morag and Matt were completely into each other, nose to nose in an amorous clinch. Jamie had been button-holed by a sinuously clinging female with long raven hair snaking down her back. A hungry predatory look lit her thin face.

'Are you really a policeman?' she was cooing huskily.

There was something slithery about her and I speculated whether she'd come as a serpent. Not wishing to intrude I melted away, previous bubbles of happiness popping like cheap washing up liquid. I slid behind a tall potted plant momentarily wishing I were back home and curled up in front of the telly with a chocolate bar.

A clammy hand brushed against my bare arm followed by a waft of sour whisky fumes as a short balding man made his presence known.

'Hiya sweet creature,' he leered into my face and softly belched. 'What delightful planet have you ventured from in that sexy flying suit?'

I held my breath as a whiff of garlicky vol-au-vent shot up my nose.

'Geddoff 'er Sammy,' chided another man lurching over. 'This lay-dee ain't interested in riff raff like you.'

Unfortunately my rescuer was not a knight in shining armour, more a clone of his companion, the only difference being he reeked of gin and pickled onions.

'Care to dance sexy momma?' The newcomer winked lasciviously, clearly under the impression he was God's gift.

'Well I-'

'*Dar*ling! I've been looking for you *every*where,' said a familiar voice as a firm hand propelled me away from a mixture of bad breath and potted palm leaves. 'Do excuse us gentlemen but I've come to dance with my wife.'

Speechless, I allowed Jamie to lead me away on his arm leaving the two men looking faintly embarrassed.

'Thank you,' I mumbled, spotting Snake Woman in the corner tossing venomous glances in my direction.

'My pleasure,' Jamie assured pulling me close.

I nose-dived ecstatically into his broad uniformed shoulder as we started to dance.

'It's lovely to see you again Cassie,' Jamie gave me a squeeze.

'You too,' I quickly replied. Hell, if he could say it then couldn't I?

'That's a lovely perfume you're wearing.'

'You too.' I said again before inwardly cringing. Berk. 'I mean your aftershave. Very nice.'

Jamie pulled back slightly to look at me properly. 'And while the compliments are rolling, I have to tell you that you really do look absolutely sensational this evening.'

I bit my lip to stop another *you too* from blurting out, although such an admission would have been perfectly true. He looked divine. I still couldn't decide whether he was flirting with me or just being charismatic company. I simply wasn't savvy or confident enough to be sure if it was the former. But one thing I did know was that right here, right now, I was in his arms and enjoying every second.

Occasionally we made trips to the buffet table and sat side by side to eat. I made sure I leant in toward him after reading somewhere that it was meant to be a flirtatious gesture of body language. I was delighted when Jamie copied this move and took it one step further by rather seductively hand feeding me. As he popped a black olive in my mouth I had an overwhelming urge to suck on his fingers and lick my way down his hand. The man enthralled me. Captivated me. If I'd been twenty years younger I might have confused the highly charged feelings thundering through my veins as falling in love.

'So are you still out of the dating game?' Jamie asked.

'Oh absolutely,' I replied automatically and instantly regretted it. Idiot! I should have come up with some witty little remark to let him know I was up for a date if he would only just ask.

'Livvy and Toby are coming on in leaps and bounds with their riding,' Jamie changed the subject, much to my disappointment.

'Mm, they love it. They're always talking about Petra and Jonas too and how kind they are letting them ride their pony sometimes.'

'It's nice they all get on so well,' Jamie said. 'We'll have to get together and take them out. Make a day of it.'

'Yes,' I nodded eagerly. So what if the outing was about the kids. I'd be there with him!

'Consider it a date in the not-too-distant future,' Jamie

twinkled. 'Come on, let's go and have another dance.'

I wanted the evening to never end but in time, of course, it did.

Back at Matt's house we all piled happily into the kitchen for final nightcaps and a party post-mortem, but at the last minute Jamie excused himself on the grounds of needing to return to Petra and Jonas whom he'd left with his mother. He raised a hand in farewell to the three of us and then he was gone. I almost wept. And when I got home I did. I cried relentlessly for a good two hours without really understanding why.

As the start of a new week got underway, whilst on the school run Toby gleefully informed me that Charlotte and Stevie had rowed over the weekend. My ears instantly pricked up.

'Dad told Charlotte off for exposing her boobies,' confided Toby.

Huh! So Stevie was getting all possessive about his young girlfriend was he? Presumably he didn't approve of the plunging low tops she wore. Surely he should be more concerned about the virtually crotchless and bumless jeans she favoured wearing?

'And Charlotte yelled that if she wanted to be photographed in the noddy then it was her business,' added Toby, 'and that she was seriously considering a new career as a prawn star.'

'What?' I gasped.

Liv chimed in. 'Then Charlotte burst into tears and confessed she'd only been glamour photographed to make Daddy jealous. And guess what else Mum? She accused Daddy of still being in love with you.'

'How utterly absurd,' I dropped the car into second gear and pulled up smartly outside the school gates. 'See you later kids. We're going to start packing for our holiday this afternoon.'

'But we're not going until the weekend.'

'Never leave things to the last minute,' I warned.

'Cool Mum. See ya.'

As my working day progressed, I offered up a silent prayer of thanks that very soon I would be shot of the irascible and ill-tempered Martin Henniker before the start of the long summer holiday. With a bit of luck, by the time I returned in September he would have successfully secured a permanent secretary.

The minute I was back home I set about locating three rather battered suitcases. However, I'd barely got as far as tossing sun creams into their depths when Nell turned up on the doorstep seeking coffee and gossip.

'What's that dog doing with you?' I frowned as Rocket goosed me, clearly hoping walkies or a jog might be on the agenda.

'Don't be like that Cass,' Nell shot me an injured look before settling herself down at the kitchen table.

'Sorry, sorry,' I sighed as Rocket sank mournfully to the floor.

'I simply wouldn't be without her you know,' Nell patted the dog's head.

'Me neither,' I lied.

My neighbour instantly brightened. 'And I can't thank you enough for suggesting I get a dog in the first place. Rocket's arrival ended all my broodiness.'

'Excellent.'

I placed the coffees on the table and sat down opposite Nell. By our feet Rocket gently snored and broke wind.

'Phew,' I flapped my hand about in a futile attempt to disperse the smell. 'Does she do that at home?'

'Yes,' Nell smiled fondly. 'She's just like a real baby — full of wind but thankfully without the colic.'

'And is Ben as captivated by Rocket as you are?'

Nell's brow puckered. 'Actually no. She's a bit of a sore point if you must know.'

'Why's that?'

'He's accused me of loving the dog more than him. Can you believe it? I mean what sort of a ridiculous claim is that! If anybody was going to feel jealous then I would have thought it would have been Dylan. Sibling rivalry and all that.'

'Hardly!' I spluttered. 'Rocket is the family dog Nell, not Dylan's sister.'

'She's like a daughter to me,' Nell said defensively.

'Well, sure, I know there are loads of pet owners who would agree with you to a certain degree, but don't prioritise her over your husband and son.'

'Oh for goodness sake Cass, you sound like Ben. Now get the biscuit barrel out and let's change the subject.'

I tipped some biscuits onto a plate. 'Everything is all right between you and Ben isn't it?'

'I'm not answering that question,' she snapped and promptly crammed an entire custard cream in her mouth.

The clothing level in the suitcases slowly rose. In due course Livvy and Toby broke up from school for the long summer break. Suddenly it was the morning of our Spanish holiday.

We crept out of the house just as the sparrows were stirring. A burly taxi driver hauled the luggage into his boot, huffing and puffing a great deal.

'Gawd blimey luv, wot you got in this one then? A dead body?'

Arriving at Gatwick, we trollied the cases to a bank of check-in desks. A bleary eyed female greeted us, snatching sticky labels that spewed from a machine.

'Each case should weigh no more than twenty three kilos. This one weighs thirty two.'

'Is that a problem?'

'It is if you want to take this particular suitcase on holiday.'

'Well of course I do. But I haven't got time to go home and re-pack.'

The woman shot me a withering look. 'You do it here.'

'*Right* here?'

'Right here.'

There then followed a very sweaty ten minutes rearranging and distributing the contents of the suitcases whilst holding up a disgruntled queue. Finally the hateful luggage whirred off through a synthetic flap curtain just as my stomach growled in hunger.

'Come on kids, let's grab some breakfast. Livvy? Earth to Planet Livvy?'

'Sorry Mum,' my daughter tore her eyes away from the milling crowd and gave me a distracted look.

'What's up?'

'Nothing. There was a girl. I dunno, for a moment I thought she was Petra.'

'Hardly. Come on. Let's go and attack some sausage and bacon.'

In no time at all we were forming a straggly line to board the plane. It was usually at this point that cold fingers of fear descended regarding the whole flying experience. As a familiar sensation of dread curdled within my bowels, I firmly told myself to keep chipper in front of the twins.

Squeezing myself into a bucket seat, I foraged in my hand luggage for the latest *Hello!* and quickly got stuck in. Anything to distract myself as the plane slowly trundled off to the runway.

All was going swimmingly well until I tuned in to the Captain introducing *her*self.

'Oh my God. A woman is flying this aircraft.'

'Mum! How could you be so sexist?' hissed Livvy in outrage. 'You're female yourself.'

'It's because I'm female that I'm worried,' I informed my daughter. Livvy had yet to get acquainted with the evils of PMT.

But the flight went without incident. As we stepped off the aircraft we were flattened by invisible fists of heat beating down upon us. An eager taxi driver ushered us into the depths of his air-conditioned cab delivering us to our modest but charming apartment around midday.

Swapping our hot jeans for cotton shorts and tops, we set off to investigate the whereabouts of the local supermarket.

'After we've stocked up on basic provisions we'll suss out restaurants for our first evening meal,' I chattered happily. 'Who fancies pizza?'

'Sounds good,' Livvy enthused.

'Toby? What about you? Toby I'm talking to you!'

'Sorry Mum,' my son replied, his eyes scanning the sidewalk

opposite. 'I could have sworn I just saw – oh never mind.'

After putting the essentials away in the tiny kitchenette, we enjoyed a leisurely supper at a pavement café and watched the world go by. Across the road the ocean relentlessly swished, emerald green waves tumbling over sapphire blue before bursting into frothy foam on the shell strewn sand. Holiday makers thronged the pavements wafting the bitter citrus scent of insect repellent.

I gave a contented sigh. Divorce, disastrous dates, the ex-husband's conquests, work and the hateful Martin Henniker suddenly seemed remote and faraway. Plunging into the holiday mood I ordered a jug of fruity sangria for myself and monster cokes for the twins.

'Cheers,' I toasted. 'Here's to a happy holiday.'

The following morning, armed with rubber rings and sunbathing paraphernalia, the three of us traipsed off to the beach, pale limbs conspicuous. Sand the colour of antique gold stretched out before us, dotted with sunbeds and bleached straw parasols.

Spotting three empty sunloungers grouped together, I frogmarched towards them dumping everything with a sigh of relief on the nearest mattress. Five minutes later the twins were splashing in the sea and I was sprawled on my tummy, firmly clutching a jumbo blockbuster. Two lines into the first chapter I paused and glanced around. There seemed to be an awful lot of boobs on display. Wherever I looked there they were – wobbling about in the waves, flopping sideways on sunloungers or simply bobbing up and down as their owners strolled along the shore. In fact, I appeared to be the only female wearing a bikini top. After the tiniest of hesitations, I curled a hand behind my back and unravelled the shoestring ties.

Liv and Toby splashed, swam, jumped waves and built sandcastles with moats and elaborate turrets while I simply turned one page after another, occasionally shifting position. Bliss.

Several chapters later, a shadow fell across my page blotting out the sun. I squinted through the black and white dots of light that danced across my vision. A man stood before me. An awfully familiar man. I slammed the blockbuster against my chest.

'Hello Cassie,' said Jamie.

'What are you doing here?' I squeaked, hastily rearranging my blockbuster.

'I thought we had a date?'

'We did?'

'Yes. To take the kids out all together and make a day of it.'

I stared at him in confusion. 'In Spain?'

'Well, why not?' Jamie hunkered down next to me. I clasped the blockbuster tightly. 'Confession time Cassie. I knew you were holidaying in Spain – you told me at Matt's barbecue, remember? You even regaled how lucky you were to achieve a booking because there were only two apartments left. The very next day I booked the remaining apartment.'

'I see,' I replied, not seeing at all. 'Er, why?'

'Because,' Jamie momentarily faltered, 'because at the risk of gate-crashing your private break Cassie, I wanted to see you.'

I clung to the blockbuster, aware that Jamie was probably seeing a great deal more of me than he'd actually bargained for.

'You wanted to see me?'

'Yes. Actually, I want to see you all the time.'

'You mean,' I stared at him uncertainly, 'you like me?'

'Yes. I've dropped enough hints and tried telling you so many times but there was always some interruption or another. So I'm telling you now. I like you. I like you very much.'

'Do you?'

'I do.'

'You like me as in,' I waved a hand about, 'as in *fancy* me?'

'As in fancy you.'

'You *fancy* me?' I shrieked causing several sweating torsos to shift with interest in our direction.

'Cassie you're not making this very easy for me. I want to *see* you. Go *out* with you. *Date* you. *Woo* you.'

'You want to woo me?'

'Yes.'

'Do you?'

Jamie threw up his hands. 'Stop! Just. Stop. Right. There. Look, I need to get back to Petra and Jonas. I've left them in a souvenir shop armed with a wad of Euros eyeing up an assortment of hideously oversized inflatables.'

I giggled. 'Sounds like Morag's chest.'

He grinned, but the smile slowly faded as his eyes held mine.

'So can I see you?'

'Oh yes please,' I reached out clumsily for him promptly dropping the blockbuster. As Jamie reached for the book, my arm whipped protectively across my bosoms and caught him a glancing blow on the chin.

'Ouch!'

'Omigod, I'm so sorry,' I stretched my hand up to rub the reddening area around his mouth. Jamie caught hold of my trailing fingers and kissed them one by one. I nearly fainted.

'I'll only forgive you if you agree to have dinner with me tonight.'

Needless to say I spent absolutely ages tarting up.

When the twins discovered Petra and Jonas were in Spain too they were overjoyed. They shrieked ecstatic greetings to each other before clattering off down the apartments' marble landing. Their voices echoed back up the stairwell where Jamie and I stood. Any moment now he would kiss me. I felt almost dizzy with anticipation.

'Well come along then,' he bounded energetically after the children, 'I don't know about you but I could eat a horse.'

'Oh yes, me too.' Actually I didn't think I could swallow a fly. Wasn't a failing appetite meant to be a pretty accurate measure of one's lovesickness?

Puffing after everybody in crippling high heels – which had only been worn to lengthen my legs and wow the man who professed a desire to woo me – we headed off to the taxi rank. And completely bypassed the drivers.

'Er, Jamie? Hello? EXCUSE ME!' I bellowed at five retreating backs.

'What's the matter Cassie?'

'Aren't we taking a cab?'

'Not on a beautiful evening like this.'

Marvellous. I click-clacked after everybody, my footwear reducing me to lots of tiny quick-steps. Five minutes later I ripped the offending heels off my feet and sprinted after the others.

We followed a meandering walkway that hugged the shoreline all the way to the marina. Jamie led the children into a white balconied restaurant. I rammed my feet back into the loathsome stilettos and plunged into the semi-lit room.

My goodness, this was nice. Very nice indeed. Cushioned seats complimented gingham tablecloths cloaked in flickering candlelight. I perked up a bit. Yes, this was the perfect place for a spot of flirty amour. At least it was until the children noisily appropriated tasselled menus, clamoured for Cokes and shrilly deliberated whether to eat pasta or test out one of the lobsters cowering in a nearby tank. A mournful looking waiter, who bore a striking resemblance to Bassett hound, patiently wrote down the children's indecisive requests with an air of long-sufferance.

Eventually, orders complete, the children chatted excitedly amongst themselves.

'Cassie,' Jamie turned to face me, 'I'm so sorry for gate-crashing your holiday but – no listen to me,' he waved away my protests. 'I was desperate to see you. I appreciate you came away to enjoy your own space and have time with Livvy and Toby – and I promise not to spoil that. So how about we do our own thing during the day but meet up in the evenings?'

But my concentration had momentarily lapsed as I caught the tail-end of Petra's conversation. Something about Selina – Jamie's stunning ex-girlfriend.

'Cassie? Do you agree with what I'm proposing?'

I zoomed back in on Jamie's words and nearly fainted.

'Proposing?'

'It would mean a lot to me if you'd say yes.'

'Well I – gosh. This is all very sudden Jamie. I don't know what to say.'

'Do you need time to think about it?'

'Definitely.'

'We won't see each other tomorrow.'

'Oh.' Surely this was an entirely retrograde step?

'I'll let you sleep on the idea.'

Privately I would rather have slept with him. But of course restraint had to be the order of the day. There were the children to think about. All four of them. Constantly present. In fact, would there ever be any getting away from them?

That night, back in the apartment and tucked up – alone – in my double bed, I tried to replay Jamie's conversation. If only I could remember the exact words of that proposal.

As I splashed cold water on my face the following morning, there was a light tap on the apartment door.

'Hi,' Jamie smiled. 'Hope I'm not calling too early but I was anxious to chat to you about my proposal. Have you thought any more about it?'

'Um, in all honesty Jamie, I can't properly remember what you said.'

'I was making all sorts of brash pledges about giving you space on your holiday but, in actual fact, I made promises I can't keep.'

'Why's that?' my eyebrows shot off my forehead in alarm.

'Selfishly Cassie, I want to see you all the time. And so do Petra and Jonas – although in their case they want to see Liv and Toby all the time. So would you mind terribly if we scrapped my original proposal?'

'Ah!'

As the dawn came up I thanked God for not letting me make a prize berk of myself. Although the idea of a wedding had rather appealed. Only last week I'd clocked a fantastic dress in Fairview, impeccably tasteful in the palest of pinks and perfect for a second time around bride.

'Cassie?'

'Hm?' I dragged my thoughts back from attiring Livvy in a particularly sweet dress with sleeves puffed *just* so.

'So do you fancy hanging out altogether around the pool this morning?'

'Oh absolutely. Wonderful!' I beamed.

The wedding could wait. Right now I needed to do something far more important – like making my body look ravishing in a bikini.

Half an hour later we were all gathered around a turquoise swimming pool. A mini sarong hid my bottom and dimpled thighs whilst a pair of open toed raffia wedges did their best to lengthen my legs. As the children tore down the pool's waterslide and frolicked in the shallows, any passing bystander could have been forgiven for thinking we were husband and wife with our large brood.

After a picnic lunch we moved to the beach. The bikini top stayed firmly on, but I did eventually shed the sarong. My spirits soared when an unscheduled touching session took place between Jamie and myself, even if the reality was his hands briskly rubbing sun lotion over my reddening back.

That evening, after quick showers, we met up again, enjoyed a sardine supper and then ventured to Tivoli World, a local theme park. We rode roller coasters, spun on carousels, whirled around on the gaily lit Ferris wheel and bashed and bumped the dodgems.

'Oh look,' breathed Petra in excitement. 'A haunted house!'

'That's one thing you are not trying out,' Jamie said pushing a fistful of Euros into each child's hand. 'Go and buy popcorn and cola while Cassie and I check it out.'

'Oh I don't think so Jamie,' I scoffed. 'It will take more than a few plastic skeletons and blaring klaxon horns to terrify me.'

'Come on,' he grinned.

I obeyed. After all, he'd slipped his hand into mine. Suddenly I wanted to hold that hand until the end of time.

As the battered entrance door creaked theatrically back on its hinges I suppressed a snort of laughter.

'Oooh, how horribly scary,' I mocked peering blindly into inky blackness. 'Any minute now a big bad wolf is going to leap out and – ARGH!'

A piercing scream set my tonsils waggling as a hooded figure materialised in the gloom. His bloodstained hands clutched an axe dripping red liquid. Unnerved I gripped Jamie's hand tighter. We appeared to be in some sort of narrow hallway. The door behind us banged shut making me jump. Suddenly this particular haunted house didn't seem such a joke after all.

A chainsaw roared into life causing me to scream again, but the noise was drowned out by the motor. An overhead light flickered dimly in the gloom haloing the chainsaw wielder. He crashed the throbbing machine against metal railings and a flurry of orange sparks showered the air.

Pushing forward, we entered a small chamber containing a hospital bed and a plethora of surgical machinery. An old hag lay prostrate on the mattress wired up to a respirator. It hissed and sucked with each rise and fall of her frail chest. Edging cautiously around the deathbed scene I kept my boggling eyes firmly on the witchy face. Ah yes. A plastic mannequin. And a pretty crappy one at that. The skin was so obviously synthetic and the matted grey hair framing the waxy features nothing more than a cheap nylon wig. I prodded Jamie in the back and whispered hoarsely in his ear.

'A very obvious dummy.'

Whereupon the dummy hurled itself off the bed trailing plastic tubes and thrust its warty features in my face.

'Jesus Cassie,' Jamie gasped clapping a hand to his possibly perforated eardrum.

The hag cackled hysterically stretching gnarled fingers towards our cheeks. If she touched me I just *knew* I'd faint. Spotting a handy 'Salida' sign I catapulted out into the night. Seconds later, Jamie appeared by my side.

'Well you did a fair impression of a terrified person to me,' he teased pulling me into a bear hug. 'Hey, you really were scared. I can feel your heart pounding.'

'I'll be fine in a minute,' I croaked collapsing against his broad chest. I had a sneaking feeling it was his embrace causing my aortic disruption, not the old hag.

Chapter Fourteen

As the holiday got firmly underway we all spent virtually every waking moment together. We visited the local aqua park enjoying a surfeit of watery rides. We also dared to be truly touristy and, armed with sunhats, big sunglasses and a surplus of suncream, booked a trip on a converted fishing trawler. And all the while, in my mind's eye, a part of me constantly stood back and studied the handsome golden man with the laughing sunburnt blonde as they holidayed with their four happy children. We looked like a family. Moreover, we looked like a family that had been together from the start.

Throughout the holiday Jamie repeatedly showed himself to be an adept and capable father to his children. He was also patient and kind with Livvy and Petra. If squabbles broke out he helped resolve them with the minimum of fuss. He was great entertaining the children, whether it be organising bat and ball on the beach or a local sight seeing excursion. Not once did he display impatience or lose his temper. He was so obviously a family man − one who threw himself into the role with great enthusiasm.

But apart from holding hands as we strolled to various restaurants in the evening or chaste goodnight kisses, the budding romance had yet to bloom. A part of me knew it was both impractical and unrealistic to expect anything more with four savvy children constantly around us. Instead I told myself to let things develop at their own pace, to relax and enjoy the old fashioned hand-holding and innocent kisses.

On our last evening the children went off for a late night game of table tennis in the apartment's private courtyard where an ancient ping pong table idled.

'Come on,' said Jamie slipping his hand in mine. 'Let's take a stroll round the gardens and leave them to it for a little while.'

We turned the corner and, for the first time, were properly on our own. Suddenly we were encapsulated in our own private bubble. I felt the outside world recede as if somebody had turned the volume down. The grass was wet and a million dewdrops sparkled and twinkled like diamonds around our feet. Moonlight shone and glinted off the softly rustling palm trees, turning them crystal and silver. Tiny shivers of excitement ran up and down my spine as Jamie placed a warm hand on my neck and pulled me to him for a kiss. As his lips came down on mine I felt as though I'd been waiting for this moment forever.

'You are beautiful Cassie. I love you.'

I gasped. 'You love me?'

'I do.'

'You do?'

'I love you very, very much.'

'Love me as in *lurve* me?'

'As in laying down my life and dying for you.'

'Omigod. Would you really die for me?'

'Yes.'

'Would you?'

'Stop. Right. There.' Jamie raised his hand in exasperation. 'I'm having a déjà vu moment. Would you please be quiet for a moment and listen to me? I don't quite know when I first fell in love with you – whether it was the day you ignored my colleague and appeared in your car driving through chaos-'

'Now look I've already explained-'

'Or when you left that idiotic message under my car's windscreen wiper-'

'Jamie I did tell you-'

'Or when I interrupted a hirsute workman chasing you down your hallway-'

'Oh God listen I-'

'Or whether it was that Speed Dating event where you spouted unbelievable garbage about being a mother to umpteen children-'

I shut up and hung my head in shame.

'But there's a part of me that feels like I've loved you forever. I find you hopelessly scatty, wonderfully endearing and refreshingly different to anybody I've ever met.'

There was a pause. I looked up under my eyelashes. He raised his eyebrows questioningly.

'Well?'

'Well what?' I whispered.

'Do you feel anything for me too?'

'Yes of course!' I exclaimed, 'I love you too! Love you, love you, love you!' I threw my arms enthusiastically around his neck nearly knocking the poor man off his feet. Steady Cass, don't grapple him to the ground. Not yet anyway.

As we pulled apart it was to catch sight of four faces peering around the corner, heads stacked on top of each other like something out of a cartoon.

'I think our dad and your mum might be dating,' declared Petra to the others.

'*Ew*,' said Jonas. 'At their age that is just so gross.'

As the plane juddered through its turbulent descent, I couldn't help thinking how the unstable motion mimicked my own emotions. The thought of not spending the next day and the next with Jamie and all the children had me on the verge of howling like a baby.

Later, as our homeward-bound taxi joined the M25, a horrible emptiness settled within the pit of my stomach. Even the twins seemed subdued.

Once home I immediately set about releasing piles of festering laundry from suitcases but was interrupted by the doorbell shrilly ringing. I smiled, sure that it would be Nell hoping for details of a smouldering holiday romance. Well wouldn't she be surprised!

'Coming,' I trilled releasing the door catch. 'We can have a coffee but I'll have to pinch some milk off you – oh!'

For standing on the doorstep was not Nell but Charlotte. And on closer inspection she didn't look so hot. In fact she looked decidedly wretched.

'You old bat!' she snarled, curling her lip like a Doberman on night watch. 'Where the fuck is he?'

My eyebrows disappeared into my hairline. 'I presume you mean Stevie?'

'Of course I mean bloody Stevie,' she spat. 'Did you both have a good time smooching in foreign climes together, clacking your castanets all around the bedroom and shaking your maracas in his face?'

'I really don't–'

'Where is he?' her voice cracked and suddenly she was in floods of tears.

'Oh Charlotte,' I sighed. 'You'd better come in.'

I guided her by an enviously skinny arm into the kitchen. 'Sit down. I was just about to make a cup of black coffee. Would you like one too?'

She shook her head and gulped several times. 'I'd prefer a fizzy drink.'

I popped a can of the children's favourite lemonade and placed it on the table.

'So. What's up?'

'I don't know where Stevie is,' she quavered wiping the backs of her hands across her eyes, smearing mascara everywhere. Livvy and Toby appeared in the kitchen doorway, eyes on stalks as they took in the distressed girl with panda eyes slumped across the kitchen table. I swiftly ushered them out while Charlotte grappled with her emotions.

'Last week Stevie abruptly announced he was going away and wanted me out of the house by the time he returned. I was convinced he was with you.'

'Stevie and I are in the throes of divorce. Jetting off into the sunset together is a total non-event. Look Charlotte,' I said gently, 'Stevie's not a bad man. He's just not a particularly faithful one. This might hurt now, but you're better off cutting your losses. You're young and beautiful. You can have your pick of anybody. In another five years you'd wonder what you ever saw in him.'

I patted her hand absent-mindedly. Poor kid. Even with black tear streaks and red eyes she still looked beautiful. Lucky cow.

'Yeah, I guess you're right. He might be good looking but he doesn't half stink the loo out in the morning. And I caught him picking his nose last week.'

'Disgusting,' I agreed, 'And I'll tell you something else. When Stevie thinks you're not looking he also picks his teeth, bites his nails, farts to order and scratches his balls.'

Charlotte looked horrified. She clearly had a lot of growing up to do. As far as I was aware all men did this.

The man himself telephoned later that evening confirming what I already knew and to say he couldn't see the twins for a few days. When I mentioned the state his girlfriend had been in, Stevie was extremely dismissive.

'Charlotte's just a kid. She'll get over it. I have to go now. We've a taxi waiting.'

We? Who was he with? It was only when Stevie had rung off I realised he hadn't said when he would be returning, but when I tried to ring him back his mobile was switched off.

The telephone rang again just as I'd lowered myself, groaning with tiredness, into an enormous bubble bath. The twins were already in bed fast asleep. Anxious that a ringing phone would disturb them, I erupted out of the bath trailing foamy water and dashed into the bedroom to snatch up the handset.

'Hello?' I panted.

'Are you simply out of breath or do I always have this effect on you?' quipped Jamie. 'How do you fancy a pizza tomorrow night darling?'

Darling! The endearment sent a little frisson of delight up and down my spine.

'Pizza's great. Anything. Just so long as I'm with you – darling.' I shyly tested out the endearment. It felt very right. 'But Stevie's gone away so the twins will be with us.'

'That's great because I'm without a babysitter too, so the children will have each other.'

Super. Another date where our kids came too. Would we ever be alone?

But, as we sat in *Pizza Express* the following evening, our four boisterous offspring could have been on another planet for Jamie and I only had eyes for each other.

'We need to see each other properly,' Jamie murmured. 'Without our kids in tow.'

'Mm,' I whispered back.

'I know you're off work for the summer now, but I'm back on duty tomorrow and the way the week is set to pan out I probably won't be able to see you until next weekend. Do you think you might be singularly available next Saturday night?'

'You can count on it,' I promised breathlessly.

The following morning the postman delivered the mail just as Nell was stepping over the threshold for elevenses.

'Just the one letter today Mrs Cherry,' he said cheerfully.

Walking into the kitchen I tossed the envelope on to the kitchen table. Nell sat down, launching into besotted chatter about Rocket's latest antics with a cuddly toy and bag of crisps. Ever the proud new mother.

'Anyway, enough of that,' said Nell reaching for my biscuit barrel. 'I haven't seen you properly since you got back from Spain. So come on, give me all the details. Did you get chatted up by anybody?'

'Maybe,' I smiled secretively as I set the coffees on the table.

'Ooh, I can tell by that smirk that it goes further than being chatted up. Tell Aunty Nell all about it.'

'It's special,' I said a bit defensively. 'It's a bit like a beautifully wrapped present that I want to savour before opening.'

'Oh my God,' squawked Nell. 'You've gone and fallen in love. Who is he? Some hairy Spaniard? It's just a holiday romance. Don't go getting your heart broken by some smoothie Casanova–'

'It's somebody I knew before I went on holiday,' I interrupted.

'Really? Who? I don't understand. Did you bump into each other?'

'It's a bit of a long story,' I picked up the envelope and studied the smeared post mark. 'Remember Jamie?'

'The copper you seem to periodically run into?'

'The very one and same,' I peeled back a corner of the envelope. 'We've kind of been skirting around each other for some time and – well – in a nutshell he flew out to Spain especially to let his feelings be known.'

'Omigod, that's so romantic,' Nell swooned over the biscuit barrel.

'And he declared his love for me,' I shook out the contents of the envelope.

Nell's eyes were like saucers. 'This is better than Mills and Boon. Tell me word for word how he said it.'

'Well would you bloody believe it,' I gasped as the air whooshed out of me.

'You're joking,' Nell sniffed looking decidedly short-changed. 'That's a total passion killer.'

'No it's this,' I turned the documentation around to face her. 'My decree nisi.'

'Oh Lord. How do you feel?'

'I don't know. Okay I guess. Shouldn't I be emotional or something? You know, try and squeeze a few therapeutic tears out?'

'Do you feel upset?'

'No. Perhaps I'm some sort of emotional cripple.'

I wondered how other people felt when they reached this point of divorce.

'I think you need to be alone with your thoughts for a little while,' Nell patted my hand and got to her feet decisively. 'We'll catch up on Jamie later. Meanwhile Cass, if you need me you know where I am.'

'Thanks,' I smiled gratefully.

After Nell had gone, I trailed a finger along the shelves of the overloaded bookcase in the lounge. There it was. Stretching up I reached for a decorative cardboard box, now a little tatty around the edges. Inside was our wedding album. Sitting cross-legged on the hard wooden floorboards I thumbed through each individual page.

The first glossy image was of a radiantly glowing Cassandra Haddock on the arm of her terribly proud father. My eyes filled with tears. Thank goodness my parents hadn't lived to witness the sparks flying as suspicions, distrust, tears and rows punctuated the last couple of years. Each argument had ended in my apologising to Stevie for being a possessive doubting wife. I snorted with contempt at my previous gullibility.

The next picture was standing before a flower laden altar exchanging shiny rings, followed by signing the register alongside the vicar who was a dead ringer for Ken Dodd.

Ah yes, walking down the aisle. The photographer had been forced to take this shot twice thanks to Great Aunty Dora tottering out of a side pew straight into the Hasselblad's viewfinder, hell bent on powdering my nose.

'You've gone all shiny dear.'

She had vigorously puffed orange loose powder over my face rendering me the colour of a satsuma for the remaining photographs.

The protective layers between each photograph rustled as another page turned. Stevie and I with linked arms on the threshold of the open church doorway, symbolic of standing on a brand new future together.

I spent a good twenty minutes going through the group photographs. There weren't many, but the cheerful faces of my parents repeatedly jumped out and held my gaze until my eyes flooded, hot tears splashing the images. Hastily I patted the wet marks with my sleeve. I missed mum and dad terribly. Always would.

And finally the cutting of the cake. A gloriously iced three tiered jobbie that elegantly reared up from an elaborate silver cake stand. It was a shame the fruit mixture had been such a disappointment. A cake that had been gorgeous on the outside and a let down on the inside. A bit like Stevie as it happened.

I snapped the album shut with a thud and returned the whole thing to the bookcase. The only tears I had been prompted to shed were for the memories of my beloved parents. The tears for my broken marriage had been exhausted a time long ago. Relieved that my lack of distress was perfectly justified, I carefully filed the decree nisi away.

Jamie telephoned very late that evening.

'I just had to speak to my girl.'

I squirmed deliciously. *His* girl. I was *his*. And *girl*. Knocking forty but feeling like sweet sixteen.

'I can't wait for Saturday,' Jamie whispered huskily.

'Me too,' I assured.

Which reminded me. Where was Stevie? It was his weekend to see the twins.

Throughout the week I attempted making contact with Stevie several times but his mobile was always switched off. Eventually I resorted to ringing his work place to see if they knew of his whereabouts.

'Is that Charlotte?' the telephonist barked.

'It's his wife.' Well it was only a little fib.

'Mr Cherry is currently away with his *real* wife.'

I slowly replaced the receiver. No wonder Charlotte had appeared on the doorstep with all accusatory guns blazing.

On impulse I strode over to his house looking for clues. The front lawn was unkempt and needing a mow, gasping patio plants drooped around the doorstep and a peek through the letterbox revealed a doormat littered with unopened mail. And then my eyes widened in horror. Presumably Charlotte was the author of the copious graffiti that adorned the recently decorated hallway.

Releasing the letterbox flap with a clatter, I pressed my nose up against the glass of the lounge window. Oh my. Nothing had been spared. Clearly Charlotte had exorcised her emotional pain via a can of spray paint. Obscene messages were scrawled over the once elegant mirror. The ornate fireplace had been bashed with a heavy object. The three piece suite had been upended with its guts hanging out. I stepped away from the window wondering what state the rest of the house was in. Stevie was going to have a blue bloody fit.

Back home I paced from room to room looking for my mobile phone. Where was the blasted thing? In mounting exasperation I rang my own number and tracked the ringtones to the laundry basket. What imbecile had put it in there? Foraging through muddy jodhpurs and grubby jeans, I salvaged the mobile from the pocket of my running trousers. Flipping the phone open I texted Stevie to call me urgently.

As the weekend edged nearer – still with no word from Stevie – I resorted to asking Nell if she would kindly have the twins overnight.

'Of course,' she agreed, 'on the absolute proviso you share every single detail of your night with Jamie.'

'Who said anything about spending the night with him?' I retorted prudishly. 'We are simply going out for the evening and it will probably be a late one. That's all.'

'Oh give over Cass,' Nell snorted. 'You're dating a guy who looks like a Hollywood heart-throb, has sworn undying love and made it perfectly plain that he wants you all to himself. What do you think you're going to do later on? Play Scrabble? Watch the Ten O'Clock News together over a cup of cocoa?'

'Well no but–'

'Of *course* you're going to spend the night with him. You'd be bonkers not to.'

Saturday morning dawned bright and clear. The twins wanted to see Matt regarding a little matter of securing pony rides throughout the remainder of the summer holiday in exchange for helping out.

'We can't keep pinching Petra's and Jonas's pony. It's not fair on them,' Livvy pointed out over the Rice Krispies.

Matt whooped with joy when he saw us all and embraced me in a rough bear hug.

'I hear you and Mac have finally got it together,' he winked lasciviously.

'Well, we're going out tonight,' I replied carefully as I glanced nervously in the twins' direction. The children knew Jamie and I were *good friends*. But that was all they knew.

'Well you have a great time. Morag's up at the house working on some legal papers. Why don't you pop in and say hi?'

I found Morag in the kitchen gazing dreamily at the ceiling, an untouched A4 legal pad sitting on the table in front of her.

'I kid you not Cass,' she sighed, 'I think Matt is The One.'

'Don't you think you need to be divorced first,' I reminded her.

'Oh but I am! Sort of anyway.' She rummaged around in her smart leather briefcase and produced a well thumbed piece of paper.

'Decree Nisi!' she grinned, flapping the document about like a Union Jack flag on Jubilee Day. Goodness. This lady was a far cry from the sobbing heap a few months previously.

'Snap! Mine came last Monday.'

'And Matt's received his Absolute. I think a celebration is on the agenda.'

With promises to dig out our respective diaries for a get-together, I hastened back home again to knuckle down to the serious task of extreme transformation. I only had six hours. What I really needed was six weeks, preferably encompassing a slot on Ten Years Younger with some wardrobe inspiration from Nicky Hambleton-Jones. Naturally I'd give her some invaluable advice in return. Like switching to contact lenses and binning those frightful specs.

Eventually I was flossed, glossed, groomed, perfumed and sporting a pair of reupholstered bosoms with an hour glass figure courtesy of a new girdle contraption in which I could hardly breathe. Slipping into a plunging lace sleeved shirt with endless tiny buttons leading tantalisingly downward, I teamed it with a floaty silk skirt. Oh yes. Very feminine and romantic.

Swiftly retrieving the twins from the stables, my expensive perfume clashing wildly with the twins' own aroma of Pony Pong, I frogmarched them into the bathroom before chucking fish fingers and chips under the grill. Leaving everything to cook, I rushed back upstairs to stuff pyjamas and toothbrushes into an overnight bag.

'Something's burning!' yelled Livvy.

'Dinner's ready,' I yelled back.

Twenty minutes later I delivered the children to Nell – narrowly avoiding a doggy snog from Rocket – just as Jamie's Rover purred up the drive. A swarm of butterflies instantly took flight in my stomach. At last we were going to be alone. Nell gave me a quick hug.

'You look fab. Go and have a wonderful evening and don't worry about the twins, they'll be absolutely fine.'

I gave her a grateful smile, smoothed down my skirt with damp palms and then tottered over to Jamie's waiting car. As I lowered myself into the passenger seat I was reassured to discover the inside of Jamie's car was almost as much of a tip as mine.

'Sorry about the mess,' Jamie apologised sheepishly. 'Keeping the car pristine with kids like mine is virtually impossible.'

I laughed. 'Know the feeling.'

'You look absolutely stunning by the way. In fact, I just want to sit here for a moment and look at you.'

'Don't be daft,' I muttered self-consciously.

'I mean it. And without the distraction of noisy kids and chattering friends and busy places and crowds of people. I just want to sit and absorb your lovely face and commit it all to memory.'

Well if he could do it, surely I could too?

My eyes travelled over his streaky honey hair, the broad forehead, light blue eyes flecked with tiny dots of brown and green, the irises very black and dilated. Chocolate eyelashes curled almost girlishly up and out toward the laughter lines that lightly fanned around his temples. The nose was straight and regular, the mouth generous. We moved towards each other and our lips touched. He tasted of minty toothpaste and smelt of citrus aftershave. I breathed the scent as if it were nectar.

'You are a very special lady Cassie. I want tonight to be both magical and memorable.'

I squirmed with pleasure. Here was an Adonis wanting to give *me* an unforgettable evening. I had an overwhelming urge to rub my hands together and cackle gleefully.

We went to a little Italian restaurant in picturesque Ainsley Brook, Jamie's village. Listed cottages crouched in a huddle and hugged the narrow road where *Luca's* was situated.

The restaurant was cosy, intimate, perfect. Despite the food being delicious I struggled to eat as I half fretted and half fantasised what might be on a later menu.

Afterwards, without even asking, Jamie drove me to his house. It was a compact detached family home on a winding hill surrounded almost entirely by farmland. No doubt in daylight it afforded the most wonderful views of the tiny ancient church and picturesque postcard village below.

A courtesy light shone cheerfully by the front door. Jamie rattled his key in the lock and strode in, touching switches on table lamps which immediately suffused the rooms with soft light.

'Won't be a minute.'

He bounded up the stairs two at a time. Was he off to the loo? Perhaps I should go too? Powder my nose or fiddle with my hair. I pulled a compact mirror from my handbag and inspected my lipstick and teeth. Good. No herby bits stuck anywhere. I hurriedly snapped the compact shut as returning footsteps thumped down the stairs. Wordlessly Jamie took my hand. Led me up the staircase. To his bedroom. This was it. This was finally *it*.

As I crossed the threshold I stared around in astonishment. The room was lit with about sixty or seventy beautiful rose scented candles. Their soft flickering sent shadows leaping across the walls. A large bed stood in the centre with turned down cotton sheets which almost crackled with that first laundered freshness. Across one pillow lay a cream rosebud, a gold ribbon tied around the stem.

'I love you Cassie,' Jamie whispered.

He softly kissed one side of my mouth, then the other.

'I want to show you how much I love you.'

'Mm, mm,' I agreed, enthusiastically matching him kiss for kiss.

He made very quick work of all the tiny fiddly buttons on my shirt.

'Lovely boobs,' he murmured eyeing up my new cleavage control bra with appreciation.

'Thank you.'

I slapped his hand away from the bra's clasp.

'Cassie, what are you doing?'

'Leave it alone.'

'Why?'

'Because if you undo–'

Too late. My breasts leapt from their ramped up prison and yo-yoed down to my navel.

Fortunately Jamie's attention had diverted to my right earlobe which he was busily nuzzling while his hands searched out the zipper of my skirt.

Suddenly he froze. 'What's this?'

Sod it. 'A girdle.'

Why the hell had I worn the damn thing? And why in God's name had I got to the age of thirty nine and not mastered the art of undressing seductively – preferably in a pitch black room?

'I'll be honest Cassie. This sort of gear doesn't do it for me.'

'It wasn't meant to. I mean, I didn't know for sure we would be doing this otherwise I wouldn't have worn it. I was trying to impress you with a toned figure.'

'I saw enough of you on holiday in your bikini to know what your body looked like. You don't have to impress me Cassie. I love you. And I love your body. I love everything about you and most of all I love you just the way you are.'

'Oh what a beautiful thing to say,' I fell backwards on the bed swooning in relief. 'In that case I'm all yours – help yourself.'

As Jamie tripped over trailing trousers and hopped about on one foot peeling off socks, I privately delighted in his own awkward undressing.

A long time later, as we lay side by side, I ran my hands over his beautiful body. The honey curls on his chest. The muscled upper arms. Strong firm thighs.

'Cassie, can I ask you something?'

'Mm,' I mumbled contentedly.

When I first met you, why did you keep calling me Mr Pitt?'

Colour flooded my face. Surely he knew? Didn't he? Hadn't anybody ever told him for goodness sake!

'Um, well I'd have thought it rather obvious actually.'

'Not to me.'

'Because, well, because you look like Brad Pitt of course!'

Jamie hooted with laughter. 'I hardly think so but that's a very nice compliment all the same.' He kissed me gently on the nose. 'Well if I'm Brad Pitt you must surely be Jennifer Aniston.'

This time it was my turn to whoop with ridicule but then I froze, horrified.

'Oh no. You mustn't say that. That's a bad omen.'

'Why?'

'Because they split up. Brad went off with Mrs Smith.'

'Mrs Smith?'

'Yes you know – she has a cloud of dark swingy hair, high slanting cheekbones, pumped up lips, pumped up boobs, a pert bottom – that's probably pumped up too – and she's just a teensy weensy bit stunning.'

In fact, she was an awful lot like Jamie's ex-girlfriend. My stomach lurched.

'Hey, hey, listen to me Cassie. I'm not Brad Pitt, you're not Jennifer Aniston and we're not going to split up. Okay? I'm crazy about you. I know its early days yet but I seriously believe we have a future together. I certainly *want* a future with you, all of us together one day under one roof.'

'You mean living together?'

'Well yes, although I really meant *married* and living together.'

'Are you proposing?'

'Kind of,' Jamie grinned. 'Although I'd rather give you a proper old fashioned proposal when the time's right. Down on one knee and all that sort of thing. And preferably when you are fully divorced and had some time on your own.'

'Are you worried I'm on the rebound?'

'Of course.'

'Well I'm not. I rebounded disastrously some time ago.'

'Is that so?' he teased.

'That doesn't mean I've been, you know, putting myself about!' I spluttered. 'I'm not that kind of girl.'

'I know you're not Cassie, don't fluster yourself so,' Jamie twinkled. I had a feeling he was laughing at me. 'We've both been married before and have four children between us. Nonetheless I reckon you and I would make a great team and collectively we'd be a cracking fam–'

Jamie ground to a halt. He looked appalled.

'What's the matter?'

'Cassie I'm so sorry. I've leapt way ahead here and I'm coming on too strong. I've probably terrified you. I just wanted to try and express how you make me–'

I put my finger to his lips and smiled. I felt as if my whole body was smiling.

'We'll be fabulous together. All of us.'

'I have one small confession.'

'What's that?'

'My surname.'

'Mac?'

'Yeah. Well, it's actually an abbreviation.'

'Don't tell me. You have Scottish blood running through your veins and in a minute you're going to confess you're Jamie MacTavish, the laird of umpteen highland acres with a castle to reclaim.'

'Er, no. Do you remember telling me that your maiden name was Haddock and how much you hated it?'

'Y-e-s.'

'Well, if you marry me you'll have another awful surname.'

'Oh?'

'My surname is Mackerel.'

'So one day I'll be Mrs Mackerel?'

'Yes. From Miss Haddock to Mrs Mackerel.'

'Sounds like we're made for each other,' I grinned.

Inevitably I stayed the night although neither of us achieved a great deal of sleep. I awoke with a start around seven and briefly wondered where on earth I was.

'Wow,' Jamie grinned at me. 'Do you always wake up looking this beautiful?'

'Oh yes,' I replied airily. 'The dishevelled look is my speciality.'
Despite the lack of sleep I actually felt wide awake and sparkly eyed.

We shared a power shower together before breakfasting on warm croissants and orange juice. If only every day started in such a romantic and civilised fashion.

Back home, seconds after my key opened the front door, Nell bustled up behind me, Rocket at her heels.

'You don't have to worry about Liv and Toby. They're watching *Meet The Fockers* on DVD with Ben and Dylan.'

I frowned. 'Is that suitable viewing.'

'Probably not. Meanwhile we have – ooh – a good ninety minutes all to ourselves. I'll put the kettle on while you sit down and spill the beans.'

I sighed in resignation and sat down, Rocket flopping to the floor under the table.

'So!' Nell exclaimed. 'What's he like in bed?'

She was given a heavily diluted account of the bedroom activity and absolutely no mention of the *marriage* word. Instead I gave her lots of extravagant detail about the scented candles and rose on the pillow, just so she didn't feel too deprived of details.

'How wonderful!' Nell sighed. 'What I wouldn't give for a bit of romance.'

'Well go and grab some!' I urged. 'Book yourself a nice weekend somewhere with Ben and I'll look after Dylan for you. And Rocket,' I added hastily catching my neighbour's arched eyebrow.

'No,' Nell wrinkled her nose. 'I don't want romance with Ben thanks very much.'

I was suddenly concerned. 'Things are okay with you and Ben aren't they?'

'Sure,' she gave a tight smile. Subject closed.

The following morning I dropped Livvy and Toby at the stables and spotted Jonas and Petra grooming their pony. Realising with a jolt that they might one day be another son and daughter, I decided it would be a good idea to muster up some interest in their pony.

'What's her name?' I nervously patted the noble tossing head.

'Smokey,' Petra smiled. 'But he's a gelding.'

'That means a male horse whose balls have been chopped off,' my son informed me gleefully.

'*Thank* you Toby,' I heaved a sigh. 'Well I'll leave you all to it. See you later.'

As I walked back to the car, the tail end of Petra chatting with Livvy floated across to me on the breeze.

'I really like your mum,' I heard her say. 'As parents go, she's quite cool.'

Unlocking the car, I realised I was smiling.

Chapter Fifteen

A few days later Stevie telephoned absolutely raging.

'Have you seen my fucking house?' he screamed.

'Ah, you're back.'

'Yes. And I've returned to vandalism and destruction courtesy of bloody Charlotte. Somehow I need to oversee an entire house refurbishment when I'm due back at work tomorrow. Can you help me out?'

'Never mind your blasted house for a moment. What about asking after your children who haven't seen or heard from you in quite a while?'

'Sorry, sorry. I'll come over right now.'

Stevie arrived just as I was making coffee.

'I'll have one of those too. *H-e-y* kids!' he flung his incredibly brown arms wide as both children hurtled into his embrace.

'How about a proper get-together,' he grinned down at them, 'just as soon as I've sorted out my house?'

'What's wrong with your house?' asked Livvy.

I shook my head imperceptibly.

'Nothing that can't be put right with a little help from your Mum.'

Stevie then went on to tell me he already had a team of decorators lined up who had agreed to pull all the stops out until the job was finished. My input was to let the boss man into the house the following morning.

'So! How was the holiday?' I asked nosily.

'Fabulous thanks. We had a marvellous time cruising around Cyprus, Egypt and Israel.'

'We?'

'Simone and I.'

'I'm staggered you dumped somebody as young and stunning as Charlotte.' I put a plate of biscuits on the table next to the coffees.

'We didn't connect on anything other than a horizontal level, if you catch my drift. I seriously thought about pressing criminal charges against her, but on reflection I guess she was simply expressing her angst.'

'That's an understatement,' I muttered.

'Simone is everything that Charlotte isn't,' Stevie enthused. 'She's mentally stimulating, extremely cultured, widely travelled and highly educated.'

'I see.' I couldn't resist taking a sideways snipe. 'What's this one then – a gap year university student?'

'Simone is a fifty-eight year old marine biologist.'

I nearly choked on my coffee.

Bloody hell. I mean bloody *bloody* hell.

The high powered painting and decorating team turned out to be a chap who bore a striking resemblance to Del and Rodney's Grandad with a motley entourage of younger male relations. Grandad – or George to give him his correct name – was in no hurry to start the job and keen to pass a minute or ten gossiping.

'Ooh 'ave yer seen all the mess his young lidy made?' George sucked his cheeks and pulled his flat cap over his eyes, even though it was nudging almost thirty degrees outside.

'Ah've bin in the decoratin' bizniss forty years and I said to my missus last night, I said I ain't niver seen nuthin' like this.'

'Yes it is a bit of a challenge George,' I agreed, privately wishing he would get on with painting over the mess rather than reading it.

'Bit of a wag was she? Had a sense of humour like?'

'I wouldn't know George,' I replied removing lids from paint pots. Surely he'd take the hint soon?

'Wot's this bit say?' George adjusted his half moon spectacles with a gnarled hand. 'My hamster has a bigger willie than Stevie Cherry. Aw, that's not very nice is it?' He broke into wheezy guffaws of laughter, his smoker's lungs crackling with the effort.

I straightened up from the paint pots. 'Well George, I won't hold you up.' Surely that remark couldn't be any clearer. 'See you later.'

The heat of the day gave way to a gloriously warm evening. Jamie came over with Petra and Jonas for an impromptu garden barbecue. As Jamie stood over the smouldering griddle, an arm slung casually around my shoulders, I gazed adoringly up at him. And failed to spot Stevie standing stock still by the side gate.

'Daddy!' Livvy squeaked excitedly.

I glanced up to catch Stevie's frozen expression, his eyes hard as flint, and found myself jumping like a scalded cat.

Twittering nervously I introduced the ex-husband to the boyfriend. It was a seriously weird moment. The two men politely shook hands but without any warmth. The air around Stevie hummed with hostility. Jamie's face was an expressionless mask. I inwardly cringed, fussing about needlessly with lemonade bottles and plastic wine flutes.

'Sorry to interrupt happy families.' It was said lightly but I knew Stevie well enough to detect the edge in his voice. 'I dropped by to give you the new key to the house Cass. The locksmith's been,' he added by way of explanation. 'See you later.'

After he'd gone Jamie gave me a curious look. 'Cassie I hate asking you this, but why would your ex-husband give you a key to his house?'

I explained the Charlotte problem and my overseeing the decorators. Jamie slowly exhaled, a relieved expression on his face.

'You surely weren't thinking something else were you?' I folded my arms across my chest, head on one side enquiringly.

'Not at all. Well yes actually. Just a little bit. I'm very aware you haven't been separated for that long Cassie. There's a deeper part of me that fears you and Stevie could reconcile. I don't want to get caught up in a triangular relationship – or for that matter get hurt.'

Knocking the burger prongs from Jamie's grasp I grabbed his hands tightly in mine.

'The only reunions I want,' I said earnestly, 'are with you – whenever you're off duty and whenever we can get together, be it with or without our children. I love you Jamie like I've never loved any man before,' and with that I hurled myself at him, kissing him full on the mouth.

'*Ew,* they're snogging again,' Jonas' voice drifted across the garden.

Despite George and his boys initially getting off to a slow start, it became apparent over the next few days that there was no stopping them.

One afternoon I popped over to Stevie's house and was amazed at the swift transformation. Clean bare walls were almost reinstated and the battered fireplace had been repaired.

When Jamie telephoned that evening it was with the suggestion of staying at his house for the entire weekend.

'Ooh yes please,' I agreed happily. 'So Petra and Jonas will be at their grandma's overnight?'

'No, not at all. Mum's going rambling for the weekend with her crowd of golden oldies so the children will be here too.'

'Oh. Oh. Right.' I struggled to get my head around this arrangement. It was taking our relationship in front of the children from a slow and steady introduction to top gear overnight. The idea of sleeping in Jamie's bed with Petra and Jonas just across the landing wasn't a comfortable thought. And what would Livvy and Toby say when they found out?

'Um, Jamie, I'd rather not do that just yet. It's too soon.'

'Sorry darling, I'm coming on too strong again aren't I! It's just me being selfish and wanting to take every opportunity to be with you.'

'So, er, did other girlfriends stay overnight when the kids were in the house?'

'Other girlfriends?'

'You know – other lady friends. Did the children ever wake up to discover another woman in the house with Dad?'

I was aware that voicing the question out loud had made me feel irked. One could even say *jealous.*

'No. Never.'

'Not even Wossername?'

I had a childish urge to refer to her as Semolina.

'Selina? No way.'

'So what did you do when you – you know – wanted to get together?' I persisted, even though the mere *thought* of the ravishingly gorgeous Selina lying in bed with *my* man was causing mental havoc. Vivid pornographic pictures were unfolding in my brain and I couldn't find the remote control anywhere to flip the image off.

'I'd go to her place.'

I was seriously uptight now. Couldn't help it.

'Just as an aside – and I really hope you don't mind me asking this,' I snarled into the handset, 'why *did* you split up with Selina?'

'Because, with the exception of work, we had very little in common. She was absolutely *not* into children and when she did meet the kids she could hardly be bothered to say hello. I also found her incredibly vain, attention seeking, boring and shallow.

Excellent news.

'So why did you go out with her?'

'Well, she suited my life at that point. I was happy to have occasional female company but I was never in love with her – and she knew it. In fact the catalyst for us breaking up,' Jamie hesitated, 'was you.'

'*Me?*'

'Yes you! Selina figured I had a soft spot for you when you crashed on the ski slope. I was adamant about staying with you and told her to go on ahead, remember? She was apoplectic with rage and we had a big row about it later that evening. And once back in England I insisted on detouring to your house to see how you were. You may recall she was in the car. It was the last straw for her and the massive argument that followed was our last. But never mind Selina. She's the past. You're my future Cassie and I want our children to start getting familiar with that.'

Jamie had said *our* children. That had sounded so nice. Like his children were my children and mine were his. They were *ours*.

As things turned out, I did end up staying the night at Jamie's house. Morag and Matt had telephoned with an impromptu invitation to celebrate their respective Nisi and Absolute insisting we join them for dinner and to bring Petra and Jonas too. Matt had the children from his second marriage staying the weekend who were good pals with Jamie's two.

'Let them stay overnight with us,' Matt suggested. 'They'll have a load of fun watching unsuitable DVDs and feasting on popcorn.'

'Don't you mind having all these kids staying when you're after private time with Matt?' I asked Morag buttonholing her in the kitchen.

'Of course not,' she replied peering into the depths of the overloaded dishwasher for free space. 'The children don't really want to hang out with Matt or me very much anyway. They think we're a pair of old fogies!' she laughed.

'Doesn't Matt worry about his kids being emotionally screwed up seeing you practically installed in the house and spending nights with him, not to mention all those step-children? It's not what I would call a stable home environment.'

'Of course it is!' Morag reversed out of the dishwasher looking most indignant. 'All Matt's kids and step-children are just fine with it. They've all endured watching their parents split up, meet other people, re-marry, split up again, meet someone else, live together, split up. But Matt's always been here for them with the door wide open. Fortunately there have never been any access struggles so each child has never lost sight of their main parent and is perfectly capable of taking the comings and goings of lovers or step-parents within their stride. Don't fret so. Kids are far more adaptable than you think.'

The incredible joy of waking up with Jamie by my side was an unexpected heavenly treat. I rolled over kicking the cumbersome duvet off and gazed lovingly at his handsome face in sleep.

'You're staring at me,' he mumbled, eyes still tightly shut.

I grinned and flopped back happily against the feather pillows. 'Do you ever sometimes experience a really bizarre sense of déjà vu about us?' I stared up at the ceiling making cloudy pictures in the uneven paint swirls. 'Ours is a fledgling relationship and yet I feel like I've known you for such a long time. Forever in fact. It's so weird.'

Jamie reached out and pulled me across the rumpled bedclothes into his arms. 'That's because we're right for each other.'

Later, when I'd returned home, Stevie unexpectedly turned up on the doorstep.

'Mind if we talk?' he asked pushing straight past me.

'Why don't you come in,' I muttered to his retreating back.

I followed him through to the kitchen.

'I'll come straight to the point Cass,' Stevie leant back against the sink, arms outstretched either side of the draining board. 'What's with you and Boy Wonder?'

'Who?'

'Mr Cop Man,' Stevie spat. 'The chap who seems to have made one hell of an impression upon *my* kids. When I last saw the kids they couldn't stop prattling on about him. I gather you all jollied off to Spain together and played ecstatically happy new families. Took your little buckets and spades down to the beach and made dear little castles in the sand. Re-enacted *We're All Going on a Summer Holiday* starring Cassandra Cherry and PC Flat Foot. Don't you think you should have asked my permission first before electing this guy to step unasked into the father figure role?'

'I beg your par-?'

'And what was he doing here the other day in *my* house sitting on *my* patio drinking out of *my* glasses eating off *my* plates with *my* SODDING FAMILY?' Stevie bellowed.

'Oh give me a SODDING BREAK,' I bawled back. 'For starters Stevie this is *my* house now and who I invite into it is nothing to do with you.'

'It bloody well is where my children are concerned,' Stevie jutted his chin out. 'You know nothing Cass. You're just a silly little woman with your head up your arse. If you want to cheapen yourself with other men then that's up to you, but don't involve *my* children,' he took a step forward and thrust his face into mine, 'DO YOU FUCKING UNDERSTAND?'

'I can't believe I'm hearing this. What about *you*?' my voice cracked. 'Did you ever stop to think about the impact *your* love life was having on Livvy and Toby? In the space of a few short months they've seen you bed hop from Cynthia Castle to Charlotte and now Simone.'

'They haven't met Simone. She's not into children.'

'No I don't suppose she is. I expect *grand*children are more her scene,' I replied scathingly.

'Don't be a bitch Cass, it doesn't suit you.'

Frustrated and furious, words failed me. There were so many things I wanted to vocally lob back at Stevie but instead I found myself incapable of verbalising it.

'We've been down this path before,' I eventually said.

'Oh no we haven't,' Stevie's eyes narrowed, 'not where my children are concerned.'

'They're my children too you know. And I have a damn sight more regard for their emotional welfare regarding relationships than you will ever have.'

'Oh so it's a re*lation*ship is it?' Stevie pounced. 'You and Plod are an item are you?'

I hesitated. Part of me wanted to scream *yes, yes, yes* but I wanted to discuss things with Livvy and Toby first, not Stevie.

'It's early days,' I said dismissively.

'Well just make sure that whatever happens between you and this bozo, you keep the kids firmly out of the equation. Got it?'

With that Stevie stalked out of the house slamming the front door so hard the letterbox flap fell off its hinges.

How *dare* he speak to me like I was some sort of good time girl when it was as plain as the nose on his face that he was the one who behaved like a promiscuous tart?

The anger stayed with me until gone bedtime. I finally fell asleep a little before dawn. I awoke exhausted, the tangle of bedclothes bearing testament to the night I'd had.

'Kids?' I foghorned from my bedroom. 'Can you come here for a moment please?'

'No, I'm looking for my riding crop,' Livvy's muffled voice floated up from the depths of the shoe cupboard.

'I'll help you find it in a minute,' I shouted back.

The pair of them finally appeared, Toby shambling in with odd socks on and Livvy clearly impatient to be off.

'Guys!' I beamed at them.

They cast doubtful glances at each other. I rarely called them *guys*.

'Sit down,' I patted the bed. 'I want to have a chat with the two of you about, well, something delicate.'

'Oh Mum if this is to discuss the birds and the bees we already know everything.'

'It's about Jamie. And me.'

'You want to tell us you're dating,' Toby gave me a bored look.

'Well, yes but-'

'And that you've fallen in love,' added Livvy.

'How-?'

'It was obvious to all of us,' Toby continued.

'Good heavens,' I stared at them both, utterly pole-axed. 'And, er, how do you feel about it?'

Toby shrugged. 'We like him, don't we Liv?'

'Yeah. He's pretty cool, especially being a policeman and everything. Can we go now?'

'No, this is extremely important.'

I focussed my attention on Toby.

'It's not that long ago you gave me a lot of grief simply for being friends with Matt.'

'Jamie's different.'

'Why?'

'He just is. He's a bit like having another Dad I s'pose.'

'But he's *not* your Dad Toby.'

'No I know that, and nobody can replace my real Dad. I'm just saying that I don't mind having Jamie around. Does this mean the two of you will now be having sexual intercourse?'

My mouth dropped open.

'Don't be ridiculous Toby,' Livvy interrupted, 'Mummy and Jamie are far too old for that sort of thing.'

Naturally I brought Jamie up to date on my talk with the twins adding that it had been Stevie's ranting remarks that had prompted the conversation.

'I think it might be a good idea for the two of us to see Stevie together for a frank chat. That way he can address any issues and concerns directly to me. I'm not on duty tomorrow evening so ask him if we can have a bit of a get together.'

'Are you kidding?'

'Why would I be kidding?'

'Er, no reason. Right, I'll do that.'

'Good.'

I didn't summon the courage to ring Stevie until quite late. He was curt to the extreme.

'Would you be available for a chat tomorrow evening only there's some-'

'Come over at seven,' Stevie snapped.

'Okay. I'll be bringing-'

But the line had gone dead. Terrific.

The following evening Nell kindly stepped into the breach to mind Liv and Toby for half an hour or so. With mounting apprehension, I nervously walked alongside Jamie to Stevie's house.

'When you mentioned your ex-husband lived nearby Cassie, I didn't realise it was the very same road.'

'It's a bit of a story,' I muttered.

Jamie stepped up to the doorbell. He squeezed my hand reassuringly. 'Ready?'

'No.'

The door was answered almost immediately by an elegant brunette who I'd have judged to be in her mid forties. Seconds later the penny dropped with a clang. Goodness, this must be Simone. She certainly looked exceptionally well preserved. Perhaps she'd had a bit of nip and tuck?

'Yes?'

I scrutinised her taut jawline. Hm. Hard to say with that hair curling under her chin.

A second later Stevie erupted into the hallway, hastily trying to usher the woman away.

'Simone darling,' he was saying, 'I'm so sorry but I completely forgot the children's mother wanted to–'

The words died on his lips as he took in Jamie's presence.

'Why don't you both come in,' he invited stiffly.

Simone smiled graciously and led the way into the lounge. An echo of fresh paint hung about the place.

'It's lovely to meet you,' Simone dimpled, her husky tones bearing testament to a long relationship with cigarettes. 'I've heard a little about the children and they sound delightful.'

'Ha ha,' I laughed, nerves making me sound like a braying donkey. 'Jolly good!'

Jamie gave me a discreet glance, his expression clearly saying *settle down*. I collapsed weakly into one of the leather sofas and flung an arm across its length in an attempt to appear relaxed. Unfortunately my timing was off and I inadvertently whacked Simone in the face as she made to sit down beside me.

'Oh God I'm so sorry!'

'Couldn't matter less,' she assured pressing a lace handkerchief to a streaming eyeball.

'Would anybody like a drink?' Stevie glared furiously at me, 'or will you not be staying long?' he added pointedly.

Jamie answered for both of us. 'A drink would be very nice. Thank you.'

Looking extremely put out, Stevie opened a trendy chiller cabinet in the corner of the room. A heavy silence ensued. I sat squirming uncomfortably while a reluctant cork slowly squeaked its way out of a bottle. Wearing a pained expression, my ex loaded a tray with glasses.

'So!' I chirruped into the insufferably tense atmosphere causing Stevie to nearly drop the tray and Simone to visibly jump. 'Stevie mentioned you're a marine biologist Simone. How absolutely fascinating!'

'Yes,' she smiled delightedly, before taking a glass from the tray Stevie was handing around, 'and a very keen one at that. Does the subject interest you at all?'

'Oh absolutely,' I nodded catching sight of Jamie's incredulous face.

Simone wriggled happily within the depths of the sofa. 'How marvellous! So many people haven't a clue.'

'No!'

Jamie rolled his eyes.

'Oh but it's true,' Simone confided. 'When I discuss my work with people and tell them how fascinating it is to study the marine environment with all its rich beauty and complexity, so often I'm rewarded with blank faces.'

I instantly contrived my features to look unblank.

'Do tell me about some of your work.'

'Certainly my dear,' she beamed delightedly. 'What is it you want to specifically know?'

'What about, um, what about what about what about,' I gabbled sounding like Jimmy Saville on speed, 'the watery bit!'

'Absolutely,' Simone laughed happily. 'After all it's the,' she posted quotation marks in the air, '*watery bit* that covers three quarters of the Earth's surface,' she twinkled at me, 'and yet – shockingly – we are more acquainted with the surface of Mars!'

'Oh yes Mars! I just love the corrugated chocolatey bit,' I smacked my lips appreciatively.

'Ooh you are funny,' Simone giggled.

Hell. She meant the planet Mars. Not the sweet.

'Ha ha, just joking!' I brayed.

Jamie appeared to be intently studying his fingernails.

'Well now, in the not so distant past our beautiful oceans were seen as both an inexhaustible resource and a bottomless sink for our wastes. Yet the increasing and combined pressures of overpopulation and pollution have dangerously threatened our natural environment, which means there is an increasing need for scientists who can understand how it all works, monitor how it affects us and, in turn, how *we* are affecting *it*. And this monitoring ranges from global warming right through to the tiniest plankton and from small local issues to vast global concerns. We now know that the marine environment is inextricably linked to our lives and indeed to our future survival.'

'Amazing.' Were we still speaking English?

'It takes a multi-disciplinary approach to explore and understand the marine environment. One needs to know about marine eco-systems, pollution, coastal navigation and oceanography.'

'Ah yes, oceanography,' I nodded sagely.

'Do you actually know what that is Cass?' Stevie asked sarcastically. Bastard.

'Yes of course,' I spluttered. 'Oceanography is...well it's like geography but...of the ocean.'

Simone clapped her hands gleefully. 'But my dear! I'd be more than happy to show you around my harbourside marine laboratory. I'm currently doing project work and I'd love to show you what's planned for a trip to Belize later this year. I'm going to be heading up a team studying tropical marine environments. Why don't you join us?'

'I'm afraid that simply isn't possible Simone darling,' Stevie smoothly interrupted. 'Cass is far too busy as a mover and shaker around the high-powered world of sparring solicitors and barristers in court room dramas.'

Stevie's mocking tone completely by-passed Simone.

'How terribly interesting,' she smiled. 'A bit of a legal beagle are you?'

'She is,' Jamie interrupted. 'But first and foremost Cassie is a mother. And an absolutely brilliant one too.'

'Now that's an area where I totally lack qualification,' Simone inclined her head graciously towards me in defeat. She seemed completely unaware of the multi-stranded undercurrents running through the gathering.

'And it's actually the mothering and – indeed – the fathering side of things that both Cassie and I were hoping to discuss with you tonight Stevie.'

I gulped.

'The fathering side? What exactly are you talking about?' Stevie glared at Jamie.

Simone finally registered the sour atmosphere and stood up.

'I think this is a suitable moment to powder my nose,' she tactfully excused herself.

Stevie waited until Simone's tread on the staircase had receded and a distant door firmly closed.

'What exactly is this all about?' his eyes glittered dangerously.

'I'd have thought it obvious given the conversation you had with Cassie earlier this week,' Jamie replied mildly. 'You indicated a wish to be consulted before any man had anything to do with your children. Therefore I'm here to discuss Livvy and Toby.'

'You leave *my* children out of it,' warned Stevie. 'They're absolutely nothing to do with you.'

'Oh but they are – through circumstance. I have a son and daughter myself so I know and understand where your feelings are coming from, but hope you'll agree it's important we try and get along. It would be a shame to let your personal feelings impact upon Livvy and Toby. Especially when they become my step-daughter and step-son.'

'Your *what*?' Stevie's eyes bulged like a frog's, his mouth opening and closing like a goldfish.

I almost called Simone back down to investigate.

In the circumstances I thought Jamie handled Stevie brilliantly, but inadvertently the twins' father now knew ahead of the children that Jamie and I planned to marry one day.

Stevie telephoned the following morning demanding to speak with the twins on the matter. Thankfully both children were at the stables.

'I'm warning you now Cass, if you do anything to change *my* kids's family structure, you will bitterly live to regret it.'

'Don't you threaten me Stevie,' I warned. 'It's a pity you didn't think more about family structure when you were chasing other women and bonking for Britain.'

But he'd hung up.

'I think,' said Jamie during our usual late night telephone conversation, 'that it's now imperative we talk to all the children. The sooner the better.'

'Okay,' I anxiously twiddled a strand of hair.

'How about all of us having this weekend together – preferably at my place. I don't fancy Stevie bashing the door down and creating a scene if he sees my car on your drive overnight.'

'Can you fit us all in?' I asked tucking the cordless phone into my shoulder and letting my other hand have a twiddle too.

'No problem. Petra and Jonas both have pull-outs under their beds, so the girls can gossip all night and the boys can play computer games. You and I, of course, will be in my double bed.'

'Together,' I added, fingers twiddling fretfully.

'Together.'

'In front of the kids,' I pointed out, twiddling faster.

'In front of the kids. Don't worry so Cassie. Goodnight my love.'

'Goodnight.'

It took me several minutes to free my hair from the handset.

Chapter Sixteen

In due course my collection of Liv and Toby from the stables was timed to coincide with Jamie retrieving Petra and Jonas.

As the car bumped along the dirt track to the stables I caught sight of Jamie parked up ahead and getting out of his car. I tooted my horn and drew up alongside.

'Let's leave the kids for another ten minutes,' Jamie suggested as I locked up the car. 'Matt's asked us to join him for a quick drink.'

'Okay, that's nice.'

'You're even nicer,' he lowered his head and kissed my lips.

Naturally Morag was at the house. I left Matt and Jamie chatting on the terrace and sought her out.

'Have you moved in?' I grinned as she poured cold shandies for everybody.

'I'm still to'ing and fro'ing – but not for much longer. Can you keep a secret?' she glanced furtively about.

'Go on.'

She hastened over to the kitchen door and quietly closed it.

'I'm not meant to say anything yet Cass, but I can't help it. Guess what? Go on guess!'

'Gosh I don't know. You're up the duff?'

'Not yet but that's on the cards. Go on. One more guess!' she hugged herself in excited anticipation.

'I give up.'

'Matt's asked me to marry him,' she squeaked happily, 'and I've said yes!'

'Oh Morag, that's wonderful news!' I hugged her warmly, no easy task with two barrage balloons in the way. 'I just know you're both going to be deliriously happy together because you're so right for one another. But why all the secrecy?'

'Well it's only for a few more days, just until Matt has told all the children. He wants them to be the first to know.'

Ah yes. I could certainly identify with that. I held back from confiding my own news on the marital subject. I didn't want to eclipse her moment.

Livvy and Toby were most surprised when, later, we followed Jamie's car to his house rather than going home.

'What's occurring?' asked Livvy.

'Oh nothing much. Just a sleepover,' I announced airily. 'Jamie and I thought it would be rather fun.'

'But we haven't packed our stuff,' said Livvy.

'I popped a few things in an overnight bag earlier on. It's all in the boot.'

'Cool,' said Toby. 'So what time will you pick us up tomorrow?'

'Er, well actually I thought I'd join in. Grown ups like a bit of fun too you know,' I smiled.

'You're having a sleepover too?' Livvy frowned.

'Yes.'

'What – with Jamie?'

'With Jamie,' I nodded.

'But where will you sleep?' asked Toby.

Oh for goodness sake.

'W-e-ll, we'll sort that out when we get there.'

'Why don't you share Jamie's bed?' suggested Livvy.

'What an absolutely *brilliant* idea,' I exhaled with relief.

As I cut the engine on Jamie's driveway, Jonas leapt excitedly out of his father's car.

'Breaking news! We're having a sleepover – including my Dad and your Mum – but they'll have to squash up and share the same bed.'

Jamie had evidently phrased everything just so. Only Petra, lounging against the Rover's grubby wing, cast me a sly knowing look. I had the grace to blush.

Jamie grinned as I walked towards him.

'Mission One successfully accomplished,' he gave me a quick hug. 'Mission Two will follow tomorrow.'

'What's Mission Two?'

'Meeting my mother.'

Waking up beside Jamie the following morning and knowing our four children were about felt both strange but right. But there wasn't time to languish. Jamie's mother was due at midday.

Edna Mackerel was absolutely everything that I wasn't. Screamingly punctual, she arrived in a pristine Micra just as the big hand of the clock was edging past noon. As the engine died there was a brief pause before the driver's door swung open and a pair of well shod size threes alighted on the tarmac. The legs, still shapely and encased in silk stockings, were followed by a small woman with a strong jaw. As I monitored her progress from behind the violently twitching kitchen curtains, it was glaringly obvious that this was a pensioner capable of leading armies.

As Jamie welcomed his mother in the hallway I hastily dropped the curtain and threw myself down on a seat at the kitchen table. Feeling an urge to do something with my hands, I grabbed one of the children's abandoned lemonades and fiddled with the glass. As Edna walked into the kitchen I leapt to my feet and stuck a hand out in welcome, promptly knocking the lemonade over.

'Oh bugger,' I greeted.

'Leave that darling,' Jamie instantly took control with a wet J-cloth. 'I'll clear up while you and Mum get acquainted.'

Gazing into Edna's piercing blue eyes I perceived the sort of shrewd intelligence only the very gifted are born with. As we shook hands I felt as if I were standing before a pint sized female version of Arnie from The Terminator. I just *knew* Edna was scanning, assessing and digesting my every pore.

Jamie busied himself cooking Sunday lunch leaving me badly parodying his efficiency. I messed about with napkins, laid and re-laid the table, moving cutlery about unnecessarily. Not that Jamie was the next Gordon Ramsay or anything. Far from it. A bog standard chicken had been placed in a roasting tray surrounded by supermarket prepared roasties, parsnips and Yorkshire puds, and the steamer was loaded up with a mixture of frozen veg. He was almost a kindred spirit to my own easy-does-it cuisine, although my expertise was more akin to slaving over a hot tin opener and bunging things in the microwave.

I instinctively knew that Edna Mackerel had never resorted to convenience foods in her entire life. I surreptitiously studied her throughout the afternoon, collating my own data bank of information.

Edna had been tragically widowed in her early thirties but, whilst privately devastated, had refused to wear a public mantle of grief and gone on to magnificently raise three small children single-handedly, run a home and hold down a busy job as a highly reputable seamstress. As if that wasn't enough to be getting on with, she'd also grown fruit and veg in the family's manicured garden, baked her own meat pies and apple puddings and set about gaining a thorough knowledge in DIY.

With a mixture of admiration and horror I listened to fondly regurgitated tales of knocking up desks for homework and even wiring light fittings. I could barely change a light bulb, never mind a light fitting. And my prowess in the needlework stakes was limited to school cross-stitch which had, in latter years, been reluctantly re-employed for stitching name tags in school garments.

When Edna eventually declared it was time to be off she hugged her grandchildren tightly and even swept Livvy and Toby into a warm embrace. Jamie towered over her as he bent down to kiss her floury cheek. Suddenly it was my turn to say farewell, but just as I stepped forward her piercing blue eyes locked on mine.

'Cassandra dear, do please keep me company while I walk to my car.'

'Certainly,' I warbled. Jamie winked and gave me a little prod in the back.

Edna pressed a button on her key fob and the central locking sprang into life.

'Let us sit inside for a moment dear.'

'Sure.'

Reluctantly I opened the passenger door and slid in beside her.

'Now then Cassandra.' The blue headlamps swivelled in my direction. 'We are both grown women and I don't bandy words, so you must forgive me for coming straight to the point. What exactly are your intentions with my son?'

'M–my intentions?'

Gosh, she wasn't telling porkies about being direct.

I cleared my throat. 'Er hum. Well now. I love him,' I croaked.

No response.

'I really *really* love him.'

Oh Lord. Edna could either accept me or reject me. I rallied.

'You're probably thinking that I've known your son for all of five minutes, but in fact it is much longer than that. At least ten minutes actually…ah ha ha ha!'

She didn't laugh back.

'Er hum hum. Well basically we've known each other for much longer than we have actually, um, you know, *known* each other. What I mean is, we met each other *ages* ago – well earlier this year actually not years and years ago – and recently, *ree*-cent-ly we started dating. But–'

God this was excruciating and I seemed to be making a total pig's ear of it. Edna had asked a direct question. Why, for just once in my life could I not respond likewise? I ran a hand through my hair.

'Look Edna, in a cack-handed way what I'm trying to say is that I feel like I've known your son forever. And I must confess I certainly want to be with him forever.' For a moment I studied my hands fluttering about in my lap. 'What more can I say?'

There was an interminable pause.

'There is nothing more you can say dear,' she eventually answered. 'Like me, Jamie was tragically widowed young in life through dreadful and unexpected circumstances. I was aghast that history should so cruelly repeat itself. Jamie went to hell and back. The children were bereft without their mother. Slowly and painfully they travelled the road of devastation and grief until a form of healing eventually took place. Of course Jamie has kept female company from time to time – I know that. But I have never been privy to meeting any of his lady friends Cassandra. Not one. Until now. Clearly you are exceptionally special to him. If I may be so pertinent, I would hazard a guess that one day you might be my daughter-in-law?'

'I certainly hope so Edna.'

'You have my blessing.'

Her words exploded into my brain. I had her blessing! Shakily I exhaled. Edna patted my hand and started the engine. The meeting was over.

As I walked slowly back to the house, I tried to see things from Edna's perspective. Yes, things were happening quickly. The last few weeks had been akin to hurtling through life as if on a roller-coaster. In the space of just a few weeks I had fallen madly in love. And it must be a mad love too. Of course Edna should rightly scrutinise me and question my intentions. The ink was barely dry on the Nisi of my previous marriage. I had appeared from nowhere with two children in tow, apparently poised on the threshold of uniting two fractured family units into a single one.

I nibbled my lip. I had been so recently caught up in keeping Livvy and Toby shielded from Stevie's ranting threats of bitterness and recriminations, I hadn't stopped to think about the impact on them if things went pear-shaped with Jamie at some point. I gulped. What if our relationship later floundered? The twins had already suffered the break up of their parents' marriage. What if they had to suffer the break up of a second relationship? And what about Petra and Jonas? They'd already lost their natural mother. What if the step-mother turned out to be a hopeless case and got the sack?

Calm down Cass, calm down.

Changing the perspective again, I tried evaluating the situation through Jamie's eyes. Widowed, his children left motherless, everybody grieving. I realised that having suffered such dreadful tragedy, he wouldn't risk playing with the emotions of his children if he wasn't absolutely sure about us.

Finally I attempted looking at things through my ex-husband's eyes. Was he fearful of competing with another man for the affection of his own children? I knew the twins loved their father unconditionally and that nobody could replace him. I'd just have to underline that fact to Stevie. He'd freely displayed his own love life – a pretty fickle one at that – in front of the children. Surely he could now be generous of spirit for their sake if not mine?

At teatime Jamie conjured up some pizzas from the deep freeze. After the earlier formal dinner with Edna present, supper was a laid back affair with fingers rather than knives and forks. As I fielded requests for squash and cola, he gave my bottom a discreet pinch before turning to address all the children.

'Isn't it nice all of us being together like this?'

On account of all four mouths being crammed with pizza, they were only able to nod, albeit enthusiastically.

'And I think it would be even nicer if we could do this all the time,' Jamie casually sliced up an enormous Hawaiian, dropping bits of pineapple over the table as he served. 'How about we buy one big house and all live together?'

Four rotating jaws froze. Toby was the first to recover.

'You mean,' he swallowed frantically, 'live together as in all under the same roof?'

'That's it!' Jamie nodded while I held my breath.

'We'd need an awfully big house Dad,' Jonas frowned.

'Yep, it would have to be a bit of a whopper.'

'What do you think Mum?' asked Livvy.

'Well it sounds like a lovely proposition to me,' I responded carefully, 'but I think I'd prefer to know what you kids feel about the suggestion.'

'I love the idea,' Petra declared firmly. 'Livvy would be like the sister I've always wanted. Not so sure about having another brother though Tobes,' she laughed good-naturedly.

'S'okay,' Jonas mumbled through his pizza. 'I'm happy to exchange Livvy for Toby. At least he doesn't spend hours gibbering rubbish about soppy lip gloss and whether to crimp his hair or braid it.'

'Does that mean we're all in agreement?' Jamie's eyes were

dancing with merriment. Everyone looked at everybody for affirmation and suddenly we were all leaning over the half-eaten pizzas cheering and hugging.

'This definitely calls for a celebration,' Jamie's face was flushed with happiness. 'Ribena all round?'

Needless to say the sleepover extended into a second night and all the children wanted to talk about was shopping for a new family home.

Having felt faintly miffed about Edna's capabilities, the following morning I decided that anything she could do I could at least attempt to do too. I handed out breakfast plates loaded with bacon, sausage, egg, baked beans and toast – a total turnaround to the usual mundane cocoa pops and cereal bars.

'What a fabulous feast Cassie,' said Jamie as my hands, encased in oven gloves, set a heaped plate before him. 'Mm, smells heavenly. I'll have to marry you.'

Once again there was a frozen pause as four pairs of eyes swivelled from Jamie to me.

'Dad, are you seriously proposing to Cass?' asked Petra, 'because if you are, I don't think much of it.'

My heart began to thump uncomfortably. Oh God. I knew things had been too good to be true. This was it. The first sign of the dream beginning to crumble. Jamie and I exchanged fleeting glances before Petra continued disdainfully.

'You're meant to go down on one knee.'

Jamie immediately got up from the table and went down on one knee – right in the middle of the kitchen surrounded by four boggle eyed children and a greasy mountain of breakfast paraphernalia.

'Darling Cassie,' Jamie grabbed my oven mitt. 'Will you marry me?'

'Yes,' I squeaked.

Livvy and Petra looked at each other in stunned amazement before erupting into each others arms.

'We're getting married,' shrieked Livvy deliriously.

'Blimey, we really are going to be brothers,' said an incredulous Toby to Jonas.

Before Jamie went off to work he drew me close and held me tight.

'I'll leave you to ferry the kids to the stables when they're washed and dressed. Any problems Cassie, just give Mum a ring. Her number is on the corkboard. She'll pick the kids up from the stables later this afternoon and I'll have a one-to-one with her this evening.'

'Okie-dokie,' I grinned and kissed my future husband goodbye. Mm. He looked so handsome in that dark tailored cloth. There was something about a uniform on a chap that oozed authority and alpha maleness. There were distinct possibilities for that attire, particularly those shiny handcuffs.

I smirked and floated off to the kitchen. Whoever coined the phrase 'walking on air' knew their stuff all right. My body might be standing over the kitchen sink with my rubber gloves whisking about in soap suds, but a part of me had risen right up over the draining board, wafted through the open window and even now was sailing towards those fluffy clouds surrounded by silver linings.

'Mum?' Toby fog-horned down the stairs, shattering the moment. 'I think I've blocked Jamie's loo.'

I sighed ruefully. There was nothing like one of my son's bowel motions to bring the real world back into focus.

Once all the children had been deposited at the stables, I caught up with Nell. As we sat in her kitchen nursing our coffees, I brought her up to date on Jamie's kitchen proposal.

'Good heavens Cass, you certainly don't let the grass grow under your feet. Are you sure you're not,' she hesitated, 'being a touch impetuous? After all it's only eight months since you booted out Husband Number One and already Husband Number Two is on the scene,' she gave me a kind look. 'Is it possible you could be rebounding?'

'I know on the surface it would appear so. But don't forget I went out with Jed a couple of times. Then I had a disastrous fling with Euan. If ever there had been a rebound situation then surely that was it. And let's not forget that incredible blind date you yourself engineered.'

'Clive was a sweetie,' she said defensively.

'He was pompous, arrogant and egotistical. Not to mention camp. Privately I would question which way he swings.'

'He's straight,' Nell sniffed.

'I wouldn't bet on it.'

'Well I think he's utterly divine and–'

'And then,' I cut across her, 'let's not forget Matt Harding was also considered for a little while. He'd certainly been eager and willing until I bailed out at crunch time.'

'More fool you.'

'I'm just not into casual sex.'

'More fool you,' Nell repeated.

'Are you deliberately trying to wind me up?'

'No,' Nell feigned innocence. 'Didn't you also have a blind date with a fascinating octogenarian?'

'You *are* trying to wind me up,' I scowled.

Nell grinned. 'Tell me again what he was like.'

'A poor chap clutching a pension book in one hand and the dregs of faded youth in the other.' I arched an eyebrow at Nell. 'Sorry, what was that you were saying about rebounding?'

'Okay, point taken. Don't be so tetchy.'

'I won't be if you open another packet of Hob Nobs.'

That evening Jamie telephoned for our goodnight pillow talk ritual. I mentally heaved a sigh of relief when he relayed that Edna had not been remotely surprised to hear about her son's long term plans for a married future. She had assured Jamie she was more than happy to relinquish the daily input with his home and children once we were all living together. Clearly she was anxious not to be seen as interfering.

'You must assure Edna that she can still be involved. I would hate her to think she's not wanted,' I told Jamie. 'I know! Why doesn't she live with us?'

'Oh Cassie, no, I don't think so. Firstly, we'll be newlyweds and everybody will be adjusting to the new set up. It wouldn't be a wise to have a mother-in-law permanently on the scene. Secondly, quite apart from anything else, Mum is fiercely independent. She wouldn't *want* to live with us.'

'Well so long as she doesn't think I don't want her around.'

It was important to maintain good links with the mother-in-law, especially one as highly qualified as Edna. Who else could knock up a handy book case in between making half a dozen steak and kidney pies for the deep freeze? The fact that Edna's practical abilities considerably eclipsed my own was neither here nor there. Good heavens no!

And, in retrospect, Jamie was right. If Edna lived with us I'd probably have daily panic attacks and end up a hyperventilating lunatic. Certainly my days of serving up beans on toast would be numbered.

Morag telephoned mid-week.

'Come over for supper this evening with Jamie,' she invited. 'Bring all the kids too.'

Naturally Matt and Morag were thrilled to hear that, one day, wedding bells would ring for us too.

'Have you seen this?' Morag proudly thrust her left hand under our noses. On her third finger glittered a serious diamond.

'Ooh very nice Miss McDermott, very nice indeed,' I complimented peering at the beautiful stone.

'Where's yours?' she asked peering at my bare fingers.

'Gosh, well, I'm not sure,' I spluttered with embarrassment.

Jamie hadn't mentioned anything about an engagement ring. My general presumption had been that a policeman's pay packet was rather thin for diamonds when bricks and mortar were more pressing.

'We haven't had a chance to get around to it,' Jamie picked up the conversation. 'But we will.'

My heart did a few skippy beats. Oh goodie. I didn't want to be materialistic but a twinkly stone or three were most agreeably my sort of thing.

'Cass,' Morag said, suddenly shy, 'over the last few months

you've been a wonderful friend to me and I've come to regard you as the sister I never had.'

'That's a lovely thing to say,' I smiled at her warmly and squeezed her hand.

'So I'm very much hoping you will agree to be my Maid of Honour?'

'Oh my goodness, yes please!' I clapped my hands with delight. Things were seriously looking up – the promise of both a rock and a frock!

'And you're the best man,' Matt nodded at Jamie, 'so you'd better get yourselves a couple of tickets to the Bahamas.'

'Why?' I asked.

'Because that's where Morag and I are planning on getting hitched.'

'Fantastic,' I squeaked, absolutely horrified. No way could Jamie and I afford an engagement ring *and* a trip to the Caribbean.

'Darling,' I broached the subject tentatively on the drive home, 'I don't see how we can possibly muster up the funds to attend a wedding in the Bahamas or an engagement ring when we're planning on buying a home altogether.'

Jamie gave me a sideways look and squeezed my thigh with his free hand. Was it my imagination or did he look faintly amused.

'Fancy doing a bit of shopping next weekend?'

'Well, okay, what do you want to buy?'

'Ooh let me see now,' he pretended to ponder, 'what about a diamond ring for starters?'

A couple of days later Morag telephoned me with a hot property tip. One of her legal cronies wished to downsize the family home. It had six bedrooms.

'You must go and see it,' Morag urged. 'It's in Lavender Hill.'

'Lavender Hill?' I gasped. 'We can't possibly afford a property in that area.'

'Well there's no harm in having a nosy-parker Cass. I've been inside and it's a stunner.'

'How much is your friend selling for?'

Morag mentioned a figure so colossal my eyes watered.

'The house is called Lilac Lodge and actually overlooks Lavender Common – spectacular outlook but on a private unmade road. There are a few potholes here and there but that's all part of the charm.'

When I relayed Morag's tip-off about Lilac Lodge to Jamie he was delighted.

'But that's great news!' he enthused. 'Why don't you check it out tomorrow?'

'Don't you want to know the price first?'

'Cassie just go and give it an initial once over. You might hate it.'

'And if I love it?'

'Then we'll view it together.'

'But what's the point when it's too pricey?'

'We'll negotiate.'

In the end I did check it out of course and, as Lavender Hill was only a twenty-five minute walk away, I took Rocket for company. After all, I reasoned as I strode across Lavender Common, a woman with a dog on a leash would look completely natural to any Neighbourhood Watch vigilantes...whereas an individual walking backwards and forwards in front of a house could be misconstrued as casing the joint.

'Be a good girl for Mummy,' Nell instructed as she handed me Rocket's leash. For one ridiculous moment I thought she was talking to me. She playfully grabbed the setter's ears and waggled them backwards and forwards.

'Aw, you're such a cutie tootie boofley woofley-'

'I'd better get a move on Nell,' I gently prised my neighbour's fingers off Rocket's hearing apparatus.

We catapulted off, Rocket's nose instantly zig-zagging across the ground. Twenty minutes later, I puffed my way around the rugged green edge of the Common and Lilac Lodge curled into view.

The house was one of six imposing red-bricked Victorian properties, all standing behind their own individual gated systems. I noticed that four of the properties, including Lilac Lodge, had CCTV cameras discreetly tucked into nooks and niches. A natural screen of privacy was provided from enormous oak trees that hugged the Common's borders. The sprawling pile was, by any standards, pretty striking. As the name suggested, climbing vines of wisteria grew up from one side of the main portal and clambered along strategically placed wires. Large locks of mauve blooms tumbled around enormous sash windows which gazed out at the Common's stunning vista.

I breathed in deeply, closed my eyes and briefly permitted myself a secret day dream. Ah yes, there was our newly acquired family wagon – which looked a bit like a clapped out mini-bus, but never mind – bouncing along the rutted road. Now it was sweeping over the gravelled driveway and parking just…about…there, under those weeping willow fronds. And now the children, *our* children, were scrambling free of the vehicle to race each other to the front door, hair flying, broad grins on their faces as they shot indoors. Nice. Very nice. But there wasn't a chance of it happening – not with that price tag dangling off the terracotta chimney pot.

'So what did it look like?' Jamie later asked.

'Gorgeous.'

'Tell you what. How about you and I take a stroll over there together in the morning?'

'But what's the point?'

'I thought the idea was to buy a house together.'

'Of course, but preferably one that's affordable.'

'It's only window shopping. No harm in that.'

Oh well. I could do window shopping. Not a problem.

Chapter Seventeen

Three months later I was very much Lady of the Manor. Or rather Lady of Lilac Lodge. I ran a finger over the granite worktop of my incredibly tasteful bespoke kitchen, enjoying the sparkles that shot off my engagement ring as overhead halogen lights caught the diamond. Jamie had insisted on buying our wedding rings too.

'Nothing like forward planning,' was all he'd said on the subject as he later tucked them away in his underpants drawer.

The irascible Martin Henniker, who I *still* hadn't managed to shake off at Hemple Braithwaite, had taken one look at the diamond ring and curled his mouth into a mocking smile.

'Ah, I see you're betrothed Mrs Cherry. Congratulations. Quite an accomplishment to be engaged to Husband Number Two whilst still officially married to Husband Number One.'

Bastard.

But that had been prior to the divorce becoming Absolute.

Stevie hadn't been too thrilled about the house move or engagement. When the 'For Sale' board had gone up on the marital home, he had arrived on the doorstep one evening in high dudgeon.

'A quiet word if you don't mind,' he'd hissed barging straight past me.

'You can have several noisy ones if you like,' I'd quipped following him into the kitchen.

Stevie had leant against the kitchen worktop, feet planted wide, arms folded belligerently across his chest.

'What's with the sale board?'

Just at that moment the twins had burst in shrieking with delight upon hearing their father's voice. After initial hair ruffling and bear hugs, Stevie had suggested they go and have their showers.

'I need to talk to your Mum for a few minutes but I'll pop up in a bit to say goodnight.'

As soon as the twins had disappeared upstairs, Stevie had slumped down on a stool and stared at me abjectly.

'Well?'

'Well surely it's pretty obvious. The house is on the market.'

'And what about me eh?' he'd snarled, jabbing a finger at his chest. 'Have you thought about that? I've just bought a fucking house to be near my kids and suddenly you're upping and leaving.'

'Look Stevie, you knew this was on the cards. And we're not going far. Jamie and I talked to you about-'

'Don't you mention that berk's name to me! You're not thinking straight – rushing into the arms of some goon you've known all of two minutes-'

He'd abruptly halted his tirade upon catching sight of the gleaming engagement ring.

'You're *marrying* him?'

'Well not just yet obviously but-'

'You're married to me!'

'Stevie, this is absolutely ridiculous. Jamie and I talked to you about our plans, remember? You were with Simone.'

'Who?'

'The marine biologist lady.'

'Oh her. I'm seeing someone else now.'

'For goodness sake!'

'Cass, don't marry him. Please. No other woman truly matters to me – not like you – they don't compare. I still love you! We can put this behind us and start again. I'll have some counselling. Check into one of those sex clinics like Michael Douglas did. He was a bit of a lad wasn't he? But he's all sorted out now, married to the lovely Catherine Zeta-Jones and had some babies. We could do that Cass. Have another child. You'd like that wouldn't you, hm?'

'Stevie we're practically divorced. You spent almost the entirety of our marriage hopping from one woman's bed to another. That's not love. You don't constantly hurt somebody over and over again if you love them. What you did was repeatedly the ultimate betrayal. And yes, I might have known Jamie for a short period of time, but by golly I don't need a ruler to measure the depth of his love. He cherishes me in a way you couldn't begin to comprehend.'

'Don't do it Cass. And please don't move.'

'We're only going a couple of miles away. Nothing will change. The children will still see you just as they do now.'

Toby had re-appeared, hair damp from the shower. His impromptu diversion had let me slip away. I'd quietly locked myself in the bathroom and had a long hot soak. When I'd come out, Stevie had gone.

Days later the Absolute had arrived through the post. I'd stared at the innocuous piece of paper in detached fascination. It was over. I was officially divorced. Once again Stevie had turned up on my doorstep, but this time meek and conciliatory and clutching a bottle of chilled Chablis.

'Peace offering?'

'Okay. Fancy sharing it?' Just to show I could be magnanimous too.

The next hour or so had been a little surreal. Together we had sat at what had once been *our* kitchen table in *our* family home, peeling away the layers of a past which had been our family life together. And as we'd sat together, we'd reminisced about the years we had collectively shared. The good times. And the bad. But no blame. Which one of us had been culpable of what was no longer relevant. As Stevie shared the last of the wine between our glasses, we put the lid on long-ago and instead toasted the future.

'Cass, I wish you all the luck in the world. I truly mean that. Your Jamie isn't a bad guy, I know that really. I'm sure he'll make you extremely happy and no doubt be a good step-father to our kids, just as you'll be a great step-mum to his two.'

I'd looked at this man, the father of my children, now ex-husband. Incredibly we'd found ourselves smiling at each other with genuine warmth.

I think what we achieved in that moment was called *closure*.

Sighing contentedly I rummaged around in the huge American fridge and pulled out a couple of vast shepherds pies that my future mother-in-law had made. Edna had been staying with us in the few days since moving into Lilac Lodge on the grounds of 'helping'. I twiddled some knobs on the kitchen range and shoved the trays inside. I knew Edna was fiercely independent and didn't want to live with us. Despite that, she currently showed no signs of going home.

I sensed that Jamie was anxious for his mother and I to bond, but Edna's presence petrified me because she was so damn good at everything. She was either whisking up delicious home cooking, weeding umpteen flowerbeds, plumbing in the new washing machine or assisting Petra with trigonometry homework. Super Gran. Even now she was probably hastening into a telephone box and twirling around, emerging seconds later with a pair of red pants over her support tights. Why did I always get that sinking feeling when I thought of my future mother-in-law?

The telephone rang. I banged the range door shut and picked up the receiver.

'Hello?'

I was met with a lengthy wall of silence until the connection clicked off. Frowning, I replaced the receiver. There had been several dropped phone calls since moving into the new house and they were starting to rattle me. It touched a nerve and reminded me of the past – like whenever Stevie had been having a fling.

Outside Jamie was barrowing early November leaf fall down to the compost heap. I smiled at his retreating broad shoulders. My man was everything Stevie wasn't. He'd nurtured my shattered trust and bolstered the shaky self-esteem. Jamie treated me like priceless porcelain – and I loved it.

I moved to the window and watched my fiancé tip leaves from the barrow. He shook it a few times before trundling back towards me.

'Coffee?' I mouthed when he was close enough to lip read.

He smiled and gave the thumbs up.

I took the lid off the kettle and ran it under the tap. The other wonderful thing about Jamie was that he was financially solid – unlike Stevie who'd periodically nagged me to release my money bond so he could help spend it.

'We could put the money towards a bigger house,' he'd once suggested.

'But I like living here,' I'd countered.

'Well let's go on a few Caribbean holidays.'

'What's wrong with Majorca?'

'Do you know Cass, sometimes you are such a boring old fart. You want to live a little – you could drop down dead tomorrow.'

'Gee thanks.'

'I'm just hypothesising. After all, you can't spend money *up there*.'

Every spare penny Stevie had earned had been frittered away on gadgets and boys' toys without much consideration for the rest of the family.

Thank God Jamie was different. When Philly had died so tragically, he had collected a substantial sum of money on life insurance. When he'd emotionally recovered enough to deal with monetary matters, Jamie had taken financial advice. A number of highly successful investments had been made with lucrative returns. That money, together with my not inconsiderable bond, had resulted in us being able to buy Lilac Lodge outright. The financial future was looking even rosier because Jamie had New Year plans to go into partnership with an ex-officer offering specialist security consultancy to major City banks.

'If this comes to fruition Cassie,' Jamie had said only last night, 'and I'm pretty sure it will, then we'll be living like pigs in clover.'

Well I was all for that. The more clover the better.

The phone rang again. I plugged the kettle in and hastened to the handset.

'Hello?'

Another wall of silence.

'Who is this?' I demanded.

The response was whispered so softly that at first I wasn't sure I'd heard correctly.

'*Bitch.*'

My jaw dropped. 'Wha-?'

But I was talking to nobody. The line had gone dead.

'Who was that Cassie?' asked Jamie coming in through the back door. Cold air from the updraft blasted my bare arms making the tiny hairs stand up.

'It was that silent caller again. I've had two in the last ten minutes.'

Jamie frowned. 'They're getting to be a bit of a nuisance.'

'The person spoke this time.'

'Oh?'

'She called me a bitch.'

'She?'

'Yes, it was a woman.'

I felt thoroughly upset. Stevie's teenaged girlfriend had come at me all emotional guns blazing earlier in the year. Was it her calling me? But surely not. She knew I couldn't care less about Stevie any more. So if it wasn't somebody to do with Stevie, was it perhaps somebody to do with Jamie? And, if so, whom?

'Why is a woman ringing this house and why is she calling me a bitch?' I asked shrilly.

'Steady darling,' Jamie put his arms around me. 'If the calls are getting distressing then it might be best to change our telephone number. I'll sort it out,' he dropped a kiss on my forehead. 'Meanwhile something smells good,' Jamie rubbed his hands together in anticipation. 'One of mum's shepherd pies eh?'

'Yes. Good old Edna,' I smiled gamely. 'After dinner I thought I'd pop over to Nell's for a catch up. Is that okay?'

'Of course it is. How is she?'

'Well okay on the surface but,' I hesitated searching for words best to describe my old neighbour's current frame of mind, 'she's just not the same since that miscarriage business.'

'In what way?'

'Well for starters she's bonkers about that loopy red setter of hers.'

'Ah yes. Raucous Rocket.'

'The very one and same. And to be perfectly honest I'm wondering if she and Ben are going through a rocky patch.'

'No way,' Jamie pooh-poohed. 'Ben adores Nell.'

'Yes I'm sure he does. But I'm not so sure Nell adores Ben anymore.'

A few hours later I turned into my old cul-de-sac, bumping slowly over the sleeping policemen whilst looking for somewhere to park. The road was full of stationary vehicles at this time of night. Reaching the end, I negotiated an awkward five point turn before driving back towards Nell's house. Oh good. It appeared she had some extra space on her driveway after all. Grinding the gear into reverse, I shot backwards straight into a parked car.

'Bloody hell,' I screeched as I lurched towards the windscreen and then back into my seat. 'What was that?'

I appeared to have driven into a visitor's dark motor that had been invisible in the blackness of night.

Gnashing my teeth in fury, I slipped out of the car intent on a discreet inspection. There wasn't a blemish on either vehicle. Thank God for small mercies. Suddenly a man shot out of Nell's house, arms waving like windmills.

'Hey you!' he yelled. 'What have you done to my car?'

'It's okay. There's no damage.'

The man fussed about, peering intently at an area over the front bumper, examining the chrome, standing back and then immediately leaping forward again to rub an imaginary scuff from the nearside headlight with the sleeve of his cassock. I did a double take. What I'd originally thought to be a long black overcoat was indeed a cassock and – yes – around his neck was a Roman collar. He seemed horribly familiar. My brain whirred backwards through memory cells, defining data. Vicar. Quite a few months ago. Matchmaking attempt. Self-righteous prat. Clive! Oh hell.

I had an inkling that I'd insulted Clive regarding the bible and compared Jesus to a magician. Had it been Paul Daniels? I struggled to remember. Had I, perchance, suggested that the Son of God wore a hairpiece and was married to Debbie McGee?

Clive straightened up. 'Ah, it's you.' He looked at me with disdain. 'I presume you are over the limit.'

'Excuse me?' I sucked my breath in, outraged.

'I seem to remember you being partial to excessive consumption of alcohol. No doubt you over-indulged earlier this evening and now your driving skills are impaired. Please furnish me with your insurance details.'

'But there's not a mark on either vehicle!'

'Appearances can be deceptive,' Clive narrowed his eyes. 'God works in strange ways. He tests things. Can you guarantee that when I drive off the suspension won't collapse as a direct result of your car's impact?'

'Don't be ridiculous,' I snorted.

'My vehicle is of paramount importance,' Clive's chest swelled. 'How else am I to get out and about, spread the Word and visit my people?'

'Oh I do beg your pardon. I didn't realise I'd reversed into the Pope Mobile.'

Nell suddenly appeared on her doorstep. 'Coo-ee. Is everything all right?'

'No it's not,' snapped Clive. 'This woman is a drunk driver and I'm calling the police.'

'Surely there's no need for that?' Nell looked anxious. Wrapping her cardigan about her, she came over and began inspecting both cars.

Clive whipped out a mobile phone from the depths of his cassock.

'Well if you're going to call the police then I will too!' I trilled rooting around in my handbag. Viciously I punched out our home number.

'Why don't we all go inside and have a nice cup of coffee and discuss this like sensible adults?' Nell reasoned.

The line connected and started to ring. 'Where's Ben?' I hissed in Nell's ear. 'Can't you get him to sort this fruitcake out?'

'He's not here,' Nell whispered back. 'He's at the pub. He's not Clive's greatest fan these days.'

'I'm not surprised.' I rolled my eyes. I could hear Clive talking urgently into his mobile demanding a posse of police to come to his assistance *right now*.

'Hello?' I heard Jamie's familiar voice.

'Oh thank God! Darling, please can you drive to Nell's as soon as possible. I'm about to be arrested for drink driving.'

'Cassie what on earth are you talking about?'

'Just get here quick,' I urged as a panda car glided into the cul-de-sac, blue light flashing ominously. I snapped the handset shut as the driver's door opened. And out got Selina.

Her eyes widened slightly when she saw me and then her mouth twisted into a grim smile.

'Well look what we've got here,' she mocked. 'If you're not causing chaos on ski slopes then apparently you're causing chaos on driveways.'

'How dare you!'

'Oh I dare Mrs Cherry because I'm a police officer. And I'm on the right side of the law,' she got out a notebook and pen, 'whereas you are on the wrong side. Okay. Let's start off with you Sir. Name?'

Selina turned to Clive leaving me mouthing like an indignant goldfish. What a bloody bitch! Just at that moment another car swung into the cul-de-sac. I swooned with relief as Jamie got out.

'Hello Nell,' Jamie strode up the driveway, 'Cassie what the devil is going on here?'

Selina swung round to face Jamie. 'Hello lover boy.'

Lover boy?

'Selina,' Jamie nodded. He looked very guarded.

Clive straightened up. 'Are you a policeman too?'

'Yes, albeit an off duty one.'

'You've come as back up!' Clive's eyes lit up as he smiled adoringly at Jamie.

'It's all just a silly misunderstanding,' Nell chimed in.

Five minutes later one disgruntled vicar had been reassured and soothed.

'Thank you so much Officer for explaining things to me,' he gushed, hands fluttering about in a camp fashion.

Selina was far from happy and wanted to throw the book at both Clive and me for wasting police time.

'I'll talk to you in the morning – *darling*,' she hissed at Jamie before stomping off down the driveway.

'Jeez Cassie,' Jamie sighed when Clive had finally driven off. 'How do you do it?'

'Thank you so much for your support,' I snapped. 'I've had a lunatic vicar harassing me and on top of all that your charmless ex-girlfriend to contend with.'

I rounded on Nell. 'And what was that moron doing here in the first place?'

'He came to talk to me about baptism.'

'Well couldn't you have popped along to his rectory to discuss Dylan being christened?'

'Oh it's not for Dylan,' Nell smiled beatifically. 'It's for Rocket.'

'Your dog?' asked Jamie in surprise.

'Yes! Clive is one of those trendy vicars who consider pets to be proper family members. He recently started up a funeral service and pet cemetery. Now he's thinking of introducing a baptism service. Rocket is a pilot scheme.'

Jamie scratched his forehead. 'You mean Clive is going to splash water on Rocket's muzzle and absolve her from chasing next door's cat and failing to come to heel?'

'Well there's a bit more to it than that, but you're on the right track.'

'I see,' said Jamie. 'Well girls, if you don't require me any longer I'll be getting back and helping Mum.'

'Helping?' I asked. 'What's Edna doing that she needs help with?'

'Oh nothing much really. She's jig-sawing a horse shaped corkboard for the girls to hang their rosettes and pony stuff on. See you later.' Jamie planted a kiss on my rigid cheek.

'Great,' I hissed after my fiancé's departing back. 'Just great.'

'You are so lucky having a future mother-in-law like Edna.'

'I must remember that the next time I feel like Edna has totally taken over my home, my fiancé, our children and our lives.' I followed Nell down her hallway into the kitchen.

'Oh Cass don't be like that. Come on, park your bottom and calm down. I'll put the kettle on. Here, have one of these too,' Nell put a plate of gingerbread men on the table. 'Who was the sultry female cop who seemed to know you?'

'You've met her before.'

Nell looked at me blankly. 'Really?'

'Yes, remember when we were uproariously drunk at your mate's fortieth birthday bash several months ago? Selina was in the police car with Jamie when he took us home.'

'I thought she looked familiar.'

'She's also Jamie's ex-girlfriend,' I snarled biting the head off a gingerbread man.

'Oh.'

'Yes. Oh.'

'Well don't let her bug you. You're tonnes prettier than her,' Nell said loyally. 'Now let's talk about Clive. Don't you think he's very distinguished looking?'

'Guess what?' said Jamie the following evening as I cleared the dinner table. 'One of my colleagues is having a house warming bash in a couple of weeks. We're invited.'

'Ooh a party,' I smiled happily whilst scraping leftovers into the bin, 'I'll have to buy a new dress!'

'It will probably be more of a jeans and T-shirt thing in all honesty. I must say, all the lads are dying to meet you.'

I suddenly froze mid-scrape. As a fellow colleague, Selina might be on the guest list. I was still smarting from our impromptu meeting yesterday, not to mention the 'lover boy' remark.

'What's with the sudden glum face?' Jamie asked.

'Oh you know,' I shrugged and resumed the plate scraping, 'this and that. My period's late and I seem to feel constantly worn out.'

'Come here,' Jamie took the plate off me before wrapping me in his arms. 'Of course you're tired Cassie. It's only to be expected. After all, there's so much happening at the moment.'

'Such as?'

'Well think about it. This year alone you've divorced, returned to work, met me, sold your home, moved house, committed to a large ready-made family and now we're planning a wedding.'

'Are we?'

'Are we what?'

'You said we're planning a wedding. Are we?'

Was it my imagination or did Jamie suddenly look shifty?

'Well, figuratively speaking. I mean, as soon as we've settled into Lilac Lodge properly, then yes, definitely. It would be nice to know our wedding is the next thing on the agenda. And of course we have Morag's and Matt's nuptials coming up. Which reminds me, they want us to have a get together this weekend – social and pleasure – but predominantly to discuss a date, flights and so forth.'

'What are we doing about the kids?' I could feel my stress levels soaring. 'It isn't feasible to take them to the Bahamas with us.'

'No, probably not. We'll sort that side of things out in due course.'

As Saturday night dawned, we left Edna – who still showed no signs of going home – with the four children and drove to Matt's. Morag had now fully moved in and rented out her own place.

'Fantastic to see you both,' she trilled undulating over, her bosom reaching us several seconds before the rest of her caught up. 'Mwah, mwah,' she kissed the air between us just as Matt appeared from the kitchen where the most delicious aroma of garlic and herbs pervaded.

'Cassie! Mac! Come in – grub's almost ready,' greeted Matt handing us both a brimming glass. 'Get your tastebuds around this full bodied red. It's almost as cheeky as my full bodied blonde,' Matt winked at Morag who immediately smouldered and blew her fiancé a kiss. Jamie gave me a sidelong grin.

'Stand back,' he murmured, 'Morag's pants are possibly about to detonate. Cheers Matt,' Jamie turned and took his glass of wine. 'Here's to our future bride and groom!'

We all then knuckled down to the serious task of working our way through Matt's scrumptious Spaghetti Bolognese. Eventually the topic turned to the forthcoming nuptials. Morag was absolutely determined everything was to be different this time around, not just for her but Matt too.

'This marriage is for keeps. Forever and ever. A marriage made in heaven and betrothed in paradise.' She dropped a brochure of the Bahamas on the table. 'This is a complete wedding package and everything is so easy. All we need to do is agree a mutually convenient date. How about we fly out on the twenty-ninth of December with the marriage taking place on the thirty-first?'

'Oh!' I exclaimed, 'that's my fortieth birthday.'

'Perfect. So we can also celebrate the Big Four Oh and New Year's Eve at the same time,' Morag clapped her hands delightedly. 'Now then Cass, I would like you to look bridal rather than bridesmaid.'

'Isn't that inappropriate?' I protested. 'Two of us dressed in white?'

'I thought cream with gold overtones actually, what with us both being blonde. I've told you before, this wedding is going to be different. No peach chiffon. No flower girls. What do you think of this?' Morag shoved a thick magazine under my nose.

Haughty looking models posed in everything from tight corsets to floaty meringues, feathers and even rags. Very expensive rags needless to say as my eye caught upon the Designer's astronomical price tag. Ah, I see, there was a real diamond stitched onto each artfully frayed piece of fabric. Morag thumbed through the pages and stopped at a simple column dress, piped in gold. It was very Grecian and extremely elegant.

'That,' I salivated, 'is without a doubt the most fantastic, totally incredible-'

'Mm,' agreed Morag, 'and absolutely *you*. I thought this one here for me.' She pointed to another column dress with a variation to the neckline, the main body spattered with a clutch of gold sequin. It complimented my coveted dress perfectly.

'I'll set up a fitting date. Next Saturday okay? Boys, you're coming too – might as well get us all sorted out in one go.'

'Aye aye Sir,' Matt touched an imaginary forelock.

Jamie smiled. 'So that's that. I had no idea it was so easy to organise a wedding.'

'Surely you've missed something out!' I spluttered. Where was all the hype? The fuss? Arguments over a photographer? A chap with a video camera on his shoulder promising to get under everybody's feet? And could one even get a bouquet of roses in the Bahamas?

Morag waved the brochure at me. 'This is a complete package – everything is organised for you. All we have to do is fly there. Now then, who would like a deliciously gooey cream cake for dessert?'

'Not for me sweetheart,' Matt declined. 'In fact, if you don't mind girls, I'd like to take Mac down the yard. I've got a new horse I want to show off.'

'Fine by me,' Morag said as the men stood up to go. She went to the fridge and pulled out a laden plate.

'Ooh yummy,' my eyes travelled greedily over the high calorie goodies.

'Shall we have one, two or three?'

'Definitely three,' I giggled. 'Might as well totally pig out on the cream and risk cardiac arrest or Alzheimers.'

'Do you know,' said Morag taking a bite and looking thoughtful, 'there's more money spent today on silicon implants and Viagra than on Alzheimer's research.'

'That's disgraceful,' I crammed half a chocolate éclair in my mouth.

'Mm,' Morag agreed, hoovering up cream with her tongue. 'In twenty years time there'll probably be a geriatric population with large breasts and humungous erections but absolutely no recollection of what to do with either.'

The following morning, feeling terribly bloated, I stood on the bathroom scales and felt shockwaves course through my system. Half a stone heavier? Surely yesterday's cream cake binge could not have wrought such swift damage? Irritably I stepped off the scales. I'd have to go on a diet now. How tedious.

But despite existing on nothing but tinned salmon and mixed salad over the next few days, by the following weekend I'd only lost one pound in weight. And whilst this was a very encouraging start, the weight loss was not enough to alter my body shape as I stood in the wedding shop's dressing room stripped down to my pop socks.

'That looks fabulous,' Morag assured as the assistant shoe-horned me into the Grecian column dress.

'My tummy's sticking out.'

'You have plenty of time to lose a couple of pounds between now and New Year's Eve. Are you constipated?' she asked bossily.

'Morag!'

'I knew it. Here.' She rummaged through her jumbo handbag. 'Take this.'

'I'm *not* constipated,' I hissed waving away the proffered chocolate medicine.

'Marvellous stuff if you need to shift weight quickly.'

'Really?' I was suddenly interested. 'You've talked me into it.' I snatched the chocolate bar and shoved it in my mouth.

'Cass, you're not meant—'

'Mm. Mm. Not bad. Not as good as Cadbury's of course.' I nonetheless smacked my lips appreciatively. 'What else are you hiding in that portable suitcase of yours? Got any high fibre bran? I need to shift six pounds for a party tonight. I want to be draped on Jamie's arm looking thin and full of fragile beauty.'

'Er, I think what you've taken will do everything required.'

She wasn't joking.

Chapter Eighteen

By nine o'clock we were ready to go.

'Wow – love those jeans on you,' Jamie nodded approvingly.

'Do you think?' I tugged at the denim. 'They're a bit tight.'

'Well in that case they're hugging all the right places.'

Hugging was an understatement. I'd only managed to get into them by lying absolutely flat on the floor. I sighed. Only a very small sigh however – I didn't want the zip suddenly unravelling.

The party was in full throb when we arrived. The hosts, Hugo and Ginnie Maxted, were friendly and charming. Ginnie pressed an enormous glass of punch into my hand. One could *smell* the kick on it at ten paces. I sipped cautiously, anxious not to upset my battered entrails. Suddenly I caught sight of Selina on the other side of the room. Exactly on cue, her eyes swivelled and met my gaze.

She glared, open hostility marring her beautiful face. Unnerved I swigged the punch. To hell with it, there was no way I could get through tonight without a drop of Dutch Courage. The alcohol descended noisily through my guts, like washing-up water whooshing down the plughole. Somebody refilled my glass and I switched to autopilot, smiling and shaking hands as Jamie introduced me to colleagues and friends, moving around the room, another introduction, another drink, until the music's volume went up a notch and suddenly I was *getting on down*. The punch must have been excellent stuff because my innards went numb. Along with my lips, nose and tongue.

Much later I excused myself from conversation with Jamie and some florid faced colleagues and made my way unsteadily to the bathroom.

Zipping my jeans back up was a challenge. I hopped around the bathroom struggling valiantly until the wretched zipper finally knitted together. Turning to the washbasin, I pumped soap into my hands. All four of them. Peering fuzzily at my reflection in the mirror, I realised a touch of lipstick was required. Extracting the tube, I applied colour to my shifting lips. I snapped the lid back on the tube, squashing the lipstick in the process. Lurching out of the bathroom I nearly tripped over Selina.

'Cassandra isn't it?'

The chilly smile failed to reach her eyes. There was a short pause while my lips and tongue struggled to articulate a response.

'Yeth,' I stared at her defiantly.

'I hear you're engaged. To Jamie.'

'Yeth.'

'I hope he doesn't do to you the same thing that he did to me.'

I arched an eyebrow enquiringly. Any further attempt at speech was out of the question.

'So he's told you that you're the woman he wants to spend the rest of his life with, hm?' She smiled maliciously. 'That's exactly what he did with me. Told me he loved me, couldn't live without me, wanted to marry me – oh yes he did,' she assured as I shook my head disbelievingly. 'You're in for a nasty surprise, you mark my words,' she gave a tinkle of derisive laughter. 'I actually feel quite sorry for you Cassandra. I could say more, but this isn't the right place.'

I stared at her, horrified. As if on cue my zipper chose that precise moment to give out. It slithered down its metal track, exhausted from containing so much spare flesh for the last few hours. I stared at it sorrowfully. By the time I looked back up, Selina had turned on her heel and was heading back to the party.

'Are you okay darling?' asked Jamie over breakfast the following morning. 'You seem terribly subdued.'

'Oh, you know,' I shrugged listlessly, 'the morning after the night before.'

'But you did enjoy yourself didn't you? Ginnie thought you were terrific. She thought how very well suited we were.'

'Really? That was generous of her.'

'That's because it's true.'

'Is it?'

'Of course! Cassie, what's the matter?'

I licked my lips. 'When I came out of Ginnie's bathroom last night, Selina was waiting for me.'

'And?'

'She told me that you once proposed to her and then unceremoniously dumped her,' My lip wobbled dangerously, 'and that one day you'd do the same to me.'

'You don't honestly believe that load of poppycock do you?'

I hung my head as hot tears welled up. Jamie leant across the Cornflakes and grabbed my hand.

'Cassie, listen to me. After I lost Philly I never thought I'd fall in love again. Sure, I went out with a few women here and there. Selina was one of them. But they were no more than female company. Some were better company than others, but none of them made me feel–' Jamie paused struggling to find the right word, '*alive*. I thought I was some sort of emotional cripple with a heart of stone. And just when I least expected it, I *did* fall in love. Deeply. With you. Only ever you.'

I looked up at Jamie, my tears spilling over now and running in hot rivulets down my cheeks.

'I couldn't bear to lose you,' I wept wiping the backs of my hands across my face.

'And you're not going to. Whatever Selina said, it's simply sour grapes.'

I sniffed and stretched a damp hand down to stroke Wallace and Gromit, our recently acquired cats from a local Animal Shelter. They weaved around my crossed ankles under the breakfast table, looking hopeful that a saucer of milk might be in the offing.

'Tell you what,' Jamie winked, 'as all the kids are at the stables, why don't I whisk you back upstairs and show you exactly how much I love you.'

Oh Lord. I hastily stood up and started clearing the breakfast bowls. Now why did the thought of rumpy-pumpy suddenly leave me feeling totally exhausted? This wasn't good. Not good at all. There was a time – and not that long ago either – when I'd fizzed and sputtered all over the place. Jamie had only whispered my name and – *bam* – down I'd gone, legless with lust. Where had my libido gone? I gave a little yelp of worry.

Just at that moment there was the sound of a key turning in the front door.

'Damn,' muttered Jamie. 'Looks like Mum's back already.' He got up and stood behind me, wrapping his arms around my waist and whispering in my ear. 'You'll have to stay on ice until tonight my darling.'

Hell. Perhaps I could pop a couple of sleeping pills in his cocoa? Oh my God! What was I thinking of? Drugging my fiancé? What sort of woman was I to even consider such a thing?

I yelped again, this time in terror.

'Steady darling. Don't you worry – I won't let you down. You'll be begging me to stop.'

Yes, definitely sleeping pills. If not for him, then for me. Good idea. And if I made sure the light was out he might possibly mistake my inertia for languid compliance. Brilliant Cass. Just make sure you don't snore.

As luck would have it, our romantic evening tryst was scuppered when Petra let out a shriek of horror just before bedtime and confessed that she'd forgotten to do her weekend homework.

'Well it's too late to do it now,' said Jamie. 'In future young lady can you please get homework done on the Friday evening?'

'But what am I going to do?' wailed Petra. 'I'll get double detention. Please Dad, let me do it before I go to bed.'

'It will take too long.'

'Not if you help me,' Petra wheedled.

'Oh for goodness sake,' blustered Jamie. But I could see he was fighting a losing battle.

'Darling,' I caught his arm as he went off to Petra's bedroom, 'I'm feeling absolutely whacked. Do you mind if I have an early night?'

'Of course not,' Jamie dropped a kiss on my nose. 'You do look a bit peaky actually. I'll be up later.'

Sighing with relief, I kissed all the children goodnight before shutting myself in our bedroom.

But the following morning, far from feeling refreshed, I felt totally depleted of energy. Arriving at Hempel Braithwaite early, I decided to seek Morag out.

Shouldering her office door open, I instantly launched into a diatribe about my libido anxieties.

'Am I glad to see you,' I declared rolling my eyes dramatically. 'I've completely lost my sex drive – haven't had a bonk all weekend. What's wrong with me? And what am I going to do? Jamie likes to roger me senseless. You have no idea what he's like sometimes. It's as if he's one big sex-mad hormone, a permanently switched on pneumatic drill – *bbrrrrrrrrrrrr*,' I made my body go rigid and juddered up and down on the spot by way of demonstration.

Suddenly I registered Morag's frozen expression.

'What's the matter?'

Morag had opened her eyes very wide and was clearly trying to convey a silent message. She gave an almost imperceptible nod in the direction behind me. My eyes widened back at her. She gave a tiny nod of confirmation at my silent query. I closed my eyes and swallowed.

'Good morning Mrs Cherry!' said Martin Henniker coldly. I slowly turned to see my grim-faced boss seated in the sofa area reserved for clients. 'I *was* in the middle of a meeting with Miss McDermott.'

'And a very good morning to you too Mr Henniker,' I smiled sweetly. 'I was just referring to that new docu-drama on the television last night.'

'Oh really? What was it called?'

'Er, Raiders of the Lost Libido. See you in five.'

Bugger, bugger, bugger.

At lunch time Morag, Julia and I sat on our favourite park bench. The late November sun shone weakly through the trees, soft white light peeking through bare branches.

'I had terrible trouble keeping a straight face after you'd left Cass,' Morag snorted. 'Oh Julia, if only you'd been there – Henniker's face was an absolute picture!'

'Laughter aside,' I said grimly, 'what's wrong with me? I love Jamie. Fancy the pants off him. So why has my body ceased rejoicing?'

'Maybe you're going through the menopause,' suggested Julia. 'My friend Maisie went through it in her late thirties. Almost immediately she went right off sex and-'

'Thank you Doctor Julia,' Morag interrupted, 'but I think I'm more qualified than you to give advice.'

'Which is?' I asked.

'You're simply run down!' Morag exclaimed. Emotionally, mentally, physically. We've all experienced it at some point and suffered the screaming heebie-jeebies when our fannies have failed us.'

'Morag!' Julia and I gasped in unison as a passing jogger overheard and nearly cannoned into a tree.

'What you need is some of these.' She reached into her enormous Dr Doolittle handbag and pulled out a bottle of tablets.

'Oh no, not more of your home prescriptions,' I groaned. 'You nearly murdered my intestines last time around. I'm not having you bumping off my private parts too.'

'Don't be silly.'

'Are they legal?'

'Of course! Take some of these and you'll soon perk up. In no time at all you will be completely perkified and wanting to perky all over the place.'

'What's in them?'

'Only ginseng and herbs from my Chinese therapist. I'll let you have these but if you want any more you'll have to go to him yourself. Now do you want them or not?'

'Do they definitely work?'

'Cross my heart.'

'In that case I'll take two of them right now.'

'Cass, you only need one. They are very powerful.'

'I know my body. Trust me, I need two.'

'And you wonder why you get extreme results,' she flung her hands up in exasperation. 'On your head be it.'

After work I detoured to the local supermarket to pick up some convenience meals for dinner. However, when I staggered into the kitchen trailing carrier bags, it was to find Edna already in situ. Having briefly gone home for a few days, she was now back 'visiting'. Edna was somehow managing to strain sprouts, make gravy, baste roast potatoes and slice up an enormous joint of beef all at the same time.

'Hi,' I cranked up a smile just as one of the carrier bags split and shed its load all over the floor.

'Hello Cassandra dear. Dinner won't be long. Would you like to get washed and call the children down? Jamie has telephoned and he'll be home any moment.'

'Er, yes. Right. Will do. I'll just sort this little lot out before–'

'Leave it dear, I'll put your shopping away. You go and freshen up.'

'Right,' I said again. Just at that moment the telephone rang. I snatched it up possessively. Edna might be cooking in *my* kitchen and putting away *my* shopping but she wasn't answering *my* telephone as well. 'Hello?'

Silence. Oh not the anonymous caller again. I thought Jamie had said the new telephone number was in hand?

'Who is this?' I demanded. But I was talking to myself. The line had gone dead. I punched out one four seven one, but an automated voice advised the caller had withheld their number.

'Sorry darling,' Jamie later apologised, 'I completely forgot to sort out the number business. Tell you what, why don't we just get a blocker put on so withheld numbers can't get through? In fact I'll do it right now.'

That night I quickly cleaned my teeth before miserably swallowing two more of Morag's capsules. Slipping under the duvet I pulled it over my head, feigning sleep as Jamie came into the bedroom.

At work the following morning, something peculiar happened.

Martin Henniker was, for once, late. He strode into the office in a filthy temper demanding coffee *right now*. For some perverse reason he came across as strong, commanding and – dare I say it – *masterful*. And for one brief moment I went a bit funny. Kind of *swooned*. Only for the teeniest moment you understand, but there was a definite warm rush of – well, just a warm rush.

Even more peculiarly, when Morag, Julia and I later congregated on our park bench for lunch, I caught myself leering at the regular lone jogger as he pounded his well worn path.

'Why are you looking all lustful?' demanded Julia, eyes sharp and watchful.

'Don't be ridiculous!' I snorted tearing my eyes away from the jogger's buttocks. Suddenly I was feeling hot and seriously bothered.

'You've gone bright red!' exclaimed Julia. 'You're having a hot flush. I knew it! Didn't I tell you she was going through the menopause Morag? That's exactly what happened to Maisie after she'd gone off sex. Within days she was having hot flushes. You'll be sweating buckets next,' Julia waggled a finger in my face, 'with soggy sheets and manky armpits–'

'Oh for goodness sake Julia!' barked Morag. She shifted position to take a better look at me. 'I told you not to overdose on those herbal pills,' Morag waggled her own finger under my nose. I slapped her hand away.

'Will you two stop remonstrating with me! I'm just a bit warm that's all.'

'Seriously Cass, cut back the dose. It's working.'

Before going home I detoured to the High Street. Edna had insisted on picking all the children up from school so I could start on Christmas shopping. However, buying cards and wrapping paper was the last thing on my mind. Now that my libido seemed to be back, I needed to make my body look the part.

I pushed open the door to the beauty salon.

'Good afternoon!' trilled the beautician. 'What are we doing today?'

'Lots of things – starting with my chin.' The beautician adjusted her spectacles and peered at where I was pointing. 'It's gone all whiskery see? Confession time, I've been plucking.'

'Hm, I see. Okay, come and lie down on the couch for me.'

'Can I have a bikini line too?'

'Have you been plucking down there as well?' she frowned.

'No,' I lied. 'I want a really svelte result. Like a lap-dancer, but I can never remember the name. A Denmark Doo-flip or something.'

'I think you mean a Brazilian.'

'That's the jobbie. Although actually,' I hesitated, 'on second thoughts take the lot off. Yes. I'll have a Baldie.'

As the beautician got down to business, I distracted myself from the self-inflicted pain by telephoning the twins' father.

'Stevie?'

'Hi Cass. Kids all right?'

'Yes fine. I wanted to talk to you about arrangements over Christmas and-'

'Ah yes Christmas. I'm at home at the moment so why don't you pop over.'

'Oh, right. Be with you in half an hour.'

When I arrived at Stevie's I was greeted by a dishevelled young woman wearing nothing other than a man's shirt which just about covered her backside.

'Charlotte!' I gasped.

'Hello again,' she had the grace to look a bit embarrassed and tugged at the shirt's tails.

'Er, hi. Is Stevie there?'

'STEVIE!' she squawked. 'Your ex-wife's on the doorstep.'

Nice to know she hadn't lost the ability of reminding me who I was.

'I don't mean to rush you Charlotte but I'm in a bit of a hurry. Got to get back home and get the dinner on.' Before Edna produced another show-stopping mega feast and the children got up a petition insisting that she live with us forever.

'Cass! Come in,' Stevie bounded down the stairs zipping up his flies. 'Now I'm perfectly aware that you're off to the Bahamas and-'

'Are you? How do you know that?'

Stevie suddenly looked shifty. 'Oh. Um, one of the kids mentioned it.'

'Really?' I scratched my head, puzzled. I wasn't even sure I'd discussed the Bahamas trip with any of the children. Well not properly anyway.

'Now don't worry about a thing. I'll look after the twins, sort out the cats, so all you have to do is get on a plane and have a wonderful time.'

'Well it will only be a whistle-stop visit. But it's just too much taking all the children with us. So Edna will look after Petra and Jonas–'

'And I'll look after Livvy and Toby. Of course. We're looking forward to it. Aren't we sweetheart? Charlotte?'

But Charlotte had stomped off upstairs.

'What on earth is she doing back here?' I whispered.

'In a nutshell we bumped into each other and things rekindled.'

'You've forgiven her for the galloping graffiti session?'

Stevie smiled benevolently. 'Yeah, she's promised not to do it again.'

'Blimey,' I shook my head in wonder. 'Must be love.'

Unfortunately I hadn't quite managed to pip Edna to the post regarding evening dinner.

'Did you have a successful shopping trip dear?'

'Oh! Er, yes thank you.'

'What did you buy?'

'Something for Jamie,' I smiled secretly.

'Ooh lovely. Can I have a peek?'

'Ah. Best not Edna. It's a surprise you see.'

'I quite understand dear.'

Privately I didn't think Edna would remotely understand if she glimpsed my newly acquired bald spot.

The telephone rang. Edna got to it before me.

'Hello? Yes. Yes dear. Just a moment and I'll get her for you. It's for you Cassandra dear.'

'Hello?'

Silence.

My heart began to beat a bit faster. It was the anonymous caller again. And this time they'd asked for me by name.

'Why are you doing this?' I demanded, but I was talking to a dead connection. I spun round to Edna standing over the range. 'Was that a man or a woman you just spoke to?'

'A woman dear. Is there a problem?'

'Er, no, we got cut off that's all.'

'Perhaps they'll call back dear.'

'Yes.'

I walked out of the kitchen taking the handset with me. I knew that Jamie had now put the blocker in place on withheld calls. In which case – I excitedly punched out one four seven one – it meant the caller had left their telephone number! Sure enough an automated voice began to reel off the numbers. I hit the number three button on the handset to return the call. There was a pause and then a click as the connection was made. At last I would find out the identity of my tormentor! Nervously I listened to the ring tone.

''Ello?' said a rough male voice.

I nearly dropped the handset in shock.

'Hello?' I ventured cautiously.

''Ello!'

'Who is that please?'

''Arold.'

'I see. Do I know you Harold?'

''Ow the bloody 'ell should I know?' the voice demanded.

'Well you keep ringing my home so presumably you know me?'

'Listen love, I don't know who you are but this is a public payphone. I just happened to be walking by as it rang. I only answered it 'coz curiosity got the better of me.'

I rocked back on my heels in dismay. 'Oh. Can you tell me the address of this payphone please?'

'Why? Are you gonna write it a bloomin' letter or sumfink?'

The receiver crashed down.

I gnashed my teeth in frustration. No matter. I would get to the bottom of this. Sooner or later. I looked up at the sound of a key turning in the front door.

'Darling!' Jamie greeted me with a smile as he wiped his feet on the hall mat. 'How's my beautiful fiancée this evening?'

I tossed the handset onto the hall table – prank phone call instantly forgotten – and flew into Jamie's arms, smothering his handsome face in kisses.

'What's got into you?' Jamie laughed.

I knew exactly what had gotten into me. Oh yes! And in the process of re-awakening my own sleepy libido, I'd unwittingly unearthed the secret of Morag's ability to untiringly sizzle and spit sexual energy.

'I've got a surprise for you.'

'Lovely. Can I have it now?'

'At bedtime,' I whispered huskily.

'Are you making me wild reckless promises?'

'Yes.'

Later that evening, instead of me darting up the stairs ahead of Jamie and feigning sleep the moment he crossed the bedroom threshold, we went upstairs together hand in hand.

'So what's the surprise?' asked Jamie shutting our door and turning the key for good measure.

'This for starters,' I leant in and kissed him full on the mouth.

Mm. Nice. A thrill of awakening rippled through my body. Mm. I kissed Jamie again. Ooh lovely. As a third lingering kiss unfolded, Jamie broke off.

'To the bed!' Jamie ordered hoarsely. 'And now,' he declared pushing me back on the duvet and tugging at my jeans, 'I'm going to make mad passionate–' he stopped abruptly.

'What?' I sat up startled.

'Good God!'

'*What?*' I repeated.

'What have you done to yourself Cassie?'

'Oh yes. That's my surprise. It's called–'

I hesitated. I was fairly sure it wasn't called *Baldie*.

'Um, Monty.'

'Monty?'

'Yes. As in The Full Monty. Do you like it? Jamie? I said do you – ooh. I'll take that as a yes.'

God bless Morag's little pills.

At work Martin Henniker was still without a permanent secretary. Susannah Harrington summoned me to her office and surprised me with the proposal of considering the post myself.

'But he hates me!'

'On the contrary my dear. Martin is fully aware that a floating position suits you with the children and so forth, but nonetheless asked me to approach you.'

She then mentioned a salary so inflated my eyes bulged.

'Bribery,' she purred.

'Oh Susannah, I don't know.'

My brain whirred. On the one hand, with a new house and the looming Bahamian trip, the extra money would be welcome. On the other, what about the children? And school holidays? There was no Nell living next door to step into the breach and I really didn't want to ask Edna for help. And there was another little matter too – like exactly how long it would take on a full-time basis before Martin Henniker provoked me to the point of no return? What if I ripped the computer from my desk and bashed it very hard over Martin Henniker's head? Especially when it was *that* time of the month? I could almost see the newspaper headlines:

Secretary Brains Boss in Broad Daylight

Sandra Cherry, 93, a legal secretary with respected law firm Hemel Breathweight, was arrested in the early hours in connection with the murder of her boss, Mr Martian Henniker, 24. A colleague of the deceased, Maura McDuff, who did not wish to be named, confided that Mrs Cherry was menopausal and suffering from diminished hormones.

I licked my lips. What to do?

'Let me have a think about it Susannah.'

On the drive home from the school run I glanced at Liv and Toby in the rear-view mirror.

'Kids, how would you feel about me working full-time?'

'What precisely do you mean by *full-time?*' asked Livvy.

'Exactly that. Being at the office every day – including school holidays. And you'd have to catch a bus home from school,' I pointed out.

'Cool,' Toby nodded his head in approval.

'So who would look after us in the holidays?' asked Liv.

'Good question.'

'Nanny Edna could be our childminder,' suggested Livvy.

'No darling, Nanny Edna is an old lady.'

'Rubbish!' snorted Toby. 'Nanny Edna is as fit as a fiddle. She's currently making me and Jonas a special desk for our PlayStations and games.'

I blanched. Good grief. It simply wasn't normal for a woman of seventy-something to be power drilling all over the place, glue gun at the ready, raising her hammer in a salute to DIY. The only thing I was good at raising was my voice.

'Well I've yet to discuss the idea with Jamie. We'll see what suggestions he has about it over dinner.'

Later, Jamie listened while I ticked off the pros and cons.

'So what do you think?' I finally asked.

'Honestly? I think juggling four children, a big house and working full-time for a man who sounds like a living nightmare will burn you out in no time at all.'

My hackles rose. 'Are you saying I can't cut the mustard?'

'No darling, not at all,' Jamie soothed. 'But you asked my opinion and I'm giving it to you. We are a brand new family – a ready made family – and now that we're all getting down to the nuts and bolts of living together, it might be more sensible to invest your energies into this period of transition.'

'But think of the extra money.'

'Cassie if you wish to work – full-time or part-time – that's up to you. I would just urge you to think carefully before you put yourself through unnecessary stress. Money is not a problem. Remember me telling you about the partnership proposal with Ethan Fareham for the security venture?'

I nodded.

'Well I'm happy to confirm that it's definite.' Jamie's face slowly lit up. 'Everything is going to kick off in the New Year. Trust me – it's going to be a gold mine.'

And so, the following morning, I informed Susannah Harrington that I would be happy to continue assisting Martin Henniker but not on a full-time basis. As I walked down the corridor back to my office, I bumped into Morag.

'Guess what, guess what?'

Hadn't we had this conversation once before?

'You're pregnant,' I ventured.

'Not yet, but I reckon it won't be long.' She cast a furtive glance up and down the corridor and lowered her voice. 'It's not official – and I'm only confiding in you – but Matt has agreed we can start trying for a baby. Just think!' she peered over her mountainous cleavage and stroked her flat tummy, 'there could be a little baba in there right now.'

I gave her a quick hug. 'That's lovely news. How long before you know?'

'Oh at least another couple of weeks. Currently I'm at my most fertile so Matt's blanket bombing my eggs at the moment,' she giggled before rummaging in her shoulder bag. 'And I have a stash of these little darlings,' she extracted her hand and waggled a home pregnancy test in my face.

'Goodness, how many of those have you got?'

'I figured I'd get impatient waiting to know. I'll probably test early and keep testing up to the day my period is due. These little sticks will get used up in a trice.'

'But Morag, these test kits cost a small fortune.'

She shrugged. 'I'm doing some private legal work for a pharmacist mate and he's paying my fees with ovulation and pregnancy kits. I'd better get my skates on – I'm off to see a client. Catch you later.'

I sat down at my desk glad that Henniker was in a meeting and to have five minutes to collect my thoughts. At that precise moment the phone rang.

'Mr Henniker's office, how can I help you?'

Silence.

I swallowed. Was this some sort of massive coincidence?

'Hello?' My ears strained to hear the soft whispering.

'*I hate you.*'

Chapter Nineteen

That evening I lay in the bath fretting. Who was behind the dropped phone calls? Calls that had now taken something of a sinister turn. I nibbled my lip. I knew a few things about my tormentor. Firstly, the person was female. Secondly she knew where I both lived and worked. Finally – and most worryingly of all – she apparently hated me. A part of me reasoned that I should tell Jamie about the latest call at work but, for the moment, I wanted to handle this my way.

My period was late and I knew stress was probably to blame. Apart from the anonymous calls, I was in a continual state of anxiety working for Henniker and edgy at home with Edna once again re-installed in the spare room.

I sighed and blasted some more hot water into the bath, resolving to discuss my problems with the girls.

'So who would you say has an axe to grind?' asked Morag the following day.

We were sitting in the local crowded Costa Coffee clutching our Skinnies and low-fat blueberry muffins.

'Well clearly somebody who isn't terribly keen on Cass,' said Julia. Nothing like stating the obvious.

'What about that Cynthia woman?' asked Morag.

'Yes I did initially wonder if it could be her. But if Cynthia was going to harass anybody then surely it would be Charlotte – bearing in mind Charlotte took Stevie off her.'

'Well maybe it's Charlotte,' said Julia. 'She once accused Stevie of still being in love with you. Perhaps she feels you're a threat to her happiness.'

'No, I don't think it's her either. From past experience I would say she'd simply march straight round to the house and say what was bothering her to my face.'

'Well who else can it be?' asked Julia.

'What if,' my throat was suddenly dry, 'what if this is nothing to do with Stevie?'

'What do you mean?' Morag said sharply.

'What if it's more to do with Jamie?'

'Cass what are you implying?'

I took a deep breath. 'I'm wondering if Jamie is having an affair and the *other woman* is harassing me.'

'Don't be absurd!' Morag spluttered. 'I can't believe you've even considered that idea. Your fiancé is besotted with you for heaven's sake. Apart from anything else, after everything he's been through he wouldn't dream of betraying either you or the children. Jamie is an honourable man Cass.'

'Yes I know,' I said in a small voice, ashamed for voicing my fears out loud. 'It was just a fleeting thought. I guess I'm still paranoid after all the deceit with Stevie.'

'Of course,' Morag patted my hand sympathetically, 'that's perfectly understandable. However I really do think you should talk about it with Jamie.'

'Yes. Meanwhile Jules, would you monitor all calls into my office. Anybody outside of the family and asking for me by name, tell them I've left.'

'Sure,' Julia nodded. 'But try not to get too stressy about it Cass.'

'I'm stressy over everything. The anonymous caller, blasted Henniker, Edna not going home-'

'You should definitely talk to Jamie about that,' Morag arched an eyebrow, 'I couldn't begin to put up with Mama Mia under my feet every day in her widow's weeds radiating disapproval every time I tell her son we're having an early night.'

'I thought you liked your future mother-in-law?' asked Julia.

'I do! Just in small doses that's all.'

'And on top of everything else,' I picked at a loose cotton thread on my cuff, 'my period's late.'

'I keep telling you but you won't listen,' sighed Julia, 'it's the menopause.'

'Oh for goodness sake, it's *stress*. How's Miles?' I asked rather cruelly.

Julia flinched. 'I'm thinking about dumping him actually. He's just not doing it for me at the moment.'

'Doing what?' asked Morag.

'Proposing.'

Morag then felt too guilty to bring up the subject of her impending nuptials, so instead switched to the topic of pregnancy.

'I'd like a baby girl. A darling blondie with big blue eyes and I'd dress her in pink from head to toe. Do you like the name Boo?'

'No, she'd get teased at school and called Boo Hoo,' said Julia. 'Is it possible you could be pregnant Cass?'

'Don't be daft,' I snorted.

'You see!' Julia crowed, 'it's the menopause!'

'How many periods have you missed?' asked Morag.

'Only the one.'

'It's the menopause,' Julia intoned.

'Get yourself off to the doctor Cass and find out what's going on in your nether regions.'

'I'm feeling so irritable I'm sure my period can't be far away.'

After lunch Susannah Harrington summoned me to her office. I mounted the stairs with a sense of foreboding. Had Henniker complained about me?

'Cassandra, do sit down,' Susannah indicated the chair opposite her desk. 'Good news! I've secured yet another new secretary for Martin Henniker – this time an extremely mature woman who I'm confident will whip him into shape once and for all.'

I had a mental picture of an aging dominatrix, complete with a corrugated grey perm, smacking a riding crop against Martin Henniker's backside.

'The bad news is that she can't start until the New Year. Now my dear, I have an enormous favour to ask. I know your lovely children are on the threshold of breaking up for the Christmas holidays, not to mention Morag's impending Caribbean wedding getting ever nearer, but Martin has an urgent deal to complete before you go away and he really does need full time assistance until Mrs Haslemere can start. Is there just the tiniest chance you could accommodate Martin until you go off to the Bahamas?'

'Well–'

'Double pay of course,' she gave me a beady look.

'If it's just for a few days then I'm sure it won't be a problem Susannah. Let me square it with Jamie and,' my heart sank, 'the children's grandmother. I'll confirm with you tomorrow morning.'

'Of course my dear, of course.'

I had a sudden flash of déjà vu as a picture of me spectacularly losing my temper with Martin Henniker swam before me. What if I lunged at my boss's jugular with the stapler – that enormous one for particularly stubborn documents – clicking away until his main artery was sealed up and brought instant aneurism? *Ew.* Sometimes I amazed myself at the lurid depths of my imagination.

'Are you sure you want to do it?' asked Jamie over dinner. 'From the sound of this guy, you don't owe him any favours.'

'Yes but Susannah Harrington has been very good to me and it's more her I'm thinking about.'

'Well I'm happy to hold the fort for you Cassandra dear,' said Edna popping a soft fluffy potato into her mouth. Naturally she'd peeled and cooked them herself. Along with the tender carrots, freshly minted peas and succulent roast lamb. I had a sudden urge to weep. Would I ever bung a convenience meal in the microwave again? 'I was going to go home this weekend but what with Christmas coming and you now working full time for the moment, I'll stay on a bit longer and get your Christmas larder sorted out for you.'

'That's awfully good of you Edna,' I said weakly.

'But in the New Year I really must go home once and for all. Leave you young things to get on with your new life together.'

In an instant my mood lifted. 'You're welcome to stay whenever you like Edna,' I smiled magnanimously. Well why not? She was a super lady wasn't she? I suddenly felt ashamed at my earlier misgivings.

Jamie's mobile phone chirruped into life on the worktop.

'Excuse me folks,' he said getting up from the dinner table. 'Hello?' There was a brief pause before Jamie's voice dropped an octave. 'I'm at home,' I heard him murmur before cupping his hand over the mouthpiece. 'Sorry everybody – work.'

He strode out of the kitchen. Seconds later I heard the study door click behind him.

'That was lovely Edna.' I put my knife and fork together and wiped my mouth on the paper napkin my future mother-in-law always placed around the table. Unlike me. At best everybody got a piece of kitchen towel. I stood up and started to clear the plates from the table.

'Leave that Cassandra dear, I'll do it. You go and get the baths running for the children.'

'Oh, right.' I gave a tight smile, trying to dismiss the feeling that Edna was organising me as well as the dirty dinner plates.

Walking past the study I paused. I could hear Jamie on the other side of the door sounding very uptight.

'I've told you before not to ring me when I'm at home. What if Cassie had answered your call?' My ears pricked up. Instantly I flattened one of them against the study door. 'No, I can't I'm sorry. It's over. No. How many times do you need telling? I don't want to see you any more.'

'Mum?' Livvy yelled from the upstairs landing, making me jump guiltily. Instantly I moved away from the study door. 'Are you coming up to run my bath?'

'Be right with you darling,' I warbled.

Jamie suddenly erupted out of the study, clearly agitated.

'Everything okay darling?' I called after his retreating back.

He stopped and spun round. 'Yeah I – sorry Cassie. I'm a bit distracted.'

'What's wrong?' I walked up to him and put my arms around him.

'Nothing. Just work,' he pulled me to him and hugged me hard.

I rested my head on his shoulder for a moment.

'Who was that calling?' I asked lightly.

'Ethan. You know, Ethan Fareham. The guy I'm going into the security partnership with.

I nodded. 'Is everything still on – no change of heart?'

'Definitely not. I can't wait to start working with the guy.'

'*Mum!*' Livvy called again.

'Go on,' Jamie kissed my forehead. 'I'll catch up with you in half an hour. We'll have a nice glass of wine together.'

'Lovely.'

As I walked up the stairs to the bathroom I felt slightly sick. Jamie had just lied to me.

As the weekend got underway, I dropped all the children off at the stables before diverting to Nell's.

'How's married life?' I asked over our ritual coffees and Hob Nobs.

'Don't ask,' she pulled a face. 'Tell me instead how the great romance is going,' she popped half a biscuit in her mouth.

'W-e-ll,' I pulled my own face.

Nell's rotating jaw froze. 'What do you mean *w-e-ll*? What's going on? Is everything all right?'

Miserably, I brought her up to date with the anonymous phone calls culminating in Jamie's own mystery caller.

'He blatantly lied to me Nell.'

'Cass this is ludicrous,' my old neighbour shook her head in disbelief. 'There's no way Jamie is cheating on you. No way!'

'In my heart of hearts I don't believe he is. But I can't think of any other explanation. Why else was Jamie telling somebody *it's over* and voicing concern about whether I could have picked up the call?'

'Why don't you just confront him then?'

'What, as in "Oh by the way darling, you're a bloody liar because I checked your mobile phone while you were languishing in the bath and your caller's number does not match Ethan Fareham's mobile number". Then what?'

'Well I'm fresh out of any other suggestions,' Nell shrugged apologetically. 'Did you make a note of the caller's number?'

'What sort of person do you think I am?' I rounded on Nell. 'It's bad enough that I'm sneaking about eavesdropping on my fiancé's private telephone conversations, doubting his loyalty, riffling through his mobile phone contacts-'

'Where's the number?'

'Here,' I said sulkily extracting it from my handbag.

'I'm ringing it.'

'No!' I snatched the bit of paper back.

'Why not?'

'Ignorance is bliss. For the moment.'

'You're joking,' Nell gaped at me incredulously. 'Okay,' she threw up her hands in despair, 'do it your way. For now.'

The following day I drove into Fairview to buy some new clothes for work. I returned home to find Edna already in the throes of cooking Sunday lunch.

'Bought anything nice dear?'

'Just some clothes for the office.'

Jamie wandered in and slung an arm around my shoulder. 'Let's see.'

I shook the clothing on to the kitchen table.

'A roughed up leather jacket, a T-shirt and a pair of combat trousers. And you say these clothes are for work?'

'Why not! I'm about to embark on a three day full-time stint with Henniker. It will be like going to war. Therefore I need to be dressed appropriately.'

'I see.'

'I also figured that something less tailored might make me more relaxed.'

My fingers caressed the combat's numerous pockets, zips and distressed bits. I'd had to buy the next size up as my tummy was still full and round. Only the other day Julia had prodded my stomach and cheerfully enquired if I was embarking on middle age spread as well as the menopause. Cheeky cow.

'That's very anti-establishment,' Jamie pointed to the T-shirt. It was covered in a mix of silver and white scribbled graffiti.

'Do you like it?' I asked nervously.

'Absolutely love it,' he enthused, 'especially the trousers,' he lifted up the flaps and undid a zip or two. 'Do these lead anywhere interesting?'

The remainder of the weekend passed without incident. There were no dropped phone calls and Jamie's mobile remained silent. His attitude to me was loving and attentive. The mystery caller's telephone number languished inside my handbag. I was positive my fiancé wasn't having an affair. Well, fairly positive.

On Monday morning I slipped into the new clothes feeling almost liberated. Walking the short distance from car park to office, a piercing wolf whistle shrilled out from a passing van.

'You're a bit of a yummy mummy ain't'cha darlin'!' yelled a cheeky chappie.

I experienced a bit of a head rush. Fancy that! I bowled into Reception feeling incredibly *hip*.

'I've just been wolf whistled,' I giggled to Julia.

'Good for you!' she grinned.

I headed off to Martin Henniker's office feeling more than a little smug.

'Good morning!' I trilled shrugging off the trendy jacket.

Henniker boggled at me. One could almost feel the series of exclamation marks emanating from the area around his desk. Clearly my appearance had knocked him sideways.

'*Mrs* Cherry!'

Ah. He'd recovered. Wait for it Cass. Wait for it.

'*What* an extraordinary outfit. Tell me, where's the fancy dress party?'

I blanched. 'I beg your pardon?'

He raised his eyebrows in a parody of astonishment and pointed to my graffiti T-shirt.

'Well presumably there is a reason for you coming to the office dressed like a hooligan?'

The effect was instantaneous. Like a pricked balloon, my shoulders slumped. Two seconds ago I had felt on top of the world. Now I just felt ridiculous.

'Fortunately my client isn't coming into the office today Mrs Cherry, but I must ask you to revert to appropriate sober attire tomorrow.'

'Yes Mr Henniker. Of course Mr Henniker.'

Twenty-four hours later things had gone from tricky to downright sticky as Henniker grew more and more enraged. The client telephoned to say he was running late which didn't improve my truculent boss's mood. As the day wore on I found myself getting increasingly stressed as Henniker repeatedly flung paperwork back at me, derided my knowledge of Power Point and finally erupted into a furious outburst over a missing comma.

As the third and final day of working full-time for Henniker dawned, I offered up a silent prayer of thanks that I would soon be reverting back to part-time status.

'And where the bloody hell did you disappear to yesterday afternoon?' my boss roared by way of greeting.

Calm Cass. Do *not* retaliate.

'Home of course Mr Henniker,' I trilled. 'Much as I love working for you, I do have four children waiting for their Mummy.'

He narrowed his eyes. Suddenly a stack of documents bound with only an elastic band catapulted through the air and landed with a heavy thwack on my desk. The band instantly snapped sending loose pages spilling to the floor.

'That little lot requires urgent amending, so pull your finger out.'

I stared at him, fighting rising anger. I caught sight of the heavy stapler and mentally shivered at my previous imaginings involving that particular contraption. How easy would it be to punch it against the throbbing vein in his temple leaving a particularly pretty cross-stitch? Or reach for my monitor and bash seven bells out of his head?

'My pleasure Mr Henniker,' I smiled brightly and stooped to gather up the fallen papers.

The client arrived and instantly picked holes in several clauses. It was gone three o'clock before everything was signed, sealed and delivered. I felt shattered and my stomach was growling hungrily. It had been a long time since breakfast. I reached for my handbag.

'I think we both deserve something nice,' I said cheerfully. 'Can I treat you?'

But my boss didn't deign to respond or even look up from his work.

'See you in a minute then,' I addressed his bald spot before slipping out.

As I stood in the queue at the delicatessen, I decided that this sort of stress simply wasn't on. I felt exhausted. So damn tired. I still hadn't had my period and there never seemed to be a spare moment to sort myself out. Along with a trip to the gynaecologist, my dental check up was overdue, as was a sight test and when was I going to get time to visit a hairdresser for some urgent highlights and a restyle before Morag's rapidly approaching wedding?

As I handed over a five pound note in exchange for two plastic triangular containers, I determined that I would hand in my notice. Tomorrow. I would draft it first thing in the morning. Jamie was right. I was lucky enough not to *need* to work, so why was I knocking myself into a cocked hat?

I walked back to the office feeling much calmer, a restored sense of being in control of my life again.

In the tiny kitchenette I opened the plastic containers and set the contents on two plates. Two enormous pieces of rich brown cake stared up at me. Something as stickily moist as this needed a cup of coffee to wash it down. Moments later I elbowed Martin Henniker's door open, tray aloft, and placed the cake and china to one side of his ink blotter.

He glared furiously at me. 'Where the hell have you been?'

'Buying you this,' I beamed. 'I told you – my treat.'

His gaze dropped to the plate.

The cake was heavily iced with soft fudge fondant. Henniker dug his fingers into the mixture to keep it from slipping and greedily opened his mouth to crocodile proportions.

'It's called *Death by Chocolate*,' I informed him as his cheeks ballooned to alarming proportions. And may you bloody well choke on it, I silently added.

Two seconds later, he did.

From that point on things became hazy. I vaguely remember Henniker fighting to swallow the contents of his overfull mouth. His face went through the colour spectrum of pink, red, fuchsia and finally deep purple as his eyes bulged. There was a spluttering noise as he inhaled and choked at the same time. Everything slipped into slow motion. Somebody was screaming – presumably me – as Martin Henniker nose-dived into the remains of his chocolate cake sending the coffee flying in the process. The incessant screaming continued as frantic footsteps pounded urgently down the hallway. Moments later Julia burst in. The blood drained from her face as she took in the gruesome scene.

'I didn't do it!' I yelled at her wild eyed. 'Look – my monitor is still plugged in. And see here?' I grabbed the stapler and waggled it in front of Julia's frightened eyes. 'Witness all the staples are present and correct.'

'What are you talking about Cass?' Julia whispered. She glanced from me to Henniker. A pate on a plate. I had a terrifying urge to break into hysterical laughter of the unfunny kind. Julia lunged across me and grabbed the telephone.

'I didn't do it,' I repeated, swaying giddily. 'I'm innocent and my hormones are not diminished.'

And with that I passed out.

I didn't go to work the following day. After Martin Henniker's literal Death by Chocolate, I was reliably informed by Julia that I had spouted incoherent garbling before dropping to the floor, eyes rolling to the back of my head. Thinking that she now had two dead bodies on her hands, Julia had frantically rung 999.

An ambulance had arrived. Paramedics had removed the body. *The body.* Just thinking about Martin Henniker morphing from living to dead before my very eyes produced violent shudders. One of the paramedics had helped me up, draped a blanket over my shoulders and pressed hot sweet tea into my shaking hands. Two policemen had materialised and assured it was unlikely I would be charged with murder. Jamie was duly summoned and whisked me home.

That evening Julia and Morag visited, both riding high on morbid fascination.

'You should have seen Henniker's face Cass when one of the paramedics pulled him out of the chocolate sponge,' Julia gasped.

'Yes, I can imagine,' I rubbed my aching head.

'His eyelashes were smothered in chocolate sauce and there was all this fudge goo everywhere – on his nose, around his nose, up his nose-'

'*Thank* you Julia,' I clapped a hand over my mouth. It was likely that I would never eat chocolate fudge cake again.

Morag, never one to bandy words, got straight to the point. 'This does of course mean there is an available Senior Partner position up for grabs.'

Julia and I stared at her, shocked.

'I'm a businesswoman,' she reminded us. 'Don't think Henniker would be grieving if either one of us had been taken by the Grim Reaper. Let's face it girls, he was a pain in the tubes and nobody's going to miss him too much.'

'Apart from his wife,' I pointed out.

'That reminds me,' Julia rummaged in her bag. 'Sign this please.'

It was a sympathy card for Martin Henniker's widow. I scribbled listlessly.

'And anyway,' continued Julia, 'why would you want a senior partner position when you're about to embark upon wedded bliss, hang up your dictation machine and plan to get big with child?'

'We'll see. One never knows what the future holds.'

Julia retrieved the sympathy card. 'For heaven's sake Cass, I can't give Doreen Henniker this.'

Morag leant across and peered at the card. 'Congratulations and all good wishes for the future.'

'Sorry,' I rubbed my eyes. 'If only I hadn't bought that blasted cake.'

'If. But. Maybe,' Morag shrugged. 'It's not your fault Cass, end of subject.'

'You don't understand,' I gulped, tears springing to my eyes. 'I actually made a wish as he bit into the cake. I *wished* him to choke. And he did. And then he died.'

'Do you honestly believe,' Morag rolled her eyes, 'that you made a wish which came true? If life were that easy the world would be awash with millionaires, everybody would be famous and nobody would do a day's work. Julia, find Jamie and ask for stiff drinks all round.'

'There are dark and evil forces at work in this world,' I muttered.

'Have you been overdosing on Doctor Who again?' asked Morag sharply.

Five minutes later we were working our way through a bottle of scotch.

'Go easy Julia, you're driving us back,' Morag said bossily.

'Oh cheers.'

'The only good thing to come out of this,' I ventured, 'is that the shock jump-started my overdue period.'

'About time,' commented Morag.

'Mind you, this afternoon it stopped again. Weird.'

'Menopause,' Julia muttered.

As December got underway I retreated into a twilight world, seemingly too shocked to function properly. I didn't go into Hempel Braithwaite for a few days. For once I was glad that Edna was around. An unofficial pattern was established whereby Edna would surface at the crack of dawn and I would later shuffle into the kitchen, still in my dressing gown, to find her standing over the kitchen range.

On this particular Friday morning my future mother-in-law was frying hash browns and tomatoes. Great hunks of buttered wholegrain bread were set upon the table.

'Good morning Cassandra dear. I should have told you last night but I clean forgot – silly me – I was too preoccupied hanging the new curtains in the lounge.'

I blinked. What new curtains in the lounge? I'd wanted Roman blinds. 'Er, told me what Edna?'

'A lady telephoned for you last night but you were in bed.'

'Was it Morag?' She'd been ringing me on an almost daily basis, anxiously monitoring my emotional progress.

'I'm afraid she didn't tell me her name and by the time I'd thought to ask she'd rung off.'

'Oh.' Perhaps it was Nell. Typical of ditzy Nell to forget to say who was calling. 'Was there a message?'

'Yes dear. She asked if you could meet her for dinner this evening. She said she had a problem that couldn't be aired at home.'

Ah. Definitely Nell. Obviously the marital troubles were ongoing and she needed to get something off her chest.

'Here's the address.' Edna moved away from the frying pan and picked up a piece of paper. 'The Planet Restaurant, Ainsley Ford.'

'Thanks Edna,' I tucked the paper into my dressing gown pocket. 'Meanwhile I'm going to get ready for work.'

Jamie came into the kitchen and caught my last sentence.

'Is that wise darling?' He grabbed a loaded breakfast plate with one hand and ruffled my hair affectionately with the other as he sat down. 'I think you're still traumatised over your boss's sudden death.'

'Jamie's right,' said Edna, 'and lately you've been looking terribly tired dear.'

I sighed. 'I feel constantly exhausted. Actually one of the reasons I want to go back to work is to hand in my notice.'

'Excellent idea,' said Jamie tweaking my bottom as I brushed past him. 'Once Mum goes home you're going to have a full-time job running this place.'

I gave my fiancé a wan smile. 'Oh, by the way, I'm out with Nell this evening.'

'Ah,' Jamie frowned. 'I'm out too.'

'Are you? You didn't say.'

'Sorry, it slipped my mind. Can you rearrange with Nell? This is something I really don't want to put off. I'm meeting up with Ethan Fareham. Business.'

'Don't worry dear,' Edna interrupted. 'I'll babysit the children. You go and have a nice time with Nell. Do you the power of good.'

'Okay, thanks. Meanwhile I'd better get my skates on and get to work.'

It was strange to be back at Hempel Braithwaite and not have Martin Henniker breathing fire down my neck. Susannah Harrington wasn't surprised when I handed her my written resignation.

'Terrible business,' she murmured *sotto voce*, 'but not altogether unexpected.'

'Well I was absolutely pole-axed Susannah,' I said in shocked tones.

'Yes but he did have a very stressful job Cassandra.'

'What's choking to death on chocolate cake got to do with Martin Henniker's stress levels?'

'But Cassandra, Martin Henniker didn't choke to death – he died of a heart attack!'

'Heart attack?'

'Yes!'

My face broke out in a huge grin. I was innocent! 'But that's absolutely brilliant news!'

'Sorry?'

'Fantastic!' I jumped up and punched the air with delight.

'Cassandra I know you didn't see eye to eye with Martin but I really wouldn't let your *joie de vivre* be on general display. Rather bad form and all that.'

'Sorry,' I beamed. 'Terribly sorry, but you don't understand. Up until just now I'd been blaming myself for his death, but now you're telling me his ticker tocked out. Don't you see? I'm off the hook!'

Susannah gasped. 'Good Lord! Well I can certainly assure you his death was absolutely nothing to do with your chocolate cake.' She glanced at the unopened letter in her hand. 'Do you still want to tender your resignation?'

I hesitated, but only for a second.

'Yes. I want to concentrate on my family. My *new* family. Life's too short for stress.'

'I quite agree dear. However, it would be tremendously helpful if you could stay for the remainder of the month and assist Morag who is initially taking over Martin's clients.'

This meant my last day at Hempel Braithwaite would literally be the day before flying out to the Bahamas. Oh well, I reflected, there would be plenty of time in the New Year to catch up on the little things in life – like sleep. I hid a yawn in the palm of my hand as Susannah thanked me for my co-operation. Taking this as my cue to leave, I waltzed into Morag's office.

'Hiya!' I trilled. 'Isn't life just *fabu*lous! Just look how the spine of those tatty files are frayed to fluffiness and the way the wallpaper peels so attractively over the dirty air vent. Beautiful.'

'Are you taking happy pills?' she gave me a sharp look.

'No of course not!'

'Final fitting tomorrow.'

'Final fitting for what?'

'Our dresses. For the wedding?' she added when I looked at her blankly. 'Honestly Cass, sometimes I wonder what planet you're on.'

'That reminds me,' I fished inside my handbag for my mobile phone. 'Got to text Nell, she didn't give me a time for our rendezvous this evening.'

I quickly tapped out a message.

C u tonight @ 7

Seconds later my mobile bleeped a response.

OK but make it 7 30 – more convenient

At lunch time Julia joined us and we remained in Morag's office, unwilling to brave the freezing elements of the park or squash into Costa Coffee.

'Glad to be back?' asked Julia tucking into a hot bacon sandwich and dripping grease down her chin.

'Feels a bit weird,' I replied sinking my teeth into a peanut butter and sweet corn bagel which, for some strange reason, I'd been craving all morning.

'Bound to,' Morag nodded her head in recognition of this.

'So what have I missed out on while I've been away?' I turned to Julia. How's your love-life?' I grinned.

'Actually I've been dumped.' Julia's bottom lip wobbled violently.

'What?' Morag and I chorused together. 'Why?'

'Oh you know, the usual male thing. Miles couldn't take any more of being frogmarched past jewellery shops stuffed with engagement rings or listen to hints about Spring being a marvellous time to get married.'

'Ah. Men,' I nodded sagely.

'Let's face it,' said Morag, 'all women's problems start with men. There's *men*tal illness, *men*strual cramps and *men*tal breakdown.'

I joined in gamely, '*Guy*nocologist and *his*terectomy.'

'And don't forget *men*opause,' Julia added giving me a pointed look.

Cheeky mare.

Once home I saw Jamie only very briefly.

'Do you want my bath water darling?' I asked emerging from the bathroom with a fluffy towel around me.

'No, I haven't got time. I'll have one later,' said Jamie discarding his uniform and plucking a denim shirt from the wardrobe. 'I'd better get a move on as I'm running late,' he said, fingers quickly doing up buttons. 'Give my love to Nell.'

'I will. By the way Mr Mackerel,' I called after my fiancé. Jamie turned and looked back at me.

'You are incredibly handsome in that denim shirt. Brings out the blue in your eyes.'

'If you play your cards right,' Jamie winked, 'I'll let you take it off my back later.'

'You're on. You'd better go darling, don't keep Ethan waiting.'

'Ethan?' Jamie stared at me blankly.

'Yes. Your business meeting?'

'Oh. That Ethan. Yes, of course. Will do darling. See you later.'

'See you,' I gazed after Jamie, suddenly disconcerted. How many Ethans did he know?

Chapter Twenty

I drove down the narrow winding lanes of Ainsley Brook and arrived at The Planet bang on half past seven.

Walking into the bar area I searched for Nell's blonde head in a sea of faces. There was no sign of her. Suddenly I noticed a horribly familiar pair of broad shoulders encased in a check shirt. The owner caught sight of me and blanched. It was Euan. The love rat kitchen fitter. Even worse, his flame-haired wife was perched on a stool next to him. She had clocked her husband's frozen expression and was already following the direction of his disbelieving gaze. Her eyes hooked on mine and widened as recognition dawned.

Horrified I darted off towards the restaurant area. Where was Nell? Ducking and diving between tables and diners stuffed into the restaurant's candlelit nooks and crannies, I hurriedly searched for the whereabouts of my friend. She was nowhere to be found. And then suddenly, like a bad television repeat, I noticed another pair of familiar broad shoulders, except these shoulders were heart-achingly well-known and encased in the denim shirt he'd put on less than an hour earlier.

I ground to a halt and stared in utter disbelief at Jamie. He was engaged in earnest conversation with an Angelina Jolie look-a-like seated opposite him. Selina.

As if on cue Selina caught my eye. She acknowledged my presence with the tiniest inclination of her head. A malicious grin played about her mouth. For a moment I could only gape. And then everything fell into place. This was my anonymous caller. This was the person who had whispered I was a bitch – who had dared to ring my work place and declare her hatred. This was the person who had telephoned Jamie's mobile when I'd eavesdropped outside the study door. And this was the person who'd rung our home last night to send me on this evening's wild goose chase.

As I stared at her beautiful face, the bottom of my world fell out. Jamie of all people. My Jamie. The man I'd thought so decent, so honourable, who'd professed to be heartbroken over his dead wife. The man who had fooled me into believing that I'd been the woman to mend his shattered heart. Not only was I reeling from the hurt of his betrayal, I was staggered at his disregard for our children and the effect our splitting up would have upon them – for make no mistake, I wasn't sticking around to be betrayed by another philandering Casanova.

A red mist descended as fury washed over me. How dare he? And how dare *she*! Enraged I marched over to their table. I'd been a participant in this scenario before. However the last time had seen me sitting down at the table with Euan while his wife made free with the table contents. This time there was a change in characters and my role was now standing room only, but no matter. I could remember how the play unfolded and would rework the lines.

'You *bastard*!' I shrieked, swiftly weaving through the dining room's obstacle course of customers, tables and chairs. Once again the background babble dropped to a highly charged silence, this time all eyes firmly on table twenty-six.

'Cassie!' Jamie looked up, appalled.

'*Cassie*,' I mimicked.

'Sorry you had to find out this way,' Selina murmured.

'What the hell are you talking about?' Jamie growled at her.

'You lied to me,' I prodded Jamie hard on the shoulder. 'And what I want-'

prod prod

'Is for you-'

prod prod

'To sod off-'

prod prod

'You WHORE!'

Bugger. I should have started the prodding with Selina. Was it too late to start again? Yes, certainly with that army of waiters gathering over there.

I squared my shoulders and looked around for the handy ice bucket that should have been on the table. Disappointingly there was only a single glass of wine. Hers. No matter. I picked it up and flung it in her face. Before she could even react I'd flipped her dinner plate into her lap. For some strange reason Jamie didn't have a dinner plate in front of him. A buttered bread roll sat forlornly on Selina's side plate. That would do. I grabbed it and stuffed it inside Jamie's denim shirt.

'What the-?'

As previously, a collective gasp sounded around the restaurant followed by an electrified buzz as diners began nudging each other. But before the waiters could frogmarch the raving blonde out of the restaurant, I'd already spun on my heel and sprinted off, very aware that Jamie had now leapt to his feet and was charging after me, complete with bread roll décolletage. I dashed back towards the bar area – straight towards Euan who was heading my way. Oh *God*.

Swerving to the left I spotted the Ladies and catapulted through the door… smack into Euan's wife. It was too much. Cornered from every direction, I flattened against the wash basins and burst into tears.

'Please don't cry,' she implored grabbing one of my trembling hands. I shrunk away from her. 'I'm so glad I've bumped into you,' she babbled, 'I owe you such a massive apology for the awful time I gave you in that restaurant. I know it wasn't your fault. Euan and I had a huge row and he confessed everything and promised me you were totally innocent. I'm so sorry about the humiliation you suffered. It must have been dreadful discovering that your boyfriend was a liar and then enduring his wife on the warpath too.'

'That's very decent of you,' I dabbed some paper towels over my wet eyes. 'And I'm sorry too for being part of your pain, even though at the time I was blissfully ignorant about the true marital facts.'

'What I did to you in public was unforgivable.'

'Oh I don't know,' I gave a shaky laugh. 'I've just taken a leaf out of your book and done exactly the same thing to my fiancé.'

'Oh Lord. Why?'

'I've just discovered him dining with his-' I choked over the word, 'mistress.'

'Oh dear. I know exactly what you're going through. But you *must* talk about it with your man because things might still work out. Euan played around because he thought – mistakenly I might add – that *I* was having affairs. But I wasn't. It was work that got in the way all the time. I'm an accountant,' she added by way of explanation.

'Well I'm nothing as high flying as that. I'm just a part-time secretary and mother.' I took another paper towel and blew my nose. 'I divorced my husband earlier this year because of his constant infidelity. I rebounded horribly with Euan believing him to be a free agent – and now I've been cheated on *again*,' my voice rose to a shriek.'

'Oh you poor love,' she swooped and pulled me into her arms. At that moment there was a commotion outside the Ladies followed by banging on the door.

'CASSIE?' Jamie yelled on the other side of the wooden panels. 'I know you're in there. Please come out and talk to me. I can explain everything.'

'You see!' Euan's wife smiled encouragingly, 'It's time to kiss and make up.'

'Hardly. Apart from anything else I've just ruined his favourite shirt.'

'Shirts can be replaced, relationships can't. Go and talk to him.'

'CASSIE!' Jamie bellowed again, 'I LOVE YOU DAMMIT!'

'Go on,' Euan's wife nodded in the direction of the door. 'Go and sort it out. I'm really glad to have met you again. My name's Maggie by the way.'

'RIGHT!' yelled Jamie, 'I've had enough and I'm COMING IN!'

'Thanks,' I gave Maggie a watery smile. 'It was nice to meet you properly too. And I'm Cassandra.'

She hugged me tightly, just as Jamie barged in. His eyes widened as he saw his fiancée in an apparent clinch with another woman.

'This is Maggie,' I said to Jamie, pulling apart.

'Hello Maggie,' he said warily.

'I'm Euan's wife.'

Jamie nodded, none the wiser.

'I'm Euan,' said the man himself standing behind Jamie and looking rather sheepish. 'Are you ready Mags?'

'Coming honey-bunny. Bye Cassandra.'

'Bye Maggie.'

'Cass,' Euan inclined his head.

'Euan,' I nodded coolly back.

'Bye pal,' Euan patted Jamie on the back.

'Er, bye mate.' Jamie turned to face me. 'What the hell is going on?'

'*You* tell *me*,' I snarled just as my mobile phone began to ring.

'I will if you'd only give me a chance,' he howled.

I flipped the phone open. 'Hello?'

'Cass where the devil are you?' squawked Nell. 'I've been sitting at my kitchen table with two coffees and a plate of Hob Nobs since half past seven.'

'So what happened after that?' asked Morag as we stripped to our undies in the bridal shop's dressing room on Saturday morning.

'After that,' I sighed, 'Jamie explained to me that Selina had been harassing him for months. Ever since they'd split up apparently. She just couldn't believe that he didn't want to go out with her anymore, a beautiful free agent with no emotional baggage.' I wiggled into my Grecian column dress. Heavens. It only just did up.

'So she started stalking him,' said Morag.

'Well, that's probably a rather strong way of putting it — they did work together after all. But certainly the work place became an emotional minefield hence Jamie being keen to get the partnership with Ethan Fareham going sooner rather than later.'

'So why were they having a meal together?'

'Apparently Selina had asked Jamie to join her as she had something to tell him in private. She promised that if he did as she asked then she'd stop bothering him. So Jamie agreed to meet her but not to have a meal together. That's why it was only her eating at the table.'

I breathed in hard. If I held my breath, the dress was comfortable.

'So those phone calls that had you jittering all over the place and the cosy restaurant scenario were a ruse to undermine your confidence and get you believing your fiancé was having a love affair with his ex-girlfriend.'

'Yep.' I exhaled noisily and experienced a bit of a head rush as oxygen levels returned to normal. 'It's no good,' I sighed.

'Don't be silly,' bossed Morag. 'Selina is gone. Out of your hair. You can carry on living your life with Jamie in peace now.'

'No I mean this *dress* is no good. I've put on weight.'

'The seams can be let out,' Morag assured. 'You look beautiful.'

'You too,' I smiled giving her a hug.

At bedtime I snuggled up with Jamie under our duvet.

'How's my darling fiancée?' he asked.

'Happy. And relieved,' I added.

'Cassie, nobody is ever going to come between us. Right?'

I nodded my head. 'I just wish you'd told me about the problems you were having with Selina. I'd have understood.'

'You think?'

'Of course!'

'I don't,' Jamie shook his head. 'Cassie, you were so vulnerable when I met you. You'd not long emerged from a marriage that had all but crushed your self-esteem. Your confidence was slowly on the up but you never gave me the impression that you believed in yourself. You're better than all the Selinas in this world put together, but you still don't believe that. The last thing you needed to hear about was a woman hell bent on destroying our relationship. I wanted to protect you.'

'I know darling,' I kissed Jamie tenderly. 'Let's not talk about her any more. She's history.'

'Absolutely. Come on, let's get some sleep. You were snoring for England last night.'

'I do *not* snore,' I retorted. 'And you can jolly well talk. Some of the sounds you make are quite incredible.'

'Oh?' Jamie raised his eyebrows. 'For example?'

'Phew-ee, phew-ee,' I imitated. 'It must be something to do with the acoustics of your nasal passage and nostril hair.'

'I don't have nostril hair!'

''Fraid so darling. You're sprouting fluffy ears too. Sign of old age,' I nodded sagely.

'Oh God.'

'Never mind. I'm right behind you. You are looking at a woman who has started the menopause.'

'Don't be daft, you're too young.'

'Apparently not. I'm going to make an appointment to see a gynaecologist for a thorough overhaul.'

Having firmly made the decision to sort out my defunct baby-making machinery I made an appointment with one Mr Rafferty, naturally recommended by Morag. Mr Rafferty was so booked up there wasn't a chance of getting near his speculum until well into the New Year.

'Shame it's so far ahead,' I said to Julia and Morag, 'but at least the matter is now in hand.'

We were squashed into Costa Coffee, steamy windows obscuring the sight of harassed office staff battling for pavement space with energetic Christmas shoppers.

'Old Rafferty is the best,' Morag assured. 'And if my next pregnancy test isn't positive, I'll be visiting him to get my fanny fixed.'

'Such a delicate way of putting things,' murmured Julia as a pinstriped suit sitting in close proximity shifted uncomfortably in his seat.

'He's seriously sexy,' Morag waggled her eyebrows. 'Think Robert Redford in his prime.'

'Oh splendid,' I grimaced. 'I'd much prefer an ancient professor type. I hope his good looks don't cause me to have a hot flush.'

That evening as the family congregated around the dinner table, I relayed how busy the High Street had been with pre-Christmas shoppers.

'Ah yes, Christmas,' Jamie rubbed his chin thoughtfully. 'I think we should start thinking about preparing for the Festive Season. Have we got balls?'

Toby sniggered.

'As in *baubles*,' Jamie sighed.

'No,' I replied. 'I seem to remember us chucking our respective Christmas decorations before we moved into Lilac Lodge. Everything was either tatty and broken, or totally naff.'

'Well, Christmas is meant to be naff isn't it?' said Jonas.

'Actually Christmas is meant to be a time for remembering our Lord Jesus,' said Jamie, 'not whether Father Christmas will be shoving a sack load of Nintendo Wii's down the chimney.'

'Oh yes please,' Toby bounced up and down excitedly in his seat.

'I propose we go to Midnight Mass this year.'

My fork froze in mid-air. I wasn't really into religion. Not that I didn't believe in God. On the contrary. But I preferred to say my prayers quietly, at the end of the day tucked up in bed. The fact that I was usually asleep within moments of addressing Him was neither here nor there was it?

'Is Midnight Mass a wise idea darling? Very late. Don't want the children exhausted on Christmas morning.'

'Nonsense,' Jamie said. 'We'll go to St. Michael's. The service shouldn't be more than thirty minutes. It will give you youngsters something to think about this year.'

'Lovely,' I gave a bright smile. 'I take it we'll still be having a Christmas tree?'

'Of course! In fact, I'll pick one up tomorrow evening on my way home from work.'

True to his word, the following evening Jamie positioned a glorious blue-green fir in the hall. Regrettably it remained devoid of tinsel, baubles and fairy lights because I had neglected to nip out in the lunch hour and buy up Boots.

'Why didn't you get the decorations?' Livvy pouted.

'I was snowed under with urgent work,' I lied.

In actual fact it had been cold and chucking down with rain. I'd also felt overcome with exhaustion. Again. The thought of elbowing and shoving through the lunchtime foray was enough to bring me to a swift conclusion that decorations could wait until the weekend. Although it was probably debatable whether the tree would even survive the next twenty-four hours. Wallace and Gromit had taken to bungee jumping off the landing and crashing into the Christmas tree below.

The children broke up from school and suddenly it was the weekend. Jamie and I visited Asda and virtually bought up the remaining stock of Christmas decorations.

'We'll let the kids decorate the tree while we sit down with a glass of wine.'

He flung a free arm around me as we walked along the pavement together and I leant my head against his shoulder. It was at times like this that the feel-good factor ran right off the top of the scale.

'Have you any idea what you're giving Petra and Jonas for Christmas?'

'Yep. As a matter of fact I was discussing it with Matt only this morning when I dropped the kids off at the stables. He just happens to have a pretty chestnut mare for sale, a little over fifteen hands and the perfect size for both of them.' Jamie looked sideways at me. 'What are you buying?'

'Haven't a clue actually,' I confessed. I had been as disorganised as ever. It was far too late to claim a couple of those Wii wotsits that Liv and Toby would have loved. Indeed, only recently a spotty youth in Game had haughtily informed me that the entirety of Great Britain was currently sold out.

'I have an idea,' said Jamie.

'Go on.'

'Why don't they have Smokey? Petra and Jonas are too big for her now and she's the perfect size for Liv and Toby.'

My eyes filled with tears.

'Hey, what's the matter?' Jamie ground to a halt in the middle of the busy pavement causing shoppers to cannon off us.

'Sorry,' I blubbed. 'I don't know what's the matter with me. I seem to be constantly over-emotional at the moment. It's a lovely gesture darling, the twins will be overjoyed.'

Jamie wrapped his arms around me, as best as he could with so many carrier bags strung about him.

'Don't cry Cassie. Come on, let's go and have a hot chocolate somewhere. You can give me some ideas on what to buy the woman in my life for Christmas. Oh and tell me what you want too,' he joshed.

The children threw themselves into decorating the Christmas tree with gusto. It was definitely an artistic monument. There could be no other in the land that screeched with such vulgarity or riotous colour.

'Now all we need are some presents to go underneath,' said Petra.

Which reminded me. What could I buy Jamie?

Once back at work, Morag, Julia and I united as one in the lunch hour. Three abreast, we linked arms, put our heads down and strode forcefully down the centre of the pavement, intent on a successful mission. We bulldozed our way into Next and Game where I resorted to buying a wad of vouchers for all four children. A totally unimaginative cop out. I tried to make up for it by buying all the stocking presents for Jonas and Toby in the Gadget Shop and splurging wildly in Claire's Accessories for Livvy and Petra.

Edna was easy to buy for – Marks & Sparks gift vouchers plus a food hamper, just to prove one didn't need to be welded to the cooker to enjoy excellent cuisine.

Morag and I dumped our shopping over her client sofas and flopped down, exhausted.

'Sod work for five minutes Cass,' said Morag sprawling her legs out. 'Go and stick the kettle on and we'll have a nice cup of coffee.'

'Martin Henniker would never have let me get away with this.'

I trundled happily off to the kitchen and even managed to find a couple of choccy biscuits going begging.

'So,' I said five minutes later, setting the tray down. 'What are you getting Matt for Christmas?'

'Good question,' Morag rolled her eyes. 'He jokingly said he'd like a Ferrari.'

'Wouldn't all men,' I replied. 'Why do they have this fascination for speed?'

'It's the Sex Factor. They know that if they're driving a Ferrari they can get away with having a face like a constipated chicken and still be a babe magnet. A car like that is the pinnacle of male motoring.'

'I know!' I squeaked excitedly. 'Let's buy Matt and Jamie a Ferrari *experience*! You know, one of those jobbies where they go out for the day and roar around a race track.'

'Clever girl Cass, you've cracked it! Now, forget that pile of tapes sitting over there. I'll tell Susannah that you're stacked out and need some extra help. You meanwhile are going to get on the blower to Silverstone and sort out the little matter of two Ferraris.'

When Jamie came home from work I was so excited about the Ferrari business I almost gave the game away.

'How was your day?' I asked, anxious to be distracted from the lure of the racetrack.

'Not bad. Quite by chance I happened to run into Stevie,' Jamie said bending slightly to peck my cheek. 'And I've invited him to Christmas dinner.'

'You did *what*?'

'Well Livvy and Toby are his children Cassie.'

Jamie chucked his coat over the banister. Gromit immediately strolled over and disappeared amongst the folds of the material.

'Yes but the twins are seeing their father on Boxing Day.' I followed Jamie into the kitchen. 'It was all arranged.'

'Well they can still go to Stevie's on Boxing Day, but he's coming here on Christmas Day nonetheless. Oh, and he's bringing Charlotte.'

'Oh jolly good,' I folded my arms across my chest while Jamie washed his hands at the kitchen sink. Wasn't Stevie going to be just *thrilled* when he watched Jamie opening his Ferrari experience. I'd never done anything like that for him in all our years together. But then again, I miserably concluded, he'd never done anything special for me either.

'Well can you and I at least exchange our Christmas presents in private, without an audience?'

'Of course darling,' Jamie agreed, 'first thing in the morning when I bring my beautiful fiancée breakfast in bed.'

'Oh well, put like that how can a girl resist,' I grinned. To hell with Stevie and Charlotte.

When I walked into the office the following morning Morag was slumped over her desk. I rolled my eyes.

'Heavy night again?'

'The wedding's off,' she mumbled into the ink blotter.

'*What?*' I rushed over and put my arms around her shaking shoulders. 'Has Matt done something wrong?'

Morag nodded, fat tears rolling down her cheeks.

'Really awesomely terrible?'

More head nodding.

'The bastard!' I closed my eyes, grimly assuming the worst. 'I know exactly what you're going through. It's like millions of tiny knives piercing your heart and then some masochist twisting them for good measure.'

Morag's face crumpled with emotion. How *dare* Matt do this to her!

'Do you want me to go round and chop his balls off?'

Men who got it out and put it about needed castrating.

'N-no, *huh-huh*, it's worse, *huh-huh*, than that,' she gasped.

'Sweet Jesus. You mean–'

We exchanged a meaningful look and she nodded.

'He's bonking another man?' I croaked. Oh Lord. I needed to sit down.

Morag instantly recovered. 'Of course he's not bonking another man you moron,' she yelled. 'The lazy bugger's not pulling his weight!'

'Not pull-?'

'No he's not! I can't possibly marry a man who takes me for granted.'

Surely this was rather over the top in the reaction stakes? But one thing was very clear. Morag was about to offload and under no circumstances should she be stopped.

'Do you know Cass,' she spat, 'last night I was working on some papers and Matt popped his head around the door with some bloody men's magazine tucked under his armpit. Then he blew me a kiss — like this.' She puckered up and planted a smacker on the palm of her hand which she sensuously blew across the room, albeit with a very wild look about the eyes.

'Ah well, that seems nice and romantic-'

'AND THEN,' she cut across me, 'Matt told me he was going to relax in bed where he would wait for me.'

I nodded in acknowledgement. Best just to stick to head movement.

'So I said I'd be along in two minutes. But before going up I went into the kitchen to check the back door was locked and — da da!' she made a noise like a fanfare of trumpets. 'Washing up in the sink, a dishwasher that needed emptying and the kids' dirty jodhpurs just chucked on the floor. *His* kids' dirty jodhpurs,' she waggled a finger at me. 'And I thought to myself, hang on a minute Morag — he's upstairs relaxing while you're down here with chores outstanding. You get my drift Cass?'

'Why didn't you just go and ask him to give you a hand?'

Morag put her head on one side as if to consider. 'Hm. Possibly I'm a bit hormonal because certainly that thought didn't occur to me.'

'So what happened next?'

'Next I was overcome with incandescent rage. I made a stupendous racket crashing about hoping he might realise that something had upset BOUNCY BUNNY,' she shrieked.

'Bouncy Bunny?'

'That's me – on account of these,' she prodded her heaving bosoms. 'So I cleared everything up and stomped up the stairs,' Morag thumped her high heeled boots up and down on the office floor to illustrate her point, bouncy bunnies nearly blacking her eyes. 'Then I banged around in the bathroom before finally slamming into the bedroom where Matt was happily engrossed in Miss December.'

'Oh dear.'

'And do you know what Matt had the audacity to say?'

I shook my head.

'He told me to chill. BLOODY CHILL,' she screeched putting both hands to her temples and massaging viciously. 'So I've told him the wedding's off.'

'Oh come on, surely you don't mean that?'

'Yes I do. Well, no. Not really. I feel all mixed up at the moment,' her lip wobbled again.

'I think you're suffering a touch of pre-wedding nerves. Give Matt a ring. Tell him you over-reacted and still want to get married.'

'I did *not* overreact,' she said stubbornly.

'Then just explain that you need a bit of help now and again and that you had a touch of PMT. Everything will be fine. You'll see. I'll go and make a nice cup of coffee while you ring him.'

She nodded meekly and picked up the receiver.

God. All I needed was a cancelled wedding putting the cat amongst the New Year pigeons. Clearly Morag was stressed. Perhaps I should invite her to Christmas Dinner with Matt. Yes, good idea. We owed them heaps of return invitations and Matt had come to the rescue so many times having the children at the stables in the school holidays. I'd tell him to bring his children too. I gulped and wondered exactly how many children there were when the register was taken. I couldn't expect Edna to cook for all those extra mouths. I'd have to raid Marks & Spencers.

That evening, as soon as the children were in bed, I cornered Jamie en-route to the television.

'Darling, I want you.'

'Splendid. In here all right? Only the footie's on in,' he glanced at his watch, 'six minutes, so it will have to be a quickie.'

Jamie's finger hovered over the remote control, eyes flickering anxiously between the television screen and my chest. It occurred to me he'd probably be quite happy to watch the footie whilst actually on the job. Annoyed I struck a pose, hands on hips.

'In case it had escaped your attention, in exactly four days it will be Christmas.'

'No, no, fully aware,' Jamie cast another anxious look at his watch.

'And we haven't written out one single Christmas card.'

'Haven't you?' he seemed genuinely shocked.

'I said *we* Jamie – as in *we* haven't written out any cards.'

'Cassie no!' protested Jamie as I strode across the floor. 'DO NOT SWITCH THE TELEVISION OFF!'

'Only if you agree to help me.'

'Okay, okay. I'll write cards out with you, but leave the telly on. I can multi-task.'

I split open the first packet and shared them out.

'I've invited Matt and Morag for Christmas Dinner too.'

'Oh for goodness sake Ref!' Jamie slapped a Christmas card against his thigh in annoyance. 'Don't you recognise a foul when you see one?'

'Four of Matt's children are coming too.' I added.

'Oh right,' said Jamie looking up in surprise. 'Which ones?'

'Haven't a clue,' I shrugged licking down an envelope.

'For heaven's sake, would you look at that stupid referee – stop arsing about Ref and send the tosser off!'

'Oh my goodness!' I clamped a hand to my mouth.

'It's okay Cassie, he's given him a red card.'

'I can't possibly ask Morag without asking Nell. She'd be so hurt if she found out. Which means asking Ben and Dylan too.'

But Jamie had leapt off the sofa, fists clenched, bellowing with joy as his team delivered a goal.

'YES! YES!'

'Do you think she'll bring Rocket?'

Jamie sat down, high on his team scoring.

'Of course. Rocket is Nell's daughter, even if she does happen to have four legs and halitosis.'

On the drive to the office the following morning I illegally clamped my mobile to one ear whilst weaving through heavy rush hour traffic.

'Hair by Design,' a harassed voice spoke over the background noise of hairdryers and in-house music.

'Hi, can I book an appointment with your top stylist please?' I yelled into the handset as a car angrily beeped me. Now what was that for? The driver stuck a middle finger up. Not to be outdone, I took my free hand off the steering wheel and stuck up all my fingers. Waggled them about for good measure.

'Sorry, he's fully booked,' was the reply.

'Okay, is the bottom stylist available?'

There was an indignant pause. 'All our stylists are highly qualified hair technicians.'

'Okay, well I'll have one of them please.'

'There are no available appointments until the New Year.'

'I see. Well what about the shampoo girl? I'm desperate,' my voice cracked.

A brief pause. 'How desperate?'

'Desperate enough to pay double,' I offered sensing weakness.

'W-e-ll. I could fit you in tonight, after hours. What sculpting had you in mind?'

Sculpting? I just wanted a hair-do.

'Nothing drastic. Just a re-style and a bucket of highlights.'

'That's the best part of three hours work,' squawked the voice.

'Oh please help me,' I begged pathetically. 'I have to fly to the Bahamas for a wedding on New Year's Eve.'

'Oh, a member of the jet set are you?'

'Well I don't like to brag,' I answered coyly. 'If you give me your business cards I'll happily pass them around for you.'

'Who will be there?'

'Top secret at this stage, but it will be in January's issue of *Hello!* They'll be holding the front page.'

'Get yourself over to me for seven this evening. And that will be four hundred quid. Cash.' The phone went down.

That evening I left the salon with a halo of blonde highlights and a sheet of hair waterfalling over my shoulders. In my handbag were a stack of business cards proclaiming *Nikki, Style Director* for distribution amongst the rich and famous.

I flushed with shame as I recalled my biggest porky – that I knew the cousin of the sister of the best friend of the wardrobe dresser for Madonna and guaranteed the Queen of Pop would descend at some point in the future imperiously demanding hair sculpting.

Meanwhile the larder was swelling with home cooking that Edna was producing on a daily basis. Maybe I could avoid Marks & Sparks after all?

'There's enough fodder to feed an army in here,' Jamie sniffed appreciatively.

'Heaven only knows where we're going to seat everybody,' I pulled some hidden Christmas stocking presents out of a cupboard along with rolls of shiny wrapping paper.

'We'll shove the kitchen and dining room tables together and tell everybody to squeeze up.'

'Not sure if that will be possible with Morag's assets,' I arched an eyebrow while breaking cellotape with my teeth. 'Come out of that larder Mr Mackerel and give me a hand with these presents.'

Just after midnight we surveyed with satisfaction a sea of colourful packages.

'Nightcap?' asked Jamie.

'Please,' I stretched my arms up above my head, unkinking muscles. Neatly written name tags were taped on my pile of stocking presents. I glanced at Jamie's contribution and froze.

'Um, darling? Which present belongs to whom?'

Jamie looked in bewilderment at his pile. 'Gosh I don't know Cassie. I just did as I was told and wrapped the blasted things.'

'Yes but you were meant to label them. As in: *To Jonas Love from Father Christmas.*'

'Well never mind. The children will just have to open them on Christmas morning and do swapsies.'

'Uh-uh,' I shook my head. 'I'm not having Third World War breaking out because Livvy has unwrapped Toby's Play Station game or Jonas has opened Petra's lip gloss and nail polishes.'

'Jonas is displaying all the signs of full blown rebellion. I'm not entirely sure he'd be displeased with lip gloss and nail polish.'

'Get unwrapping.'

'You're joking.'

'Am I laughing?'

'You're not laughing.'

'So I'm not joking.'

Suddenly it was Christmas Eve morning. Morag and I met up outside the Bridal Shop at Fairview. Morag had insisted we try on the dresses again to be absolutely sure the alterations were correct.

'Well if they're not, it's too late to worry about it,' I pointed out as I wiggled into the soft sheath of fabric. 'Good heavens, did the seamstress alter this dress?' I gazed in dismay at my abdomen. Carrying off a gown like this required a flat tummy.

'Both ge-owns have been altered,' the Manageress looked down her nose.

'We'll go to the lingerie shop,' said Morag. 'They do fabulous all-in-one body supports.'

An hour later my figure was sorted.

'Thank goodness for that,' Morag heaved a sigh. 'I must dash Cass, I've got a few last minute things to buy. See you tomorrow for Christmas dinner.'

Back home, I unpacked my figure-saving secret weapon and laid it reverently upon the bed. The nude-coloured all-in-one was an ingenious work of engineering moulding bosoms aloft, tummies inward and botties upward.

'What's that?' asked Livvy bursting into my bedroom without knocking.

'Do not touch!' I shrieked as her hand hovered over the all-in-one. 'It's special lingerie to make me look slimmer.'

'Aw, you're not fat Mum.' My sweet child. 'You're just a bit saggy.'

Livvy was right. I needed to join a gym. I'd make it my New Year's Resolution. Sit on one of those rowing machines and whip the oars backwards and forwards so frenziedly that the blasted contraption would break its metal moorings and set sail right across the gym floor. My irritation was interrupted by a commotion coming from the kitchen downstairs.

I hid the all-in-one under the duvet and went downstairs to investigate. All four children were excitedly clamouring around Edna who had set down on the kitchen table a whopping homemade Yule log so richly decorated that the very thought of putting a slice to my lips made me want to heave.

By early evening all the Christmas presents had been stacked around the tree. There was such a glut of parcels we resorted to bricking up the tree with blocks of presents so that, eventually, only the star at the very top remained visible.

Wallace and Gromit, instead of swinging from the banister, could now simply step off the staircase onto the uppermost ledge of parcels. I held my breath as the pair of them daintily tip-toed along, damp noses sniffing and exploring, waiting for instant demolition, but it never came. With nimble dexterity they concluded their investigation and threaded their way back between the staircase spindles. I slowly exhaled and sent up a silent prayer that both tree and presents would remain intact for the next twenty four hours.

Chapter Twenty-One

Dinner that evening was a jolly affair until Jamie reminded us to wrap up warmly for Midnight Mass. The children instantly groaned. I almost groaned with them. All I really wanted to do was snuggle up in front of the telly cuddling a cushion and holding the remote control.

'I'll give it a miss if you don't mind Jamie dear,' murmured Edna. 'It's been a long day one way or another.'

'Good idea,' I nodded. 'I'll stay behind and keep you company Edna.'

'Don't be daft Cassie. Mum's going to have an early night. There's no need for you to keep her company.'

Edna smiled. 'Of course you must go Cassandra dear, I wouldn't dream of spoiling your family time.'

'Oh. Well, if you're absolutely sure.'

Jamie was in high spirits as we drove to St Michael's.

'Isn't this wonderful?' he enthused, seemingly impervious to the wall of stony silence within the car. 'We're about to pay our own personal homage to Baby Jesus.'

'Will it take long?' asked Petra as the car swung into the church's grounds.

'About half an hour,' replied Jamie ignoring his daughter's sulky face as he led the way into the church.

Ignorantly I'd been expecting a meagre gathering. Instead the church was packed with people. The congregation sat, eerily quiet, heads bowed, palms pressed together, as they silently conversed with Him. The air was thick with the smell of incense and the only light was that which issued from hundreds of flickering candles. The very pores of the ancient stone walls reeked of holiness.

I glanced about fearfully, half expecting Angel Gabriel to swoop low and soar over my shoulders. Instead I spotted Nell in the front pew and – good grief – wasn't that Rocket sitting next to her? I couldn't see Ben and Dylan but that was hardly surprising as church wasn't Ben's cup of tea. Nell's pursuit of religion had intensified recently, along with her crush on the funky vicar who counted pets amongst his faithful followers.

My eyes pinged back to Rocket. No! Surely a dog wasn't here to take Communion! Sure enough, a second sweeping glance of the congregation revealed a few other pooches sitting quietly by owners' feet. There was even the odd cat blinking owlishly within its travelling basket. Which could only mean one thing – the ghastly Clive was about to take Midnight Mass.

I opened my mouth to tell Jamie but at that precise moment he pushed me toward the last available pew and, before I could utter one word, the choir appeared at the entrance. They launched into a chanting incantation so hauntingly beautiful the hairs on the back of my neck prickled.

Dressed from head to toe in long red gowns, white collars and cuffs, the choir walked in a steady line with hymn sheets held aloft before filtering both left and right of the altar, all the while maintaining their melody. Somewhere a lonely flute joined in and a few bars later a piccolo struck the higher sweeter notes. For a while I was completely lost.

Half an hour later a monumental desire to fidget took over. The choir were still chanting. The children had fallen asleep. Eventually three bespectacled men appeared at the rear of the church, dressed not dissimilarly to the choir, but bearing what appeared to be copper buckets attached to fishing rods. I watched as they glided down the aisle, buckets clanking, wafting incense. The scent caught in my throat and I immediately went into a paroxysm of coughing.

'Ssh,' whispered Jamie as a woman in front turned to glare disapprovingly.

I'd just about recovered when Clive made his entrance. A vision in cream damask and gold stripes, he stood framed in the imposing archway looking like a cross between the Archbishop of

Canterbury and a games show host. Mincing imperiously down the aisle, he ascended the pulpit as the choir ceased their song.

We were now forty-five minutes into a service that had clearly only just begun. Clive opened his mouth to speak but for some reason his speech came out as song. Not melodious you understand. No. It was just the one note. Initially I didn't understand a word. It sounded like 'Give me an Eeeeee'. The congregation were all knowing because, pitching perfectly, they responded likewise. Except instead of singing 'Eeeeee' they sang 'Aye'. Or possibly 'Yea'.

I concentrated on the tuneless mumbo-jumbo. Ah. Clive appeared to have welcomed everybody to St. Michael's. And pets too. He then monotonously sang out his best wishes hoping the congregation would have a warm and wonderful Christmas in the bosom of their families. I immediately thought of Morag and wondered what effect her bosoms would have on Stevie over Christmas dinner.

Hymn after hymn unfolded broken up only by bible readings. The children slept on. Eventually Clive invited the congregation to form two lines for Communion and a blessing. I noted with alarm that even the animals were queuing. First in line was Nell with Rocket sitting obediently to heel.

'Come on,' Jamie nudged me.

'I'm not drinking from that chalice after Rocket's slobbered in it.'

'Rocket isn't taking Communion, she's just having a blessing.'

'Well I'm still not drinking from that vessel,' I dug my heels in. 'The thought of all these people,' I waved my arms expansively, 'slurping from the same cup with their gingivitis and germs–'

The woman in front turned round indignantly. 'Why did you bother to come?' she bristled furiously.

'I *do* apologise,' Jamie soothed whilst steering me into the aisle. 'She's not quite herself at the moment. Brought her here for healing as a matter of fact.'

'Jamie let go of my arm!' I hissed as he manoeuvred me to the far side of the church.

'Cassie would you just stay here and try not to upset anybody, okay? I'm going to wake the children up.'

We drove home in silence, everybody shattered. Jamie ushered four white faced children up the stairs while I retrieved hidden Christmas stockings. But as I walked through the kitchen I let out a gasp of dismay. Edna's chocolate Yule log, left on the kitchen table, had been dissected by Wallace and Gromit. They looked at me guiltily from under the table. Chocolate sponge had been dragged across the worktops and fondant paw prints smudged across the floor. The robin, made entirely of marzipan, had been mistaken for the real thing and lay in a mangled mess next to Gromit.

'You naughty cats,' I admonished just as Wallace regurgitated a sprig of plastic holly.

It was gone three in the morning by the time I'd cleared up and staggered, exhausted, up the stairs. Jamie was still awake.

'Father Christmas has delivered the stockings,' he grinned.

'Yes, I spotted them hanging off the kids' door handles,' I replied kicking off my shoes.

'And ho ho ho! What is Father Christmas hiding under the duvet?'

My shoulders sagged. The last thing I wanted was a sexual marathon. I would have to bully Morag into another supply of aphrodisiac pills. I'd bet my last pound that even now she was bonking an exhausted Matt absolutely senseless. Probably dressed in a baby doll Santa outfit with strategically placed pom-poms.

'It's only tiny Cassie.'

'Is it?' I asked in surprise.

Jamie flipped back the duvet revealing a small square box.

'For you darling,' he nudged it toward me. 'And what's this little mound hiding under the cover? A gift from Mrs Christmas? Good Lord Cassie, what on earth is this?'

'Give that to me,' I snatched the all-in-one dangling between his thumb and forefinger. 'That cost the best part of eighty quid.'

'But what is it?'

'My body.'

'Your body?'

'It's a special item of clothing to make me look thin,' I tucked the garment into a bedside drawer.

'Er, right. Well are you going to open this? Happy Christmas darling!'

I lifted the lid and bit my lip.

'Oh Jamie. It's gorgeous.'

'Try it on.'

The platinum eternity ring contained an uninterrupted circle of diamonds. I slipped it onto my third finger where it beautifully complimented my engagement ring.

'Wow,' I exhaled slowly.

'I know Christmas Day will be manic so I wanted to give this to you in a quiet moment. After Christmas we'll sort out our wedding, okay?'

'Okay,' I smiled up at him. 'And now for your present darling.'

'Is it that body thing?' asked Jamie nervously, 'I mean I'm chuffed to bits if it makes you feel thin and fab Cassie, but really and truly it's not my cup of tea. I'd much prefer the sexy French Maid approach or even a Naughty Nurse or – *ouch* what are you doing? I didn't mean it – *aargh* – geddoff, I love your body, especially the all-in-one body, just stop beating me with that pillow.'

And suddenly it was Christmas Day proper.

After four hours of sleep, I was awoken by excited whoops and shrieks issuing from various bedrooms along the landing. Seconds later the children burst in with Jamie bringing up the rear, bearing a breakfast tray.

'I didn't hear you get up,' I rubbed the sleep from my eyes.

'Not surprised, you were snoring for England.'

'Look Mum!' squeaked Livvy biffing me on the nose with her lumpy stocking.

A happy ten minutes followed as all the kids quickly emptied their stockings. Thankfully the Gadget Shop and Claire's Accessories did their stuff.

Jamie emerged from the bathroom, washed and dressed.

'Right,' he rubbed his hands together enthusiastically. 'A quick trip to the stables I think. You're coming too Cassie.'

At Matt's yard it was almost like any other day as stable girls whisked about swiftly mucking out looseboxes, but there was an added sparkle in the air. As Jamie led us down the L shaped yard he paused between two stable doors. As if on cue, Smokey stuck his head over the door, munching hay and dropping it untidily everywhere. His ears pricked forward dislodging some tinsel decorating his head collar. A handwritten label dangled from the collar's buckle. Seconds later a larger and rather more superior equine head emerged over another door. This horse also wore a decorated halter with an identical label.

'Happy Christmas kids,' said Jamie gruffly.

'Oh my God!' screeched Petra. 'It's Honey. Oh Dad! Is she really ours?'

Petra flung her arms around the mare's neck. 'Matt's been letting us ride her, she's wonderful.' She kissed the mare's nose delightedly as Jonas, his face wreathed in smiles, patted the mare's neck.

'Liv? Toby?' prompted Jamie. 'What do you think?'

'You mean Smokey is ours?' asked Livvy in disbelief.

'Have a peek at that label and see what it says,' replied Jamie hugging me tight. I squeezed him back. Hard. Resorted to rapid blinking as my eyes seemed to be watering rather dramatically.

Back home, Edna had already manhandled two turkeys into the range and was up to her efficient armpits in potato peelings.

'When can we open the rest of the presents?' the children clamoured.

'When our guests are here and after dinner,' said Jamie.

The children made themselves scarce whilst Jamie and I pushed tables together, arranged chairs and stools, folded napkins, polished crystal and decorated the table centrepiece with an enormous phallic candle.

The doorbell rang. Heavens, were guests arriving already?

Morag and Matt came into the hall, four teenagers trailing in their wake. Morag was already rosy cheeked with a head start on alcohol. She tripped over the doorstep and giggled tipsily before rearranging her ample décolletage within the confines of a plunging sweater. Our children greeted Matt's offspring like long lost soul mates and spirited them away upstairs. Seconds later the sound of Florence and the Machine reverberated through the house.

'Let's go into the lounge,' Jamie invited. 'It will be quieter and a little more civilised.'

'Oh let's not be too civilised,' gushed Morag prodding Jamie playfully in the chest. 'It's party time. Let's crack open the bubbly eh?'

Matt dumped half a dozen bottles of ice-cold champagne on the sideboard.

'Chilled and raring to go,' he declared as the first cork shot off with a bang.

The doorbell rang again. This time it was Stevie and Charlotte.

'Enchanté,' gushed Stevie taking Morag's hand and bending over to impart a lingering kiss on her knuckles. His eyes immediately swivelled up and alighted on her enormous attributes. There is only so long a man can boggle at bosoms without being over obvious. Regrettably, words like *tact* or *discretion* were never part of Stevie's vocabulary. His expression was an open book as his face registered the more simplified jargon of *tits, big tits* and *whopping great tits* of which Morag's were most definitely the latter.

His behaviour was not lost on Charlotte. She stood there looking pretty amazing herself but wearing a distinctly chilly expression. Sensing trouble, I zoomed over and pressed a champagne flute into her hand just as the doorbell rang again.

'Nell!'

'Cass!' she shrieked as we hugged.

Ben and Dylan followed Nell in with Rocket bringing up the rear, wagging her tail politely. And then my eyes alighted on an unexpectedly familiar man's face. A man that surely Jamie hadn't invited and I certainly hadn't.

'I hope you don't mind,' Nell hissed in my ear, 'but he has no immediate family.'

'Hello Clive,' I said stiffly.

'I told you she wouldn't mind,' Nell beamed up at Clive. 'The more the merrier eh?'

The more the merrier? With the Ratty Reverend? I was

amazed he'd even deigned to dangle a polished brown brogue across my threshold.

'Clive!' Jamie stepped in to rescue the awkward moment. 'Jolly good to see you matey,' he pumped the vicar's limp hand. Clive appeared to swoon.

Not for the first time I wondered which way the vicar swung. Nell also appeared to be swooning. Her pupils were dilated with eye lashes batting faster than a cricket team as she visibly palpitated in Clive's direction. Clive appeared to be mimicking Nell, but his own hot looks were being lobbed in Jamie's direction.

I cleared my throat and addressed Clive. 'So, are you not in church today delivering sermons and converting lost souls?'

Clive reluctantly tore his eyes away from Jamie. 'Not until this evening.'

Oh super. So we were stuck with him for several hours.

Jamie directed everybody to the dining room. My failure to provide any sort of seating plan resulted in Stevie swiftly sitting himself next to Morag. Charlotte looked outraged and squeezed in next to Clive, wrongly presuming him to be flirt material. She'd have been better off sitting next to Matt. Nell, livid that a mere stripling had bagged a prime spot with her idol, instantly abandoned Ben and Dylan and positioned herself on Clive's right. Morag, overjoyed to be sandwiched between her attractive fiancé and a handsome Casanova, was clearly high on alcohol and aphrodisiac pills. As she sat down, her bust overhung the dinner table. I pondered briefly how the patch of table before her would accommodate both breast of turkey and breast of Morag.

Eventually everybody was served. Clive called for attention by tinkling his fork against his champagne glass.

'Let us say Grace.'

'Grace,' Petra and Livvy giggled together.

I shot them a warning look.

For a moment or two all one could hear was the scrape and clatter of cutlery on china. The children had grouped together down the far end of the table and struck up conspiratorial chatter, Petra whispering about Midnight Mass at St. Michael's.

Clive's ears pricked up. Crowbarring his way into their conversation, he proceeded to tell the Christmas story, all the while shovelling food in his pink mouth. Spitting bits of masticated runner beans across the tablecloth, he finally got to the bit about Mary finding herself with child.

Livvy piped up. 'Oh, I remember this, we did it school. Mary had an immaculate contraption.'

Clive turned puce and choked on a roast potato. Nell quickly got up to pat his back adoringly, at the same time picking up the reins of conversation.

'I love discussing the bible and talking about God's rules,' she beamed.

'What rules?' Jonas snorted, all set to ridicule.

'The Commandments.'

'Oh yeah, I know,' chimed in one of Matt's daughters. Her face bore a strong resemblance to a tomato and mozzarella pizza. Was her name Margarita?

'Things like Thou shalt not admit adultery.'

Nell tinkled with laughter. 'Not quite, but jolly good try. Christians are meant to be loyal and true to their spouse. Who knows what this is called?'

'Monotony,' muttered Stevie.

Morag, quite drunk now, creased up with laughter and slapped Stevie playfully on the hand. It was the perfect excuse for him to cosy up to her cleavage and laugh uproariously with her. Charlotte was visibly grinding her teeth.

Nell tried again. 'Who knows about the epistles?'

Petra hesitated. 'Um, I'm not sure, but weren't they the wives of the apostles?'

Meanwhile Clive had disentangled the remnants of roast potato from his tonsils and was raring to go again.

'Here's a nice easy question for you. What was the special name given to the people who followed our Lord?'

Margarita stuck up her hand, for all the world looking like a contestant who'd reached the £250,000 question on *Who Wants to be a Millionaire* but used up all her lifelines in the process.

'I'm going with The Twelve Decibels,' she quavered nervously.

'Oh bad luck,' replied Clive as Margarita retreated in despair, out of the game.

'Okay, who can tell me another name for marriage?' Clive glanced around as the children conferred.

'Acrimony,' Stevie replied to which Morag gave such a burst of laughter one of her heavy breasts unexpectedly popped out. It bounced joyfully onto her dinner plate and wobbled in a puddle of gravy. Stevie was immediately the helpful gentleman, octopus hands everywhere.

'Oops, hold it there Morag.'

He brushed a carrot off her nipple and gently mopped gravy from her cleavage just as Matt, who had been in deep conversation with Edna, came alive to the situation.

But Charlotte was one step ahead. Leaping to her feet she furiously flung her champagne at Stevie. Unfortunately her aim was appalling and instead she drenched Morag. Outraged, Morag lurched upright causing her second breast to make a break for freedom. Stevie, mesmerised, paused mid-mop to stare lustfully at Morag's appendages. Matt, frantic to shield his fiancée, simply grabbed the tablecloth noisily upending everything on the dinner table.

As plates clattered off and glasses tipped over, Rocket zoomed in to hoover up food remnants. Wallace and Gromit materialised from nowhere to join in the impromptu freebie lunch. But Rocket was having none of it. She turned on the cats, snarling like a savage. The cats puff-balled like porcupines and made a run for it. Rocket momentarily dithered, torn between food and a cat chase. The latter won.

A furry red streak catapulted out from under the table in hot pursuit of Wallace and Gromit. Not missing a beat, the moggies nimbly shot up the wall of stacked presents around the tree in the hall. Failing to put the brakes on, thirty five pounds of dog crashed into the gift wrapped mountain which instantly fell, like the colourful marbles in a game of Kerplunk, scattering in all directions. The cats, utterly terrified now, disappeared into the branches of the Christmas tree. It began to sway violently, as if caught in the grip of some terrible storm. Within seconds the whole thing had toppled in a tinkling heap of smashed fairy lights and broken baubles.

There was a moment of stunned silence. Edna carefully patted her mouth on a napkin covered in galloping reindeer before giving everybody an enquiring look.

'I think we were all just about finished. Now who'd like dessert? There's traditional Christmas Pud or Sticky Toffee Pudding.'

'Edna me old darlin',' Morag slurred, 'gimme some of yer Stiffy Tocky stuff.'

'Never again,' I exhorted over the cornflakes the following morning.

I silently pondered how many other homes in Great Britain had ousted their Christmas tree as early as Boxing Day? It was amazing how quickly the mess had been created. From the moment Charlotte had lobbed her champagne to gazing with dismay upon a wrecked dining room and hallway, no more than thirty seconds had elapsed. Half a minute of mayhem but two hours to clear up.

Livvy had been in tears. 'Bloody Daddy flirting with Morag.'

Bloody Daddy had immediately apologised, but not for *his* behaviour. Good heavens no. He had apologised for *Charlotte's* behaviour.

'Don't know what came over the stupid girl,' he'd shaken his head in bewilderment. 'I'd better go after her.'

Within moments Matt had given the nod to Jamie that he was taking Morag home. Margarita and the other children followed in their father's wake. Ben immediately stood up, retrieved Rocket and declared that the time was getting on and they'd better drop Clive off at St. Michael's.

I slammed the coffee pot down on the table. 'Everything was spoilt,' my voice wobbled dangerously.

'Hey, it was only a bit of mess,' Jamie leant across the breakfast paraphernalia and kissed my cheek. 'I can't remember the last time Christmas Day was so entertaining. Do you know what the best bit was?'

'Spare me,' I shuddered.

'The best bit was having you there by my side Cassie,' Jamie took my hand in his. 'I couldn't have cared less if the whole house had imploded. Just so long as you and I are together, then every day is Christmas.'

After that, I really did cry.

That evening I telephoned Nell.

'I'm so sorry about Christmas dinner ending in upheaval. Was Rocket okay – no sickness after gobbling up the Christmas tree's chocolate decorations?'

'Not at all. She's fine, frisking all over the place!' I could hear the smile in Nell's voice.

'And you?' I asked cautiously. 'Are you *frisking* all over the place?'

'I am as it happens.'

'Nell,' I sighed heavily, 'you can tell me to mind my own business, but I couldn't help noticing yesterday that you seemed terribly smitten with Clive. Is everything okay with you and Ben?'

'Oh yes,' she chuckled. 'Everything is just fine between me and Ben – now,' she added. 'Your invitation to dinner was an absolute blessing.'

'How's that?'

'Well I'm not ashamed to confess that I did have the tiniest crush on Clive.'

'I'd never have guessed,' I said dryly. 'I'm sure he's gay Nell.'

'Yes, well, you could be right about that. Anyway, Ben couldn't help noticing me looking at Clive all starry eyed over the Brussels sprouts and later – after quaffing quite a bit of your lovely champagne I hasten to add – I made a disastrous pass at Clive.'

'No! When?'

'When we dropped him off at St Michael's.'

'And?'

'I insisted on kissing Clive good-bye.'

'Well there's no harm in that.'

'Except I wrestled him to the ground and stuck my tongue down his throat.'

'Oh God!'

'That's what Clive kept shrieking.'

'Whatever did Ben do?'

'He was absolutely furious. The minute we got home and Dylan was out of earshot, Ben demanded to know what the hell I'd been playing at.'

'So what did you say?'

'Everything just tumbled out Cass. All the hurt and anger I've been carrying these last few months since the miscarriage, the ever widening emotional chasm between us and the fact that I felt he just didn't care any more. Ben ended up in floods and said I meant the world to him and he couldn't live without me. Actually he said some really heady stuff and before I knew it we were kissing passionately and declaring how much we loved each other.'

'Thank goodness for that,' I breathed. 'And has Clive forgiven you?'

'He has now. He staggered into St Michael's thoroughly traumatised and was assisted into the vestry by Burly Barry who happened to be passing by.

'Who's Burly Barry?'

'The verger. He also does a regular stint with the Samaritans as a counsellor.'

'So he gave Clive an impromptu spot of therapy?'

'It would certainly seem that way. They're going to the pictures together tomorrow tonight when Clive's finished drafting his sermon.'

'So everything has worked out for Clive too!'

'Yep. And even better – remember me telling you about Ben's client that went bust? Well he's back in business, has repaid Ben all the money he owed *and* stumped up a hefty advance against the next project. Things are booming again – so much so that we're going away on a last minute romantic holiday to the Caribbean.'

'Oh Nell that's fabulous news! I'm so pleased for you – both of you. Have a marvellous time. On New Year's Eve make sure you have your mobile phone on and I'll ring you.'

'Ah yes, a very special day if I'm not mistaken.'

'Don't remind me,' I groaned mockingly. 'It's just another birthday.'

'If you say so,' Nell chuckled.

Returning to work, I felt as though I'd gone back for a rest. The delicious realisation that the day would be spent parked on my butt instead of bog deep in domestic chores had me bursting through Hempel Braithwaite's doors with a broad grin on my face.

In Reception Julia was fizzing with excitement. Leaping off her receptionist's stool she shoved her left hand in my face.

'Look at my ring!' she pointed happily to a green plastic monstrosity on her wedding finger. 'You'll never guess where that came from!'

'A Christmas cracker?' replied Morag striding into Reception.

'Yes! But it came from Miles' Christmas cracker and he's given it to me.'

'But I thought you and Miles were finished?' I asked, puzzled. 'You told me you were spending Christmas with your family.'

'We were and I was,' Julia's eyes were dancing. 'But on Christmas Eve, just as I was leaving for the station, Miles turned up on my doorstep. He implored me not to go, said he'd made a terrible mistake and wanted us to get back together.'

'And?' Morag and I chorused together.

'He begged me to talk to him over dinner at Farrugia's.'

Morag gave a low whistle of appreciation. 'Very nice.'

'It was. The tables were laid up beautifully with festive candles and Christmas crackers. When we pulled Miles' cracker this ring fell out. He took my hand, slipped it on my finger and asked me to marry him. I said yes!'

'Oh Julia that's wonderful news!' I threw my arms around her. 'Congratulations!'

'And at the earliest opportunity,' Morag smiled, 'get that ring changed for a three carat jobbie. Meanwhile Cass,' Morag turned to me, 'have you packed yet?'

'Don't be ridiculous.'

'Well get a move on.'

The thought of flying to the Bahamas filled me with dread. A nine hour flight wasn't something I relished. Nor travelling such a distance from the children. In fact, the moment I started to consider the invisible umbilical cord being stretched thousands of miles, my bottom lip started to wobble.

I gave myself a mental shake and told myself not to blub.

But the following day all I did was blub. It was my final day of employment with Hempel Braithwaite, a workplace which – one way or another – had seen rather a lot of drama.

At five minutes to one, the entire staff squashed around my desk as Susannah Harrington dispensed largesse and hugged me hard. Moments later an enormous bouquet was pressed into my arms accompanied by a *Sorry You're Leaving* card. I immediately burst into tears. As I stood there clutching my flowers and crying, for a brief moment I felt like an award winning actress at the Oscars. Gushing like an oil well I thanked everybody for everything, from the remaining senior partner who I'd barely exchanged a good morning with, down to the office cleaner who I'd almost certainly never met.

And suddenly it was All Systems Go, and go we did. To Gatwick Airport. Eventually anyway. In the car, I buzzed down the window and waved frantically.

'Good-bye. Bye. Be good. Miss you. Bye-ee.' As I mopped my eyes, I had a sudden flash of deja-vu. I seemed to be doing another Oscar winning performance. How strange. Perhaps I'd been an actress in a past life?

Edna, framed in the doorway of Lilac Lodge, had an arm apiece around Jonas and Petra. Stevie stood close by, having come to see us off before taking the twins back to his place. They all waved and grinned manically. Tears streamed down my face as I blew frantic kisses. Yes, very probably an actress in a past life.

'Bye-ee. Don't squabble. Don't forget to clean your teeth. Oh God, I love you all so much.'

Stevie looked a bit startled at this.

The arm waving was flagging a bit and we hadn't even left the driveway. Jamie finally started the engine and the car rolled backwards.

'Stop!' I screeched.

Jamie hit the brakes so hard I nearly head banged the dashboard.

'What's the matter?' he cried in alarm.

'I need to kiss my babies one more time,' I choked.

'Oh God Cassie. Go on then, hurry up.'

I leapt out of the car. Everybody looked slightly unnerved as I hurtled towards them, arms outstretched. *Definitely* an actress in a past life. Probably a damn good one too.

'My babies!' I swooped theatrically on Livvy and Toby who looked mortified.

Eventually Stevie prised my fingers off the twins and I flung my arms around an unsuspecting Petra and Jonas.

'I'll miss you two as well,' I snuffled and snorted attractively.

Jamie tooted his horn. With great reluctance on my part and huge relief on everybody else's, we finally drove off.

We joined up with Morag and Matt at the airport but at boarding time I took one look at the size of the plane and nearly went into reverse. How the devil was that enormous lump of metal going to get off the ground?

'I need a whisky,' I bleated.

'Come with me,' ordered Morag hauling me off to the Ladies. She shouldered me into a quiet corner, shielding me from onlookers with both her body and massive handbag. 'Hold out your hand.'

'What's this?' I screwed up my eyes suspiciously.

'Really Cass, you are terribly ungrateful at times.'

'You're giving me *three*?' I gasped. 'Are you trying to kill me?'

Half an hour later, as the aircraft charged down the runway and threw itself into the sky, I smiled serenely and slipped into a drug induced slumber.

Chapter Twenty-Two

I wasn't entirely sure what time we eventually arrived at our hotel. All I wanted to do was crawl into bed and sleep off jet-lag and tranquillisers.

Much later, when we awoke a little less bleary-eyed, we were able to fully take in the unadulterated opulence of our villa. We had slept in a vast four-poster bed, canopied and curtained in rich emeralds and gold. Two enormous cream sofas bearing a row of plumped up pointed cushions snuggled up to an occasional table bearing flowers, a tray of sweets and an overloaded crystal fruit bowl. French doors issued onto a large bright balcony affording stunning views of white sand, pale turquoise sea and an abundance of softly swaying green palms.

'Paradise,' I murmured, leaning over the balustrade and drinking in the vista.

'Let's go and explore,' said Jamie.

The hotel was a vast architectural structure designed like a sultan's palace, its stone walls constantly changing colour according to the time of day and angle of the sun. The colossal building stood against a backdrop of white sand and turquoise ocean.

In the hotel's grounds – a mere seven acres – there were half a dozen pools each with swim up bars offering mouth-watering Caribbean cocktails. The pools were watery works of art, meandering under an assortment of ornamental bridges through lush tropical gardens.

Morag preferred the recreation of the water park, treating fellow swimmers to the spectacular sight of a large breasted woman hurtling down water chutes and slides squealing her head off with girlish excitement. Wherever Morag ventured, a rush of enthusiastic males discreetly followed in her wake.

On the morning of Morag's and Matt's wedding, a combination of jet lag and time disorientation almost made me forget what day it was.

'Happy Birthday darling,' Jamie kissed me, 'the big Four Oh!'

'And on this landmark occasion I am about to fulfil a lifelong ambition – a bridesmaid no less. Well, Matron of Honour actually. Talking of which, what time do we need to be ready?'

'One hour.'

'One hour?' I shrieked.

'Just kidding. Two hours.'

'Two hours?' I shrieked again flinging back the bed covers and scampering off to the shower.

'Move over, I'm coming in too.'

As we blasted ourselves with the power shower's numerous jets, I mentally took a step back. Back to this same day, but exactly one year ago.

On that particular day, just like now, I had showered and taken care with my hair and make up to celebrate both my birthday and New Year's Eve. But the man by my side had been a very different one. A very adulterous one. And exactly one year ago today my world – as I had then known it – had crashed devastatingly around my ears. At the time, I'd thought I'd never recover.

Jamie stepped out of the shower, towel slung around his midriff. He caught my eye.

'That's a rather serious face. Penny for your thoughts?'

I wrapped my own towel around me before kissing him tenderly.

'I was just thinking what a lucky lady I am to have you in my life. You're just – well – perfect I suppose!' I gave a shaky laugh which caught in my throat. Tears suddenly spurted from my eyes like the power shower's water jets.

'Hey, there's no need to cry,' Jamie gently kissed me back. 'I can't help it if I'm perfect, can I?'

I grinned through the tears. 'Silly. I love you.'

'That's good, because I love you too. More than words can ever say, do you know that? Cassie, look at me.' He put a finger under my chin, tilted it up so he was looking directly into my eyes. 'Cooking aside, you're pretty much perfect too you know.'

A little later, as Jamie sauntered from the dressing room, I felt the air whoosh out of my lungs.

'You look amazing,' I stared at my handsome Brad Pitt look-alike, every inch as good as a Hollywood Superstar.

'My God,' Jamie gazed back at me. 'You look absolutely stunning.'

The all-in-one body hadn't let me down and was perfect under the Grecian column dress which softly clung to every voluptuous curve. My hair was swept up in a simple twist and threaded with fresh flowers. For once my skin was glowing, either from the Bahamian sun or the outrageously expensive new make up I had splurged on. As I stood in that room with a man who was the stuff of fairytales, I felt gloriously happy.

Wedding parties took place almost every hour on the hour at the hotel. The sight of wedding guests milling around or bustling off to a particular venue was not an uncommon sight. As Jamie and I came out of the elevator and crossed the vast reception area, our attire therefore caused no stirring reaction from other guests save for the occasional smile or nod of good wishes.

We walked across a sun terrace just as Matt and Morag emerged from a palm fringed pathway, both looking resplendent in their wedding finery.

'Howdy-doody folks,' Matt grinned and gave us a hug. 'Are we all ready? Anybody want a swift glug to steady last minute nerves?' he extracted a slim flask from his inside pocket with an exaggerated jittery hand.

'Quit fooling you daft bugger,' grinned Morag.

'Lead the way Ms McDermott,' said Matt impersonating a condemned man, 'before I change my mind.'

'Before *you* change *your* mind?' snorted Morag. 'If anybody should be anxious it should be *me*! Do you realise I am about to become the *fourth* Mrs Harding?'

'And the final,' Matt assured patting Morag's bottom. 'You're the real thing and I'm never going to let you go. Not even when you're nagging me,' he grinned.

'No more fishwife,' said Morag firmly, 'just wife.'

'Come on then. Let's go and get married.'

We strolled off toward the appointed wedding venue, a grand decking area with soaring arbours smothered in rippling ribbons. The scent of floral arrangements floated on the air with the ocean providing a breath-taking backdrop.

As the dashing Bahamian minister greeted us, I couldn't help thinking how much fun the children would have had if they'd been here with us. I felt a lump rise in my throat. Oh no Cass. Don't cry. Not now. I blinked and gulped, hastily swallowed. This was Matt's and Morag's big day. All the same, it would have been lovely to have the kids here with us too. Look at that little girl over there – she was probably no more than Livvy's age and clearly having the time of her life, grinning away.

I gazed at her through my watering eyes. How weird. She looked remarkably like Livvy. I stared hard. Harder. My God. It *was* Livvy! And there was Toby. And Petra and Jonas. And – oh my goodness – there was Edna. Good grief, what were Nell and Ben doing here? And there was Dylan, but thankfully no sign of Rocket. No! Not Charlotte and Stevie too! I turned to look incredulously at Jamie, but he'd dropped down on one knee. There was a sudden hush.

'Darling Cassie. When we first talked about getting married, I promised that when the time was right I would give you a proper old fashioned proposal, but it ended up being in the kitchen surrounded by dirty pots and pans. So here I am down on one knee again, but this time surrounded by our children, family and friends. Will you marry me?'

I gasped and began to laugh and cry all at the same time. Whoever invented waterproof mascara, at that moment I silently thanked them from the bottom of my heart. Speechless, I could only nod my head as I waited for my voice to return.

'Yes,' I whispered. 'YES!'

Everybody cheered and clapped and suddenly we were all rushing towards each other, hugging, clasping hands, laughing, the men awkwardly clapping each other on backs, the way men do. The minister gave us all a minute or two before discreetly clearing his throat.

'Ladies and gentlemen, let us begin.'

'Oh, but we don't have our wedding rings,' I interrupted.

'Yes we do,' smiled Jamie fishing in the silk lining of his suit.

And so it was that two radiant brides and two handsome grooms stood side by side to solemnly repeat their respective marriage vows in a carefully orchestrated double wedding.

Afterwards we converged as one, congratulations ringing in the air as a photographer snapped away, eventually taking us to one side for some spectacular shots against the shoreline. All that remained was to celebrate with our nearest and dearest at the wedding feast before dancing the night away and enjoying fireworks to welcome the New Year.

Much later, I slipped away to the Rest Room, desperate to take the shine off my nose and re-apply fresh lipstick. Morag was hot on my heels and crashed through the door looking incredibly elated.

'Congratulations on keeping a monumental secret,' I beamed at her glowing reflection in the ornate mirror.

'Can you keep a secret yourself?' she whispered furtively, 'just until I can buttonhole Matt?'

'Spill the beans.'

'I'm pregnant!'

'No! Are you sure? Have you done a test?'

'Of *course* I've done a test,' Morag tipped her bridal bag open conjuring before my very eyes a test kit confirming a positive result. 'God knows how many of these sticks I've widdled on over the last few months. Ovulation tests. Pregnancy tests. Thank goodness for my pharmacist friend.'

'Ah yes, I remember you saying,' I nodded. 'Perhaps I should buy one of those menopause tests. I don't know why I didn't think of doing that before actually.'

'Well I expect your gynaecologist will do that along with a pregnancy test, just to rule out any possibility-'

Our eyes collided as the obvious dawned on us both at the same time.

'Um, I don't suppose you have a spare test on you by any chance?' I quavered.

'What a ridiculous question,' Morag huffed. 'You shouldn't even need to ask!' She instantly produced a fresh kit. 'Go on. In you go,' she shoved me into a cubicle, squashing herself in behind me.

'Morag!' I hissed. 'What on earth are you doing? If somebody came in right now-'

Too late, footsteps were approaching. The Rest Room's door swung open just as Morag pushed me backward, slamming the cubicle door shut. Oh terrific. I eyeballed her furiously and snatched the tester stick from her proffered hand. Morag jerked her head towards the loo. I frowned and shook my head in the negative, then likewise jerked my head indicating she turn around. She rolled her eyes but obliged. The minute her back was turned I hitched up my gown. Elsewhere a toilet energetically flushed.

'All done?' she whispered over her shoulder.

Moments later a hand dryer whooshed into life and then the door banged back on its hinges. We were alone again.

'Just give me a sec,' I murmured.

I stared at the twin windows, watching, waiting. Inexplicably I was holding my breath. Goodness, this was weird. And surely ridiculous. Whatever was I doing jammed in a toilet cubicle with Morag's chest taking up most of the available area, peering at a pregnancy stick when I was simply menopausal?

'Well?' she asked, turning around.

I didn't answer.

'*Well?*' she repeated impatiently.

I met her gaze, my face expressionless. 'Well, well, well.'